"Benson reveals a formidable talent... Benson's debut is assured and accomplished in both the past and the present."
—*Publishers Weekly* (starred review)

"Cleverly narrated... iterate, chock-full of curious lore and considerable suspense."
—*Entertainment Weekly*

"A harrowing medical novel that will give readers both nightmares and thrills... a carefully woven page-turner."
—*Library Journal*

"Lively descriptions... sympathetic characters."
—*The Boston Globe*

THE BURNING ROAD

"Gripping... Appealing on many levels, this exciting and complex tale will please sci-fi and historical fiction fans as well as readers interested in millennial themes."
—*Booklist*

"Ms. Benson skillfully presents a tale that spans seven centuries and has what every reader dreams of—intrigue, suspense, romance, and drama. A definite must for the medical thriller fan."
—*Rendezvous*

"Fresh and vivid... Those who love richly textured historicals, edgy speculative fiction and suspenseful medical thrillers will enjoy Benson's books."
—*BostonHerald Sunday*

"A riveting medical thriller."
—*USA Today*

Also by Ann Benson

THE PLAGUE TALES

THE BURNING ROAD

THIEF SOULS

a novel

ANN BENSON

A DELL BOOK

THIEF OF SOULS
A Dell Book

PUBLISHING HISTORY
Delacorte hardcover edition published December 2002
Dell mass market edition/December 2003

Published by
Bantam Dell
A Division of Random House, Inc.
New York, New York

Library of Congress Catalog Card Number: 2002067394

ISBN 0-440-23629-0

Manufactured in the United States of America
Published simultaneously in Canada

OPM 10 9 8 7 6 5 4 3 2 1

For Gary

with love

ACKNOWLEDGMENTS

I am grateful for the help and encouragement of my agent, Deborah Schneider, the sublime guidance and patience of my editor, Jackie Cantor, and the support of my husband and daughters, all of which was, as always, lovingly tendered. In addition, I thank the many law enforcement officers, including my husband, who offered technical advice, as well as the Connecticut Juvenile Court judge who helped me wade through the intricacies of certain legal procedures. Professor Arnold Silver was more than generous with rare research materials from his extensive library.

AUTHOR'S NOTE

This is a work of fiction based in part on actual events that took place in the fifteenth century. Lord Gilles de Rais, the real-life figure on which the fairy-tale character Bluebeard is based, actually committed the heinous acts described in the historical section of this book. He was a comrade-in-arms to Joan of Arc, and at one time owned more of what is now France than any other person had before or has since. He did, in truth, squander his fortune on debauchery. His arrest, trial, conviction, and subsequent execution are well documented, and I have tried where possible to portray the events as they actually happened. The judges, codefendants, and victims are represented with their real names. Most of the other peripheral characters in the historical portion were of my creation. However, Guillemette La Drappiere was the name of his actual childhood nurse, though little is known of her beyond that.

The new portion of the story is entirely fictional, but the detectives in Los Angeles and Boston are named for real police detectives, both active and retired.

THIEF of SOULS

one

THE DEAR LITTLE COTTAGES that were the gate-
keepers to Nantes were receding rapidly as I slipped into
the tunnel of trees—the worst part of the journey to
Machecoul. Out of the light, and into the darkness. One
cannot help but feel very small among these barked giants,
whose gnarly underbranches could reach out at any moment like the devil's fingers to draw me into the dark ric-
tus of some knothole, where I would melt in the eternal
agony of my own sins.

As always, I pray, for there is little else to do. Dear
God, do not let them take my thumbs, for without my
thumbs I shall not be able to grasp the needle, and a life
without embroidery is unthinkable.

With each step, I shove my hands deeper into the
folds of my pocketed sleeves. My precious fingers disappear completely, safe again.

They find the letter. My fingertips discern small
wear spots along the folds in the parchment, despite the
relative recency of its arrival here from Avignon. It came

among other important papers sent from his Holiness to my own *maître,* Jean de Malestroit, who as Bishop of Nantes is privy to so many of God's deepest secrets. Though I am his closest companion, I cannot begin to understand the weighty matters that his Eminence is bidden to consider by his Holiness, nor in truth do I wish to. I am driven by some desperate maternal urge to bypass the cares of the world in favor of the precious thoughts of my firstborn. The date, written in my son's sweet strong hand in one corner, was March 10, 1440, seven days previous. I skip his long-winded blessing—he is a priest, after all—and recite the rest in my head as I walk.

There is most excellent news, abrupt and unexpected. I am now fully a scribe to his Grace; no longer must I work under another brother, but instead answer directly to the Cardinal himself. Increasingly I am called to his chambers to record important business. He seems through some miracle to have taken me under his wing, though I fail to understand why he finds me fit for such an honor. It gives me hope that I will be anointed with official advancement sooner rather than later. . . .

How wonderful, how precious, how … how abysmally insufficient; I would rather have had the man himself by my side. But his Eminence Jean de Malestroit abhors complaint, so I shall not indulge therein, may God forbid that he should abhor me for that weakness. I continue my recitation, which is perhaps not appreciated by the squirrels and foxes, who are my only listeners. It gives my steps a reassuring firmness, however false it might be.

I think of you every day and rejoice in knowing that you will be here in Avignon in not too many months, to see firsthand how rich my life has become. I am forever grateful to Milord Gilles for his influence in securing this position for me when I was but a young brother with limited prospects. . . .

My own gratitude is tinged with bitterness. Lord Gilles de Rais's beneficence was such that I, once his own nurse, must remain here in Brittany, and my son, practically his own brother, is many days' ride away in Avignon. It seems almost as if he had some purpose in separating us.

But how could that be?

You must report more of the goings-on in Nantes in your next letter, Maman; *we have had a pilgrim here recently who spoke of events in the north, of this nobleman's tribulations and that lord's triumphs and that lady's romance; we are eager to have these bits of news. But I find myself especially intrigued to know the meaning of a ditty he recited—the entirety of the lyrics escapes me, but in part it was* "Sur ce, l'on lui avait dit, en se merveillant, qu'on y mangeout les petits enfants."

. . . as for that, someone had told him, marveling, that they eat small children there . . .

I did not know what it meant, nor, in truth, did I wish to. Certainly not in this moment, when I was in sure danger of being eaten myself, by God alone knows what vile and monstrous beast. I know better than most that such beasts are here, often unseen, their evil jaws patiently agape.

A blessed sliver of light snuck through the trees and flickered—had a bird settled on a branch, or was it merely my own long-held breath, expelled too rapidly? I am always desperate for light; all the world speaks with hope of the time after the wars end, if they ever do, when illumination will not be such a luxury as it is now. We seldom waste unnatural light in looking upon each other when there is the thinnest thread of daylight left, for there are wiser uses—indeed, there always are for the little graces of life than what we foolishly choose to spend them on.

Once light was supplied in abundance at the pleasure

of Lord de Rais in his residence at Champtocé, and I—in those days, Madame Guillemette la Drappiere, wife to Milord's loyal retainer Etienne—could bathe in it almost at will. Now I depend on God to supply radiance, though I do not like God these days as much as I did before I became *la Mère Supérieure,* or, as the stern Jean de Malestroit is fond of calling me, *ma soeur en Dieu.* A better woman than I might appreciate the sanctuary of an adequate—nay, even abundant—existence. With so many women spitting out their teeth for lack of nourishment, I ought to be overjoyed at my good fortune. But it is not the life I long for, not the life I had and loved. Nevertheless, when my beloved husband died, practically all but myself agreed it was the best thing for me.

My sweet Etienne fought bravely with Lord de Rais under the banner of the Maid in the great battle of Orléans on a day when many valiant men were lost. He was pierced through the thigh by an English bowman, God curse their uncanny skill. His leg festered, as it often goes with deep wounds. The midwife—alas, we had no physician, though no one should doubt that she was near as good as one—insisted that to save his life the limb must be removed. But he would not consent.

How can I, a soldier and woodsman, properly serve my Lord de Rais as a cripple? he said to me.

His was not the honorable battlefield demise that all warriors crave in their secret hearts, but a lingering slide into pain and degradation. When he was finally summoned to the soldier's reward, my neglected place of service in Lord de Rais's house had already been given over to a less distracted woman. Had I inherited property, I would have been assured of another husband. God got me instead.

I am careful to make myself useful now, for I could not bear to be displaced again. I am a quiet shadow to his Eminence, who as both Bishop of Nantes and Chancellor of Brittany serves two demanding masters: one unspeakably divine, the other brutally mortal. Which master rules him more completely is often determined by which one's interests are more compatible with his own at the moment, but in the thirteen years of my service here I have come to respect him greatly despite that regrettable flaw of character, which few but I can see.

Still, it is not the life I long for.

"I must go to Machecoul," I told him that morning. "A few small tasks, some supplies ..." I explained. "All can be found in the market there."

"Well, Machecoul is not an overly long journey, but perhaps you should consider sending one of the younger women."

I did well in hiding my annoyance. "It is a good walk, but the day is turning out to be lovely, and I shall be quite fine, I am sure. And I would rather choose the things I need for myself than trust another's eye."

"*Frère* Demien can be spared from his regular duties today.... Perhaps he might help you carry your purchases."

I had sleeves enough for whatever I might buy. "He will resent being parted from his trees. And nothing will be heavy—I need needles, and a few threads. Some of your surplices require repairs in certain colors, ones we cannot seem to dye properly ourselves."

"Ah, yes, well, those are things about which I understand very little, may God be praised. I will happily leave it all to you." He raised one side of his unbroken eyebrow. "And whatever other business you might have beyond your acquisitions."

He waited for my reaction. I could almost feel his desire to press me further on the matter, but I responded with only a contained nod.

"Well, be about it, then, but take care not to overtax yourself."

"Of course, Eminence. I shall not ruin myself for my duties here."

"Indeed," he grunted. He dismissed me by returning his attention to the text before him, but when I was halfway out the door I heard, "May God go with you." It brought a smile to my face.

Our abbey is an ancient building, and when it was raised, the people were somewhat smaller-limbed than we are now, or so we glean from the bones that lay moldering in our crypts. One can learn a lot from bones, and teeth—one of my sons had a chip in his tooth that I would know anywhere. In any case, the proportions of my room, and within it the bed, are quite close. I chose it for its position on the inside of the courtyard, as the daylight is always strong. In the winter one of the brothers stretches an oiled parchment over the opening to keep out the drafts, for I could not bear to have it darkened by a tapestry for so many months. There is not much to see, in truth, but there is light, and I am not subjected to the sound of cart wheels rattling by in the predawn hours as farmers go to market along the outer wall.

But it is not always intrusions from outside that tarnish one's sleep. Things I did not wish to think about had disturbed my rest through a long and fitful night—ghosts, demons, cruel monsters in the dark forest—the nightmares of a child in the grips of an imagined witch. I am long past the time when withering menses compel a woman to rise wide-eyed in the smallest hours and then pace in a state of agitation until the cock crows; those indignities have come and gone, and now my sleep is seldom interrupted, either by wakefulness or dreams. But when I awoke this morning, my eyes were crusted shut. I must have wept in what sleep I managed, but I could not recall having done so.

Often I will kneel beside my pallet at bedtime, then squeeze my eyes tightly shut and clasp my hands together as a child would do. I leave the door to my chamber open, so that if someone should happen by I would be seen in what appeared to be a fervent state of devotion. On most occasions I do it for appearance's sake, but last night my devotion bordered on fervency as I pleaded with God to let Madame le Barbier find her son, if God is not the cruel jest I lately think Him to be.

As I towed a column of my sisters back to the convent to break our fast, *Frère* Demien caught up with me.

"God's blessings on you, Mother."

He always said *Mother* as if he truly meant it. I was unspeakably grateful. "And you, Brother."

"It is a fine day, is it not? Though there is a chill. Last night as well."

He had a galling exuberance to him, but it was simply an expression of his youthful vitality, and therefore completely forgivable. I often forgot that he was a priest; minus the robes he would be a young squire in full flower—had there been more to inherit from his family, he might have had a small estate of his own. For a man who had not chosen his own vocation, he performed his duties admirably—and with annoying vigor.

"When you are of an age with me, you will like the morning chill less than you do now," I promised him. "But the sun will burn it off quickly enough."

"A good thing—his Eminence says you shall be making a journey to Saint-Honoré today. A quaint parish. But I was surprised that our *maître* would release you."

So Jean de Malestroit had already enlisted my young cohort to accompany me. I was, confoundingly, a bit pleased for a moment—that is, until the annoyance set in. "This is a veil, not a chain," I said. "May I not go on a journey of my own choosing?"

"Well, with Pax so close at hand, I wonder at the reason."

After a pause, I said, "No reason beyond the purchase of a few necessities."

"Ah," he said. He made a wise little smile. "I only ask," he said, "because this morning you seem . . . drained. Tired, perhaps. As if you were carrying some burden."

I had not inspected myself in our one glass—but I guessed that the sleep-tears of the previous night had taken their toll on my face. I lowered my gaze and kept silent as we walked.

"Is there something you would like to confess, Mother?"

Bless me, Brother, oh thou who art younger than my own son, for I have committed the grave transgression of excessive curiosity, and also the sin of overabundant emotion.

"No, Brother, but I thank you. My sins are not too momentous today."

"The day is young," he said.

"And there is hope yet for misbehavior." We laughed on parting.

Thereafter, the morning's housekeeping tasks fell to my sword of determination, for which there were dark looks aplenty from the young brides of Christ who labored on the church's behalf under my orders. As I made my way through the markets of Nantes before leaving the city, I could not help but notice that everything I supposedly needed was available right there, probably in greater assortment than I would find in Machecoul. No doubt Jean de Malestroit knew this, despite his declaration of happy ignorance. *I should have been more clever,* I chided myself.

The chunk of cheese and slab of bread I had stowed in my sleeve began to thump against my leg. I ceased my recitation of my son Jean's letter and began to hum a little tune in time with the rhythm. Sounds emerged from between the trees—crackling twigs, rustling leaves, the odd animal chirp. With every step, I half-expected the unknown that waited in the thickets on either side of the path to leap out and claim me. I thought of Madame le Barbier, who must have traversed this wood the night before after her futile plea to Jean de Malestroit; accommodations along this route were scarce and likely too dear in price even for a prosperous tradeswoman. She had left the abbey well after sunset by the light of a single torch. Surely her arm must have ached abominably by the time she reached this point.

I was afraid—fear in these woods was reasonable and right, for there are beasts everywhere. Not the legendary gilded lions of Ethiopia, nor the white bears of the northlands that our brave knights had slain with jeweled swords, tales of which thrill us before the hearth on cold nights. Here in the forest there are foul beasts with tusks and matted hair, who snort and claw the earth, whose fiery anger glows from wet eyes too small for their massive, misshapen heads.

It was in such thickets as these near the palace at Champtocé that Guy de Laval, father to Milord Gilles de Rais, met the boar that brought him to his end.

His sojourn into the forest that day was ill-fated from the start, or so Etienne would later tell me. A favored horse had turned an ankle, and his usual warden was ravaged by *la grippe* and could not come out of the latrine long enough to pray for a cure, never mind ride out to hunt. These cruel circumstances, we all eventually came to believe, were the devil's work. As must have been the assailant, a certain pugnacious boar. He was a tough-hided, heavily scarred animal whose capture Guy de Laval craved, since the beast had eluded him for an embarrassing length of time. Had Milord Guy not been overcome by a desire to make something of a frustrating day, he might not have done what even a novice hunter knows not to do, allowing the boar to face him with his tusk and thus becoming the prey himself.

His two unfortunate gamekeepers had dragged him over the rough terrain on a rude carrier while he held his own viscera in place. *He would not take his hands away from his belly! We could not put him on the horse. . . .* I shall never forget the sight of him, the pain and terror on his face, foreign to a brave huntsman, one who always kept our tables so well supplied with succulent treasures. Rumors ran wild, and there was much blame to be passed around but no clear shoulders on which it might be settled.

Etienne, I said, when the thick of the scandal was upon us, *can it be true what they say? Might Jean de Craon have arranged this?*

It would not have been beyond the brutal and acquisitive old man whose daughter, Marie, then had the misfortune to watch her husband die. I heard things said that I did not want to believe, whispers of treachery. *Jean de Craon crossed the palms of the gamekeepers with a bit of gold, and when the moment was right, they looked away. . . .*

Gilles stood to inherit his father's vast holdings, save those brought to the marriage by his mother, who, as Jean de Craon's compliant daughter, would do what her father bade her do with her property in the absence of her husband. Milord Jean de Craon was a cruel taskmaster who knew he could more easily control the inexperienced young Gilles de Rais than the boy's mature and intelligent father. Speculations, rumors, whispered accusations flew; none of us knew what to believe, only that power within Champtocé would soon change hands, which notion could not help but be unsettling.

It was difficult not to conclude that Jean de Craon had indeed played some part in Guy de Laval's demise, and that all kinds of evil can dwell unseen in a man's heart. How otherwise had these gamekeepers and squires, all faultless in their previous years of service, suddenly found themselves too far away to help?

Still, the animal was a demon and must have known that the pain of his old wounds was brought about by Milord Guy.

As if he were possessed by a demon of the most unholy kind, the beast tore deeper still into Milord Guy's innards and thrashed his tusk about viciously, pulling out great lengths of entrails . . . which Milord Guy desperately shoved back within.

And then, according to these witnesses, the boar simply disappeared, his evil task having been completed.

Though I also watched my Etienne die many years later, I must confess I will not be able to understand the terror of standing on death's threshold until my time actually comes. *Mère de Dieu,* it was horror enough to observe! For the first two days, Guy de Laval was desperate for the services of anyone who might help him and sent riders out in all directions. He who had such power, wealth, and influence could find no one who would give him the slightest hope, not for all the gold in Brittany. Our wonderful midwife gave him opium to dull his pain, but she would not speak falsehoods—he would die, she avowed, as surely as the sun rose and set. And there would not be many more risings and settings of the sun for him to savor.

As the truth of this avowal became clear to him, he began to behave like the great fighter he had always shown himself to be. Milord Guy launched into preparations for his own passing with great decisiveness. Through substantial pain, he gathered to him all those men on whom he would depend to carry out his will regarding his sons, including the sons themselves.

Young René de la Suze was yet a child and could barely understand the significance of the events that swirled around him. He did little more than stare blankly at his father with no true comprehension of what lay ahead.

But Guy's firstborn son, Gilles de Rais, who was then but eleven years old, seemed to take it all in with understanding beyond his years. While René was frightened of being in the presence of his mutilated father, his older brother, Gilles, would not allow himself to be removed but stood and watched at even the most terrible moments. He made it known that when his father's dressings were changed and fresh poultices applied, he wanted to be present. As all the others began to abandon Guy de Laval and cleave to Jean de Craon, Gilles remained at his father's bedside.

I, who knew him so well, might have been the only one who noticed that the son's noble devotion to his failing father was tinged by a disturbing fascination. And despite my tender tolerance for what must have been youthful misunderstanding of our plight's gravity, I was equally disturbed to observe this in him.

The boy is far too captivated by all of this ghastliness, and I fear for his soul's purity, I told Etienne. *The midwife complains that he will not leave her to her work but would put his hands on the wound itself as she dresses it.*

It sent a powerful chill through me to recall this curiosity in one of such a tender age, who ought to have been innocent still of morbid preoccupations. All the ladies of the castle spoke against Marie de Craon behind her back, as if she herself had created that strange interest in her son.

That is, until she herself died, suddenly and without explanation, not quite a month after her husband. Then she became a saint, and I, his nurse, the fiend who had spoiled her son.

❧

Suddenly I was aware of standing still in the forest; I wondered how long I had been doing so. The dry, crystalline sound of rubbing leaves and the low of the wind sent a shiver through me, which brought me out of the grips of my dark memories. Unshakable images of that powerful boar still coursed through my mind—his thrashing heavy head with its long tapered snout that ended in an exquisite weapon, the sharp cloven hooves that could tear up great clods of earth with a single swipe and rip flesh to shreds.

The rustling of leaves, the crackling of twigs, the noises behind me in the trees ...

I told her she should have sent one of the younger women. That was what his Eminence would say when they finally came upon my torn and bloody corpse. *She might have allowed* Frère *Demien to accompany her. But she would not listen. Guillemette would never listen.*

The thought of him wallowing in such sanctimonious exactitude was all the inspiration I needed to rediscover my legs, which carried me handily away from that place of danger and brought me into a small patch where the trees were sparse and the sun shone blessedly through. I rested in the safety of that dear light until my heart had calmed itself and I had breath enough to continue, which I then did with renewed purpose. The sun was already high in the sky when I emerged at last from the forest path to the flat open meadow outside Machecoul. Not far ahead was the market square, where the day's bustle would be well under way, and there I would find the safety of the crowd—farmers, notioners, smiths, and bakers all hawking their wares, women bargaining for advantageous prices, the occasional whore whom I was not supposed to notice. One could tramp through an expanse of mud to buy a soap cake with which to later remove that mud from the hem of a gown or robe, a pointless and circular journey but one all wives, save those of the nobility, made at some time in their lives. Those same wives might be gossiping beneath a favored open window or marketplace stall or, more likely, at the common well. Such comfortable familiarity always set me to longing for the days past when I had something to talk about myself: husband, sons, the intrigues of the castle.

I chided myself for the delusion. After so many years in seclusion, I no longer had sociability of that kind in me. I stopped and stood quite alone in the tall grass. No one else was about, so I removed my veil and pulled the pin out of my hair. It tumbled down my back in waves the color of storm clouds. I leaned my head back and closed my eyes and shook it loose.

Ah, Guillemette, my husband would say, *your hair . . . it can make the birds sing. . . .*

I opened my eyes and saw not songbirds but a falcon circling lazily overhead. It dipped to follow some hapless mouse or shrew, which was oblivious to its imminent rendezvous with a beak. How Etienne could bear to have such a cold creature as a falcon sit upon his arm was beyond me, but as Milord Gilles became more enamored of birding, it fell to Etienne to accommodate the requirements of his lust for that sport.

It was too easy to dwell on such memories when God's hat was off my head. So even though the bareheadedness was blissful, I replaced the veil and rearranged myself properly. Thoughts of Milord's lusts were banished and I continued into the village.

The anticipated bustle was everywhere in evidence, for Pax was coming, and there was much to be done in preparation. I spoke to the first friendly-looking man I encountered, bidding him good day.

"Good day to you, Mother," he replied, quite pleasantly.

"I am looking for a certain woman, one Madame le Barbier, a seamstress from the parish of Saint-Honoré. Can you tell me, please, where might I find her?"

The man's face reddened almost immediately, and by

the expression he wore, I half-expected him to reach up and cross himself.

"Over there," he answered after a weighty silence. He pointed eastward and I had to shade my eyes to see anything because the sun was so strong. "Go past the well and then between the first two cottages you come to on the left. Just beyond them is a round cottage. She lives there," he said.

I nodded my understanding and began to thank him, but he interrupted me.

"May God watch over her," he said, "and you."

He hurried away. My hand was raised and my mouth open; jumbled words of gratitude and confusion poured out of me. But he could not have heard a bit of it, for he was nervously whispering, almost a song.

Something about small children ...

There was more I wanted to ask; I made a half-hearted attempt to hail him, but he was too far gone by then, considering that I did not know his name. To summon the man back as "Sir" would have turned a dozen heads, and I did not want that attention.

His directions were excellent. Madame's round house faced into a common courtyard with two others, though both of those were longhouses that would shelter animals as well as people. Madame le Barbier's trade could be lucrative as bourgeois trades go, and at one time she could probably afford not to have animals inside her house. The woman I remembered from so many years before would have been proud of her prosperity.

But today she had the same mud in her courtyard as every other resident of the village outside Machecoul; it was a universal affliction, especially at this time of spring. I tiptoed through the ooze with my skirts raised and knocked on the plank door, then stood, clutching my robes about me, and waited.

And waited.

"Who calls?" I finally heard from within.

"Madame le Barbier?"

After a pause, I heard the same inquiries repeated, though less muffled this time.

It seemed futile to stand on ceremony. "This is Sister Guillemette. I was present when you called on his Eminence last night. I would have a word with you about the matter in question."

There was a decided bustle within and then the door opened. Madame le Barbier looked disheveled, as if she had just arisen from her pallet; had she still been in the straw at an hour when industry, not sleep, was supposed to be the rule? I could not help but think so.

"What do you want?" she demanded, her voice full of suspicion.

"I would speak to you of the matter that brought you to the abbey last night."

♛

We were preparing for Vespers but had not yet lit the torches in the cathedral itself when Madame le Barbier came to call—the Bishop will not light a candle in the house of God until he can barely see his own hand, for he insists that God sees all even in darkness. How different from Milord Gilles, who adored notice and would cast brilliant light upon himself the whole night through despite its great cost. His enormous wealth made it possible for him to behave so recklessly, a quality of which I distinctly disapproved. Even well into his adulthood, I would take every opportunity to chide him for wastefulness. He would always laugh affectionately in his dismissal of my concern. He had a strange affinity for lesser folk such as myself, though it was no wonder, for he came into this world and settled into common hands, those being my own. Lady Marie could not hold back her convulsions; the midwife had been summoned too late. Were I not there to catch him, he would have made a far less dignified entry than befits an infant who would grow up to own more of France and Brittany than their respective rulers.

It was as violent a birth as any I had ever witnessed; we all thought it a terrible portent. When she finally arrived, the midwife had much work to do in repairing his poor exhausted mother. Still, he was as perfect-looking as one can hope for in an infant, the unifying member of two powerful families whose wealth and holdings were already unimaginable.

Mine was the first face into which he gazed, and mine was the first teat on which his hungry little mouth would settle. I recall thinking at the time that his eyes were so dark and deep, and that if nature played her proper role, he would grow to be a handsome lad as befit his fortunate station. Those were days of great promise and joy.

Madame Agathe le Barbier, Frère Demien had said to announce her.

And immediately I had recalled a hearty woman of substantial wit. But the woman who entered was small in comparison to the memory and anything but hearty. She wore tattered garb, quite incomprehensible for someone who had been a prosperous tradeswoman. She was all bones beneath the voluminous folds of her skirt.

When I had a child at the breast—many years running, it seems, since I nursed my own two children as well as Milord Gilles—I could not seem to hold an ounce of flesh on my bones for what it took from me. My hips just seemed to melt away, and my own skirts would have dragged had I not fastened them in tighter. Etienne managed to pad me out a bit with ale, God bless him—he liked me lush. But Madame le Barbier was not of an age where she would still be suckling babes.

I had felt compelled to speak. *Your Eminence, I beg a word before we proceed.*

Immediately he had furrowed his magnificent eyebrow, surely the seat of his power, in frank disapproval. Such handsomeness was sadly wasted on a cleric—he ought to have been a courtier.

This woman is known to me, I had whispered out of her earshot. *A seamstress quite skilled at her trade, enough so to attract the personal business of Milord himself, who takes notable pride in his appearance.*

"Too much pride," he said with a grunt.

"She has aged far more than her due," I told him. "She was once a handsome and robust woman. One wonders—"

And then the Bishop's impatience got the better of him. "Guillemette, if you have nothing more substantial than gossip to tell me, I shall proceed to hear her."

I blurted out unsolicited insight into the stated purpose of her visit.

"Her son would have to be fifteen or sixteen years old now." A brief pang of regret for how time separates us from our fondest memories passed through me. "He was a beautiful babe and, oh, so vigorous! If childhood was decent to him, he would have grown into a handsome youth, perhaps unusually so."

Madame went frequently to Lord de Rais's apartments with bolts of fabric and samples of buttons and other such trimmings, for as his Eminence had been quick to point out, and not with approval, Milord loved finery. One such occasion stayed with me and haunted me still. Milord was late for the appointment he had made with Madame's employer—not an uncommon occurrence, since he craved the fuss that was made when he swooped in so dramatically. Madame had given the little boy to a young girl to watch over him, but at that moment the child was ill and could not be quieted. The girl had been forced to bring him inside. No sooner did Madame have him calm than Lord de Rais strode briskly into the room. She turned away to hide the child from his view so as not to offend him, but Milord Gilles saw the infant. He came directly over to Madame and plucked him off the breast. The boy began to wail again, this time as if he were being tortured.

Lord de Rais bounced the boy up and down with a fascination that distressed me, though I could not say exactly why.

"Why, little angel," he said, "what have you to fear? I am no demon." Then he laughed, and tousled the boy's fine yellow hair.

How unseemly that attention was, if one gave it any thought—a great lord in the glow of manhood, bouncing the baby of a tradeswoman in his arms, when so much other business awaited. But I did not think on it further at the time, for the girl whisked Madame's child out of the room, and, after all, had I not done the same to that lord himself when he was just a babe? More so than his own mother, I daresay. Then we were caught up in the bustle of tasks: measuring, fitting, the selection of trims and fancies—it was all so very engaging that my concerns slipped away. There was Lady Catherine's wardrobe to be seen to as well; it would not do to have Milord looking fine and his wife shabby, though he hardly took notice of her that I or anyone else could see.

As was often the case, Madame and I had exchanged pleasantries that day—that is, when she had recovered from her agitation over the incident. She had little awe of those above her station, having seen the naked gentry often enough to have a certain ease about it. Now, so many years later, she no longer seemed to have that ease. She stumbled at first when directed to speak.

"My son is a lad of sixteen, just last month."

I was correct, then, in my recollections of his age.

The Bishop had seemed perplexed, rightly—this was not a matter for him, but for the Magistrate. Still, he queried her. "What seems to be the matter with the boy?"

"That I cannot say, for he has simply vanished. I sent him out thirteen days ago with a set of breeches for delivery and he never returned."

I had opened my mouth, wanting to speak, but Jean de Malestroit's flashing glance stopped me. I knew what he was thinking, that the boy had just run off as young boys sometimes do, or that the money he was supposed to collect had been squandered or lost. I remained silent and still against all my inclinations. Then he did precisely what he ought to have done; he advised her to see the Magistrate.

She had turned back at the door to say, "Other children have disappeared and he has not answered the complaints of their parents."

They eat small children there, Jean had written.

For a few moments thereafter, the Bishop and I had remained silent.

Finally, I summoned the courage to speak. But before my words came out, he said, "It is not lost on me, Guillemette, that you must have great sympathy for this woman. But she must do as I have advised her. You must know this better than most. Now, let us proceed, for God is impatient."

One does not keep a deity waiting.

Another unsettling moment of silence passed, this time at Madame le Barbier's door. Finally she said, "Have you some authority that was not revealed last night?"

"None more, I am sad to say. But I come in sympathy and a desire to help you if I can."

"May God forgive my impertinence, Mother, but

you had the chance to help me already and you did not."
Her words were harsh and her expression angry, and
there was little I could say in my own defense. It angered
me as well that I had remained silent during her plea.

"I am as much an underling to his Eminence as anyone else is. But I did speak on your behalf after you left."

It was a limp offering, but her expression softened
on hearing it. "And did you know success?"

"Well . . . not precisely."

"Then why are you here? You will only taunt me further."

"No, Madame, I swear I will not taunt. That would
be cruel."

We had not moved from our relative positions, she
just inside the door, myself still in the mud outside it.
"Please," I said, "may I come in and speak with you?"

A deep bitterness seemed to overtake her; she looked
hard at me and said, "What good will it do? You, an
abbess, have as much as said you can do little for me, and
you cannot possibly understand how my heart breaks
well enough to offer any true sympathy." She started to
close the door.

I put out my hand to stop it and, to my own surprise,
succeeded. My skirts dropped into the mud.

"You are wrong, Madame," I said. "I am here because I *do* understand. And because there are things I
would know."

chapter 2

FUNNY HOW SOME WORDS just sound like what they mean.

Dirrrrrrrrrggggggggge.

The mournful dirge "Scotland the Brave" looped in my head, complete with snares and big drums. I could feel a headache coming on. But by now our fellow detective Terry Donnolly was at the blue gates of cop heaven, toward which he had been piped on this rare gray day in Los Angeles. Everyone agreed it was just the right kind of weather for a funeral. Thank God, because sunshine at a funeral makes no sense to me at all.

The mourners had disbanded and most headed toward the mass of units parked along the narrow driveways of the cemetery. Benicio Escobar was at my side, shaking his head. We walked slowly past a small group of brass, all huddled together and sharing some deep secret known only to those of elevated position.

The only word we heard of their whisperings was *himself*. He drank himself to death.

"They make it sound like he killed himself. He didn't. The job killed him."

"Ben ... come on. Don't do this. It's not going to change anything."

The autopsy had been performed almost immediately. The tissue and fluid samples had been carefully collected and catalogued, and results were coming in quickly.

"He had a heart attack, for God's sake. There's no question about that."

Word had spread quickly around the division when it happened. They'd kept him breathing until he got to the trauma center, where one of the doctors had immediately cracked his chest.

His heart had basically exploded. There was massive damage, and, breathing or not, he was dead the second it happened. He died of an irreparably broken heart.

"You know, I hated that big Mick when we first paired up, but he grew on me, you know? We got to be friends. *Good* friends."

I touched Ben's arm to comfort him. "Let it rest."

Escobar sniffed and wiped a few tears away with his fingertips. "Maybe if Terry had just let a few things rest he'd still be here today."

I had no argument.

We walked in synchrony to the echo of the drone. The pipers had already packed up their gear and were gone, but their music hung in the air. By the time we reached the car, I'd managed to shut down "Scotland the Brave," but no sooner was it banished than "Minstrel Boy" slipped in to take its place.

It took "She Loves You" on the radio to finally send it away for good. I went home and tried to relax before my shift started at six.

When I got back to the division room, things were inordinately quiet. No ringing phones, no wisecrack banter, no crackling radios or shrill cell phones. It often happens that way when there's a sad official occasion; for some unknown reason, the perverts shut down, as if it were against their sense of fair play to grab a kid while the members of the Crimes Against Children division were all at a funeral.

It didn't last long. The phone rang on Terry Donnolly's desk. I heard the desk sergeant call out, "Who's here?"

I took a quick look around. Escobar was in the head, and no one else seemed to be there.

"Dunbar," I called out, reluctantly.

"Well, you better get that phone, Pandora."

I wish they wouldn't call me that. But it isn't a fluke, sad to say; I always seem to get the cases that are loaded with all the troubles of the world. So I looked at the phone and I thought, *Don't touch that thing, it's going to be a box full of trouble,* a moronic notion because we don't get calls in this division from folks who just want to say, *Hi, how are you.* They have to go through channels of referral first, patrol cops, detectives, maybe a sergeant or two, and then it's gonna be, *They stole my car and my baby was in the backseat; they're cooking up something that smells really bad next door and there's a four-year-old in the apartment;* or, *someone's using his kid for a punching bag.* Not, *Hello, ma'am, how are you today, and would you like to try our incredible six-pound vacuum cleaner for ninety days, risk free?* Always something, never pleasant.

And it was creepy that the phone was ringing on Donnolly's desk, just after we'd planted him.

"Crimes Against Children, Detective Lany Dunbar," I said.

"My son is gone."

Trouble.

"How do you mean, gone?" I asked the woman.

"Missing. Disappeared. Just gone."

I hate to tell you what we usually think when we first

hear "missing kid," and I hate to tell you how many times we hear it. Kids take a walk on the wild side for all sorts of reasons, and it's not always just the screwed-up ones. Lots of nice, normal kids bolt, and they do it for the most bizarre reasons you can imagine. For that reason we don't spring right into action until we eliminate a few of the more common possibilities first.

I asked the caller to tell me her name.

She snapped it out. "Ellen Leeds."

"Ms. Leeds—"

"Mrs."

I could understand why she might be feeling a little bit tense at the moment. "Mrs. Leeds, has a patrol officer been to your home yet?"

"No. I called 911 and they sent me right to you."

It had to have been a new operator. "Give me your address and phone number, please."

She blurted it out.

Escobar's desk was the closest one. I had to dig around to find a scrap of paper—his work space is always so disorganized. But he's amazingly productive, against all probability. I scribbled, then said, "I'm going to put you on hold for just a moment. I'll be right back with you."

I called the patrol sergeant for that district and asked him to send a car to that address to wait for me. The call would give her a few seconds to settle down, but I didn't want to leave her holding too long. She was about to go through a series of highly insulting questions designed to hack right through the bullshit—*when was the last time you punished your child physically* is one they all just love.

My own desk is pathetically neat. When I need a pencil I know just where to put my hand, and if it's dull there's an electric sharpener in the right-hand drawer. I used to keep it on the corner of my desk but it walked a couple of times. It's only because I'm a detective that I figured to look in Frazee's cubicle for it.

There's a stack of fresh notebooks in the lower right drawer, which no longer squeaks because I oiled it the day before. There was a nice, soft *whoosh* when I opened it, and it made me smile.

That might have been the last time I smiled.

Notebook open, pencil sharpened, I pushed the button. "Mrs. Leeds," I said into the phone, "I'm sorry to have kept you waiting."

"Detective Dunbar, my son is out there somewhere, alone and afraid. Every second is precious."

Stuff like that still stings me, but we have to follow procedures, especially in these cases, because the sad fact is that it's almost always a close friend or intimate—we can't say "relative" anymore because family structures have changed so much—at the bottom of a kid's disappearance.

"I understand your anxiety right now. I'm sorry to say that I have to ask you a number of questions, some of which may be upsetting to you. But I hope you'll also understand that we have to determine a few things right away to know how we should proceed in the case of a missing child. It saves a lot of wheel-spinning later."

"Get on with it, then. But I can tell you right now that somebody took him. Just took him."

So much for procedures. "What makes you think that?"

"He's not the kind of kid who would run away."

They never are. "I'm sure that's true, but we do have to eliminate that possibility. So please, just bear with me. This will take only a few minutes and then we can get to the specifics. Does the boy live with you?"

"Nathan. Yes, he does."

"What about his father?"

"We're divorced. He lives in Tucson."

"Any other children?"

There was this little hesitation, then she said, "No."

"Any other adults in the household?"

"No. Just me and him."

"How old is Nathan?"

"Twelve last July."

"What grade in school?"

"Seventh."

"You say you are divorced. What is the nature of your relationship with Nathan's father?"

"Tolerably cordial."

She'd been asked that question before and had a ready answer. I wondered who had done the asking and scribbled on my notepad a reminder to ask.

"How about his relationship with Nathan?"

"They adore each other."

"How often do they see each other?"

"Not often enough. Maybe once a month. My ex flies in as often as he can. And Nathan spends summers in Arizona."

"When did they last see each other?"

"About a week ago. Nathan's father came here."

"I'll need contact information for him before we finish."

"Of course."

I took a long breath before asking the next question. I'm sure she heard it. "Mrs. Leeds, do you have a regular companion of any kind?"

I always hate that question. My first impulse is to say *boyfriend,* but we can't do that anymore either. It's getting silly, the way we have to talk now. Frazee had a great call once—female-sounding voice says, *My lover is missing.* After the usual round of questions Frazee asks for a description. It took him about twenty minutes to figure out that the caller was a cross-dresser, and the missing lover was *actually* a woman but was being described as a man, the point of the whole story being that you can't always assume things about people by looking at them or listening to them, because people do all sorts of things to make themselves look different than they really are.

"I don't have a boyfriend, if that's what you mean. I date occasionally, but there's no one special or significant. And no one who's had any contact with Nathan."

"So he wouldn't have gone with anyone else and not told you."

"No. Not that I can think of at all." Then her voice got really hard. "Detective, don't you think I've already exhausted all the other possibilities on my own?"

I let the comment pass without reaction. "When did you first begin to suspect that something might be amiss?"

"Just a little while ago. He left for school this morning at the usual time and that was the last anyone saw of him. He generally meets up with a couple of other kids on the next corner, but not always. When they do meet they walk the rest of the distance together. It's only three blocks from here."

When she told me the address I recognized it as an apartment building in one of the better sections of the precinct. There had been a suicide a couple of years ago before I came to CAC, and I'd been the primary on it.

"I know that building." I didn't tell her how. "Nice and clean."

"And safe, or so I thought," Ellen Leeds said.

But not safe enough.

So began another quest for the proverbial needle, the one that has the nasty habit of leaping into the haystack at the most inconvenient time. Nathan's description went out immediately to all the patrols and precincts. Adolescent male, about five feet six inches tall, slight of build, dark-blondish hair, blue eyes. Probably wearing a red or maroon jacket and jeans. Sneakers, but they all wore sneakers—it would have been noteworthy if he had anything else on his feet. Beat cops all through the city would hear his description over the radio, and for a couple of hours they'd really be vigilant about looking for him. Then another call would come in, and a description would be sent out for the next needle, and Nathan's image would begin to blend with that of every other missing teenager. He would enter into that great neutral amalgam of unfound children, *those* kids, whose smiling images on milk cartons make us all feel so smug about our own success in raising children.

Just before our initial phone contact ended, Ellen Leeds asked me, "How long do you think it will take to find him?"

"There's no way to answer that question until we do. We'll try our very best." Anything else would have been an ugly lie, not that the probable truth was exactly pretty.

All the way to her neighborhood I brooded over that truth. Sometimes we get lucky and they turn up. Sometimes they just walk through the door after staying out all night and we get a "never mind" call from the parent, who's not only angry but really embarrassed to have missed the signs that the kid had it in him to do that. More times than I like to tell you we get no call at all when they turn up at home, and we expend all sorts of effort looking for a little lost bird who's already back in the nest. That really annoys me.

But when it's the real deal, our success rate is humiliatingly low. The likelihood of us finding Nathan Leeds if he didn't want to be found—or his abductor didn't want us to find him—was really small. We just don't have the resources to get out the kind of search that will turn up a grabbed kid if he's still alive—big *if* there. Volunteers are the best bet, but they still have to be organized, and that takes manpower. We just don't have it.

There were a couple of patrol cars parked outside

Ellen Leeds's apartment building. I talked with the guys briefly—I knew one of them, but the other was too new. When I was on patrol myself, I had lots of reasons to associate with my brothers and sisters in arms. The locker rooms were a great place to hang out. But detectives wear street clothes, so I rarely go there anymore.

A few people were standing around, curious about the presence of patrol units. Good security; it took two buzzes to get past the lobby. The Leeds apartment was on the fifth floor, at the back of the building, what I imagined was probably the quieter side, since the street that ran behind was narrow and one-way.

There was a hand-painted welcome sign hanging on the door, a cheery, homespun kind of thing. The woman who answered the *ding dong* was surprisingly small and thin, leading me to wonder if this was the same woman who'd made the call. Her voice had sounded bigger.

"Mrs. Leeds?"

"Yes."

"I'm Detective Dunbar." I handed her one of my cards. She took it quickly but didn't bother to look at it.

"Come in."

I stepped into the apartment; it was immaculately clean and decorated in warm colors. Very homey and safe-looking. She closed the door behind me, and I heard the turn of a dead bolt and the slide of a chain. She was careful. "You have good security in the building lobby, and up here too," I said.

"I wish they would put a guard at the front door, though, at least after dark. I picked this building in part because of the security. And I asked for something above the second floor so no one could come in and grab my son out of an open window."

It was a bitter and ironic reference to the high-profile abduction of twelve-year-old Polly Klaas, who was dragged out of her bedroom window as three slumber-party friends watched in horror. The mother was asleep in a nearby room at the time—can you imagine the balls of this perp? There was never any doubt about what happened to her— she didn't just decide to take a little break from *no video games until your homework is done*. Her parents were articulate and pretty well-connected, and right away a whole bunch of very visible people got behind the search. The shame of it is that she was probably still alive and only about fifty yards away while a pair of cops questioned her abductor after he had car trouble. Lucky son of a bitch. We got him in the end. Too late for Polly, but we got him.

But if Ellen Leeds thought that her son's disappearance would bring about the same kind of response, I was going to have to disappoint her.

She pointed me to a couch and offered something to drink, which I refused politely. We can't get too sociable, because it's tough to stay in charge if you're acting like a visitor or a guest, especially if you're a woman. We sat opposite each other on separate couches, and I opened up my notebook. "Please recount the events of the day for me, if you would."

I watched her speak. You can tell if people are lying sometimes; their eyes get shifty and their faces really tighten up. We're trained to look for certain signs when we do interviews. A person who isn't telling the complete truth will often glance away, because it's hard to look someone in the eye and speak an outright lie unless you're a complete sociopath, and contrary to popular belief, they're pretty rare.

But in parents whose kids have disappeared, another factor sneaks in—they blame themselves, whether or not that's appropriate, and that kind of guilt clouds the picture. Ellen Leeds stared down at her hands as she spoke, which made it more difficult to read her.

"I got home from work this evening at about the usual

time. Nathan has a classmate whose mother and I take turns with the kids. Today was his day to go to George's. His mother and I have our schedules coordinated so one or the other of us is around every afternoon. Thank God we can both work from home. The kids don't need to be watched directly, they just need an adult available. It's a good arrangement and it's worked beautifully. Until now."

"How does Nathan get back home from there?"

"He calls and I go pick him up. Usually around six-thirty or seven, because dinner is included in our setup."

"Makes sense."

"Yeah." She pulled a tissue from a box on the coffee table that was between us and wiped her nose. "It's nice not to have to rush home and throw dinner together."

I wanted to smile and say, *yeah, I know,* because that was exactly what I did each day when I worked my normal day shift. This past week I'd been moved to evenings temporarily because a whole bunch of detectives were out of town for bioterrorism training and we needed the night coverage. I started back on days tomorrow. My own kids were staying with their father for the week and *he* was rushing home to cook their dinner for a change. It was nice to know that he was going to have to listen to a chorus of *but I don't like meat loaf mac and cheese chicken.* Evan is a truly pathetic eater; he hates everything. Frannie eats everything in sight but nothing that's good for her. Julia I still haven't figured out. Thank God they're not allergic to any foods, or I think I'd have to give up.

It was not the time to drift off into my own troubles.

"It got to be almost eight," I heard Mrs. Leeds say.

"Did he usually call before then?"

Guilt spread over her face as she nodded yes, clouding her expression even further. "I didn't call because I was really liking the quiet. Working full-time, I get so behind in my life, you know? I don't have time to do any of the things that make *me* happy. I took out my needlepoint tonight for the first time in months."

Poor woman; she probably would never do needle-point again.

"But when it started to get so late I called their house, and George's mother told me—"

She choked up for a few seconds; I did nothing, said nothing, just watched.

"She told me that George said Nathan hadn't come to school today at all."

"Do you generally communicate when that happens?"

"No. Not usually. I mean, if the kid's not in school, the automatic assumption is that he's home sick and the parent knows, right?"

That was the mistake she would have to live with for the rest of her life. "Right," I said quietly. "We'll need to get a time line set up for everyone who saw Nathan today. And everyone who expected to but didn't."

"I called the school principal as soon as I got off the phone with Nancy—George's mother. He called Nathan's team teacher and she told him that Nathan had never been in school."

"They're not computerized?"

"Not yet."

Principal, teacher, I scribbled in the notebook. "We'll need to make a contact list. But go on, please."

"That's it. He just didn't show up where he was sup-posed to be."

"The school doesn't have a policy of contacting the parent in that situation?"

"No."

Hard to believe, but the regulations didn't mandate it yet. The policy would be in place the next day. I would make sure of it.

———

Ellen Leeds directed me along the route Nathan would have taken to get to school. I needed her to travel it with me once to get it right, and then I would take her back home again and go over it again without her watching. It took only a minute or two in a car, during which I kept an eye on Mrs. Leeds to see if she reacted to anything in particular. All I could see was that agonizing expression of distress.

As I brought the car to a stop outside her building, she asked, "Will you be coming up again?"

It was almost a plea. "Not right now. I have to get some things going right away. But I'll be in touch with you tomorrow, and as leads develop." I pointedly did not say *if* leads develop. "I'll be calling you for additional details."

"But what will you be doing right now, while my son is God knows where, maybe hurt, maybe in the hands of some monster?"

Scratching my head and wondering what to do.

"Mrs. Leeds, please don't jump to conclusions." Unfortunately, it was a logical conclusion. "I already sent Nathan's picture back with the patrol officer. He'll have it out on the cruiser computers within a few minutes along with a description. They'll also send it out to the other departments in adjacent communities. All those officers will be keeping an eye out for your son."

"You're not going to organize a real search?"

I took a moment to formulate my response. "In the morning, when it would be fruitful, we'll get something organized if the leads we develop tonight warrant it."

"I'd like to come to the station with you. I want to help in any way I can."

No, no, no. "Mrs. Leeds, I don't think it would be wise for you to do that."

"But if something should come up and you need me, then I would be there—"

"I'll call and send a car if something develops. Right

away. I promise. You probably don't want to hear this, but the best thing you can do right now is go back to your apartment and try to get some rest."

"Do you think I'm actually going to be able to sleep?"

I didn't. "I know this is difficult, Mrs. Leeds. But you'll have to just wait now."

"Just wait."

"Yes. And if Nathan should call—"

She cut me off. "So I'm supposed to go back upstairs into my apartment, where my son lives with me, and I'm supposed to just wait there for him to show up or call."

"Ma'am, I'll be back in touch with you as soon as I can. But there are things I have to do to get this investigation rolling properly."

She got out of the car, but before she closed the door, she turned and glared accusingly. "What am I supposed to do right now, will you tell me that? I'm going to go up there and look around my home and nothing will look familiar to me, because everything has changed."

"Mrs. Leeds, I'm sorry, I truly am, but we do have procedures in place—"

The door slammed. She ran toward the main entry to the building. I watched as she unlocked the outer lobby door, and then the inner one. The big modern building swallowed her.

It was midnight. Too late to call my children at their father's apartment to tell them that I love them like crazy. Their father, Saint Kevin, would be righteously indignant, and their own belief that Mom was just a little whacked would once again be reinforced. So I did the next most satisfying thing I could do—I got to work.

I called for two units to join me in the parking lot. We left our cars there and, flashlights waving, searched both sides of that first street. What we were looking for I couldn't really say; if there was minuscule evidence or blood, we weren't going to see it until daylight. But we all knew the scene wasn't going to get any fresher than this, if it was in fact a scene. That needle-in-a-haystack feeling crept through me again. Hurtling through the universe in search of one specific asteroid. It always makes me feel so small and stupid.

But we have to start somewhere. We picked up a lot of paper scraps, but nothing that looked like it would have anything to do with a middle-school student, no official school notices, nothing that might be discarded homework. But we tucked the papers into an evidence bag anyway, because you never know. A decent detective is almost always a pack rat—I certainly am, even if I am neat about what I gather.

There had been little or no wind over the last day— thank God it was too early for the Santa Anas, but we were all complaining anyway. Right at that moment I was grateful for the dead air, or whatever *was* there might have blown away.

We turned onto the second of the three streets. From where we stood I could still see the upper two-thirds of the apartment building Nathan had left that morning, which meant that someone could have seen something.

This street was more residential than the first one we covered—fences, bushes, wider sidewalks. We divvied up the territory and separated. I poked my light into brush and moved branches around with one hand as I looked into little spots where squirrels are usually the only observers. My back hurt from bending so low, but I denied the ache and concentrated. Once or twice I saw the red glow of eyeballs reflected back. There were little scurrying sounds as assorted quadrupeds headed for cover. A June bug screamed and put a crack in the thin veneer of calm I'd managed to maintain. I shoved aside the dried palm husks that invariably got swept under covering brush, but carefully, because they can have sharp razor edges. They rustled like peanut shells.

It all went silent when one of the patrols yelled out, "I got something."

three

IT HAD BEEN MANY YEARS since the evil day on which my Michel had simply disappeared at the flower of his youthful vigor and beauty, and I had only succeeded—through nearly constant flagellation of my own soul—to dull the ache somewhat. One never forgets the agony of losing a child; one can only hope that the memories will diminish in time. That is as it should be—the spirit of a lost child should remain forever in the hearts of those who loved him, so it may be kept alive. Often I have wondered why it was that God put this task to me, that the essence of the boy who was Michel la Drappiere should have been given to me to preserve. How is one to preserve the sweet innocence, the lovely curiosity, the growing depth of his character? I had not even one portrait of him, save the one that parades daily through my waking mind on its way to my dreaming heart. He is tall and slender, but his limbs show the promise of later strength. He has eyes the color of a clear sky in April. How does one capture his warmth, the tenderness of his embrace, the humor of his cracking voice? There have been many moments when I feel that I am simply not strong enough.

Madame le Barbier at first gasped when I told her, then swore the bitterest of oaths; she clutched my hand so fiercely that I feared for the bones in my fingers. The tattered woman embraced my shoulders with surprising violence as tears of unspeakable grief poured out, for me, for herself, for our lost sons, for all the tortured days that I had known and she would come to know. A swoon overtook her to the point that I began to fear she would collapse. I guided her inside to a cushioned bench, where she fell against my shoulder and allowed the sobs to claim her. When her will to weep actively was spent, she laid her head in my lap and hitched in a long series of uneven breaths until she finally dozed.

I knew, though others might not, that there were no words to ameliorate her pain, no expressions of sympathy to soothe the ache that began in the moment of her loss and would never, if my own journey had revealed any truth, come to a proper end. What Madame needed was someone to sit silently by her side while she endeavored to empty her soul of its misery, which might seem to her a fruitless effort for a very long time. A similar kindness had been done for me in my own desperate hours, ironically by a bride of Christ who had entered into service (though voluntarily, unlike myself) when her husband died. She was known for her generosity and proved it with her gift of uncritical time to me; when the other ladies of the castle had no more patience for my weeping and lamentations, when even Etienne's tolerance was growing brittle, she was the one in whose presence I could always find solace. She compelled me to enter the light I so dearly loved once again by simply refusing to allow me to vanish into the sweet, uncomplicated darkness that beckoned after Michel's disappearance. To live in the light seemed too much then; I felt I would always wear the mark of unspeakable shame, one that would separate me from the fellowship of those who were not similarly scarred.

I had convinced myself beyond all doubt that Michel's disappearance must have been the result of some fault of mine, some dire failing, and that the tragedy could have been averted had I only been more vigilant, more attentive, a better mother, a hawk to my fledgling son. To believe that it had simply been a random occurrence, that God for some reason had spared Milord Gilles and had laid his hand upon my son instead, was too much to bear, for it took away all hope of safety in this world. It was so much more comforting to tell myself that there was a reason for it and that my own failure to be watchful was the cause. We must always find someone to blame, after all. But my dear sister in God made me understand that what He sets in motion cannot be altered, despite our desperate efforts to thwart His will with our own good actions. In time, I have been able to forgive myself to some degree, but it has been brutally slow in coming.

My hand rested on Madame's head; I half-expected to feel those same self-incriminations through her hair. I was determined to do for her what had been done for me so many years before, as we were but two links in a long, unbroken chain of sorrow. I sat while she slept, her head heavy in my lap, and considered how there were days when my own grief still felt fresh to me, though it was ancient to everyone else.

When she finally stirred and raised herself up, her face was stained and streaked with tears and her eyes were pitifully swollen. With one corner of her apron I wiped away what wet remained. She stared at me as I did this, her eyes begging to know, *Will this ever end?* I wished I could have told her *yes*. But it would have been a lie.

She got up from the bench and began to pace. I watched her in silence, though there were many things I wanted both to say and to ask. When she finally spoke, her voice was shaky, though in and of itself this did not alarm me greatly—it was many months after my son's death before my voice was firm enough to sound beyond my own ears. Etienne was always telling me to speak up, sometimes rather more brusquely than I thought kind. He seemed through the natural characteristics of his sex to recover more quickly than I did, though there was a hardness to him after Michel's death. I could never seem to break through it entirely, the armor that men often put up around themselves to ward off deep emotions that do not serve them well in the tasks they are required to do, most especially the unsavory task of war. How can a man feel sorrow for the warrior whose head he must remove and still make the bloody cut? It would be impossible.

"Your son, what was his name?" I heard her whisper.

"Michel," I answered. "La Drappiere."

I waited; she gave no indication that she knew me. After a few moments I said, "You do not remember me, then?"

She looked at my face. "No," she said. "I regret to say I do not. Do we know each other, Mother?"

Of course we both looked very different—thirteen years takes its toll by the natural order of things. God does not want us to be as attractive as the younger widows, who might yet bear children and ought to have first claim on what men the wars have not taken. "We met now and again when my husband served at Champtocé, and I with him," I told her.

Though my fingers were stiff from Madame le Barbier having clutched them, I reached up and removed my veil. I set it on Madame's table and smoothed back a few errant strands of hair.

She looked at me, and slowly came the spark of

recognition. "Madame la Drappiere," she breathed. "Of course."

"*Oui*," I said. "*C'est moi.* Once you called me Guillemette."

"But ... I would not have thought you—"

—could tolerate a life of service in the church, I thought in my own mind. Strangely, that sentiment felt like a compliment.

"It is not a life entirely of my choosing." I clenched and unclenched my fingers a few times to restore the feeling to them. "My husband died from his wounds after Orléans." I did not need to explain any further.

Madame le Barbier shook her head slowly back and forth as she continued to sniff. "Well, at least you are provided for."

"That I am," I said. "And I am not as lonely as I was in my last days in Milord's service. Everyone I knew and cherished there—by then they were all gone. The abbey is a pleasant place where I can be useful; I am a confidante of his Eminence, who depends on me in small ways."

"Indeed. I saw that last night."

It surprised me to learn that she had observed anything in her state of distress, but once her memory was prompted by recognition, she began to recall other things as well.

"I remember your son ..." she said, "but he was older than what I would have thought him to be."

"You are thinking of my firstborn, Jean," I told her. "He is—*was*—older than Michel. He is a priest now. In Avignon."

"A priest?" Her surprise was marked. "This was allowed?"

Unthinkable, Etienne had said when Jean first voiced his desire to enter the priesthood. *It will not be considered.*

You will soldier as I have. Let your brother, Michel, enter God's service, as befits his secondary position.

"He had no aptitude for the arts of war," I said, "nor a whit of interest...."

Michel would gladly take up the sword. I beg you, Etienne, for the good of our sons, let Jean take the cloth instead.

"It was a mountainous task, but I did manage to prevail upon my husband to allow Michel, instead of our firstborn, to be the one to learn weapons. In time he came to see that the arrangement suited them both well. Michel was only just beginning to practice with armaments when he—"

So many years had passed and still I could barely say it.

"He ... *vanished*," I whispered.

My voice abandoned me for a few moments, during which time Madame joined me in a comforting silence. "So Jean is in Avignon ..." she eventually said, "a fair city, *à bon temps,* I have heard. But so far away ..."

"I have never traveled there, though his Eminence has had audiences with the Holy Father many times during my service to him. He says it is a comely place indeed, especially the palace where his Holiness lives. I miss Jean terribly, but he seems happy in his work—and there are finally plans for me to visit him in a few months when his Eminence travels to Avignon."

I saw genuine pleasure in her expression. "How wonderful to have such a journey ahead of you! The traveling will be hard, but—"

"I have never feared setting out into the world—indeed, I have always viewed it as something of a pleasure. What awaits me at the end of this road makes the journey itself seem a mere trifle of inconvenience." I patted my sleeve. "He writes often; I carry the letters on my person until I have memorized them. But it is not the same, Madame, as reaching out and touching his cheek."

"Please," she said, "my given name is Agathe." Then came another bitter smile. "We are true sisters, *n'est-ce pas?* With something as strong as the souls of our sons to join us, we ought to be on quite intimate terms."

Her tears flowed again. I put my arm around her shoulder until she stopped weeping.

"Well, then, Agathe," I said to her, "you must tell me all that you know of what happened to Georges."

She bit her lip. "Ah, Mother—"

"Guillemette," I corrected her.

"Guillemette." She tried to smile, but it was a half-hearted gesture at best. "There are times when I cannot seem to stop speaking of it, but right now, it is as if you have just told me I must walk to the Holy Land and back again in a fortnight."

I said nothing but lightly touched her hand in reassurance. She sniffed once again, then began her sorrowful recitation. "My employer—the tailor Jean Peletier, a well-respected man—still dresses Lady Catherine sometimes, although the woman seems a veritable ghost to me, for all that we see of her. Sometimes, when the occasion arises, he will outfit Lord Gilles himself, though we have done much less of that since Milord took to traveling so much."

Stories of his entourage were legendary, of lavish trains, multitudes of retainers and servants, all impressively attired. "He seems never to stay in one of his own castles for very long," I said. "One wonders at his nomadic tendency. He did not show it as a child."

"Ah, but he saw it—in his father. We were always outfitting Lord Guy for one journey or another. How his traveling garments became so worn so quickly I will never understand. But now Milord Gilles stays in Champtocé for good stretches, or so Monsieur Peletier says; he has heard this from a tailor he knows there. We serve him only when he is in Machecoul." She added, hesitantly, "And there is difficulty in collecting what is owed from him, so we do not directly seek his business."

Thank God it had not been my responsibility to teach the boy Gilles how to manage money—I cannot imagine the battles we would have had. That gruesome chore fell to Jean de Craon, who terrified his grandson into obedience on all matters with consummate cruelty but still somehow did not manage to impart sound fiscal sense to him. I could almost hear Jean de Malestroit saying, *If one gives a man a fish, he will eat it and then be hungry again, but if you teach him to fish, he shall never want.* This was never more apropos than regarding Milord's wealth, which was given to him without tutelage, so when he reached his majority and could no longer be restrained, he was as profligate as any man could be.

"Perhaps all his traveling is an attempt to outrun those to whom he is in debt," I offered.

"No doubt. Nevertheless, Monsieur Peletier will still consent to do work for Milord now and then; he says that he would keep his wares in the eyes of the nobility so additional business might be acquired from those who actually will pay. He considers it a reasonable investment. My Georges is—"

She stopped in mid-sentence and caught a breath as I had done in speaking of Michel, then let it out slowly before continuing, this time with more care in her choice of words. "Monsieur Peletier took my Georges to apprentice, before ..."

Again, she stammered to find the right words. "In any case, the boy has been going into Milord's castle here at Machecoul with him regularly. What he has told me is unsettling—fantastic tales of how he is treated within, sometimes by the page called Poitou, but on occasion by Lord Gilles himself. The man does not pay his debts, yet he lives lavishly and treats his guests, even commoners, as royalty. And why such an interest in a mere apprentice—"

She did not recall that day, so many years before, when Milord took the infant Georges away from her.

Why, little angel, what have you to fear?

I held my own recollection within and said, "It is unseemly, I agree."

"Georges was beginning to speak covetously of all the luxury he saw. I did not approve and told him to accept his own fortunate position with grace. Of course he resisted my advice, but what could I do? He was apprenticed. Almost a man. Out of my control."

"When one is a tradesman, it is difficult not to covet such a life as Milord lives."

"I myself saw it all, and yet still I knew my place. But the youth of today, they seem to have forgotten that prosperity comes through hard work and diligence." She shrugged wearily. "What does one know at that age beyond his own desires? He could be swayed by the tickle of a feather. He was certainly influenced by the one called Poitou—a character the likes of which I cannot describe, except to say that he made me feel uneasy in my own skin, like a thousand spiders were crawling all over me. Georges would come home and speak of the promises of benefit the page made to him on behalf of Milord, of compensation for tailoring, even though my son is not yet accomplished. Of materials and goods, needles, expensive scissors—I thought it too far-fetched to be trusted. The last promise I heard him repeat was that he would be given a horse."

"A horse?" It *was* far-fetched. "Quite an excellent gift."

"*Oui, Mère,* it is. Too excellent. Naturally he was enthralled."

"As would be any young man."

"I told him that he must be suspicious of such

unmerited generosity. But he went to the castle anyway, against my wishes, to take possession of the animal on the appointed day. A fortnight ago. Before he left I gave him a pair of breeches to deliver en route and bade him collect the money for them. He laughed and told me that he would make the delivery on his new horse, that such tasks would henceforth be a pleasure and that he would gladly do them for me." She lowered her head and a tear fell down one cheek. "He is a good boy. A good son to me."

I did not wish to disturb what good thoughts of him she had managed to salvage from his disappearance, so I stayed quiet for a moment. When it seemed proper to do so, I asked, "And there has been no trace of him since?"

"Not one."

"Did you inquire at the castle?"

"My husband would not allow me to do so. He said it was his place as the boy's father. He went forth to Machecoul but came back with only the word that Georges had never arrived to collect the horse and that the animal had been given to someone else."

"Did you ask who told him that?"

"Again it was this Poitou, Milord's page."

"And he did not question him further?"

"My husband does not find it necessary to be suspicious of anyone but his own son."

Her resentment was plain. Not only had she lost her son, but she had also lost confidence in her husband—a desolate situation.

"Have you inquired as to whether or not anyone else saw him that day?"

"*Mais oui,* Mother. Of course."

Not Guillemette this time, or the more familiar *Mère,* but *Mother.* Our young intimacy was already being strained by my pointed questions. And what a fool I was to have even asked her this question—I myself had plagued everyone around Champtocé until they came to dread me like the disease itself.

"André Barbé told me that he saw Georges picking apples early that afternoon. He saw him behind the house in which *la famille* Rondeau lives, where they keep an orchard. He was not especially fond of apples himself. When I heard this I thought he must be doing it for the horse."

"And no one else speaks of seeing him ..."

"No one."

How many times had I retraced Michel's last hours from what had been told to me by others? Too many to count. "This man Barbé, did he tell you anything else about having seen Georges?"

"It was all he saw. He did not see Georges leave the orchard. Nor did anyone else, for that matter. And I have asked aplenty. But Barbé did have something else to tell me." She took in a long breath. "He said to me that he met a man, a stranger, on the road between Machecoul and Nantes. When Barbé revealed that he was from Machecoul, the stranger became agitated and told him to watch his children, for they were in danger of being snatched. He sang this little *chanson* he had heard; the words were, '*Sur ce, l'on lui avait dit, en se merveillant, qu'on y mangeout les petits enfants.*' "

I was stunned. It was the very phrase that Jean had written to me, the recalled words that initially piqued my interest in her plight, the same ones I had vaguely heard from the nervous stranger who had directed me here. But Georges was sixteen years of age; he was not a *small* child, certainly not small enough to be eaten. But not all sixteen-year-old boys were man-size. "Agathe," I said quietly, "was Georges of small stature?"

"He had yet to reach his full growth."

"Did this Barbé tell you where this stranger came from?"

"Saint-Jean-d'Angély."

A good-enough distance. But then, shocking news travels quickly, especially on dark roads.

☙

I stayed with Agathe le Barbier for another hour at her insistence, though there was little more to be said on the matter that had brought me to see her. She found the wherewithal to feed me and I accepted her offer; it would have been an insult not to do so. In the deepest period of my grief over Michel, walking ten paces had been nearly unimaginable until someone forced me to do it. Madame le Barbier had walked from the village, through the forest, and to the abbey church; she had presented herself, albeit shabbily, to the Bishop and myself and told an ill-received tale. Then she had found her way home again in the vile darkness. Today she had withstood the sting of my questions. This was a woman of admirable substance, who had my complete respect.

Now it was my turn to show such substance. As I hurried through the darkening forest on my way back to the abbey, through the shadows and pitfalls and grabbing branches, I held my own terror at bay with an altogether different distraction: What unpleasant shape would Jean de Malestroit's magnificent eyebrow assume when I spoke to him later?

☙

" '... someone had told him, marveling, that they eat small children there.' "

"You heard this said?"

"Yes, in a ditty, Eminence, from a man who told me the way. And it was told to me by someone to whom it had been previously told, who heard it from another ..."

I did not mention Madame le Barbier's part in this chain of news, nor Jean's; both seemed superfluous and would divert him from the heart of the matter. "But that was exactly what the man said to him, not one word different from what he told me, or so the witness swears—"

"Guillemette, I have told you many times that gossip is not to be tolerated—"

"This was *not* gossip," I said firmly, though my knees were nearly trembling. "It was told to me in the course of my inquiries." Finally I pulled Jean's letter from my sleeve and opened it, more roughly than I ought to have. "And look, here it is, all the way from Avignon, written by my own dear son. And all of this relates directly to the purpose of my going there in the first place."

I gasped. I had given myself away. An almost wicked smile crept onto the Bishop's face. "I must have heard wrong, then," he said. "I believe you said you were going to Machecoul for threads and needles."

Caught in a falsehood—I groped for an explanation. "Indeed, Eminence. That was my original purpose."

"Guillemette, you need not lie to me. I am not a difficult man for whom a woman must tamper with the truth."

By all the saints, the man fairly invited lying with his strictness. But it was not the time to speak on that matter; that could only be done in a relaxed and quiet moment, when he might be more receptive to helpful criticism. I lowered my head submissively and hoped it would work. "Please allow me to apologize, Eminence, for my lack of confidence in your fairness. I confess that I longed to speak to Madame le Barbier again, and I ought to have told you this."

His expression softened. "Yes, you ought."

"But I did have need of those things. And since I was going to be in Machecoul, I thought it would be productive to inquire about this other matter."

He looked at my empty hands. "You have put your parcels away before coming here, then."

Blessed Virgin, save me! "No—"

"Then, where are they?"

"There are none!" I cried impatiently. "There was nothing to my liking. The market seemed rather bare for some reason."

The eyebrow dipped lower on one side again. "None at all?"

"None," I said sheepishly.

"Hmm. Perhaps all the vendors were here in Nantes today; such a pity. Often you come back from your forays with more purchases than you intended. And then you spend hours on your return chatting about the wonders of your acquisitions, in what I have come to recognize as an effort to justify what you have disbursed from the abbey's treasury, which effort I must confess I have also come to anticipate with great enjoyment, for you fairly glow and it is a pleasure to see how inventively you come up with uses for the things you buy. Today you came back with empty hands and no stories, except wild tales of children being eaten."

"At least they were at no cost—"

"—in keeping with their probable worth."

I wondered for a stunned moment if Etienne had known me as well as this man seemed to. "I confess I was a bit distracted by the matter of the missing child. But at least I wasted no money."

"No, only time. And *a bit* seems a mild expression to describe your distraction today. One hopes you will not be overtaken by it."

"Eminence, my duties were attended to before I left here. I will admit that one of my purposes got the better of me as the day progressed. But you must realize that this is a tale worth pursuing—children have disappeared and cannot be accounted for by any means. *Children.* One understands they are not noble children, but—"

"We know only of one child for sure."

"There are strong rumors of others." My voice had gone quite shrill, bothersome even to myself. "You know everything that goes on in this realm. Surely your advisers must have spoken of this."

"You exaggerate. There are many things I do not know. And my 'advisers,' as you so gently call them, have said nothing."

A man with as much power as he, with so much to protect for himself and others, would have many spies bringing him information. He would know what he needed and wanted to know with little difficulty. "It is not in the natural order of things for children to disappear," I said. "Surely you can discover what is happening to them."

"Sister, do you propose that something *unnatural* is happening to them, if there is indeed a pattern? It would make more sense that these young ones have run away or vanished due to some unfortunate oddity and their remains are not yet found. And we are talking about a few children, not dozens. Were there dozens, it would be a different situation."

"Perhaps there *are* dozens. It would be wise to determine that before we dismiss the disappearances as nothing out of the ordinary."

"Oh, bah," he said. "A waste of time."

I let a moment of cold silence pass before saying, "You would not think so were it *your* child." I cast my glance at the implements of worship that lay ready on the tray. "Your preparations are complete. With your permission, Eminence, I shall retire to my room. For private devotions. I think perhaps the journey got the better of me."

Without waiting for his response, I lowered my head and moved toward the door. Then I felt his hand on my shoulder. I turned back and gave him an angry stare.

"I apologize, Guillemette." He was all contrition, at

least for that moment. "You are right," he said. "I am ill-equipped to understand your feelings about this."

A smile of gratitude was aching to slip onto my face, but I forced it back and pressed my advantage in the strategic moment he had provided—the Maid of Orléans herself had little on me in that realm. "Eminence, let me discover if there are more, and if there are, then I would ask your blessing to pursue my inquiries even further."

His contrition, it seemed, might not extend to sanctioning such a bold request. "You have duties here, need I remind you."

"You need not."

"It would require you to go out into the countryside—a dangerous thing to do."

"I am an abbess. No one will harm me."

"An abbess is a woman. There are men out there who would ravage the Virgin Mother, given the opportunity."

I swallowed hard, and spoke. "I shall go, nonetheless. And if you forbid it, I shall remove this veil, and you will then not be able to forbid me anything but the sacraments."

Harumph. "God may curse you for this obstinacy."

"*Au contraire,* Brother, God will reward me for my bravery. You will see."

"Only He knows if either of those characteristics pleases Him. Do as you wish, Guillemette; you will anyway." Then he added with some reluctance, "If you find this worthy of your time, then I suppose I will just have to trust your judgment. But please be discreet. We do not want to cause any unnecessary upset among the people."

It was a gift, but not one without cost, for after blessing me with permission, he simply had to finish with a stern directive. "Just do not allow it to consume you," he said.

"I will do my best." I bowed slightly and made to

leave, but Jean de Malestroit took gentle hold of my arm and stopped me.

"God would be pleased to have you worship Him here rather than in your private quarters."

God, indeed. It was His bishop who wanted me there. I nodded my assent with as much dignity as I could muster.

"Good," Jean de Malestroit said. He took up the tray and started for the door but set it down again and said with a sigh, "Someday God will make me answer for the shortcomings of my memory. There is a letter for you. From Avignon." He produced a scroll.

Jean. My heart soared as my hand went out greedily for the parchment. His Eminence had been right. He would never understand my passion.

chapter 4

ELLEN LEEDS HAD SAID RED, and this jacket looked more like maroon in the thin light, so I tried not to get too excited. I was really glad for the very basic investigative training they put all the patrol cops through, because this one had known better than to pick it up. This turned out to be doubly important in this case; when I got down on my knees and looked closely with my flashlight, I saw a small, crumpled piece of paper resting on top of the jacket.

A narrow strip—a discarded receipt, maybe. It might have been blown in there, but with so little wind that seemed unlikely. I glanced around again to gauge the breeze; not one leaf stirred anywhere along the sidewalk. The little white paper was balanced precariously on one of the sleeves, near the elbow. If it had blown there, it more likely would have been caught in one of the folds or low points. But there it was, perched on a smooth section of the fabric surface. It had to have landed at that spot after the jacket did, and if it was a receipt, as I suspected, it would have a time printed on it.

We left them in place. One of the patrols walked the measuring dog and called out the numbers. I pasted myself onto the ground and snapped a couple of pictures, hoping for the best. Something scurried when the flash went off. I drew a rough little map in my notebook, showing the distance from two permanent landmarks—one a fire hydrant, the other a street lamp—neither of which was likely to be moved in the next couple of days. When it was all duly documented, I packed both items in plastic bags and labeled them. Except for a few twigs and leaves that didn't want to let go when I picked it up, the jacket looked clean and was in excellent condition.

The piece of paper, as I'd hoped, was a receipt. The printer must have needed a new cartridge, because the print was barely visible. For a moment I wondered if it had been outside for a while and had blown onto the jacket after all. But I could just make out the letters and numbers—it was for the purchase of a carton of milk and a pack of cigarettes at a store not a block away, made that morning at two minutes past eight, by which time the jacket was in all likelihood already on the ground.

I didn't find much in the pockets, at least nothing that would identify it as having belonged to Nathan Leeds. There was no name sewn or written in the label—at twelve he would be past the point of allowing his mother to do that, like my own son, Evan, who at that age nearly crucified me when he saw me with a Magic Marker in one hand and his new windbreaker in the other.

Mom, what the heck, I'm not a baby anymore.... Jeff's mother stopped doing that a couple of years ago....

I pulled out two empty gum papers and three pennies. But no wallet; that would be in his school bag. While the patrols continued their search of the area, I walked back to the car to stow the evidence and to take another look at the picture that Nathan's mother had given me. It was an outdoor shot, and I couldn't remember what he had been wearing. It wasn't the jacket in question, but a T-shirt. The design showed a toothy, malevolent silhouette of some beast, encircled with the words *La Brea Tar Pits*. It was very scary-looking.

He would be very scared by now. If he was still alive.

More patrols came out and cordoned off the scene. All night long some poor rookie would end up sitting in a unit at one end of the taped area to protect it from the ravaging effects of passersby. First thing in the morning, I would be back there with an evidence team to go over everything in the daylight. I could have had the high-intensity light sets brought in, but true daylight is the best thing in a detailed search, because you just can't see the same stuff in artificial light. And the abduction, if that was what it was, occurred in daylight, as best I could determine. There is so much more to be learned—maybe *sensed* is a better word—when the conditions in which a crime takes place can be replicated.

It was 0100 hours and I knew Nathan's mother would still be awake, probably sitting by the phone. That's what I would have been doing in her place. I smelled cigarette smoke when Ellen Leeds opened the door. A thin smoke trail rose up lazily from the glowing tip of the butt that dangled from her left hand. She tucked the hand behind her back right away. Maybe I'd wrinkled up my nose without realizing it.

"I don't usually smoke in the apartment."

"I'd be smoking like a chimney right about now if I were you."

She motioned me in with her free hand and closed the door behind me, with the same *click clack* of locks as I'd heard before. "I know it's very late," I said, a sort of apology, "but I thought you'd want to be contacted immediately if something turned up."

She couldn't see the plastic bag with its contents. It was tucked into a large canvas carryall that I keep in the car. I don't like parading evidence of a heartbreak in front of the whole world; I try to get it out of sight if that's possible.

Hope flooded her face, trimming away years. "Did you find him?"

"No, I'm sorry to say, we didn't. But there is some evidence I think you should look at."

The years returned with vicious cruelty. "What kind of evidence?" she whispered fearfully.

"A jacket."

She shut her eyes and was quiet for a few seconds. Then she opened them again and asked, "Is there blood on it?"

"No. At least not that I can see right now. A closer examination might reveal something, and we will do lab work, but it looks quite clean to me. Of course, that's just a first impression."

She reached out for the tote. I held it back and kept the top opening closed. "I'm sorry, I can't allow you to touch it just yet, because contamination will lessen the evidence value in court later. But I need for you to identify it as being Nathan's if you can."

I undid the plastic zip closure at the top of the bag and exposed a portion of the jacket for her to see. Of course her hand went out, but she caught herself and pulled it back. "I need to see the label," she said. "Nathan's jacket was made by a company called Harmony. There should be a black tag with some musical notes and the word *Harmony* on it. I think the stitching is blue."

It was.

Three hours of sleep is not a lot to go on, but between having kids who kept me up at night sometimes and my job—which either drags me out or keeps me up with annoying regularity—I guess I've gotten used to it. Evan was a decent sleeper, and Frannie did okay, but Julia didn't sleep until she was five. She didn't cry, but she wanted to play, and she would talk and talk and talk from her crib until everyone in the house was awake. All she really wanted was company, but God forbid her father should actually have gotten up to play with her. It was always me. But the older I get, the harder it is to make up for lost hours of rest. By the time I got back to the station house, filed all the necessary reports, sent out a fresh Teletype, detailed the label on the evidence, I was as wired as if I'd just had a full pot of coffee.

I was out at the scene the next morning at about 0700, an hour earlier than I usually arrive at the station. The evidence guys hadn't arrived yet, but the patrol unit was still there. I showed the kid my badge and told him I was the primary. He waved me in, as if he needed to.

Each crime scene has a personality of its own. I like to just stand in the middle of my scenes and take in their nuances. Some of the guys think I'm crazy, but my individual solve rate is better than anyone else's in the division, so they don't say too much.

The street was a quiet mix of small houses and storefronts. Not much activity, even around the roped-off portion. Most of the stores were late-opening types—a gourmet shop, a hair-and-nail salon, a wine store. I was wishing for a donut shop, so someone might have seen something. Opposite where we'd found the jacket, there was a boarded-up old theater with signs saying it was about to undergo renovation. A few people going to early jobs walked by, but only one person actually stopped and asked a question. I told her what had happened and asked her about the neighborhood.

"Mostly working people in the houses, no trouble-makers, and we all mind our own business."

"When do most of the residents leave, if you know?"

She didn't. But I was there at just about the same time of day that Nathan would have been abducted, and the place was nearly deserted. It was quite likely that no one saw a thing from within the neighborhood itself.

When I got back to the division it was barely 0800, but I was feeling very tired. It had been a night of spare sleep with my standard nightmare: I'm stranded outside in weather so cold that my snot is frozen. I'm wearing sandals and a tank top but there's knee-deep snow. I'm plowing through it on foot, to God knows where, I never seem to have a destination, I'm just running, and I can feel the sensation of my legs dragging in the snow. This time I had a horse with a kind of mutant *Star Wars* quality to it, like the beast that Luke Skywalker eviscerated and hid inside to stay warm while he waited for Han Solo to rescue him. I swear I smelled that putrid stink in the dream.

Where was George Lucas when you needed him? I could have used some special effects that morning. Bags under my eyes, hair that inspired a self-directed *oh, screw it.* I was running on adrenaline, and not enough of that. When I stood up and talked about the case at the morning briefing, I was afraid I would throw up right in the middle of it. One of the guys said to me afterward, "You sound beat."

"Yeah," I said to him. "You must be a detective."

I went straight from there into Lieutenant Fred Vuska's office to give him a more detailed report. Fred is a genuinely good man who advocates for all of us in the division with his own superiors, who can be real jerks. But he's under so much political pressure, the poor guy. He was always the link between the people who do the work—us—and the people who theorize about how we ought to do it, known in regular conversation as "them." The last thing he needed from me was a request for additional manpower to do a more thorough search for Nathan Leeds.

"All the patrols were out looking for this kid last night. No one saw him. You don't know that he got grabbed, anyway. He still might be a runaway."

"We found his jacket."

"He probably dropped it. Or tossed it because it isn't cool enough for him. I hate to tell you how many jackets my own kids lose."

"I'm just getting a feeling that this kid is not a runaway."

"Based on what?"

I wanted to say, *That girl thing you don't get, the thing we call intuition.* But it would have been disrespectful and sexist, and I have had all that bigotry trained out of me. "I saw the home, talked with the mother ..."

"You done any other interviews yet?"

"Just one with a resident of the street, but it was a real quickie and she didn't really have anything to tell me."

He gave me a good long stare of disbelief.

"Lany, go do your interviews. If you turn up anything more that makes you think he didn't just run away, then bring it to me. We'll take another look at it."

"The kid's twelve, for God's sake."

Cynical now. "You want to see some twelve-year-olds? Come on. I'll take you for a ride down to Venice Beach, and we'll ask the punks who hang out there how old they are. Get your ass out there and dig something up."

The training apparently didn't take on Fred.

I was wishing very earnestly for a key to the lobby of Ellen Leeds's building. I could buzz her and ask to be let in, but she would expect me to come to her apartment for an update and I was just a bit too brittle to deal with her diplomatically at the moment. So I waited until someone came out, flashed my badge, and was let in.

It took me a few moments of orientation to determine

which stack of apartments was the one I wanted. They would all be corner units above the third floor; everything else was too low or incorrectly angled. It made my job easier; I didn't have to canvass the entire west side of the building.

I got there at about 0930, so there weren't going to be too many people at home. I would just have to do the best I could and hope for something to break. The first apartment I tried was empty, so I scribbled *Please contact me* on one of my cards and stuck it into the door crack. The fourth-floor occupant was home when I rang his bell but mightily peeved, because he worked a midnight-to-eight-A.M. shift and had just climbed back into his casket for the day. He said he hadn't gotten home until around 0930 yesterday, by which time the deed (if it was indeed a deed) had probably already been done and the doer long gone. I got his name and the number of his employer for verification, then thanked him and apologized for waking him.

Fifth floor, not home, left a card. On the sixth floor, I was just about through writing *contact me* on the card when the door was finally opened by a very elderly lady, whose sickly-sweet perfume returned me to the sixties like a flashback. She was nicely dressed and her bluish hair looked as if it had just been done. She had her pearls on already, and lipstick—far more than I ever wore. Little tributaries of red branched out from her upper lip along the wrinkles.

"Oh, come right in," she said on seeing my badge. I hadn't explained the nature of my visit, but I got the sense that it didn't matter to her. A visitor was a visitor, and I was a cop, therefore safe. Old folks and children think that way.

"Can I get you some coffee or tea, Officer?"

"Oh, no, thank you, ma'am." I hadn't asked her name yet. She followed me with her eyes as I migrated slowly to the big window. The street I wanted to see was in full view. On a small table next to an overstuffed chair there was a set of binoculars of the sort that one might use for bird-watching.

"You have a lovely view here," I said.

"Yes, I do. That's why I rented in this building."

Ellen Leeds's reason had been quite different.

"I was just about the first tenant in here," she continued. "That was, oh, let's see, twenty years ago. They keep waiting for me to die so they can rent this apartment out to someone younger for lots more money."

I had to smile. "I'll bet," I said. I picked up her binocs. "Are you a bird-watcher?"

"I do a little, but not seriously. I had a gentleman friend—he passed away about ten years ago now—who used to love it. Those are his viewers you're holding."

I replaced them reverently on the table.

"Now I mostly just watch what goes on in the world out there."

Oh please oh please oh please, I prayed silently. "Mrs. . . . I mean, ma'am . . ."

"Mrs. Paulsen."

I scribbled the name in my notebook. "I wonder if you were looking out your window yesterday morning around seven-thirty or a little bit later. A little boy who lives in this building has gone missing, and the last time anyone can place him was on his way to school yesterday morning."

She raised her eyebrows just a bit. "So that's what all the fuss has been about."

"Yes."

"Well, I'll have to think for a moment." She sat down in her chair quite deliberately. "Let me see, yesterday morning . . . I got up at my usual time, six-fifteen, and I had my shower. Then I had my coffee and took in the paper—I have a young boy who brings it right to my welcome mat, you know—and I read that for a little while. I remember I put on the television to watch the *Today* show at seven—I like that Al Roker so much. . . ."

She went on to describe the minutiae of her morning routine and it sounded so leisurely, like heaven to me.

"You know, I was at the window about that time. I remember seeing children on their way to school. There's this one little girl who always looks so pretty; her mother dresses her so nicely and she skips along on her way—reminds me of how I used to walk to school myself. We always wore dresses, you know, not like these days when they barely wear anything at all . . ."

"You say you had *Today* on; do you remember what they were talking about or doing at the time that you were looking out and saw the kids?"

"Well, yes, I do. The lady who has all those linens and things was on and she was making some kind of decoration."

Martha Stewart. I could call the local broadcaster and get the precise timing of that segment. I took the picture of Nathan Leeds and his mother out of my case folder and handed it to her. "Did you happen to see this young boy on his way to school?"

She regarded the photograph for a moment. "Well, yes, I did. But he didn't walk all the way down the street like he usually does."

Oh please oh please. My heart started beating a little faster. "What do you mean, Mrs. Paulsen?"

"Well, he got into the car about halfway down the street, in front of the little white house."

Precisely where we'd found the jacket. But she had said *the* car, not *a* car. "Describe the car, please."

"Oh, I won't need to do that. You can just go right down into the garage and look at it yourself. Of course, you'll have to wait until later. On days when she goes out, she doesn't usually get home until suppertime."

She? I didn't understand. "Do you mean that someone from this building picked him up on that street?"

"Not just anybody, dear. His mother."

I don't know why I was so angry. She should really have been among the first people I suspected. She just didn't seem like the type.

But Susan Smith hadn't either, at least to the outside world. Andrea Yates ... well, what can anyone say about her? Smith was at least sane. She'd put on quite a show. Black carjacker, my ass, but the cops who handled that case were really good at figuring her. I read that the investigators started to suspect her of foul play after the first day that her sons went missing. *The story was too pat,* one of them said. She cried, but not when she should have. It just seems to me that there has to be something so completely wrong, so twisted, for a mother to harm her own kids. To kill them she has to be some kind of space alien.

There was an article about Smith included in one of our training sessions on perp profiling. Some shrink spent a lot of time interviewing her and analyzing why she might have done something so unimaginable as strapping her children into a car and then rolling it into a lake with them screaming and crying inside—he had all sorts of theories about genetic mandates and deeply rooted psychological compulsions. She killed her kids, he said, because the man she wanted to marry wasn't interested in taking care of them. He wanted just his own.

This shrink went on to say that this was "logical biological behavior" on the part of the man—those were his exact words, I remember, because it made me so mad. Males, he claimed, had a "reproductive necessity to eliminate rivals" for stuff that their own children might need. He said that if the mother had other kids by another man, she would devote attention to them at the expense of any children she might have with the new man, and that it would endanger the success of his own genetic material.

I say, bullshit. Men are better than that. And at least the guy was honest with her. But an honest louse is still a louse, and he should have known not to get involved with a married woman who had small kids, because there's nothing but a heartache in it. As for Susan Smith herself, I don't have words for anyone who commits infanticide.

But I would have a chance to talk to Ellen Leeds, and I would find words. Lots and lots of words. And training be damned—they would not be sensitive or respectful.

five

LE PRINTEMPS *IS WELL UPON US* here in Avignon, Maman. *The river swells with the recent rains and everywhere there is color. All the earth is preparing for the glorious rebirth of our Lord, and I am filled with joy each day as I rise up from my bed, for there is so much to thank Him for.*

I know it must still be cool in the north, but here we have already had some hot days. I long to shed this heavy robe for lighter vestments. . . .

No one was within earshot. I fingered the hem of my veil and said aloud, "Oh, my dear son, I understand this desire to disrobe quite well."

His letters were always full of sweet pleasantries, garrulous in an intimate sort of way, but they seldom contained much real news, because his position required discretion. Nevertheless, in this tome there was a wonderful enlargement on what he had previously written:

I take on new responsibilities every day and am completely trusted, by all indications; there are whispers that I will soon be advanced. . . . Sometimes I do not understand how

*this good fortune has befallen me. . . . I am once again com-
pelled to say how grateful I am to my* frère de lait *Gilles for
the help his influence has provided. . . .*

Grateful servants to Milord, both of us—Jean and I
were so alike. Far more so than he and his father, who was
the warrior that Jean could never be. But Etienne and
Michel had been father and son to the very bone—in
their mannerisms, their likes and dislikes, their expressions. The resemblance between them was striking enough
that Milord Gilles would continue to comment on it,
even long after Michel was no longer with us.

Twins, he would tell me, *more than father and son—and
both so handsome and fair. Your Michel had the face of an angel.*

So had my Etienne, but that was a matter of opinion.
Still, I could not have been in closer accord with Milord's
assessment of their looks.

Mon cher fils, I wrote before departing, *I am so proud
to hear of the improvements in your position. But I do not
wonder why. It will not be long before you write to tell me
of your elevation to Monsignor, and my heart soars to think of
the honors you are yet to receive. Lord Gilles's patronage was
helpful in securing your placement in Avignon, to be sure, but
these additional accolades are earned by your performance,
not through Milord's influence, which has waned of late.*

There is intrigue here in Nantes . . .

I told him of what had transpired with Madame le
Barbier, from beginning to end.

*I heard repeated the same ditty you wrote to me in your
previous letter, concerning the eating of small children! His
Eminence discourages me but has not forbidden me to do so,
and therefore I shall ride out into the countryside to speak to
the people and see what tale lies behind it.*

✦

I must have seemed very odd to those I encountered
and questioned—an abbess wandering the surrounds of

Nantes inquiring if any children had gone missing. Though I was in search of what his Eminence would probably try again to dismiss as gossip, I was certain that I myself would give rise to nearly as much of it as I brought back.

By all the saints, it would be revealed beneath some window or in front of some market stall, *the Reverend Mother has finally gone over the edge . . . I saw it with my own eyes. . . .*

No matter. I departed the convent of the Bishop's palace in Nantes on Tuesday of the week before Easter to find out if the traveler from Saint-Jean-d'Angély's story, the one that had already reached Avignon as a *chanson,* was the result of real occurrences or the invention of some poor lunatic, may God save those who are too heavily influenced by the moon. I had been given a donkey to ride, not a horse—*You will do better with this animal while you are unaccompanied,* the stablehand had assured me. In other words, *No one will try to steal it out from under you.* This gave me pause; for a moment I considered removing from its permanent home around my neck the fine chain of gold that had come to me in what my mother left behind. When she passed into God's hands, while my Etienne was still alive, that chain was always around *her* neck. She never said where it had come from originally—my father, or perhaps her dowry. In recent years, when it has come to seem a part of my own body, I have wondered if it might have been a gift from someone other than my father—perhaps a loyal admirer, or some previous beau of whom she never spoke. My mother was always a comely woman, at least until the final illness that robbed her of all her flesh and left her looking like a sack of bones.

She passed almost without notice, for on that day an unsettling incident occurred within *la famille* de Rais. Lady Marie de Craon de Laval had a small dog with a curled tail and very short hair the color of sand, brought as a gift by a merchant from across the southern sea beyond the Holy Land, out of a place where the skin of some of the people was reputed to be more ebony than even the darkest Moor, though I have little faith that such a crazed assertion is true. She cherished it to an almost nauseating degree. The animal could not seem to bark but instead made the most plaintive yelping noise, which displeased young Lord Gilles, who had his revenge by taunting the dog mercilessly. I know he was jealous of the animal, who got far more attention from Lady Marie than he did himself. So when the dog was found hanging dead by its curly tail, there was little doubt who had done it. There were no other marks on the animal's body, so we could not immediately tell how it had died. But it was surely dead.

He strangled it, our midwife asserted.

But how could she know this?

Look beneath the fur on his neck—there you will see dark bruises. I have seen such bruises when men have fought hand to hand and both have lost their weapons.

Often I wondered why it was that Madame Catherine Karle seemed to watch Milord so intently. She was the one who had arrived late for his abrupt birth. So many times she had said that his was an unholy arrival, full of bad portents.

Of course, Lady Marie was completely distraught, but her upset was over the loss of the dog, not her son's disturbing behavior. *He is a boy,* she would always say, as if that might excuse the vile behaviors that so often seemed to pop out of him without warning. Being a conscientious retainer, I took it upon myself to fret in her stead, concluding as would any nurse that I ought to have been more vigilant about his moral strength, more firm with him in his outbursts, a better shaper of his character.

It is not your place to shape him, Etienne would always say. I never contradicted him; that was *truly* not my place.

Guy de Laval did nothing to punish his son. It took the formidable Jean de Craon to force out the eventual confession. Young Gilles trembled in front of his grandfather, who tolerated no nonsense from anyone. He wailed out reason after reason to justify why he had left the pitiful thing for his mother to find, with its eyes staring dead straight, its tongue hanging out of a mouth agape.

The dog was so loud as to be ungodly; the dog could not be controlled; the dog was the spawn of the devil himself.

How I wish there had been just one word of remorse; none was ever said, nor was Gilles de Rais ever required to do penance for that savagery. But there was no chance for me to correct him on this matter: I had my mother's remains to wash, to dress, to prepare for her eternal rest. In any case, such a lesson from me would have had to be delivered discreetly, for the patriarch Jean de Craon would not tolerate my interference any more happily than he did anyone else's.

The gold chain I had taken from *Maman*'s neck that day bounced lightly against my skin as the donkey made its way up a hilly path. I no longer felt disappointed over the lack of a finer mount but rather fortunate as my surefooted beast negotiated the slopes and inclines with asinine expertise. But as the day wore on, that sense of fortune waned—she brayed more and more as the terrain grew more difficult, and by late afternoon she had me suffering a powerful ache in the head.

But never could I imagine strangling her for the sake of silence.

I meandered a bit, stopping in many small villages to water my beast and to give myself a moment's respite from swaying on her back. Everywhere I found a well, there was also a story to be told.

Seven years old, as beautiful as a cherub, now gone—and such a good boy, never one to disappoint his parents. . . .

We do not know what became of him, if he is alive or dead, for there has been no trace of him at all after he went begging. . . .

I had papers in my satchel from Jean de Malestroit, who was generous in his demands on my behalf, all of which would be granted if not outright exceeded. He had tried at the last minute to dissuade me again, claiming danger as the reason. But brides of Christ were seldom ravaged—why risk the immortal soul when there are so many ordinary virgins to be had, all younger? The mothers of kings are fair game—Yolande d'Aragon herself suffered the banditry of Milord Gilles in one of his more idiotic moments, when he decided to be his own "free company" and rob her while she traveled—but a nun, at least an abbess, was safe.

In the parish of Bourgneuf, not far from Machecoul, there is a comfortable convent, as convents go; I had stayed there once on a journey with Lord de Rais's entourage many years before. Though it was not a towering edifice, I saw it from some distance as the sun hovered over the treetops. The thought of sanctuary was sweet, and I urged my beast forward with whispered promises she somehow seemed to understand.

The surprisingly young Mother Superior greeted me in the courtyard just as the sun slipped over the last of the outside walls. After reading my papers, she introduced herself respectfully to me as Sister Claire, though she would be Mother to everyone else. I explained my mission briefly, which brought a look of genuine curiosity to her visage, behind which I suspected was a more-than-coincidental interest.

Had she, too, heard stories? I hoped for a truly revealing discourse.

As was expected of her, she invited me to stay the

night. When I accepted, she herself led me into the main chamber of the abbey, a commodious room with vaulted ceilings and high windows. There was no one there but the two of us, as everyone else was about the last of the day's tasks in the waning light. She brought me to a small neat room, roughly the size of my own in Nantes, and settled me in.

I thanked her, saying, "The accommodations are quite fine."

"We have not the facilities you have in Nantes, but we do well enough. And now will you take some supper?"

"If any is left, yes. But there is no need to prepare anything especially for me."

"Nonsense," she said. "A traveler will always find sustenance here."

A heavenly meal of thick turnip soup and bread was served to me by a young novice, who spoke not a word as she laid the offerings before me. The Abbess watched every move the girl made with the eyes of a mother eagle, and I was sure that at some later point the flaws in her service would be pointed out for correction—gently, of course. The meal itself was followed by a glass of hippocras, which unfortunately was not of the fine quality I knew at the Bishop's table. But I enjoyed it nonetheless and was grateful for the relaxation its intoxicating effect afforded me. When our conversation turned to the details of my business, Sister Claire was quite attentive and spoke not a word as I explained Madame le Barbier's visit.

"Why should this be a matter for the Bishop?" the Abbess asked me. "Children are sometimes lost. Especially in evil times such as these."

"That was precisely what he said himself. He told her to see the Magistrate."

"Wise advice, perhaps . . ."

"She had gone already," I told her, "but got no help. The Bishop has consented to allow me to make inquiries in the area, and when I have collected reports from all around, I will take my findings back to him."

She made the sign of the cross on her chest. "A dreadful task, if ever there was one."

"Indeed," I said, "terrible. But I do not mind the traveling." I sipped the spiced wine slowly, lest it loosen my tongue too much. "I am hoping it will not take too long. I have duties, of which you well know the scope. I hope to complete this inquiry within a few days—and I suspect I will, considering that today, at each well, I heard a tale of one sort or another of a child lost."

The Abbess raised an eyebrow to that. "I would prefer not to succeed, were this task given to me," she said.

The wine made me bolder than I ought to have been. I sat forward and said with great seriousness, "I took it upon myself, almost had to beg for it. I had little support from his Eminence."

"It *is* a job for the Magistrate," she said. "But still, one wonders why the Bishop did not see fit to pressure him. If what you have heard is true, and innocents are disappearing ... well, then, something ought to be done about it."

The accord of sisterhood is so sweet! "One does wonder," I agreed, "with some vigor. There are tales being told in Saint-Jean-d'Angély of how children are being eaten in Machecoul, spoken unsolicited by travelers in chance encounters—told as warnings by complete strangers, and then turning up in letters from Avignon. Considerable regard is being paid to this phenomenon by the common folk, but we who dance on the steps of heaven seem to have ignored it quite handily."

"Perhaps there would be consequences if the truth were revealed. Ones that cannot be seen plainly just yet."

Again, she had uncannily spoken a thought I had not yet voiced.

"I would be happy to make inquiries among the local people on your behalf," she said. "That would save you from having to gain their confidence. The folk around here tend to keep to themselves and do not trust outsiders."

It was a gracious offer and I accepted it readily. "If it wouldn't be too much bother, might I receive any callers right here in the abbey who bring news of missing children?"

"That seems both sensible and convenient." She rose up gracefully. "And now you must be very tired. . . ."

I was. Sister Claire took me by the arm and walked me back to my quarters, where she bade me good night. The narrow bed had very fresh straw and a good feather mattress to top it off, and I was suddenly aware of just how exhausted I was from my day's jostling travels. Padded though my rump might be, it was no match for a donkey's up-and-down trotting; in the morning I would be stiff, at least for a time. There were perhaps two more such days ahead of me.

Against one wall there was a chair and above it the slit of a window through which the light of the nearly full moon streamed in. I was careful to avoid it as I went to the chair to remove my dusty shoes, lest it craze me as it did so many others. I took off my veil and robe, until I wore only my white linen shift. A cross of silver hung above the head of the bed, reminding me of where I was, though I did not need the cross to remind me of why I was there.

Dear God, I prayed—almost sincerely—*let it all be conjecture and rumor. . . .*

I lay down on the bed, pulled my robe up over me, and fell into a deep sleep. Sometime during the long night, my repose was interrupted by a dream of Lady

Marie's hanging dog, but now he was Cerberus, guardian of the gates of Hades, who compelled me with fierce yelps to cross the River Styx and follow him. And I understood that I had no choice but to do so.

⚜

Breakfast was more than ample—warm milk, crusty bread, apples, and golden-green pears brought out of the sand cellar for the occasion of my visit. The conversation between us was remarkably candid and friendly for having known each other such a short time. I attribute that in part to the effects of a marvelous treat the Abbess gave me, a flagon of the fragrant and delicious concoction made by steeping the leaves of certain plants from the Orient in freshly boiled water. She had sweetened it with honey to balance out its natural flavor, which she found somewhat bitter. I found it pleasant enough, and I thoroughly enjoyed the small sense of exhilaration it gave me.

"Such a rare and worldly treat," I commented.

The fabric of her long sleeve rustled against the table runner as she reached across the table to place another section of pear on my plate. "I was once a woman of the world," she said, smiling warmly, "when I was younger, I mean to say."

Then, whether I ought to have or not, I asked, "Are you widowed?"

"Oh, no," she said, laughing a little. "I came to this veil a spinster."

"By your own choice?"

After a slight pause, she said, "It did not seem so at the time. I was betrothed in childhood, an excellent match according to my family, very advantageous for all of us. Except that my betrothed turned out to be the most loathsome man God ever created. A vile beast with despicable habits. I would rather have died than bring his children into the world."

Had this frank, outspoken woman been at the hip-pocras, so early in the day? I thought not and decided it must be the honeyed *thé* that was loosening her tongue. "So you thought to come here instead."

She smiled conspiratorially. "Did you decide to go to Nantes?"

It was a very direct question, delivered bluntly, and I fancied that she knew the answer already. "No," I said. "My husband had died; my only remaining son was a priest, who could not support me."

"Ah, yes. How often it goes that way. But I have found that the sisters who come here after living in the true world are so much wiser and more useful than those who take the veil as young virgins."

I could not and did not disagree with her.

"When I first came here it was far less"—she gestured with her hand in search of a word—"comfortable. My father wanted me to understand the consequences of refusing the match he had made for me, so he sent me into the worst place he could find. But he brought me up to be clever, and I rose quickly among the young girls. This convent was in near ruin—when I took it over I saw to its restoration."

"Quite wonderfully," I said, looking around. The stone walls were all remarkably clean and freshly mortared. Oil had been diligently applied to the surfaces of the wood, which imparted a warm glow and gave off a lovely scent. The windows of multicolor glass were spotlessly clean. Though our abbeys and convents were of a far grander scale, nothing we had in Nantes was in a comparable state of perfection. She had used her skills far more forcefully here than I had in my own realm.

"Submission and loyalty have served me well enough," I told her, "but whenever I try to be clever, it seems to work only toward my undoing."

"I have no bishop here to annoy me."

"Ah," I said. "True."

"His Eminence Jean de Malestroit is a man well known for his staunchness."

"Another truth," I mused. "But he did allow me this journey, against his own wisdom. Though I suppose, since he is a chancellor as well, that he might have made this concession to me because it was in his interest, or that of Duke Jean."

"There you have it," Sister Claire said. Then she leaned forward and whispered advice. "You must observe him and discover what drives his actions in this matter; you will find a way to make him grant you what you want. In that sense, all men—even priests—are like husbands." She laughed discreetly and added, "Or so I am told, never having had one myself."

⚜

The Abbess had sent a young nun out first thing in the morning, well before we took our meal. The girl had gone straight to the nearest village and stood at the well, as would any good crier, to spread the word that I was inquiring about lost children. She was a local girl and proved to be an exceptionally good choice of emissary, for it could not have been an hour before a woman of the village arrived. It felt like less time to me, perhaps because the Abbess had served me another flagon of her marvelous *thé,* which had the strange effect of making me feel giddy but not drunk. I was wearing a path in the handsome stones between the dining table and the privy, but I felt wonderfully alive despite my dark mission and welcomed my visitor enthusiastically.

"Marguerite Sorin," the Abbess said when the woman was brought in. "Madame is a chambermaid. She sometimes works in the *maison* that is attached to our convent, as well as for a number of prominent local families."

Madame Sorin bowed and took the proffered seat, and the Abbess, my *soeur en Dieu,* discreetly turned to leave.

"Mother, please stay, if you'd like," I said.

She looked pleased to have the invitation and sat back down in her own seat.

I turned to the woman who had come to speak with me. "Madame Sorin," I began, "how good of you to come."

The woman nodded almost eagerly. "I could not fail to, after what the young sister said."

I could only imagine the embellishments. "You have a story to tell, regarding a missing child?"

"*Oui, Mère,* I do."

My first question was "What is the child called?" It hardly mattered, but somehow I thought he would take form within me if I knew his name.

"Bernard le Camus," she said. "He is—or was, as I fear it may turn out—not a local boy. He was—is—I hardly know which to say—from Brittany. He came here last year from Brest, where his family lives, to stay with Monsieur Rodigo. The boy was here to learn French, as he was raised speaking only Breton, and his father thought it would be a great liability to have only one language, especially that one. He was ambitious for the boy, or so we have heard since."

"A wise father, in that choice at least." To speak Breton alone would get his son nowhere in this life. "How old is this child?"

"Thirteen when he disappeared, according to the father. He came here looking for the boy last year, perhaps a month after the child went missing. By now I suspect he would be fourteen, though I did not think to ask the father the month and day of his birth. He was managing very badly the last time we spoke."

I could understand that. "How did you come to know this boy?"

"Monsieur Rodigo had engaged my services to look after him while he was here. I would come every morning to serve him his *petit déjeuner,* empty the pot, look after his laundry and mending, do all the things his mother or nurse would have done, and naturally we became quite friendly, the lad and I. His French was poor yet, though improving rapidly. We managed to understand each other. I lack sons—though I've daughters aplenty—so it was a pleasant change for me."

"One senses that you took his welfare greatly to heart."

"I looked out for him as best I could. But I could not be there every moment to watch over him." There was deep pain and regret on her face.

I knew that feeling well and did my best to comfort her. "Of course not, my daughter. You must not berate yourself. God does not expect perfect vigilance."

"It is not God who expects it, but I," she said sadly. "One day I saw Bernard talking to a stranger; it must have been August, but quite late in the month, I think. The storks were already restless on the rooftops and making ready to depart. He was an odd-looking man, although *man* seems not quite the right word to use—he was very slightly built and almost womanly in his shape. At first I thought perhaps it was a woman dressed in a man's clothing—but, *mon Dieu,* who would do such a thing, save at the feasts and tournaments, where that is sometimes the fashion of the highborn? Later I learned this man's name—he is called Poitou, though I am told that is an affectation after the city where he was born, that his real name is Corrilaut. It made me uneasy to see him with Bernard, because he seemed to be putting his hands on him in a manner that was too friendly for my liking. And the boy was pure-looking, of a very good nature, and compliant. It would have been easy for someone to take advantage of him. So after this Poitou left, I asked the boy: *What did this man want with you?*"

"And he said . . ."

Her voice revealed a great frustration. "Nothing. Not a blessed thing. Only that he had been forewarned not to speak of the encounter by Poitou. I asked him again, more vehemently than before, to tell me what passed between them, but still the boy would not speak. I warned him that strangers make offers to trick young children and that he ought not to believe fine promises, for they are unlikely to come true. Again he put me off and revealed nothing. I never got another chance to ask, because that was the last I saw of him."

The Abbess and I exchanged dark glances.

"When did you realize that the boy was gone?"

"It was not I who noticed, but Monsieur Rodigo. He went looking for the boy that evening in the room where he'd been installed and found his hood, his robe, and his shoes still there. But not the boy himself."

I sat back in my chair and wondered aloud, "Where would a child go without his shoes?"

The Abbess spoke. "Where else but to some place where he had been promised new ones? To a boy of few advantages, shoes are not an insignificant offering." Then she sighed deeply and added, "If not shoes, then something else; he was enticed away by something he could not have expected to own otherwise, at least until he was better established."

Poitou. The name rang in my head like a bell. "Madame, you are saying that you did not see the boy depart with this Poitou, but that you inferred nefarious intent on his part toward the boy. I am wondering how you came to this conclusion."

Now her voice rose. "It was quite obvious, *Mère,* so shameful and ungodly the way he handled the lad . . . and what could he possibly gain from this child? I can only think he meant to do him some harm. A woman knows these things."

We do, in some incomprehensible way. Taking care not to upset her, I pressed further. "Do you suppose, Madame, that Bernard might just have run away? Boys of that age often do. Especially those who are spirited, as seems to be the case with this young one."

"Those that can almost always return, *Mère*, after they have had their fun. It is a cruel world when one walks through it alone."

How right she was. "Perhaps he abhorred his studies and did not wish to confront his father about his unhappiness."

She shook her head, quite vehemently. "He often spoke of how much he loved his studies. He wanted to learn Latin as well. As much as the father was ambitious for him, the boy was ambitious for himself."

"Could there have been *any* other reason for his sudden departure—might Monsieur Rodigo have been cruel to him, or too strict in the rules of his lodging?"

"Monsieur Rodigo is the kindest and most courteous man in this village. He was decent and generous to Bernard and was greatly distressed by the boy's disappearance."

I asked a few more questions, all of them inconsequential. We came to no conclusions about the missing boy. I thanked Madame Sorin for bringing her story to me and she left the room, bowing her way out.

I was drained by the encounter. It must have showed on my face, for the Abbess was quick to offer me refreshments—in particular, another cup of her brew. "There are biscuits as well," she told me.

I declined it all. "My stomach is a bit unsettled just now."

The Abbess said, "It would be wise to take some refreshment while you have the chance."

"But I am not yet hungry," I said.

"I think you will be," she said. "Or, on the other hand, you may lose your taste for food altogether."

Here was a new mystery. "Why?"

She folded her hands together and said, "There are some people waiting to see you."

"*Some* people?"

After a heavy sigh, she told me how many. I crossed myself to keep from fainting.

chapter 6

SMOKE WAFTED OUT when Ellen Leeds opened the apartment door. Her hair was a mess and she was still in the same clothes she'd been wearing the night before.

She hadn't been to bed, the evil bitch.

"Hello, Mrs. Leeds. I'm sorry to disturb you so early. But I was hoping I would find you home." I was solicitous and sympathetic.

"Where am I supposed to go? I wasn't about to go to work today. I mean, what if Nathan tried to be in touch with me, or someone found him and tried to contact me ..."

This wonderful actress had obviously been reading the Parents of Missing Children manual, the version edited by Susan Smith. I nodded in sympathy for her pained dilemma and walked right through the door without invitation.

"I meant to ask you more about your work situation last night, but we had other things to cover first. I'm curious about the arrangement you have with your employer."

Translation: *I want to check with your boss about the exact times of your arrival and departure yesterday.*

"I work at the Olive Branch."

"Ah," I said. "That must be an interesting place." It was a high-profile nonprofit peace-oriented organization whose M.O. was to provide start-up money for small businesses in third-world countries, the theory being that when poor people start to get fat and rich, they get very peaceful and their societies stabilize. They were aggressive in their fund-raising, sometimes to the point where there were complaints. I wondered if it was just a job to her or if there was some belief system behind her choice of jobs.

She answered the question before I could ask it. "I suppose some of the positions are interesting. But mine is a lot like telemarketing. I manage all the donor lists and oversee the computer system that we use to input donor information. I'm not out there in the trenches teaching Ethiopian widows how to keep track of their inventory. But it has some advantages, the primary one being that there's a lot of work I can do at home."

"You were there yesterday, though . . ."

"Yes," she said with bitter deliberation. "Otherwise I would have been here, and I would have known about Nathan a lot sooner."

I wanted to press harder, to see if I could trip her up on something, but it was too early. I needed her unguarded a little while longer. "Do you happen to remember what time you left here yesterday, Mrs. Leeds? I'm trying to establish an exact chronology for the events of the morning."

She didn't flinch or get that nervous look and didn't seem at all ruffled by the question. "I don't have a set time for leaving because I don't have to be there until nine and it's pretty close, only a fifteen-minute drive, maybe twenty when the traffic is bad. But it's nice to have some solitude at the office—I can get so much more done without the distractions of other people. So I generally go in at eight. Nathan leaves here before then, so there's no reason not to. Yesterday I think I probably left around seven-forty. I don't know exactly, but it must have been about then. Nathan had been gone only a few minutes when I left myself."

"And what route do you take to drive to work?"

"I take a left out of the building parking lot and then a right onto Montana."

It was east. She would not have passed by Nathan on his way to school. But it made me wonder—if they left at relatively similar times, why did Nathan walk?

"He likes to," she told me. "It gives him a sense of independence. He's lucky enough to be that close. A lot of other kids get bussed, but he likes to get there under his own power. He's a very heady kid—always daydreaming— he thinks and mutters and dallies along the way. Sometimes I think it's downright weird the way he behaves, but it seems to have some benefit to him. And I want him to have all the benefits he can get."

I recalled my own walking-to-school days in Minnesota—as I told my kids when they whined, especially Evan, my trip was nine miles uphill both ways, always in the snow. A far cry from three blocks in perpetual warmth. But I understood what she meant; there was great value in private-thinking time.

If she needed to make him disappear for some reason— the Susan Smith thing popped into my head again—why not just take him down to the garage and drive off with him, and do the deed in seclusion? Why on earth would she grab him in broad daylight on a weekday?

It was beginning to seem to me that Mrs. Paulsen had been seeing things.

I was a little miffed at myself for not remembering from my earlier visit whether she'd been wearing glasses. When she opened the door, she wasn't wearing any, but there was a pair of granny glasses suspended from a cord around her neck.

"I'm sorry to bother you again, Mrs. Paulsen, but I just wanted to review a few things with you, if you have the time."

"Oh, not at all, come right in." She smiled and winked at me. "All I have is time, dear. I was just doing the crossword puzzle, anyway."

She pointed to the chair by the window. Next to the binoculars on the small table by the chair was a folded section of newspaper and a fat old dictionary that explained the glasses.

"There are just a couple of things I'd like to clarify. If we could go to the window ..."

"She didn't hurt him, did she?"

I was a bit taken aback by the abrupt question. But she'd had some time to think about the things I'd asked her and to consider her own recollections and had come to a logical conclusion, similar to my own.

"I can't say what happened yet—it would be nothing more than speculation. That's why I'm here again. The circumstances of the boy's disappearance are somewhat confusing and I need to sort it all out properly. At this point Mrs. Leeds is not a suspect in her son's disappearance."

The elderly Mrs. Paulsen emitted a quick little *hmph* and raised her eyebrows. I half-expected her to start whispering gossip about Ellen Leeds; her expression was one hundred percent *let me tell you*.

I purposefully did not allow myself to react. "If we could go to the window ..."

She walked right over to it; her paces were short but her footing seemed firm. I wondered if she ventured out at all, or if this apartment and this building comprised her entire world.

"Could you show me approximately where you were

standing yesterday morning when you saw Nathan's mother pick him up?"

"Nathan? I never knew his name. That was my late husband's middle name."

"Small world."

"Yes, isn't it? Well, I was right about here." She turned outward. I came up next to her and looked out.

"Where did you first notice the car?"

She considered that question for a moment. "I can't say that I actually noticed the car. I was looking through the binoculars and it just sort of pulled into view. I didn't see it approach the boy, really. It just pulled into the field of the glasses."

I gestured toward the binocs. "May I?"

She picked them up and handed them to me. I had already forgotten how heavy they were. I put the strap around my neck—you could do some serious toe damage if they dropped—and brought them to my eyes. It took some adjustment to correct the focus.

"Where did you first start following Nathan?"

"Do you see a fire hydrant?"

I zoomed around. "Got it," I said.

"Count three lampposts. Right about there."

It was well before the cordoned area. The probable abduction site was still half a block away.

As if an explanation for her nosiness was required, she said, "I like to watch that little boy. He has an odd way of walking, and it's interesting. He touches everything along the way, all the fences, some of the bushes ... when he turns his head, his lips are sometimes moving. I think he sings to himself."

I pulled the binocs away from my face and let my vision readjust, then pulled out my pad and made a note to find out if Nathan was dyslexic. Like my son, who had so many of the same mannerisms.

"So the car pulled into the field of vision. From which direction?"

"Coming from this way."

So the passenger door had been on the curb side. "And as you were watching through the binoculars, the boy got into the car."

"Yes. That's just how it happened. But—well, maybe this is silly, and I don't know if it's even important—"

"Everything has potential significance, Mrs. Paulsen. Please speak freely and don't worry about anyone thinking you're being silly."

"Well, it was odd—he hesitated a little bit. Like he wasn't sure about something. And I saw that he dropped his jacket. It sort of fell off his bag."

Yes, yes, yes . . . "Did he just leave it lying there?"

"Well, yes. It sort of got stuck at the edge of the bushes. Come to think of it, I thought that was a strange thing that his mother didn't make him pick it up. But children these days don't value the things their parents buy for them like we did. I meant to go downstairs and leave a note on their door that he'd dropped it. But I guess it slipped my mind."

Someone must have come along later and kicked it all the way under the bushes. Probably another kid. Maybe the litterer who dropped the receipt on it.

"Is there anything else you can remember? The smallest thing, even if you don't think it means anything . . ."

She put one hand on her chin and pondered for a moment, with great concentration. "No, I'm sorry. That's all I remember. At least right now. Sometimes it takes me a little while to bring things back up. Not like when I was younger. I had a good memory then, especially for figures."

I was willing to bet that she would remember her first telephone number, but not what she had for breakfast that day. "Thank you, Mrs. Paulsen. You've been a great help to me."

"Oh, I'm only too glad to help. I hate to hear of families having troubles. It's awful, the way things are these days."

A mediocre defense attorney would tear her to shreds. But it was a start.

Fred Vuska was peeved; he hates this kind of thing as much as I do.

"You want Frazee to come in on this with you? He'll drag it out of her like nothing."

Spence was our Father Confessor; he could make an Eskimo confess to sweating in about five minutes. We had to watch him sometimes because he made people want to come clean so badly that they would come clean to things they hadn't done.

"Not yet. I'm building a rapport with her. And I don't want her to freak."

"What about the kid? Anything new?"

I shook my head slowly. We both sat for a minute and contemplated our hangnails. I said, "He's either perfectly fine and hidden away somewhere, or he's dead."

"Yeah, that would be my take on it too."

"Is there any money in the budget for a profiler? It would help me to understand what might motivate someone to do this. Then maybe I could approach her again and get somewhere."

"There's money—a lot, in fact. We haven't spent it because all these gurus are busy writing books for big bucks or trying to nail down terrorists. You might manage to book one for next year, if you beg."

"I hadn't thought of that."

"You might want to talk to Erkinnen, though. He's pretty knowledgeable about this stuff."

Our department psychologist was known more for

airheadedness than expertise, at least among the troops. "I didn't realize."

"Yeah. He keeps up on things. Give him a call."

It couldn't hurt, especially in view of the rarity of profilers in the postwar era. "I will, but in the meantime, I'm going to run Ellen Leeds and see if anything comes up."

"Sooner the better. I'd like to wrap this one up quickly."

He said that about every case and we all pretty much ignored him. But this time, I think he really meant it. An uneasiness sets in around here when a good kid disappears. None of us likes the things we're forced to think about, but it's our job to consider every possibility. I hate to tell you what the statistics are about abuse—it's overwhelmingly at the hands of someone the child knows. That's what makes it so unthinkable, that a human being could violate a position of trust so sacred. I mean, your own kid, or your sister's kid, or your grandchild or your nephew ... what kind of scumbag do you have to be? I can understand it more easily—well, not that much more easily—if there are rage problems or impulse control issues; those can be worked out sometimes. Kids can push your buttons on purpose; mine certainly do. There are occasions when I can barely walk away without pounding them. And I'm a cop. Also a grown-up; lots of folks just don't realize what happens with kids because they're not really grown-ups themselves when they have them.

But the ones who create trust as a way to get close to a kid, and then hurt them intentionally, well, there's a special place in hell for them. At least I hope to God there is.

I'd had only limited experience with Errol Erkinnen, our department psychologist. I recalled that he had a doctorate in forensic psychology and that he had written a number of academic books on the subject, but I forgot how friendly he was.

"Oh, I'd be more than happy to talk to you, Detective," he said. "More than happy."

More than eager, he might have said. You have to have a certain craziness yourself to diagnose and pronounce judgment on those who do criminally crazy things, and as I recalled, Erkinnen met that requirement. "All I have open today is lunch. Funny, I've been really busy for the last couple of weeks. Everyone needs a consultation *now*. Some kind of run on bizarre behavior."

I didn't have the heart to tell him that he was the overflow route for the double-booked FBI boys. "I'll bring sandwiches."

"Lovely."

As I was entering the data on Ellen Leeds, I realized that I hadn't asked her maiden name. If nothing came up, I would have to call and ask her, which would surely make her suspicious about my line of thinking. But it turned out not to be necessary.

I plunked the printout down on Fred's desk. "Ellen Leeds was investigated fourteen years ago for possible child abuse when her first child was found dead in his crib at the age of eight months. The death was eventually ruled to be from natural causes."

"SIDS?" he asked.

"Supposedly. The investigator said she told him the baby didn't wake up when she expected him to, and so she went in there and found he just wasn't breathing. How easy is sudden infant death syndrome to fake?"

"I don't know. There weren't any other marks on the baby's body, according to the medical examiner's report. But there was that woman in New York who got away with it eight times."

"That was New York."

I pouted silently.

Fred said, "Yeah, I know you hate that fat-assed, big-mouthed pitcher they have there. But they don't let baseball players do the postmortems, even in New York. They have medical examiners, just like we do. There was a big sympathy thing going on there. Everyone was saying, poor woman, lost eight kids to SIDS. Finally someone started to get suspicious. Turned out she liked the attention she got when something happened to one of them."

"I'm wondering if that's what's going on here too. The kid is way too big for SIDS, but just about the right age to get grabbed by the bogeyman. But the mother is keeping a really low profile. She's not screaming to the press or banging on the mayor's door. Doesn't seem to be looking for attention, really."

"Well, maybe she figured out how big a deal this would turn out to be after it was too late."

"If that was the case, she would just have Nathan turn up and give us some lame explanation. Threaten him if he didn't go along with it. You can make a kid keep quiet."

"If he turns up, I'm gonna want Spence to talk to him."

"Me too."

When I got back to my desk to grab my purse and gun, there was a light flashing on the phone. It was a message from my daughter Frannie. She forgot to bring her tap shoes to her father's house and needed them for her lesson that afternoon. Could I bring them to the dance school before three?

I was annoyed for a moment. But then I thought about what it would be like if she just dropped off the face of the earth.

The department's consulting psychologist is a tall, bony Finn named Errol Erkinnen. He was attractive in a sharp-faced sort of way, very angular and Nordic-looking.

His mother was a big fan of Errol Flynn, hence his alliterative name. We all call him Doc, anyway. He's a skilled listener, and it took him only one recitation of the facts to grasp the case and my concerns. You wouldn't think so to see his office—it was a jungle. Papers and journals were strewn everywhere; there were no clear flat surfaces. A number of cardboard boxes, all bulging with files, were stacked up against one wall. Bookshelves, crammed full to the ceiling. But he never had any trouble coming up with paperwork when we needed it from him. I guess he was mentally organized in a way that most of us can't understand. Smart people can be like that.

He got right to the point. "Okay, first thing is, if you've got a mother who made her own kid disappear, there's likely to be some mental illness going on there. Depression, Munchausen-by-proxy, maybe, but it may not be anything overtly visible. Remember the woman in Texas who drowned her five kids in the bathtub, one by one?"

"Well, it goes without saying that she was nuts."

"Yeah, and everyone could see it in her, and she was supposedly getting treatment. But that visibility made her the exception. Mostly they hide it. You're going to have to keep that in mind when you interview her."

"What do you mean, that I should be really tender with her?"

He smiled. "Only if you go that way."

I bristled. "Come on, Doc. You know what I mean."

"I know. Sorry. I meant to say that you'll have to remember that the questions you ask and how you ask them could set her off."

"I've read a little about that Munchausen thing, but I don't know too much about it."

"It's a pretty rare syndrome, despite all the news about it lately. In a nutshell, the parent or caretaker—it's almost always a woman, usually the mother—becomes fixated on the attention she receives when she has a sick child, so she deliberately makes the child sick to get that attention. Did you see the movie *The Sixth Sense*?"

"Yeah."

"The little girl who was poisoned by her mother and haunted the kid to get him to tell her story so her little sister would be saved: that was a classic case—fictional, but well-portrayed—of the mother with Munchausen-by-proxy. But there are other diagnoses that could fit here too. The mother could be psychotic or depressed or delusional, any one of a number of conditions that might make her harm or hide her child. In some cases, she might not even be aware that she's done it."

I thought about what he'd said for a moment as he worked on his sandwich. "You know, she looks too normal for any of that other stuff. I know it's hard to tell, but you'd think there would be *some* visible signs of being whacked out. With the Munchausen thing, you might not see it unless you were watching specifically, but these other things, you'd think you'd see something in her behavior."

"Not necessarily. Some perpetrators of crimes against children are really good at looking perfectly normal. A lot of pedophiles look like the guy next door."

It was too true.

"And don't forget, you're not seeing her under 'normal' circumstances. Her son is missing. That's a stressful situation, even to a person who's in the middle of a psychotic episode, *even* if she is the cause of him being missing."

"I suppose it would be."

"Any possibility that the ex is involved?"

"I did a quick check and he looks clean."

"I'd interview him immediately. He'll be able to give you a lot of subtle insight, if he's willing to talk. And I probably don't have to tell you that he'll give you a sense of what happened when the first one died. Hopefully you'll be able to figure out if he thinks she did it or not. Is he here now?"

"On his way, due to arrive in a couple of hours."

"Good. When you talk to him you'll be able to see his face."

Not that I'd want to, ever again—Daniel Leeds had a wart on his cheek big enough to support a hanging plant. I had a very hard time looking at anything else while we were talking, which we did very shortly after he arrived in Los Angeles.

Having seen his ex-wife, who was petite and compact, I would never have put the two of them together. He waddled into the division reception area like a pregnant polar bear, pasty white, rolls of blubber hanging over his enormous belt. He had a plumber's crack when he turned around.

But he was articulate, intelligent, soft-spoken, and clearly upset by his son's disappearance. Before we got into the difficult stuff, I needed to get him calm and to establish some kind of rapport. So after a few strained pleasantries and an expression of sympathy for his troubles, I started the interview with a question that's usually pretty safe.

"What kind of work do you do?"

"I'm a rocket scientist."

I almost had to force myself not to laugh. He just didn't look the part. "Really?" I said, quite stupidly.

"Yes. *Really.* My official job description is rocket propulsion engineer. The company I work for develops propulsion systems for high-tech weapons and airplanes. The military is our biggest customer."

"So you must be pretty busy these days."

"I am."

"You have other customers for that kind of stuff?"

"Unfortunately, we do."

"Well, that must be very intriguing work, and I'll bet you—"

"I really can't discuss anything about my work, Detective. There are security issues and I'm restricted by our government contracts from revealing anything about what I do."

So much for the safe questions. I cut to the chase; there seemed little point in trying to connect more fully. We'd already established in a phone call that he was at work in Arizona when Nathan was abducted. With the kind of security his employer was likely to have, it almost seemed an insult to try to corroborate his statement. I would, of course, but it would not be my top priority.

"Tell me about your relationship with Nathan, Mr. Leeds."

He squirmed a little. I couldn't tell if the chair was too small for his bulk or if the question made him uncomfortable. "I don't see him often enough, of course. I try to maintain a working relationship with him, be an active father and all, but it's hard from so far away. He's such a great kid. I miss him a lot."

"Have you been having any problems with him lately? I know kids and parents go through tough times no matter how much they love each other. I do with mine, for sure."

"No, nothing worth mentioning. He's doing well in school, he's pretty respectful still, although I'm beginning to see signs that he's becoming a teenager, so that may change soon."

I smiled, thinking of Evan, with his occasionally smart mouth. "It probably will. But it's manageable if you work at it."

"I can't say that there's anything specific that I've noticed. We get along pretty well. Part of that is the distance, I know. If I were in the trenches with him every day like Ellen is, I'm sure I'd have a thing or two to say."

He had given me the entrée I needed. "I also wanted to ask you about your relationship with Nathan's mother."

He let out a troubled sigh. "It's as good as any divorced couple, I guess. We don't try to make things difficult for each other, if that's what you mean."

"What was the cause of the breakup of your marriage, if you don't mind me asking?"

He hesitated, then said quietly, "There was another woman."

It was true what they said about taste—there is just no accounting for it. That any woman would have coveted this man was beyond my understanding. Except that he was obviously intelligent, well-spoken, caring, and a devoted father. None of those qualities made him any less gross to look at.

"Is there rancor between the two of you over that?"

"There was at first, but I think when it all shook down she was pretty tired of me, anyway. I don't get any indications that she's still dwelling on all that. It was almost ten years ago when it happened, and we've both grown up a lot since then."

"Have you been in Arizona that whole time?"

"No, I went out there five years ago. It was a tough decision to move away from Nathan, but the offer was too good."

"Do you stay in regular touch with Ellen?"

"Fairly regular. She keeps me informed of all his activities; he's not so good at doing that, just because of who he is, I think. He's a scatterbrained kind of kid."

The mother had said *dreamy*. "I've been getting that impression. So your communications with Ellen are generally pleasant?"

"*Cordial* would be a better word. She wants me to have a good relationship with Nathan. I've always been grateful to her for that. She's a decent woman."

"And how has she seemed lately to you?"

"What do you mean?"

"Has she seemed nervous or unusually upset at all?"

"Well, her son is gone, for crying—"

"I meant before now."

"Oh. No, not at all."

"I understand that you lost a child previously to SIDS."

"Yes. We did, before Nathan was born."

"I'm very sorry."

"Thank you. It was an awful experience, let me tell you."

"I understand. When you were going through that experience together, how was Ellen?"

He shifted in his seat again. His expression grew dark as he began to understand where I was going; the tone of his voice sharpened. "What do you mean, how *was* she?"

"Was she upset, angry, resigned, what?"

"Detective, she lost a baby. How was she supposed to be?"

"I don't know, Mr. Leeds. It's not something I've experienced myself, so I'm trying to understand. I'm also wondering how that experience might affect her reaction to this situation."

"How is that going to help you find Nathan?"

"Well—"

He struggled out of the chair and stood. "Look, if you think Ellen had anything to do with this, you're mistaken. She loves that boy and she's been a terrific mother. Just wipe out any notion of her being involved. Don't waste your time, or my son's. If he has any left."

When he reached Ellen's apartment, he would tell her that I had questioned him about her and that it sounded like I suspected her. Why, oh why, could I not be more like Spence Frazee, smooth as silk, with all the right questions?

seven

THERE WAS NO POINT in another day of inquiry in the parish of Bourgneuf, nor did I think it necessary to seek additional stories of children being devoured by unknown demons in other parishes. Between Bourgneuf and the other villages I had passed through, I had all the fuel I needed to start a hearty fire, so after another night of less-than-blissful repose, I set out early on the return journey to Nantes. The undercurrent of adventure that had rendered the journey out sufferable—though barely—was now gone. It had been replaced by urgency.

I encountered no brigands on the road, not that even the most audacious marauder would have dared to take me on—I carried a dark cloud above me that was sure to dissuade all but the most determined ravager. Still, deny it though I might, I knew the danger to me was real. *Chaos reigns everywhere,* my son had written in one of his darker letters. *We never know from one day to the next which*

duke or baron will arrive to demand that his claim on usurped
territory be legitimized with a blessing.

Conditions had improved in the south over the last
year or so but remained unsettled in the north; we are an
easy mark for the English, who naturally prefer to lay
siege to convenient Normandy and Brittany before wast-
ing supplies and arms on a long foray into Provence, despite the marked improvement in the weather one always
experiences by going farther south. How much more
pleasant it is to ravage the countryside when the air caresses one's skin like the fingertips of a lover than when
the rain stings it like arrows and needles. Duke Jean, in
either wisdom or callousness, I could not say which, had
managed to keep the English at bay in Brittany with a
tenuous alliance, the terms of which seemed to change
nearly every month, much to his Eminence's chagrin
when he wore a statesman's hat.

It was perhaps owing to that constant readjustment
of accord that we knew better circumstances here in
Brittany than they did in France herself. But even relative
peace can bring difficulties one would not expect—to
wit, the problem of the free companies: With the wars
somewhat at bay for the moment, knights and squires
who once had purpose in serving their lords now roamed
aimlessly through the countryside in search of victims to
plunder, the spoils of which might bring in enough in-
come to support the continuation of the company. It was
the irony of peace.

One could hardly distinguish between soldier and
criminal, so faded had the distinctions become. My own
countrymen were no more successful in eliminating the
blood lust from their souls than the despised English—
they made menace on children, the aged and infirm,
anyone who did not carry a weapon—perpetrating acts
of viciousness that would make God Himself weep. In
his final delirium, my husband, Etienne, had spoken of

things he would never have told me while he was still of sound mind. He had seen men chained and roasted while their women and children were forced to watch, teeth pulled out one by one until every last *sou* had been given o'er, tortures and maimings of the innocents—such atrocities as defy belief.

Now, as if that torture were not enough, what innocents remained were starting to disappear. It was beginning to seem that they had been disappearing for some time, directly under our watch yet unnoticed.

I arrived at the abbey in late afternoon and returned my donkey to her own little abode. I bade her a fond good-bye; she had been a worthy companion, always willing to listen but never to contradict. I thanked her for not swaying too much on the ride home and fed her a handful of straw.

In the fields behind the stable, I could see young monks with their sleeves turned up and novices with veils tied back, all bent to the spring's planting. *Frère* Demien would be there overseeing these labors, moving from person to person with careful instruction on the best methods for each specific crop. Later in the growing season, when the plants were well up and unveiling the first of their abundance, I would often find him hovering over a favorite, whispering encouragement like some wizard or conjurer or, better even, a mother. Sometimes I wondered how he could later eat these plants, these small children of his, that he had so carefully shepherded to fruitfulness, and with such relish.

As for that, they eat small children there. . . .

As always when he was in the garden, his mood was serene and content, unlike my own, which in the aftermath of my journey was troubled. The warm smile with which he greeted me felt like honey on a bad throat, and I found great comfort in it.

He brushed small bits of dark earth off his hands

and rolled down his sleeves. "Mother—we did not expect you for another day or more," he said. "But I am glad you have returned. His Eminence has been quite testy in your absence."

There was a sinful bit of satisfaction in having been missed, though I did not like knowing that Jean de Malestroit suffered any form of discomfort. "I am glad to be back," I said wearily.

"Did you encounter difficulties that forced your early return?"

"Only one," I said, "that of achieving too much success in much too little time. I saw no reason not to return immediately, especially with Pax so near."

He made no comment but took the small satchel in which I had carried my travel necessities from my hand and gestured toward the abbey. We began a slow walk in that direction, arm in arm.

"Naturally you will give your news to his Eminence forthwith."

"Naturally."

"Affairs of state are complex at the moment, judging by our bishop's mood of late."

"I fear I shall only add to his woes, then."

♔

Eleven, I told Jean de Malestroit. *And Bernard le Camus— so, in all, twelve.*

"Over two years, in the area around Bourgneuf alone. Not to mention the stories I heard on my way there. I went no farther; there seemed no need with so much to report in that one visit."

I waited anxiously for a response, but he remained quiet.

"It cannot be ignored," I insisted.

After a long moment of what I imagined to be reflection on the matter, he spoke. "Well, once again you have given me something to consider. Not that I lacked worries. Tell me, Guillemette, you have met these people—do you find their complaints sincere?"

I was nearly speechless. "Well, yes, Eminence, I do, and I cannot fathom why a group of disparate people would conspire to invent such stories as I have heard. It would require a good amount of cooperation and far more imagination than such people have perhaps been blessed with."

"And what do you consider an appropriate response to their complaints?"

By all the saints, what could he be thinking? Such a decision could not be made by someone like me. My purpose in going forth had been to acquire enough information to force *him* to act. I bore in mind that he had given only grudging approval of my foray in the first place, but now Jean de Malestroit's disinterest seemed so complete that I began to feel rather vexed. I held my tongue; perhaps there was something here that I was missing. He was not by nature a callous or uncaring man.

"Clearly, Eminence," I said quietly, "someone should investigate each one of those disappearances to determine if there is a common thread to them. You would do well to choose a person of keen mind, one who could be trusted to have enthusiasm for the work."

"Yes, well, there does not seem to be an excess of keen, enthusiastic people available to me for such a task at the moment."

"Only one is required." I paused briefly, then plunged. "And as I am the one who brought this inquiry about in the first place, it seems only fitting that it ought to be me who sees it to completion."

"Guillemette, you are a woman. Beyond that, you are an abbess. It would be a most unseemly activity in view of your station."

"Perhaps, but no one else could have the passion for it that I have."

"Your passion may cloud your thinking. Someone more impartial, perhaps . . ."

How exasperating! *His Eminence giveth, his Eminence taketh away.* "I believe that my deep concern will give me unusual clarity on the matter—I have an ability to understand this sort of situation that will far outweigh the benefits of ignorant impartiality."

Having failed to dissuade me with reason, he next reminded me of my responsibilities. "You cannot be spared from your duties for such work."

"Oh, bother," I said. "There are idle hands all around this place, aching for tasks."

"Very well, then," he said. "*I* cannot spare you."

"Then I shall arrange my inquiries so that you will not *have* to spare me."

One corner of his mouth turned up ever so slightly. "All right," he said, "if you wish to pursue your inquiries on a deeper level, then you have my consent."

I wanted his blessing, but consent would suffice.

"We shall give your regular duties to Sister Élène," he said. "She is very competent and is quite eager for advancement. She will take your place nicely."

He always had to have the last thrust of the sword. Jean de Malestroit saw the look of distress that clouded my face and hastened to clarify. "Of course, she cannot ever truly take your place, and we shall all suffer in your absence. Rest assured, the change will persist only until you are finished with the work before you. When you return from this quest of yours, we will be very glad to have you back again."

"Then, with your leave, I shall begin immediately," I said.

"Ah, Guillemette, do not be so hasty. It would be

better if you waited until after Pax," he said. "After all, I shall be needing you, as I always do."

For my duty of standing against the wall during preparations, one for which I could *not* be replaced. "Of course, Eminence. That would be very sensible."

I thought it anything but sensible.

⚜

Thus the most sacred week of our year began to seem to me the longest. I was eager to move forward, but I could not do so—there was holiness to be inspired, a daunting task in such a large parish as ours, where many of the communicants would benefit more from a good meal than yet another plateful of spiritual nourishment. Despite its wealth and prosperity, Nantes had many poor, all of whom had been beaten down by the constant wars and resultant levies on their meager treasuries.

Good Friday came and went; its terrible sorrow washed over us like a wave and then, under the glorious influence of the Resurrection, quickly abated. Easter was early that year, before the end of *Mars,* so the air was spring-chilled as we headed in procession to the church. Along the way long queues of worshipers lined the muddy streets, some with nothing more than rags tied about their feet, in the hopes of seeing the Bishop and his entourage in the glorious pomp and dignity of holy procession. What shoes were worn by the gawkers could not help but be wet and would stiffen later as they dried. There would be great clumps of dried mud cast off onto the stone floor of the sanctuary after the service, for which Sister Élène would now be responsible.

The sanctuary itself was already overflowing with worshipers attired in their finest raiment, brought out only on such worthy occasions. But a great deal of what was presented as finery could hardly be called so by any standard; Madame le Barbier could have been very useful among these worshipers. I craned my neck and looked around to see if she had made the journey from Machecoul, but I did not find her in the congregation.

For all the despair and poverty that most of these people could rightfully claim, they worshiped with great hope; it was a day of renewal, rebirth, of the promise of spring. The air had a freshness to it that does not seem to happen at any other time. The sunlight was thin but bright and teased of the sweet warmth to come. Birds sang as if they had been tapped on the wing by God Himself.

We had our own God-tapped birds in the loft at the rear of the church, though they were all human—boys and men, to be more specific. But some among them possessed voices that might have been stolen from the angels. I closed my eyes and let their holy chant wash through me.

Kyrie eleison, Christe eleison.

O Domine, Jesu Christe, rex gloriae, libera animas omnium fidelium de functorum, de poenis inferni, et de profundo lacu.

I lost myself in the sweet smoothness of the chant. But I opened my eyes in surprise when one voice sounded alone. I had heard it many times before.

Hostias, te preces tibi Domine, laudi suferium, tu suscipe, animas iras . . .

From my place near the front of the church I turned back to look at the singers.

"By all the saints . . ." I said under my breath.

Quarum hodie, memoriam, et jus . . .

Frère Demien was seated directly in front of me; I reached out and tugged on one of his sleeves. Apparently I had disturbed a moment of true prayer, for he turned around and gave me a rare look of consternation.

I pointed upward. "Look—in the choir," I said.

He put a hand up to shade his eyes against the sun coming in through the rear window. "God be praised," he whispered. "Buchet! But . . . why is he not at Machecoul? *Mon Dieu!*" He gave me a shocked look. "The Duke must have enticed him away from Milord Gilles."

It was an unlikely development. "One wonders by what means—Milord and Buchet might have shared a skin."

"No longer, by the looks of it."

André Buchet was famed throughout the land, and deservedly—he was young and handsome and possessed a voice that might have been an affront to God in its perfection, had it not been created by God Himself and had Buchet not used it primarily to his Creator's glory. Gilles de Rais heard him singing one day in the parish of Saint-Etienne, which parish was his own property, and had whisked him off immediately to join the choir of his own Chapel of the Holy Innocents. The ceremony with which the installation had been made was remarkable and oft recounted, though never could it be reproduced exactly, even by the same musicians and singers—the air of it was what made it so special. Buchet was but a boy at the time and still unspoiled. Now, after having been pampered with all manner of advantages, he had come to expect such treatment and was known for his impetuous temper when things were not exactly to his liking.

For a long while there was a quiet scandal among us about the way Milord doted on the boy. René de la Suze had protested his brother's expenditure of money to support the boy so lavishly.

Good trebles are rare and to be cherished, Milord had said in his own defense.

Harder still to keep and therefore a waste, Milord's brother had countered; *They grow up, and their voices deepen.*

But not Buchet. "What is his age now, would you guess?" I asked *Frère* Demien.

"Twenty and two, perhaps."

"He still sings as he did at twelve."

It was not much of an exaggeration. I wondered to myself if he had been made a *castrato*; if so, it might even have been his own choice. He would have had to decide at a tender age, before the man effects took hold of him.

We must not have been the only ones who speculated on the presence of André Buchet, for murmurs began to rise up all around us. But when he began to sing again, the congregation went completely silent. The chant flowed silken from between his lips; the melody was sweet and holy, mysterious—we were all thoroughly entranced.

Libera me Domine, de morte eternal. In die ila tremenda, quando celli movendisunt et terra, dum veneris, judicare seculum, per ignem.

Then another voice joined in, and another, then more, until finally the whole choir was singing in such exquisite unison that they seemed *sola voce,* except for the bit of Buchet's voice that could be heard floating above it all. They pleaded with God on our behalf to free us all from eternal death, to keep us from the judgment of fire. There was not a cough, not a whisper, not the whine of a child in the sanctuary, so enthralled were we all by the beauty of what graced the air.

But in the middle of the final cadence, heads suddenly began to turn. The buzz of curiosity seemed to originate at the rear of the church and was moving forward in a wave that progressed at about the pace of a man's walk. We were at the front of the congregation, so I could not see what or who had caused the commotion. All along the central aisle, heads began to nod as a small procession worked through the parting crowd.

As they came into view, I saw first a priest in white robes—one Monsignor Olivier des Ferrieres. That in and of itself was cause for comment, for he was a rogue, loose in his beliefs, known to associate with a darker element than that which his superiors would prefer. More than once his Eminence had considered defrocking the man.

"He is not attached to this parish," *Frère* Demien whispered in surprise. "To any parish that I know of."

I shrugged in demonstration of my own bewilderment. I stood up on my toes and craned my neck higher in an attempt to see farther back. The last note of the choir's chant hung in the air over all of us, in bittersweet reverberation.

"Mon Dieu," I heard myself say. I felt my hands make the familiar protective gesture on my chest, crossing first up and down, and then from one side to the other.

My heart was suddenly in my throat. Lord Gilles de Rais walked slowly behind des Ferrieres, each halting step moving him toward the front of the church. He stood out from those around him by virtue of some indefinable quality of character, which had more to do with his stature as a nobleman and hero of France than any physical attribute. He was not an overly large man, just a bit more than average of height, but he had a presence about him that demanded notice. His dark hair, fashionably trimmed just above the collar of his tunic, was stark in contrast to the pallor of his skin, which had not of late been bronzed by war. He wore red that day, a shade not unlike fresh blood. On his face there was an expression more in keeping with the day of our Lord's crucifixion than His rebirth. Milord was near to weeping, as I saw it.

No one had expected he would come here to celebrate our Lord's rising from the dead. "Why is *he* not in Machecoul, at his own chapel?" I wondered aloud.

"He is free to worship where he sees fit, Sister."

"But here, today, under Jean de Malestroit's nose, while there is still such disdain between them?"

At about the midpoint of the aisle, he stopped and turned around. His gaze went up to the choir loft, and when his eyes found André Buchet, the whole of Milord's body seemed to sag, as if a great weight had been settled on him.

Therein lay the answer to the question of his unanticipated presence.

Frère Demien leaned closer and said, "*Je regrette, Guillemette,* I know you love Milord well. But even you must admit that it is disgraceful how he stares at Buchet."

I took my eyes off the great lord who had spent countless hours on my lap as a child and looked up at the singer who held his attention. The affection and sadness in Milord's expression unsettled me. "*Regardez, mon Frère,*" I said. "Buchet is like ice up there in the loft. He will not return Milord's gaze."

Then Milord's head drooped again, as if he were in complete misery. He turned around and proceeded along the main aisle as before, following the ungainly des Ferrieres toward the confessional, a peacock towed by a squab.

Oh, Guillemette, my Etienne had mused dreamily in his final days, when he could do little more than that, *you should have seen him at Orléans! We all stood in awe of him. His armor was shiny black and beautifully fitted to his body, and when he pressed his steed forward, the white plume at the peak of his helmet would lay straight back. I tell you, Wife, he was both fierce and fine; he could call upon his violent nature at any time, more readily than any of us. I saw him plunge his sword into the belly of many an Englishman—few survived if he got a decent thrust. There was not a man in that army who fought as mightily as did Gilles de Rais.*

It was in the aftermath of that great and bloody battle that he was elevated to his position of Marshal of France. Gilles rode at the side of the Maid Jean herself, she in her pure white undecorated armor, he so splendid in black.

Coal and snow, Etienne said. *How two people could be so alike and yet so disparate is unfathomable.*

My husband was not the only one who noticed their marked dissimilarity and at the same time their undisguised comradeship. Each one's legend grew: she, an untarnished peasant girl called to arms by her "voices" (which some thought unholy, perhaps instead the whisperings of witches in her ears), and he, the epitome of worldliness, with all the glamour that his position afforded. Both were untethered in spirit and in action, though that abandon showed itself in different ways. Everything Jean d'Arc did was justified by her belief that God had given her the mandate and the means to unite France under the bastard Charles; Gilles de Rais offered no justification whatsoever for what he did, as none was required of him. He had been born to entitlement and did what he wanted to do.

They were both completely mad, Etienne would say. In view of what they did separately and together, it could not be otherwise. Yet there was a simple affinity between them that bore a disquieting resemblance to affection. They seemed inseparable while they were companions—there was even scandalous talk of "love."

But Jean d'Arc was a virgin—Yolande d'Aragon determined this herself with an examination so thorough that the Maid was said to have been deeply offended and even injured in her private parts—and Milord was a married man who had no reputation for philandering. I never heard it said once that he took a woman other than Lady Catherine to his bed; it was more often said that he took no woman to bed at all, which declaration was more troubling to me than if he had. And while Lady Catherine was a beautiful woman, she was not of a similar mind to Milord. She was quiet, polite, courtly, and gracious, unlike her rash and adventuresome mate. It seemed to me that there was nothing he would not try.

To Etienne, that was all so glorious; he could hardly stop speaking of the things he saw. *How grand it all was, how excellent we all were, both in spirit and the flesh, a massive entourage of soldiers and noblemen, warriors gathered at last into one united army. Swordsmen, bowmen, foot soldiers, and lancers, we all lined up in proper order, fresh for the fight.*

Blood lust was in the air, he said, heightened by the sudden, miraculous announcement that day that the troops were finally to be paid, by virtue of contributions from many noble coffers, Milord's included. All manner of men went into that battle behind this one small woman: good men, bad men, thieves, beggars, fathers, sons, and brothers, among them men who had secrets from everyone but God. Plenty of ne'er-do-wells went forth, two in Milord's own entourage: his cousins Robert de Briqueville and Gilles de Sille—never my favorite pair, not as grown men to be sure, not even when they were young boys. There was little to be liked in either; both had an edge that gave me pause, and I was not alone in feeling thus. No one at Champtocé or Machecoul seemed to care much for them, singly or together.

Yet for all the mischief they made in both places, the cousins were never more than shadows to Gilles. Even as a child he led them about like goats on a tether, and never did any good come of it. So many times while he was in my charge I caught myself wishing that Gilles de Rais might have chosen different playmates among those available to him; he seemed to do so well with my Michel and so poorly with the sons of Briqueville and Sille. With

Michel he could be a good boy; with his cousins, he was always a rogue, vicious and sly.

But those cousins comported themselves well at Orléans, or so it was reported; the Maid seemed to inspire all who rode beneath her banners, from the lowest peasant to the highest noble. How glorious it was to remember; how proud we all were, how quick to claim a share of Milord's honor.

"He was at his best in that time," I whispered blankly to myself.

Frère Demien looked at me in concern. "What?" he said.

It hadn't seemed so loud when I spoke. "I said"— hastily, and in a shaky voice—"he is not at his best."

"You said more than that."

I was silent. And then I looked away, back toward Milord again.

I had unintentionally uttered a bit of truth in covering my words; he was *not* at his best at this time. His exquisite attire could not hide what we all saw on his visage: He looked drawn and tired, older than his thirty-six years. The crowd continued to part to let him pass, as much in wonder at his very presence as in such courtesy being his by virtue of his position. The holy book he carried was covered in gilt leather. The hilt of his ever-present sword was encrusted with jewels of every color and shape. But the porter of all this finery was himself a worn and tired man, one weighted with some indefinable anguish.

There had been distressing rumors of late that he had given himself over to some young conjurer, a dashing rogue that the priest Eustache Blanchet had found for him on a journey to *Italia*. It seemed an awfully long distance to go when there were charlatans aplenty hereabouts, but, then, none of our local inveiglers would seem so intriguing to Milord, who always favored the exotic over the mundane.

François Prelati, this conjurer's name was. I saw them together once in the castle at Machecoul when his Eminence brought me along on some business of state. Enraptured though I was by the familiar surroundings there, I could not help but notice the young man who had found a place by Milord's side and rarely left that position. He looked to be quite a bit younger than Milord himself, perhaps around twenty and four, a stylish blade with strikingly handsome features and a slender build. Milord followed him around shamelessly, like a puppy. It gave me discomfort to see them together, for there was an unnatural ease between the two, a good deal more than God allows between men of honor. Milord was all aglow, as if the presence of this Prelati made him a young man again himself.

Now this same lord approached me with leaden steps. I felt inclined, though I did not understand why, to look away—before me was a man who was almost my own son, and yet for some unnameable reason I did not want to meet his gaze should it come my way. But temptation was too strong, the pull too great; I glanced directly toward him, and for a brief moment our eyes met. First there was a spark of recognition—how could one not know one's own nurse—and then he stopped for a moment to regard me. There was fondness in his gaze, and his expression grew more childlike as the moments passed. It was as if he were wistful about his days under my care. The eyes of those who had been watching him— nearly everyone—fell upon me as well. Milord finally broke the thread of time that connected us and moved on, but I still felt the stares of those around me. I looked around for safety and, finding only scrutiny, I turned to face him again.

But he was too far ahead to see my frantic gestures,

for I could not call out to him—it would be unseemly for a woman of my position, especially on this holiest of holy days. *Wait,* I wanted to say when I saw that he'd moved on, *come back to me,* mon fils de lait, *we must speak.* But it was too late—once again I was merely one of the crowd who stared in fascination as our sovereign lord headed toward the confessional.

I watched with trepidation as Milord and his imported monsignor proceeded toward the front of the sanctuary. When they reached the end of the queue where those who required absolution waited, all those who had arrived before him stepped aside to let him pass. He waved them back to their places in line. Many of these peasants and commonfolk looked bewildered and indecisive; would they be punished for going before their lord?

Finally, as if he understood their quandary, Gilles de Rais spoke to them. "Resume your places," he said. His voice was troubled and utterly uncommanding. "I shall wait among you and confess in order."

The whole church came alive with whispers—none of his forebears had shown such deference to his subjects. Gilles's own father, Guy de Laval, was notorious for his ill-tempered treatment of clerics, but even Lord Guy could hardly keep pace with his dastardly father-in-law Jean de Craon—and I daresay that even a steady stream of unconditional absolution might not have sufficed to save *his* evil soul.

I often wish I had found the courage to chastise him publicly before he died; my position with the family afforded me a bit of impunity, and the old man never cared for me anyway. His Eminence considered the man a despot and would have secretly been pleased to know that Jean de Craon got an unpleasant earful to entertain him on his afterlife journey, which would surely not be made in a heavenward direction.

But on this holiest of holy days, Gilles de Rais—the grandson, son, himself now a father, though his daughter was nowhere in sight on this morn—did not follow in the impatient footsteps of his ancestors. He waited with uncharacteristic humility among the lesser folk for his turn to beg forgiveness. There was little one could say to describe the feeling that permeated the sanctuary as the feared and revered Lord of Champtocé, Machecoul, and a host of other properties sat among his own trembling serfs and waited to voice all his regrets to God's representative. I feared that those who immediately preceded him would feel compelled to hurry their confessions so as not to keep him waiting and might achieve only incomplete forgiveness—one imagines the sins of these poor folk being spit out like so many mouthfuls of angry bees.

But Gilles never looked impatient or agitated, only somber and burdened. When it came his turn at last, he entered the confessional, and Monsignor des Ferrieres took his place on the other side of the screen. It was quite a while before they emerged again; Milord was as pale as a shade and the Monsignor had the gravest look upon his face. The penance was simple and brief, but, then, the sins of the highborn have always been more easily forgiven than the sins of those who serve them. Or perhaps the transgressions were so dire that the penance could only be symbolic. In any case, Gilles de Rais was not on his knees for long before he rose up again and approached our Brother Simon Loisel to receive Communion. He knelt down and stared at his folded hands as he awaited service.

Jean de Malestroit, stoic and cold, watched stiffly as the wafer was placed by Loisel on the tongue of the Marshal of France. My bishop's face was marked with a hardness that I seldom saw on it. He was a shrewd man when it was required of him, and he often showed disdain for those many he managed to outsmart, but rarely did I see on his face such a glaring look of disgust as the one he now wore. I could not help but wonder what he was thinking at that moment.

I resolved to ask him that question later, when the intrigue and excitement prompted by the day's remarkable events finally died down.

Which never did happen.

chapter 8

MY DAUGHTER'S TAP SHOES had been safely delivered. When I got back to my desk, there was a note staring up at me. On it, in Fred's small and crunched handwriting, was a name, followed by the words, *Ellen Leeds's lawyer.* The last word was underlined.

I glanced at the phone and saw no message light. For some reason this lawyer had bypassed me and gone directly to Fred.

The moment I arrived in his office he said, "Looks like you got a little problem, Dunbar. The guy called a little while ago and said forget about talking to her anymore. He was squawking about a civil suit after 'we catch the real perpetrator,' as he put it. How come you didn't say anything about liking the mother for this?"

To my momentary silence, he said, "Speak."

I told him what Mrs. Paulsen had said and then explained the ambiguity of Ellen Leeds's alibi. "The ex was pretty hot under the collar when he left here to go to her apartment. He sort of told me off and then humped on out of here. They still talk to each other, and I assume he just passed it on that I sounded suspicious of her."

Fred offered, "Maybe he was asking himself the same question."

"I don't think so. He defended her pretty vigorously." Then I sat down. "But you know what? A little while ago I was ready to put the cuffs on her. Now I'm having second thoughts. Something's not working here."

"Like what? You have a witness who saw the kid getting into the mother's car, and there are problems with where she said she was at the time it happened."

"Yeah. I know. But I just don't get her for the type."

"Oh, come on, Lany. Dispassionate review of the evidence. *That's* how we make decisions here, remember?"

"I know, I know. But the old lady—I'm just not sure about what she told me."

"Is she senile?"

"No, not really. She engaged me in a cogent conversation and was very lucid in the moment. It's all the other moments that could be a problem. Nice lady and a real busybody, very credible-looking. Just the kind of witness you want, except for her age. She has the potential to be lawyer food on the stand."

"If we ever get to that point."

I could almost hear his thought. *At the rate you're going, she'll be dead by then anyway.*

He said, "Is she taking any kind of medication?"

"I didn't ask."

"Why not?"

"I'm trying to build a rapport with her. And you don't ask an elderly lady that kind of question right away. I imagine she'd view it as impolite. She likes me, I think, but I'm not sure how much she trusts me just yet."

"You have the people's permission, as their employee, to be impolite. In fact, the taxpayers are counting on you to be that way on their behalf. Give her a call and ask her the same questions a defense lawyer would ask."

"If she is taking something, I got nothing but the jacket. Where do I go from there?"

"Beats me. I'm just a supervisor. I delegate that problem to *you,* the detective."

"So *supervise,* then. Tell me what to do."

It was as if he were waiting for that opening. "Well, I think maybe I got something here that might get you moving." He turned around in his swivel chair and picked up a cardboard box from the table behind his desk. He swiveled back again and put the box down in front of me.

Scribbled on the side of the box that faced me was the name *Donnolly.*

The bagpipes from his funeral were still ringing in my head. "Oh, jeez."

For the last few weeks of his life, before Terry Donnolly's heart blew, he'd seemed stressed and anxious and occasionally depressed; he talked incessantly about getting out. *I can't stand these tough ones anymore* was all he would say when any of us asked why.

"His last two cases. Both sort of stagnating at the moment. I looked them over again this afternoon while you were out. The thing that brought them to mind—and he was very frustrated by this—is that the initial suspect in both of these cases was an intimate, based on a seemingly reasonable eyewitness account. Just like in your case now. But the evidence directly contradicted what the witnesses said, and Donnolly came to the conclusion pretty early on that the intimates weren't involved. He didn't know where to go with either of these. One of the parents knows he died and keeps calling for the case to be reassigned."

I put my hand on the box. *Pandora Pandora Pandora,* it was screaming, *open me, open me.* Fred didn't seem to hear it. The cardboard began to feel hot, as if my touch had started some sort of chemical reaction. I pulled my hand away.

Fred saw it and frowned. "I had all this stuff gathered together because I thought it would help you. So I think you better take a look."

Which meant that they had been reassigned.

Ours is a big division. I have enough trouble keeping track of my own cases, never mind everyone else's. I knew Donnolly had two missings, but the details were completely foreign to me. The files were pretty meaty, judging by the weight of the box. In my lower drawer there were two accordion files left over from previous cases, both well-solved cases and with very good karma; maybe if I put the Donnolly cases in those folders, a little serendipity would rub off and speed things along.

The names of the victims were emblazoned on the front and side spine of each of Donnolly's thick folders. It was too late in the day to sit down and really dig in, but I read enough of each one to get a rough sense of what had happened. The first case was the disappearance of Lawrence Wilder, male Caucasian, age thirteen, height five feet three inches, slight build. Light brown hair on the blondish side, blue eyes, lots of freckles. Last seen approximately one year earlier getting into the vehicle of his mother's brother, which, according to three witnesses at a sidewalk café, was purportedly driven by same. Problem was, the uncle had an irrefutable alibi—he was a firefighter, on duty at the time, punch card, coworkers, and all. There were no real physical clues except trace evidence in the uncle's car, in which we found a few fibers from clothing known to belong to Larry. But that meant nothing—the boy had been in that car dozens of times. Believing the uncle to be innocent, the boy's family had posted a reward for information leading to his recovery. Thousands of calls had come in—they always do when there's money to be claimed—but no real leads had developed.

The bulk of the paper seemed to be the result of Donnolly's interviews with the witnesses, with family and friends, with school chums, teachers, coaches—he'd done an exhaustive job. Some of these people had been interviewed a number of times, perhaps for clarification, but also perhaps because Donnolly didn't want to stop working on the case. It's something we all do when we have nowhere new to go—we go back to the previous witnesses. Sometimes we get lucky when we do that, but usually it gets us nothing more than a continued sense of activity and involvement. It's hard to let go, especially when you want so badly to solve a case and it just isn't happening.

I could feel Terry Donnolly's frustration even in this quick scan. He was a good report writer; everything was clear and concise and, where possible, well documented. But the reports were colored with the bitter truth that it all led nowhere.

Boy number two from Donnolly's box was named Jared McKenzie. He had made his unexplained exit about six months before the Wilder boy. When I read the missing-child report, I did a bit of a double take—I thought maybe something had been misfiled from the Wilder case. His physical characteristics were remarkably similar, with the exception that Jared's hair was more red than blond. He was last seen walking off a soccer field in the company of his coach, a longtime adult friend who spent a good deal of time with the McKenzie family and often gave Jared a ride home. On the day of the disappearance, however, the coach claimed to have gone back to his accounting office after practice to pick up some papers for a later meeting with a client. Another parent reported seeing the two leave together in the coach's car and remembered the time exactly because she had just used her cell phone, which displayed a broadcast time. But the security guard at the coach's place of employment verified his arrival there precisely five minutes after the other parent reported seeing him. It was at least a ten-minute drive from the soccer field to the coach's office. Impossible.

No wonder Terry Donnolly had had a heart attack. What was he supposed to do with stuff like this?

What was *I* supposed to do with it?

Three cases where intimates were all the initial suspects and the victims were shockingly similar—all white adolescent males, slightly built. There was the relative lack of evidence in all three cases, which meant that the three perps were being very careful.

Or the one perp was.

I told Fred what I was thinking and asked him to give me someone to help with the integration of the data.

"You think we have a serial abductor on our hands?"

"Well, it's hard not to think that way. . . ."

"It's a little early yet to be saying that."

The kiss of death, so tenderly delivered.

I now had the unenviable job of contacting people who had already suffered a terrible loss, with the purpose of reopening their old wounds. Donnolly's reports were excellent, but I wanted to talk to these folks myself.

Nancy Wilder was surprised to learn, when I called her, that Terry Donnolly had died, which saved me the trouble of having to ask Fred which family had been pushing for reassignment, a detail we somehow managed not to discuss. "I figured he just wasn't getting anywhere on the case, and that's why we didn't hear from him in a couple of weeks," she said when I told her. "I'm very sorry to hear that he passed away. Did he leave a family?"

"A wife and two children."

"Oh, how terrible."

"We're all pretty unhappy about it. He'll be missed."

"I have to say, he was a very vigilant detective. Very thorough. I was always grateful for that." She sighed and was quiet for a moment. "Oh, dear," she said finally, "This is very upsetting. Such a sweet man. Are you going to be taking over the case now?"

"I've been given the task of cleaning up a few loose ends. Terry's cases have to be looked into, so they can either be closed or given out for further investigation. I'm gathering information so those decisions can be made."

A half-truth, one I hoped would sound more convincing to her than it did to me. "I just want to hear for myself what you have to say. Detective Donnolly was very good about documenting everything, but it really makes a difference to me to talk to the families. I apologize for opening up old wounds, and I hope you'll understand that this is in the best interest of the case."

"Well, I do understand that," Mrs. Wilder said. "And I appreciate your regrets. But you don't have to worry—the wound hasn't healed yet, so you're not opening anything up. It never closed, at least not for me. Larry's father is ready to just walk away and give it up, to just assume that Larry is dead somewhere and we'll never find him. But I'm not there yet."

Larry's father was probably right, but it's cruel to take hope away from people, if that's all they have left. It was all too typical for a married couple to experience difficulties in the aftermath of a child's disappearance. There is always blame on one side or the other, even if it isn't overtly stated.

"I'd like to meet with you in your home, if that isn't too much of an imposition."

I would visit the following day. I was able to make similar arrangements with the McKenzie family, though Jared's mother was quite a bit less civil. She seemed to think it was terribly inconvenient for Donnolly to have dropped dead of frustration, that it somehow served him right, that he should have moved heaven and earth on her behalf. I'll admit that there are some of us who close out property crimes as "unsolvable" just to be done with them, but Terry Donnolly always busted his hump, never more so than when there was a kid involved. His pressures were self-imposed. And he paid for it in the end.

I made some discreet inquiries around the adjacent sectors, asking for overviews of stalled cases where boys had gone missing. Then I copied all of Terry Donnolly's interview summaries and put them in a folder. Evan was waiting at the curb when I got there. Jeff Samuels, his best friend and shadow, was beside him.

He tossed his school bag and soccer bag in the way-back of the van and then slid in next to me in front, all legs and arms and straight straw hair. Just like his father.

"Did practice get out early?"

"No. You're just late."

I looked at my watch. He was right. "I'm sorry, Evan, I guess I need to replace the battery again."

I leaned closer, hoping against hope that he would forget his adolescence long enough to plant a little kiss on my cheek. With eyes rolling, he acquiesced.

"Oh, come on, that wasn't so bad, was it? It makes old ladies happy to have a little kiss now and then."

"Mom, knock it off ... you're not really old."

I could have lived without the accent he'd placed on *really*.

"What are we having for dinner?"

"I don't have a clue. I'll figure it out when we get home."

"Can Jeff stay?"

"Of course. You like a mystery meal, don't you, Jeff?"

"Yes, Mrs. Dunbar."

Frannie and Julia were both at the dance school, where

Kevin had dropped Julia so I wouldn't have to pick her up at his place. By now there would be a woman there, one of the endless stream he seemed to have going. I didn't care that he had a steady rotation of women, but I didn't want them paraded in front of the kids. He'd behaved very decently so far, at least on that issue.

I'm not sure that Frannie could look any more like my mother than she does; Julia defied resemblance classification completely. Unsolicited, each of them clambered forward to give me a kiss before settling down and buckling up. I grinned triumphantly at their brother.

"They're girls," he protested. "They're supposed to kiss their mother."

"What's for dinner?" Frannie said.

"Yeah, what?" her sister echoed.

"Whatever Jeff wants."

They were all over him with suggestions. I ended up agreeing to Spaghetti-O's and canned string beans, the classic four-appliance meal: can opener, microwave, disposal, and dishwasher. Jeff went back to his parents' nearby apartment in the same complex, and then the rest of us did our homework around the kitchen table, myself included. I woke up, after nodding out, to find Julia standing next to me, struggling to read the Donnolly report I was drooling on. She put her finger on a big word and looked at me with innocent curiosity.

I sounded it out, syllable by syllable, as I'd been taught to do. "Per-pe-tra-tor," I said.

She repeated it slowly. "Does that mean bad people?"

God bless context.

When I came in to work the next morning after sleeping ten hours straight, there was a very noticeable stack of faxes on my desk. Attached to the top one was a yellow Post-it note from Fred. All it said was *Hmmm*.

All were still listed as active cases, but in reality they were all on hold, though no one would say that officially. One was more than three years old—after that much time, a case of this nature is virtually unsolvable unless striking new evidence appears out of nowhere. Witnesses move, their memories of the crime dim. None of these disappearances were particularly horrific, at least on the surface. *I saw the car pull up and the boy got in and that was the last time I saw him or (the intimate in question) that day.*

Dead end after dead end, except for one surprise; it had been "solved." A twelve-year-old boy had been abducted, supposedly by his mother's boyfriend, one Jesse Garamond, who had a previous conviction for child molestation, the details of which were not included in the overview report. The missing boy's body was never found, but Garamond was prosecuted for the crime anyway and convicted solely on the eyewitness testimony of a middle-aged clergyman who had supposedly seen the man and the boy together about an hour before the boy's mother called the police to report him "missing" because he was late getting home.

The crime had been a violation of Garamond's parole, so he went back to jail immediately to serve the remainder of his original sentence. The new one was tacked on; he would be toothless by the time he got out.

The case grabbed me for two reasons: first, because it's so unusual to get a conviction without a body, and second, because it was Spence Frazee who had interviewed the guy.

I was kind of surprised to find Spence at his desk because he hates being there. It's not on a lake, and fishing poles are not allowed. When he's forced to work in his cubicle, he gets fidgety and short-tempered and no one can stand to be around him. Otherwise, he's a really nice guy. I think he'd still be out on the street if the difference in pay weren't so stark. We all make a lot more money pushing a desk than we did pushing a cruiser, and we don't come into anywhere near as much contact with the scumbags of the world as we did on the streets. That gets to be important at some point, especially for those of us who have kids. I always felt like I should delouse my uniform and myself before I went home so I wouldn't bring anything in.

I put the fax down in front of him.

"What's this?" he said.

"The Garamond case."

"Oh," he said.

"Well . . ."

Spence had worked Jesse Garamond like a real pro. He built up his confidence, established a rapport, created a real sense of responsibility, all the things we're trained to do to get a suspect to speak freely. By the time he got through with him, he had this Garamond saying that he'd love to confess, he wanted so badly to admit to Spence that he'd abducted his girlfriend's son and killed him.

"Problem is," Garamond said to him, "I didn't do it. Hey, if I could tell you truthfully that I did it, I would. But I didn't."

Of course, they all say that. But Garamond went one step further and bolstered his credibility when he said, "I'll cop to the first one, you'll pardon the expression. The one I got sent up for. But I didn't do this one. There's a sicko out there that you're not gonna get because you want it to be me and you'll do whatever you have to do to make it be me. So some other little kid is gonna have to suffer because you got the wrong guy."

He had no alibi because, at the time the abduction supposedly took place, he was cheating on his girlfriend—the missing boy's mother—with his brother's wife.

"Hey, what the hell am I supposed to do here? I love

my brother. I don't want his kids to suffer through this stuff. He might walk out on her if he found out I was sackin' her. I can't be responsible for that. No way. I'd rather do time."

Honor among thieves, or something like that—among adulterers, maybe. But, again, it was a story line that had been used many times before—*I have a great alibi but I can't use it because someone will be hurt or compromised*—and it was easy to discount. Usually we yawn and chuckle when we hear it.

But Spence wasn't laughing right then.

"I don't know, Lany, there's just something about this one. I don't get this guy for this crime. It's just not his style. He's a bad dude, but he's not that kind of sicko."

With a promise of secrecy, Spence got the brother's wife to corroborate the story. She would not, however, agree to testify on her brother-in-law's behalf, nor would she allow us to consult with her husband on the matter. So much for fraternal loyalty.

Spence handed the papers back to me. "Let's go get some fresh air," he said.

The Los Angeles County Corrections facility is located in Lancaster, about an hour and a half away, through the lower mountains. Sixty miles or so, but half the time is spent going the first ten miles. The second half of the journey was quite scenic, but we had to get through a forest of billboards first. I think sometimes that L.A. is a billboard museum with rotating exhibits. Just when you get used to the last big obnoxious sign, another one takes its place.

Spence was driving a company unmarked unit; I was in the front passenger seat. We had the police radio going, and I was trying to hear the garbled chatter over the AC fan. I was totally absorbed by the scratchy transmissions when a new sign caught my eye. It had a black background and a short silver sword with a jeweled hilt as the main design elements. Emblazoned in medieval-type lettering were the words THEY EAT SMALL CHILDREN THERE. Some sort of red liquid—probably a few gallons of fake blood—was dripping off the lettering.

"Look at that," I said to Spence. "Damn. Now they put special effects on the billboards too."

Spence peeked out from behind the steering wheel. "Oh, yeah, I saw that the other day. Just what we need, another weird movie for the copycats to mimic in their spare time."

I hated to admit it, but that sort of thing always caught my attention. There was a time, before it became fashionable to emulate the crimes shown in some of these films, when I was actually a little bit of a horror aficionado. I couldn't tell you why I like to be scared, but I do. I followed the sign with my eyes as we drove past it in the mid-afternoon traffic, which was heavy enough to allow a good, long look. The whole thing gave me the creeps.

"The red stuff must drip through a hose into a bucket of some sort down where the lights are attached. Gotta be a pump of some kind sending it back up to flow down again."

Spence just shook his head and sighed.

We had to check our guns with a guard at the prison gate; I hate to do that, especially when I'm going into a place that I know is full of criminals. The thing weighs a ton on my hip, but there's a certain comfort in having it there when the hand comes through the bars and squeezes your neck.

Garamond was waiting for us in one of the screened-off reception cubicles, as opposed to the glass-partitioned high-security cages, where contact was limited to the telephone.

"He must be behaving," I said quietly.

Spence *hmphed*. "Might as well make it pleasant."

Jesse Garamond wore the familiar bright orange coveralls that are so endearingly hard to miss in the outside world, where no one would be caught dead in that color. He had a few more tattoos than he'd sported the last time I saw him, which was on the day of his sentencing as he was being taken out of court. He wore his thinning hair in a straggly ponytail and had a decent-size gold hoop dangling from one ear. I wondered why it hadn't been yanked off him. You could barely see his mouth for the mustache.

He actually smiled when he saw Spence. "Man, you're startin' to feel like a member of the family."

"How ya doin', Jesse?"

"I'm okay, can't complain. They mostly leave me alone because I keep to myself. I'm writing a novel, don't you understand, so I need quiet. The other guys don't want me writing nothing bad about them, so they give me my space."

Spence grunted. "That's very interesting."

Jesse was not fooled. "So what's up with this unexpected visit, not that I mind havin' the company, especially since you had the good manners to bring me a lady to look at...."

"Detective Dunbar is working on a case similar to yours, and she wants to ask you a few questions," Spence said.

"Yeah?" he said. "Am I a suspect? 'Cause if I am, I want my lawyer."

He grinned at our expressions. A gold tooth gleamed on one side of his mouth. He gave me a lascivious once-over; it was creepy and unwelcome. Then his expression turned cold. "Your ass she's working on a similar case. You just want to try to get me to tell you I did that kid so you can sleep better, that's all. Man, don't waste no time and no taxpayers' dollars. I didn't do it. I told you that a thousand times, I'll tell you again. You're sitting still, so here goes: I didn't kill that kid. I diddled the first one, but I am not a kid killer. How many times I gotta tell you? Shame on you for hiding behind a skirt with this kind of bullshit. Now, why don't you get your sorry ass back out there and find the guy who really did it, you know what I mean? Be productive. Earn my respect."

"Mr. Garamond," I interrupted.

"You can call me Jesse, pretty lady. And don't waste your time asking me questions about these other cases. I been in here, remember? So I couldn't have done anything. And I wouldn't be hearing anything either."

"Mr. Garamond," I repeated, "I know you've already talked to Detective Frazee extensively on your own case, but I want to ask you just one more time. Is there anything you may have neglected to tell him at the time? I know that was a difficult period for you. Stress like that can make you forgetful."

"I didn't forget nothin'. I told Mr. Detective here everything I could about what happened. I was with my brother's wife. She told you so. Now I gotta do time for something I didn't do because I don't want no trouble between my brother and his wife."

"That's very admirable," I said. "But there must have already been trouble between the two of them if you were having sex with her."

"Nah," he said. "I did her a few times as a favor when he had to be out of town for a couple of weeks for that army reserves shit he does. I don't know why—he leaves his old lady and their kids all alone. She got lonely, that's all. I was just taking care of her for him."

"Very brotherly of you."

"Yeah. They should let me out early for that."

"You're doing okay here now already," Spence said. "Last time I was here, they had you in one of the cages."

"It ain't what you think," he said. He looked around furtively to see if any other prisoners were close enough to hear him. "I been telling the guys here that I got sent back on a parole violation. Most of these guys don't have a clue about what's going on outside. But then this dude comes in for embezzlement, and he's a newspaper kinda guy. Most of the dudes in here used newspapers to house-train their pit bulls. But this one actually reads them. He remembered me right away from the papers. Started telling stories about the conviction and all."

"So?" I said. "You're innocent, right?"

He sniggered ironically. "Lady, that's what they all say in here, you know that. Except in my case it happens to be the truth. Trouble is, now the guys are starting to think that I'm something I'm not. My first gig was for having sex with a girl who was thirteen. They all done that, but none of them got caught. But now they think I offed a kid. You know what they do to those guys in here?"

I'd heard a rumor or two.

"You'll pardon my language, my mother didn't raise me to talk like this in front of no ladies. But you gotta know, so you can understand my position here: They make sausage out of your dick, and then they make you eat it."

I could see Spence cringing and crossing his legs. We weren't going to get anywhere with this line of inquiry. I stood and said, "Well, I appreciate your candor and your willingness to meet with us, Mr. Garamond. Even if nothing came of it."

"Hey, no problem," he said. "*You* can come back anytime. *Any*time."

Neither of us had much to say as we threaded through the endless corridors between the interview area and the main reception lobby. There was good lighting, and the walls were all painted a cheerful soft white. Everything was simple and clean. The bars were brushed steel, reminiscent of the handrails in a modern hospital. But there was no getting around it: This was a dungeon, pure and simple. There was no natural light, and if someone wanted us *not* to get out, we wouldn't get out.

As soon as we had our guns back, Spence straightened up again, having reacquired the ability to shoot anyone with a notion of making sausage out of any part of him. For myself, I was relieved to see the daylight when we exited the front gate and headed toward our vehicle.

"Well, that was a waste of time," Spence finally said.

"No, it wasn't. I believe him now too. Unfortunately, what that means is that I probably have another case to solve. Not to mention there's an innocent man—well, maybe not innocent, but certainly not guilty—in this prison. That's not right. One of these days we're going to have to do something about that."

"You can't say anything yet, Lany—this guy was convicted by a jury of his peers. And the prosecutor knows everything I know about this case, about the sister-in-law, all the details. I haven't been exactly quiet about my feelings on all of this, but no one has done anything to challenge the outcome of the trial."

"Then we have to make a lot more noise. This isn't right, Spence."

"I know that. But it would be career suicide for either of us to stir anything up right now. And you know as well as I do that he was legitimately convicted of the crime that landed him in jail in the first place and that he probably shouldn't even have been out when the boy got grabbed. Don't think he didn't force that girl either. The only reason he didn't get convicted of forcible rape is that he pleaded guilty to statutory. And when you find the real guy, this will all take care of itself."

"*If* I find the real guy."

"You will, Lany. Like you said, you have that intuition thing going. I can see it in your face. But until then you have to leave this alone. There isn't any evidence to refute the eyewitness testimony, unless he gives up the sister-in-law. We have nothing."

Sadly, he was right, and I knew it. So now I had a new case, a perplexing, difficult case, loaded with nothing.

nine

I SQUANDERED A PERFECT DAY by wallowing in
old misery over the terrible events that had befallen me
so many years before. In my own defense, I must put it
forth that in the wake of my new discoveries, the ancient
hurt over my son's loss seemed fresh again to me.
Perhaps after two decades it ought not to have, but it did.

The sun glowed high over the castle, the courtyard,
and all the surrounds, but I could not seem to feel its
warmth. The flowers in the courtyard garden showed
their appreciation for the weather by filling the air with
great waves of scent. I sat between a peony and a rose on
a bench with a base of carved marble angels, whose
plump little arms reached up to support the wooden seat
on which the weary were supposed to find rest, though
there was little comfort to be found on the hard planks. A
few soft yellow rose blossoms had just come open, as if
signaled by their fading Oriental cousins to spring forth
and take up the cause of seducing insects and passersby.
In my lap there rested an old but serviceable surplice,

the very one whose repair had ostensibly sent me to Machecoul for the supplies I failed to buy. God be praised, I found the required threads at the bottom of my basket and was therefore not stymied in effecting the repair. But it seemed too much effort at the moment to blend my own stitches into those that had been laid down, quite sloppily, by my less fastidious predecessor.

All I could think of on this day, when I should have been living from one sweet breath to the next and enjoying the pleasant labor (it could, after all, have been the despised accounting of the expenses instead), all that filled my heart and mind was the sorrowful past, specifically my son Michel and what might have been had he not been taken from me. Another letter had arrived from Avignon from his brother, or so a messenger this morning had said; such was the depth of my despair that the thought of reading it hardly inspired me at all.

Letters from Michel would have been far different from those I received from his brother, especially in the regularity with which they arrived. Michel's would have been sporadic at best, unlike Jean's, which were more predictable than my erstwhile menses. But had both my sons survived into adulthood, Jean might not have been as inclined to ameliorate the absence of his brother with frequent missives, so who can say what he might have done under more normal circumstances? I had often mused on what the content of my younger son's letters would have been. He would first have filled them with the joy and wry humor that colored his everyday demeanor. There would have been plenty of good news and very little bad, that unlikely proportioning intended to lessen my concern over having a son who waged war for a living. All mothers of sons born to the saddle and the sword have such worries, but of course mine would be the only one who mattered. His sooty parchments would arrive tattered from some battlefield or outpost to which he had been sent by his liege lord, whoever that might prove to be.

Would he have served Gilles de Rais, his childhood playmate? Perhaps, but I think not. I always considered it possible that their diverging personalities might have forced an eventual parting of ways—Michel was so deeply good, and Milord Gilles could never seem to trust his own worth after having it beaten out of him by his grandfather, that beast of a man.

I began to notice just before Michel's disappearance that Milord often seemed lost in thought. Around this period he took to spending time alone as much as possible, though his sycophant cousins de Sille and de Briqueville were always attempting to cling to him. When he appeared to have entered one of his dark reveries, I would ask my young master what he was thinking, but it was nearing the time when he would shed me, his childhood nurse, like a snake molts a skin that has grown too tight. Usually I was ignored, but when he spoke he would often claim that he was engaged in his own imaginings, though rarely would he reveal to me what those imaginings might be. So many times I said "Ah" to him, as if I understood, which I did not.

Michel tried to draw Milord out of his grief during the period after his father and mother passed to eternity. He would tempt him with inspiring activities such as hunting or swordplay. But his earnest, heartfelt appeals— *Why are you playing at conjuring, Brother, when the sun shines so fair and bright? Come, let us ride out instead and frighten a few foxes with the noise of our swords*—were largely ignored. I suppose it is only fitting that when one has been left behind by someone so near and dear—in Milord's case, two people at one time—one would want some solitude within which to think on the nature of death and life and the like, or whatever else struck the sad one's fancy. I know this as well as anyone can.

When his principal companion was in one of these dark moods and did not wish to be disturbed, it fell upon Michel to entertain himself. This he did in reading, or in swordplay with his own shadow, or contests of martial skill with his father if Etienne happened to be in the castle and was not engaged in some other occupation. There were many such times in the unsettled period after Milord Guy passed on, because Jean de Craon was engrossed in the act of securing his daughter's holdings. He was vicious in his determination to see the estates remain as one inheritance, but no one faulted him, for we all understood that he was a father looking out for the interests of his daughter, who was completely paralyzed by her husband's unexpected death. Lady Marie then had the audacity (I once heard Jean de Craon curse her for the inconvenience) to die herself.

Milord Gilles, a tender eleven years of age, was thrust into two contradictory positions. In the eyes of the world he was the unaccountably young master of a huge realm, in which his every whim was catered to by anyone within earshot. All the while he was a puppet to his vile grandfather. At this time there came a visible separation between him and Michel. Before then, the difference in their stations had hardly mattered—they were as close as any brothers. But I suppose everything changes, given time; some folks rise, others fall, as fortune dictates. Loved ones come and go; those who go send letters if they have the means and learning to do so.

Letters from Michel ... if God would grant me just one, and if within the lines there could be some reasonable explanation for what happened to him, I would find a way to live sinlessly for the rest of my days in repayment. What would his adult hand look like? His writing as a child was spirited and loose. I knew Jean's neat inscribings; if you laid before me a pile of a thousand parchments, I would wager my soul's reward on picking out the one he had written. The fluid lines of prose that crossed the page from left to right had the same straight perfection as the sea's horizon. I cannot say whether Michel's lines would have made such orderly progress as Jean's; he was a far more rowdy boy than Jean at the same age, destined for battle as his father had been, in opposition to the birth order that dictated the church for him and battle for Jean. One cannot force a child to be what he will not be, in my opinion, though I know it has been done countless times before. But this is a modern age, where we permit our sons some self-determination. Michel was not destined to take up the cloth, and Jean would surely die in his first battle were he to take up the sword. If Michel was indeed dead, and if there is such a thing as a correct demise, how I wish he could have had the chance to die the warrior's death, which would have been proper for him.

In the midst of this dark abstraction I heard my name called, or, more accurately, my title. *Mère* was said timidly by a young priest I had seen in the abbey but did not know. He startled me so that my embroidery threads fell to the ground. The young man fairly groveled in apology and vowed that he would not have disturbed me for anything less than a summons from his Eminence. It took me a few moments to recover any sort of grace after all the threads were gathered up. Though clearly mortified, he waited patiently. I wished he would have left me alone—I would find my way to Jean de Malestroit as easily as if he had laid out a row of crumbs for me to follow.

What would his need be today? The hour gave me pause (before lunch, when he was generally preoccupied with the duties of state) as did the look on his face when I entered his hallowed lair. First Jean de Malestroit gave me the letter that had come for me from Avignon. I nodded my thanks and let the feel of it filter into my palms, but instead of slipping away at once to tear open the seal and devour the words as I would ordinarily have done, I tucked it in my sleeve and waited for the Bishop to speak on the matter that had prompted him to summon me with the day's business still in progress. I could see that he was flustered when I arrived; he was milling about his chamber and could not seem to put his thoughts in order.

"Eminence, how you have managed to be a statesman I will never understand," I said.

He sat himself down abruptly in his high-backed chair and took a long, deep breath to calm himself. "Ah, Guillemette, sometimes I do not understand it myself. I like the hat of a diplomat far less than the miter." He smiled philosophically and shrugged his shoulders. "But, then, no man has ever worn two hats at once with any ease or grace. It would require two heads. I often find myself torn between disappointing God or Duke Jean, neither of whom particularly cares to be let down."

But I had seen him switch one hat for the other with uncanny ease. It would not have surprised me to discover that Jean de Malestroit had a spare head for his other hat, tucked away someplace where no one would think to look for it. I imagined stumbling upon the grisly thing in a cabinet, one with a squeaking hinge. I would open the door in search of a wick or a thread or a whetstone, and that head would stare out at me with its one eyebrow and then quickly remind me to tend to the bothersome noise of the hinges as soon as possible.

Or maybe Sister Élène could see to it . . . the head would say with a wicked smile.

The current hat-wearer snapped me out of my fantasy by saying, "I have something to tell you."

After a pause I said, "You sound as if you think I will not be pleased."

"I cannot predict your reaction—only that you are sure to have one."

"Speak," I said. "Do not tease me."

"Very well. You will not be allowed to continue looking into the disappearances of children."

The predicted reaction took the form of unhappy knots in my belly. My donkey would remain stabled, I would not venture forth again but instead stay in the abbey and resume my duties in lieu of Sister Élène taking them over, which I will admit brought me some small relief. Still, I was acutely disappointed. My voice went up a notch as I protested. "Eminence, you granted me that privilege on good grounds. I am sorely distressed that you would change your mind so quickly."

He rose and smiled broadly. "There is quite a good explanation. Duke Jean has authorized a larger investigation to be made and has appointed someone to oversee it."

Again, he had surprised me. "But this is wonderful," I said happily. "Who has been named?"

He hesitated for the duration of one breath. "The Duke has appointed someone whom he thinks will be a capable investigator."

So many of the men who might be called to such a task were known to me because of my previous service; perhaps I could influence the work in some way. *"Who?"* I pressed him.

"Let us leave it at that for the moment. I have much yet to accomplish today. I simply wanted to let you know that you did not need to prepare for any kind of journey. We shall speak of it tomorrow and then conspire further."

"Eminence, how positively cruel—you condemn me to conjecture for the remainder of this day and then to a night of sleepless flailing."

He began to look annoyed. "You are a thorn, Sister, on the rose of my life."

I was equally annoyed, and with greater justification. "Forgive me, dear *Brother*. But what would a rose be without its thorns?"

"What would it be indeed ... ah, well, one might describe it as the epitome of perfection."

"But, alas, how bland and uninspiring."

"One could use a bit less inspiration sometimes."

"Inspiration is never to be overlooked, Eminence. T'would be a grave sin to do so, as worthy of your ire as any other sin."

"Yes ... well ... perhaps it would." Then, with quiet concern, he said, "You truly will not sleep?"

"Not one second."

He sighed. "I would not be the cause of that. Very well, then. But I must swear you to keep it a confidence."

"I swear."

"Duke Jean has appointed *me* to delve further into these matters."

All of his difficult qualities, his sanctimonious rigidity, his stubborn intractability, the aloof temperament that he so often employed to set himself apart from those around him would now permeate the course of the discoveries.

On the other hand, my influence was assured.

꘠

I put the task of overseeing the removal of dried mud from the stone floor of the sanctuary in the capable hands of Sister Élène after all; the woman seemed genuinely grateful, which I failed to comprehend. Mixed in with the brown mud were the inevitable bits of excrement that found their way into the soil everywhere from horses and cattle and goats, all of which wandered daily through every village street. In this chore I did not mind being replaced. Novices under her supervision would gather the dried ordure and remove it to the garden, where it would be distributed under the watchful eye of *Frère* Demien, who would all the while be praising God for His great bounty in delivering copious amounts of *merde* into his stewardship. We wasted nothing, lest our Creator be displeased.

A new summons from Jean de Malestroit came as the young sisters were leaving the sanctuary with their brooms and pans.

"I am ready to begin," he told me when I arrived.

"So soon?"

"As you know, Sister, I am most frugal with my hours. And yours, I daresay. Now, I would like you to repeat to me the stories you were told in Bourgneuf, with as much detail as you can recall," he said. "It will help me to determine the proper path for moving forward."

The shadows would shorten and then lengthen again before we finished. We could not foresee how many more days would belong to this as well.

⚜

Some three years before, a woman by the name of Catherine Thierry gave her brother to a certain transplanted Parisian, one Henriet Griart, so that the child might be admitted to the chapel at Machecoul. The boy was never seen again and did not become a member of the chapel, that his sister ever heard, nor was there offered any explanation of what might have happened to him.

And then there was the angelic-looking Guillaume Delit, Guibelet's son, who used to help the chef roast the meat for Lord de Rais. The master chef himself, Jean of the Château at Briand, told this child's mother that it was not a good idea for the child to be helping thus because small children were being caught and killed in the area around Nantes. The mother complained later to the chef's wife that two men came to call upon her not long after her initial inquiries and spoke quite roughly to her, telling her that she had better not complain at all, that it would do her no good, nor would it do her son any good.

The son of Jean Jenvret was a schoolchild of only nine, who frequented the area around l'Hôtel de la Suze in Nantes. His family lived in the parish of Saint-Croix in Nantes but had close relations in Bourgneuf. Two years earlier, his sister told me, some eight days before the feast of Saint John the Baptist, the Jenvret child disappeared without a word.

And in the parish of Notre Dame in Nantes, the son of Jeanne Degrepie was lost, just around Saint John's day, so it took place only a few days later than the loss in Saint-Croix. His mother speaks of a woman named Perrine Martin, who supposedly was seen leading the child away and was later seen with him again on the road to Machecoul. No one has an opinion on why this Perrine might have been taking the child to Machecoul.

A schoolboy from Saint-Donatien parish near Nantes, a beautiful child from the family named Fougere, was lost not quite two years past in the month of August. No trace of him was ever found, nor any word said of anyone having seen him.

And in the very next month of September, in Roche-Bernard, the ten-year-old son of Perrone Loessart was entrusted to a man with the odd appellation of Poitou, who promised the mother that her quick-learning son would continue to go to school. Later, this boy was seen in this Poitou's company on the road to Machecoul, as was the son of Jean Jenvret with the woman Perrine.

A gentleman from Port-Launay speaks of knowing a family called Bernard whose son set out for Machecoul one day in the company of another boy of similar age, both to seek alms, it having been said that great generosity could be found there. The hope of charity must have been strong to entice two twelve-year-olds to make such a journey—one must cross the Loire at Nantes and then continue many more kilometers. The other boy with whom he traveled waited for him at the arranged spot for three hours and then was forced to return alone to Port-Launay. So claims the mother of the lost child, who says that she complained very bitterly about the disappearance of her son to priest and magistrate alike.

In Saint-Cyr-en-Rais, a village adjoining Bourgneuf, the son of Micheau and Guillemette Bouer went begging at Machecoul on Low Sunday of last year. When the child did not return, his father made immediate inquiries in various places as to the boy's whereabouts, having heard that other children were also missing and fearing that the same fate might have befallen his own son. But then, the following day, a large man dressed in a black cloak came to call on the distressed mother while the father was out making further inquiries. She did not know the man, but when asked where her children were, she replied that they had gone begging at Machecoul, whereupon the stranger left her alone and was not seen again.

Ysabeau Hamelin, who had lived a year in the borough of Fresnay, having come the year before from Pouance, sent two of her sons, aged fifteen and seven, to Machecoul with money to buy bread. When they did not return, she thought at first that they might have been robbed and left for dead. But no evidence of foul play could be found on the route when she and others in her family searched it. The day after, two men came to see her for the purpose of inquiring about her children. She was frightened and did not mention their disappearance to them. As they were leaving, she overheard one man say to the other that two of the children were from that house, so she had great suspicions that they knew what had happened to her sons.

Just before Christmas last, Jeanette Drouet, the wife of Eustache, sent her sons of eleven and seven to Machecoul to seek alms. She said that several people told of seeing her sons in the next few days but that they never returned home again, and when she and her husband went there to make inquiries, they could learn nothing at all.

♚

Our supper lay untouched before us. A fine slab of lamb, much anticipated after six long weeks of meatlessness, lay cold and gelatinous on the platter. Neither one of us could have stomached one bite.

"Has nothing been resolved of *any* of these disappearances?" his Eminence asked soberly.

"No. None has come to any conclusion."

"No remains? Clothing left behind?"

"Nothing."

He sat straight up in his high-backed chair, obscuring my view of the beautifully embroidered cushion, which I admired greatly. He patted his hands on his knees and said, "It seems impossible."

"Indeed. Or, at the very least, unlikely."

"Well, then ..." he mused, "we shall have to see that the truth is discovered. It would be sensible for me to begin my deeper inquiries at Machecoul, I think."

"Yes, Eminence."

He spoke decisively. "We shall go there three days hence."

It was too long a wait. "Eminence, more will be lost if we delay this further."

"Guillemette, there are important things I must do first—"

"Children, Eminence—what could be more important than the souls of little ones?"

He blanched with guilt. "Very well, I shall wait on my other obligations. On the morrow, then."

I nodded. My influence was most certainly assured.

⚜

We saw to Vespers as we always do, and then Jean de Malestroit gave me leave to retire. I went to the abbey stable, where I found my little donkey placidly chewing a shaft of straw. Her jaw worked rhythmically from side to side as the yellow grass grew shorter and shorter, disappearing finally into her toothy mouth. I bent over and picked up a few fresh shoots and held them out to her. She took them gently from my outstretched hand with her worn teeth and chewed as I patted her neck affectionately.

"You are a very understanding beast, mademoiselle," I cooed. Why does one speak to an animal as if it were a small child? She shook her head to banish a bothersome fly and sprayed me with small bits of spittle. I wiped my face with my sleeve.

"And effusive as well," I added. "But I don't mind. You will listen to me without complaint, as few two-legged beasts will do. Which reason occasions this visit, my small friend. I would like your opinion on a matter of some concern to me."

Almost as if she understood, she raised and lowered her head, nodding assent.

"Good. Then let me ask you this: Why is it that when these children disappear, it always happens in Lord de Rais's realm? And why is it that his servants seem always to be present?"

She went nervous on me suddenly, and brayed.

"That is exactly how I feel myself," I said. I placed my forehead on hers and just stood there as a tear slid down my cheek.

chapter 10

IT WAS ONE OF THOSE MOMENTS when I wished I'd paid more attention in high school. We all thought statistics was just a big waste of time back then, one of those things we'd never use except maybe on a trip to Vegas, the sin city that Minnesotans would never visit because it was known to beat the wholesome out of you.

What were the statistical chances in a city like Los Angeles, where Caucasians were technically a minority group, that thirteen missing boys would all be white, blond, light-eyed, slim, and angelic-looking?

"Well, I guess we have an anomaly on our hands," Fred Vuska said.

I was quiet for a moment, then said, "I think what we have on our hands, Fred, is a serial abductor."

The brief silence inspired by my declaration was pregnant with political considerations and worries about budgetary implications. With transportation security details eating up most of the overtime budget, a manpower crunch deepened by a hiring freeze, Fred was in the same bind as just about every municipal supervisor in L.A.

"Now, don't go jumping to conclusions," he said eventually.

His about-face didn't surprise me; anytime you say *serial* in connection with a group of crimes, the expenses just multiply, sometimes exponentially. But his reticence was annoying, put mildly. "I don't know what else to think. There's a definite pattern, a huge pattern, one you just wouldn't expect to see, especially here. If the grabs were random, there'd be Hispanic and African-American kids in the mix. You saw it too, or you wouldn't have given me Donnolly's cases. Now all of a sudden you don't seem to like it."

For a moment, Fred looked troubled. Then he said, "It's not for me to like or dislike, Dunbar, it's for me to manage. And right now management is a tough business."

"I know that. But this stuff isn't always a matter of convenience."

"It never is."

He thrummed his fingers on his desk while apparently weighing his options. The option he chose was not one I liked much.

"You got pictures of all of them?"

He was stretching out the "convince me" curve.

"Yeah, in the files."

"Let's take a look at them all together."

It would take a little time to organize it. "Give me about half an hour."

"You can have all day. I got some stuff to take care of now and I won't be back until around four-thirty."

"I'll be out of here by then."

"Okay, we'll do it tomorrow."

He picked up his reading glasses and slipped them on, then picked up some papers from his desk and pretended to read them. It was my invitation to depart, which I did, with an unspoken expletive hanging on my tongue.

It cost me another lunch, this time out of my own pocket, but I was glad that Errol Erkinnen could find time to fit me in again. I only gave him an hour's notice.

Doc's eyes widened as much as anyone else's would have when I told him why I'd come to see him. Saying *serial* takes the game to a whole new level. His response was intense, enough so to make me feel a little uncomfortable. His intrigue was palpable; he was Halley, discovering the comet: the big career event you dream of but rarely get.

"A *serial* abductor, Detective. *Very* interesting. Tell me why you're thinking this way."

"Similarities in a string of victims in unsolved cases. Before now they haven't been tied together, except maybe loosely. The case I came to see you about the other day— Nathan Leeds—he's the most recent, but they go back a while—years, really. So I have to assume that if I'm correct, we have someone who's been active for a good long time and continues to be a threat. I got assigned Terry Donnolly's last two cases because Fred Vuska thought there were similarities, and then when I put out the word that I was looking for a pattern"—I dropped a stack of the copied faxes on his desk—"this is what I got back. A slew of similar dead-end cases from guys who don't know where to go with them."

He picked up the stack as if he were going to guess its weight. "How many?"

"Ten more. So altogether there are thirteen missing boys, all around the same age—preadolescent—all white, all slim and sweet-looking. One case was officially solved, but the perp has been screaming innocent since day one. He admits to another rap but won't admit to this one. I'm inclined to believe him."

"Why's that?"

"Honestly? I don't know. But he doesn't exhibit any of the physical or psychological signs of lying. And my gut just tells me that he's not."

"Hmm." He stood up and started pacing around with half a sandwich in one hand. "Striking similarities in the victims—that is a good indicator." His voice took on a droning, trancelike quality and he began lecturing. "It's a common phenomenon, this pattern of victims. Ted Bundy's choices were all very similar, at least the ones we know about—a lot of people think he may have killed twice as many women as he's acknowledged. There's always been speculation that he patterned on a young woman from Seattle, who he was engaged to for a short time. She was attractive, intelligent, from a solid, well-respected family— a really good catch for someone like Bundy. He was born out of wedlock, you know."

"Yeah, so I read once."

"His whole life was like one desperate quest for legitimacy. So when his fiancée broke it off, he was crushed. He once confided to an acquaintance that he thought her family had pressured her. Not surprisingly, the killings started around that time. She had long dark hair, parted in the middle."

As had most of his victims. "So he was killing her over and over again."

"Symbolically, yes."

"I don't remember that time too well, I was pretty young," I said, "but one of my aunts told me that a lot of women changed their hairstyles."

"They did. I was in college then and really starting to focus my attentions on psychology. So I was just as riveted by it as anyone. I think the Bundy case happening when it did had a lot to do with me deciding on forensics. Anyway, the thing that scared everyone was that he kept escaping from jail and moving around—started in Seattle and then moved to Colorado, then Utah, and finally to Florida. A girl couldn't count on being a New Englander to save her." He smiled, with a touch of sadness. "But you can never count on anything to save you, really. Sometimes you're just in the wrong place at the wrong time."

"But these kids don't appear to have been randomly chosen, that's the whole point."

"Probably not. It's likely that they were *selected*. Your perp—if you have one guy doing all of this, as it looks on the surface—likes little blond white boys for some reason. What you need to know is *why*."

I gestured with my hands as if to say, *That's why I'm here. . . .*

He smiled. "A fixation of some kind, most likely. If you can't get the real thing, you go for the nearest equivalent."

"Didn't really seem to work for Bundy," I said. "He did it over and again."

"That's because the equivalent—which can never be more than a substitute—rarely satisfies the original need that leads to the fixation in the first place. He experienced temporary release, but the original need for legitimacy remained. So he had to keep killing. That's why you see the intervals shortening in cases like that. What happens over time is that the act, whatever it is—murder or rape or abduction—loses its potency and has to be repeated more frequently. Have you established a time line for these cases?"

Yeah, in my spare time. "No, not yet."

"Well, that would be my next order of business, if I were you."

"What should I be looking for?"

"Don't look for anything. Keep an open mind and see what's there, not what you want to be there. A killer's pattern isn't always as regular as we'd like. Of course, it's helpful when it is."

He was saying *killer*. I wasn't even saying *killer* yet because we had no bodies, just holes in the ether where bodies used to be. I was vibing *killer*, though, and he was picking up on that. "Yeah," I said. "Helpful."

"Sorry. That's the best I can tell you. Patterns vary, based on a number of factors." He moved to one of his overstuffed bookcases and for a few quiet seconds he perused the vertical spines. I think he had some kind of homing device, because I could never have found anything in that mess. Saying "Ah, here we are" under his breath, he pulled out a book and handed it to me. "Not exactly bedtime reading, but this is a very good study on the psyche of serial killers. You'll get a lot of information from it. Right now, though, to speed things along for you, I can tell you that the intervals generally shrink from where they start out. If the interval is initially a couple of weeks or a month, it will shorten to two weeks, then maybe ten days, et cetera. By the time they're down to a few days, you usually catch them because they're rushing and out of control, and they start to make mistakes."

"I love it when they make those mistakes."

"Yes," he said. "Mistakes on the part of a killer can be quite welcome. But it doesn't look like your perp is at that point yet. From what you've said, this grab was pretty seamless, as were the other two you have deep dirt on. I'll be interested to see how the other cases shake down in terms of the intervals. When you do establish the pattern of his timing, you'll have two pieces of information about this guy. You already know what his fixation is, and then you'll know how desperate he is."

I was beginning to wonder if he recalled our previous conversation, the one in which we talked about Nathan Leeds's mother. "Doc," I said, "if I have a serial abductor on my hands, I'm not sure it's a guy."

He stared at me. "Is there some reason to think this is a woman?"

"The Leeds case, remember? The mother who we thought might have Munchausen-by-proxy syndrome because she appeared to have abducted her own kid?"

"Oh, right ..." he said absently. Somehow he'd made a leap to the next level of assumption and he'd forgotten to tell me. "Well, it's extremely unlikely that this would be a woman."

I was confused. "I've seen his mother up close. She really is a woman."

"Look beyond that for a moment, Detective. These crimes are almost never committed by women, and you said yourself, as I recall, that you didn't think she was 'the type.' Has your opinion on that changed?"

"No."

He crumpled up the sandwich wrapper and soft-touched it into the wastebasket. "The statistics are overwhelmingly in favor of your abductor being male. It's just not part of the basic female psyche to do this sort of thing."

All of a sudden I felt like our roles were reversed. "We're not talking about a normal psyche here."

"That doesn't really matter. Even the most aberrant female psyches rarely get to that place."

"What about that woman in Florida—" I stammered without recall, then it came to me. "Wuornos. She killed a dozen guys that they *know* about."

"I'm not deeply familiar with that case. But I do know she was atypical in many ways. And I do remember reading that there were cross-gender issues there."

"There could be here too. This *is* California."

"Land of the free," he said with a jaded smile. He came around from behind the desk and sat on the front edge. He stared down professorially and said, "Look, Detective Dunbar, of course it's technically possible for your perp to be a woman. It's also *technically* possible, but not likely, that O.J. didn't do it. I just don't want to see you spinning your wheels, especially where we have an ongoing situation. I would strongly urge you to operate on the assumption that you have a male offender here."

"But the abductor looked like a woman last time—"

He cut me off with a negative shake of his head. "Remember what I told you a few minutes ago, to see what's really there, not what you want to see? What appears to be there is a woman, but it may only have been an illusion of a woman. If that's the case, and I suspect it is, you now know *three* things about this guy: his fixation for little blond white boys, his timing when you establish it, and that he's got a wolf-in-sheep's-clothing M.O. working. It's possible that he makes himself look like something he's not to gain the confidence and trust of his victims. Woman or man, he approaches his victims as a person they believe to be trustworthy. No wonder he's gone undetected. Clever, very clever. I would like to stay very close to the working of this one, Detective Dunbar. It's a very interesting case, to say the least."

He had *copyright* and *royalties* written all over his face, along with *national recognition*. It was clinical and theoretical to him, and I could see that he was enjoying the academic exercise. But I was the one who was going to have to find this shape-shifter, who would look completely different from one incident to the next.

I went right to the files to pull out all the photos of the victims and scan them, so while I was doing that I ordered them chronologically by date of disappearance in a photo viewer. Not only would I be able to show Fred the similarities of appearance, but I would be able to establish a timing pattern as well. Killing two birds with one stone.

But by the time I'd finished, one of the birds had risen from the dead, flapped its wings, and was throwing stones back at me. The gaps between the disappearances were

big and irregular—not a couple of weeks or a month as
Doc had intimated, but multiple months with unpredict-
able gaps, the shortest of which was eight weeks. There
was no discernible pattern.

See what's really there, not what you want to see. Easy
for Errol Erkinnen to say.

I grabbed Spence and Escobar by the arms and
dragged them both to my desk. "Take a look at this for
me," I said, almost pleading.

"What are we looking for?" Spence asked.

"Nothing. Just tell me what you see."

"I see a lot of dates. You must be looking for a pattern
here."

"Well, duh."

"I hate to say it, Lany, but I don't see one here."

To my expression of dismay, Escobar said, "It could
just mean that there are unreported abductions in between
the ones we know about. Or that your guy is operating out
of another geographical location. Maybe he's bicoastal or
something like that."

I asked myself how I'd gotten from a mother with
Munchausen-by-proxy to a bicoastal serial abductor overnight. A very good question, one for which I didn't have an
answer.

Fred was walking through the squad room. He'd
wanted to wait until tomorrow, but I had them now. I almost lunged at him as he passed by my cubicle.

"I got those pics," I called out over the sound of
voices and the ringing of phones.

He was the very image of annoyance, but he gave in; I
must have looked like I was going to cry. "Come on, then,"
he said.

I picked up my picture board and followed him to
his office. I set it up on his desk as he looked disgustedly

through a stack of small papers, each of which mandated a return phone call. He regarded the board for a few moments, his eyes going critically from one to the next. "I can see your point," he said. "Looks like a multiple birth."

"So?"

A brief, noncommittal silence passed. "So I'll take it under consideration," he said finally.

"Fred, I could really use some help."

He was quiet again for a few moments, thinking hard. "If this *is* one guy, he just grabbed a kid, so we're at the beginning of one of his gaps and we've got some time before the next one. Be patient and keep investigating."

"I'll be sure to tell the next parent that that's what I'm doing."

"That's it. This meeting is over."

I slithered out, looking for someone to sink my fangs into. A few minutes later, Fred showed up at my desk.

"Look, I can do this: I'll free you up so you can concentrate on it. Give all your other cases to me and I'll pass them around."

I had trouble hiding my disappointment. "I was hoping for a little more than that."

"Not yet, Dunbar. You're gonna have to have something more compelling than this for me to show the folks upstairs before I can give you extra help. But I won't let anyone give you anything new."

For the time being, it would have to do.

I decided, as soon as Fred gave me his dictum, that since my kids were going to an exhibit with their father that evening and staying at his house for the next two nights, I would spend all of Saturday and Sunday morning going through the new cases, maybe even contacting some of the folks whose children had disappeared. But before I left the office, I called the elderly Mrs. Paulsen to ask her the question about medication.

"I need to ask you a rather personal question," I began.

"Well, I'll do my best to answer."

"If we catch the person who abducted Nathan Leeds, we're going to have to build a case. Part of that case would be your testimony. Any decent trial lawyer will try to undermine your credibility. I need to know, before we go any further, if you are taking any medications that might affect your memory."

"Oh, goodness. That's not personal. I thought you were going to ask me something about my sex life."

Please, God, let me grow old like this. "Well, no. Nothing like that."

"Detective, I don't even take aspirin."

"You're not on any blood-pressure or glaucoma medication, or anything for diabetes?" I asked, running through the typical problems that elderly people are likely to have.

"I'm healthy as that old horse they keep talking about."

"How old are you, if you don't mind me asking?"

"*Now* you're getting personal." She laughed a little. "Eighty-four down and sixteen to go."

"It's always a good thing to have goals, I guess."

"It is indeed, Detective. Keeps you going."

A goal had been dropped into my lap, one that would certainly "keep me going"; the only question was how long.

"Thanks very much, Mrs. Paulsen. Someone from the prosecutor's office will be calling you when the time comes."

That was my last task of the official day. It's my habit on Friday to straighten up my desk a bit so that it's not in total disarray when I get in on Monday. I was planning to be there on Saturday, but habits are hard to break, so I put things in order, even though I'd be messing them up again. I guess *messing up* is a relative thing—to me, it means a pencil out of place or a pad out of square to the corner. When all else fails, I clean.

The traffic was lighter than what I was accustomed to at my usual departure time. So often going home at the height of rush hour, I've been tempted to put the flashing blue light on the dashboard and just power my way through. Never did it, though. There's this thing I have about abusing my position. Other cops do it; I've seen it myself once or twice on the freeway. But not me—not enough testosterone, I guess.

Dinner was leftover chili. I missed the kids, though they were probably pretty happy, because Kevin was less strict with them and had a far better collection of video games. I worried about that sometimes, that they wouldn't do their homework and they would succumb to the influences of popular culture, which I've been fighting off since the day they were born. With some success—Frannie is a bookworm, and Julia the creative type; they always find productive things to do. But Evan could just get lost in the PlayStation, and he was a lot more vulnerable to societal pressures. He was the one I worried about most. He was my first child, and I'm certain that I made a lot of mistakes raising him.

But this weekend they could turn their brains to mush for all I cared. Their father would take good care of them—they would come back to me on Sunday night well-fed and properly loved. And that was all that mattered.

After a quick shower and a glass of red wine, I got into bed, Erkinnen's book in hand.

Serial Killers: The Ultimate Reference

Once I had the pillows just where I wanted them, I cracked the book open and perused the table of contents. The case studies were of killers who were uncomfortably familiar to me. I suspect that was probably what at least a couple of them wanted, that blazing fame and immortality. There was a section on historical killers; some I'd heard of, some not. Jack the Ripper—who hasn't heard of him; Vlad Tepes, the legendary impaler, on whom the character of Count Dracula was based; Elizabeth Bathory, the countess who thought the blood of a virgin would keep her skin from wrinkling and regularly bathed in it. Gilles de Rais, a name I didn't know, who came down through history to us as Bluebeard, according to the subtitle of the chapter.

I had always thought Bluebeard was a pirate. I guess that was Blackbeard.

There was a chapter that gave an overview of methods, another that gave detailed descriptions of the conditions that shaped men with violent tendencies into the worst kinds of monsters. I thought about that one for a moment and realized that I would probably find something in that chapter that I did to my own kids, and then I would have one more thing to feel guilty about as a parent. Not a good idea when they were off with their father. But I couldn't seem to resist it.

A lot of what the book put forth was just common sense. Take all of the qualities we consider weird or perverted and roll them all into one person. Ninety percent of them were bed wetters, and most of those reported a serious conflict with the parent or caretaker over that issue. More than eighty percent were abused as children. Most were shy by nature or, more accurately, socially withdrawn. The author theorized that physical and sexual abuse, usually by the dominant male in their lives, was at the core of that. A few of the killers studied reported that their mothers or grandmothers had fondled them or forced them to have sex.

Sick fucking bitches.

And Erkinnen was right—the strongest predictor of a human being becoming a serial killer, at least according to this author, was simply being born with a Y chromosome.

Sure, there was a lot more to it than that, or the whole world would be in trouble—they were fire starters and drug users and alcoholics and sexual addicts. But maleness was the overwhelmingly common factor.

They killed small animals as young boys and teenagers and shunned the company of others in social situations. They were loners who avoided all unnecessary contact. They were trouble in school, poor learners despite their solid intelligence. They were sociopaths who could not feel remorse and psychopaths who were beyond control.

But most of all, they were fantasizers. They thought about what they were going to do before they got up the balls to actually do it. Some reported elaborate internal preparations for their crimes. . . .

I put my finger in the page and closed the book for a moment. *Elaborate internal preparations.* My guy must have done that—it looked like he went at least two months between grabs, so he had to be doing something in that time. But what about the physical preparation? That would have to play a big role in this case, if Doc was right.

I slipped a hairpin onto the top of the page to mark my place and set the book down. It wasn't exactly bedtime reading, and now I'd polluted myself with something I was going to think about and think about until it made more sense to me. And probably dream about that night.

My last thought before unconsciousness was that I would soon be buying Doc another lunch.

A discernible sense of lightness came over me on Saturday morning as I looked at the neat stack of current case folders I would hand Fred on Monday. One of the open cases, an assault, would probably never get to court—there were credible eyewitnesses and solid physical evidence, and if the perp had half a brain or an even mediocre lawyer he'd plead to a lesser charge and save us all the headache of having to nail his ass to the wall. Either way he would get out too soon and just do it again as soon as the opportunity presented itself. Some days I wonder why I bother to show up here at all.

Who am I trying to kid—sitting right here on my desk is the reason, or reasons if you want to get semantic: Nathan Leeds, Larry Wilder, and Jared McKenzie, and the other ten who look just like them. The lightness I felt just a few minutes before dissipated and was replaced by a heavy sense of foreboding.

Of course, these thirteen cases were all individual and legally separate, but I knew in my heart they were connected, even if Fred was in denial. Slightly askew in the stack of files was that lovely little monkey wrench, the Garamond case. One ragged corner stuck out accusingly. I shoved it back in place and lined up all the edges.

Would I recognize the pivotal clue when I tripped over it in this mess? *Keep an open mind,* Erkinnen had told me; good advice, but it was a lot easier to give than to follow.

The division mailboxes were conveniently located just outside the locker room. A number of the full files were waiting for me already; they must have felt like hot coals to the guys who'd handed them over. I stood there for a moment with my arms full of detective stuff and recalled the bad old days when my job, however defiling, was pretty much over at the end of my patrol shift. I pushed the swinging door open with my rear end and went into the locker room. The benches had been replaced since my last visit; the new ones had that nonskid emery surface and were quite a bit wider. Were female cops getting broader in the behind, and did they need traction on their benches? Not like my time in patrol, when we had to meet specific physical limits.

No one was in there—it was hours away from shift change, when the place would fill up with overlapping arrivals and departures. There was always a gabfest going on in there when I was still on the streets—we would brag about our kids, complain about our boyfriends and husbands, crow over a bargain. I heard from one of the new girls—a daughter of one of the guys who was already a cop when I came on—that there was a lot of gossip, some of it pretty nasty. Things do have a bad habit of changing.

One thing that hadn't changed, though, was the midshift solitude. No telephones—if someone wanted to reach me, they'd have to page me. I sat down on one of the benches and placed the stack of envelopes next to me, thinking I would just look at a couple of them and then go back to the division room.

It was almost four hours before I got back upstairs.

Every time I opened another envelope, it was like reading the same script over and over again. A young white boy had disappeared suddenly and without explanation. This boy would be slight of build, with blond or light brown hair, a sweet face, and very fair skin. Eyewitnesses would report seeing him in the company of an intimate immediately before the abduction, but the intimate (except the esteemed Mr. Garamond) would always seem to have an irrefutable alibi. I was ready to bet my pension that when the rest of the files showed up, the same pattern would surface.

Doc's interest was beginning to make more sense to me. You always want to feel outrage over these horrors, but when things fall into place like they were just now, a guilty excitement creeps in. I pass GO pretty quickly and head straight for the *revenge is mine sayeth the detective* square. I become the huntress in lion skins; I am sharpening my spear. I am setting out at a trot with the spear in my hand. I am hungry. I will eat.

eleven

IT CAME TO PASS as I feared it would—during the course of our inquiries, which took far more time than I thought prudent, more children vanished. Even before Pentecost, a boy was lost. The widow of Yvon Kerguen, who was a mason of great skill in the parish of Saint-Croix in Nantes, put her son in the charge of the insidious Poitou, whose reputation ought to have been well-established by then, yet somehow it continued to be ignored. The boy was never seen again.

They eat small children there.

And why on earth did people keep giving their sons to him?

We were promised benefits. The same story was told over and over again. I cannot understand why any would believe him—was there some insane hope that one boy would not fall prey to the same fate as all the others, that one child would be spared by virtue of some intangible quality that all parents hope they have bred into their children but rarely do? It would have to be immortality, for nothing short of that seemed to protect them.

The Kerguen lad was fifteen and supposedly quite comely for a boy on the verge of manhood. He was said to have been small and very young-looking. He was nearly as fair as a girl, they said, and soft-spoken.

My Michel had been comely but far from small—he had long, straight legs and all the grace such favored limbs can bring. It was always a pleasure to behold him, this creature that God had seen fit to bring into the world through me. He was making his entry into manhood with far more dignity than most boys do; he had none of the ropy clumsiness that marks his sex so cruelly in the years when voices deepen and shoulders broaden. He would often slip his arms around me and hug me tightly with unconditional adoration—the lucky woman he took to wife would not lack for affection. To this day I can remember how it felt to have his arms around my neck; I need no exotic Italian conjurer to bring to mind the tightness of his grip, the warmth of his cheek on mine, the pure joy of having him close, of just having him.

But of course I could not keep him—no mother ever keeps a son, though I gave mine up much earlier than most, and with far more pain.

In the beginning of May another boy was taken, again near Machecoul; he had gone with many children of his village seeking alms at the castle there, the parents thinking there would be safety in numbers. Always the girls were given alms first and then they would depart, leaving the boys to try for themselves. On the day in question, a son of the pauper Thomas Aise and his wife, who lived in Port-Saint-Pere, went to the castle with the group but for some reason was passed over time and again as donations were made. Finally, when everyone else had already received, they gave him alms.

But this time there was a witness to his taking. A young girl by the name of Dominique had remained behind to wait for Aise's son because she was sweet on the boy and hoped to walk home with him. Her aunt had come forward to the Magistrate with the story she had been told by her confused little niece, who had walked all the way home by herself in the darkness when the boy did not return. She was too young to understand the dangers she might face, and I must admit that she seemed a bit simple—not feebleminded, precisely, but slow.

I freely confess, may God forgive me, that I took advantage of this weakness of hers. She was brought to us one afternoon, delivered discreetly through the Magistrate, after a request by his Eminence that she appear before us. We had already decided that it would be better for me than for the Bishop himself to speak with her, for she was a shy child in the presence of adults, or so her mother claimed. I wondered how she had been forward enough to wait for an older boy.

When her mother presented her, I understood.

"Move forward, Dominique," the mother scolded, literally shoving her daughter forward to stand before us. I wondered if it had been at the suggestion of this domineering mother that the girl had waited for the boy. He was young, but not so young that he would ignore a girl's flirting. I took her to be perhaps thirteen or fourteen, a bit older than the lad. To get with child might be such a girl's only hope of securing a husband.

Jean de Malestroit stayed well back in the room while I spoke to her. If I failed to get from her what we needed, he could step in.

"*Bonjour, ma chérie,*" I said.

The mother tapped her on the shoulder, quite hastily. The girl curtsied and said, "*Bonjour, Mère.*" Then she clasped her hands together in front of her white apron, which looked to have been soundly laundered for the occasion of this visit to the Bishop's palace.

"Thank you for coming here today."

"Oui, Mère," she said, dipping again.

"I am told that you know something of what happened to the son of Thomas Aise. You saw him enter the castle at Machecoul, your aunt says."

"That is true, *Mère.*"

"Did he enter alone, or in the company of anyone else?"

"In the company of a man."

"Do you know this man yourself?"

"No. But I have seen him before in Machecoul. They say he is called Henriet."

I had to be careful not to allow my distress to show. Nor my unholy and shameful excitement! I had not yet told Jean de Malestroit of my thoughts regarding Milord de Rais and these disappearances.

"Did you hear what this man Henriet said to the Aise boy?"

"His name is Denis, *Mère.*"

"Denis, then. Did Monsieur Henriet say anything to him?"

"Oui, Mère." Another hasty but unnecessary curtsy was performed before she could continue. "He said that if Denis had not had any meat, he could enter the castle and be given some."

Meat would be a powerful enticement to a hungry child. "Did Denis say anything in return?"

"No, but he went directly inside."

"Did he speak to you before doing so?"

Her head drooped slightly. "No."

She said further that she saw him led away. She was the last person who saw him outside the castle.

We gathered all of this new information together and put it to parchment along with that pertaining to the earlier disappearances. Sheaves lay everywhere in stacks and folios; I wondered why they did not burst into flame with the heat of what was inscribed upon them.

One day we stood among them, and it all came to roost.

"Guillemette." He said it with great resignation.

"Yes, Eminence . . ."

"A pattern emerges."

"Indeed, Eminence. I have been thinking so myself as well."

A moment passed while each of us dwelled on the trouble we had uncovered. "What shall we do about it?" he said finally.

I cannot describe the thoughts that traveled through my heart and soul at the time, for they are too diffuse and jumbled. I did not want them to take greater form within my mind. But they did anyway, against my will. "I am not the one who ought to be asked that question," I said quietly. "I cannot make an untainted judgment."

There was no need for me to explain myself further. He knew what was in my heart well enough. But there was no way he could understand the true nature of my anguish—it cannot be comprehended by anyone who has not raised a child with all good intent and patience, only to watch that child's character waver terribly from the true path.

"It seems obvious that Milord de Rais is stealing these children, or at the very least that someone in his service is doing so. Could he be so blind to the activities of his retainers that he does not know?"

"One hopes that he is," I said.

I breathed several times before his observation reached my ears. "But you do not think that."

"I do not know what to think," I cried, almost plaintively. "They may be taking advantage of their positions of trust with him to offer enticements without his knowledge. There is always that possibility, Eminence."

Jean de Malestroit gave me a very troubled look.

"Well, it *is* possible, and it cannot be discounted."

I could see the Bishop straining to hold himself in check. But I placed no such restrictions on myself. "I am loath to believe this of him," I went on. "My intellect tells me one thing, my heart another."

It was a lie. In my heart, I knew the truth. Even then.

His Eminence then stunned me with a nearly vicious declaration. "As for me," he fumed, "my own intellect has little difficulty with the notion that Gilles de Rais could so easily disregard all decency in pursuit of unclean pleasure."

I stood speechless for a few moments, then folded my arms over my chest in defense of my heart. "Eminence, he is a nobleman—he is not expected to comply with the rules of ordinary life. You know his history—you have known him all his life."

"As have you. Far more intimately than I. Though my lesser knowledge gives me a clearer eye than yours— it seems that you are blinded by your emotions in a most feminine mode. I had hoped for better from you in this matter."

The insult stung, but I let it pass, understanding that people sometimes use such mockery as a weapon in defending a difficult position. "You cannot deny that his life, even beyond his nobility, has been far more than ordinary."

"That I will admit, Sister, both to the good *and* the bad. But he is no more or less ordinary than any other man in the eyes of God. Still, he behaves as if he were the law unto himself. He answers to no one."

Though the acts we were investigating were worthy of such disdain, our certainty was far from absolute that the man on whom he bestowed it was truly deserving thereof. It surprised me greatly to hear such ranting from a man whose unblemished intellect I so admired, upon whose friendship I could always depend. I felt compelled to refute those rantings, right or wrong. "I know him well, Eminence. I saw him pray at Pax. His prayers are far more sincere than my own, truth be told."

"Guillemette—"

I raised a hand, rather more boldly than was prudent. "Hear me," I insisted, "though it may displease you. He answers to God, Eminence, as do we all. You yourself were present when he gave his sins to God and was absolved. We cannot know what sins those were, what deeds he—"

I had to stop speaking in mid-phrase—there was such a sudden and stark change in Jean de Malestroit's expression that it caught me short. His eyes shifted guiltily back and forth beneath the eyebrow. Somehow he must have gotten Olivier des Ferrieres to reveal the utterings of the confessional to him, and thus knew all Gilles de Rais's transgressions. I could only imagine by what means he had pried those private revelations out of the lesser priest.

I turned to leave; such was my indignation at this turn of events. He caught my sleeve in his hand.

"Guillemette, there is much you do not know about this man."

I shook off his grip and walked slowly to the window. Young boys, some of whom I recognized as sons of important noblemen, were being led across the courtyard stones by one of our teaching brothers. The first few walked in quiet single file behind the brother, who hugged some

treasured volume to his chest and stared resolutely ahead.
Those toward the end of the line engaged in far less
decorous behavior; they were skipping about and swat-
ting at one another with open hands. Gilles de Rais
would have worked his way to the end of the line so he
could partake in such friskiness; he would not have tolerated the austerity forced on those in the front positions.
He would not have had to. But Milord Guy would not allow his son to be schooled in a group; he would only
sanction the presence of my sons Jean and Michel, so this
was all speculation on my part. But it was speculation
based on deep knowledge, as were all my assumptions
about him.

"Eminence," I said quietly, "I know the contents of
his soul better than anyone alive, his wife perhaps included. I *shaped* him."

"I understand that this pains you," he said slowly.
"But you before anyone else should know that the man
defies the rules that are set out for him. There will come a
time when he will try to defy even God Himself, and that
will be his ultimate undoing. Mark my words—it will
come to pass as I predict."

In the middle of May, on a warm sunny day when the
world should have been a finer place than it turned out to
be, Milord Gilles did as was predicted. He rode out of
Champtocé to the abbey at Saint-Etienne-de-Mer-Morte,
accompanied by perhaps sixty men-at-arms with full armor and weaponry, as if a small country were to be taken
rather than an abbey and church. Milord himself was
said to have brandished a long pointed pike, though few
soldiers can use such a weapon as lethally as those of a
more innocuous appearance, or so my husband once
said. It is the fierce look of such things that frightens op-
ponents into submission, Etienne claimed. He must have

been right, because Gilles de Rais met no resistance at all, not that there was any to be encountered—the "commander" of the castle was a tonsured cleric, Jean le Ferron, a man known for the generosity and mildness of his character.

The news was brought by a swift rider, whose lathered horse fairly dropped when the man dismounted. *Frère* Demien and I were in the garden at the time, engaged in a bit of conspiracy over the location of certain plantings, which discussions were always dominated by my brother in Christ by virtue of his expertise and passion. But passion or not, when my gossip-loving brother saw the messenger fairly run into the Bishop's palace, he excused himself, after a glance that promised a quick return when intelligence on this budding mystery was properly had.

The tale he came back with sent me running, skirts in hand, to Jean de Malestroit, who quickly confirmed what *Frère* Demien had already revealed.

"But why should he take by force a property that he inherited?" I said, my bewilderment genuine.

"He no longer owns it."

"He would never sell Saint-Etienne!"

"It appears that he would. He sold it to Geoffrey le Ferron."

Duke Jean's treasurer, no lover of *la famille* de Rais. "*Dare* you say …"

"Temper yourself, Guillemette—I know this to be true. It was all arranged at Machecoul."

Affairs of state was all Jean de Malestroit would say when I asked about his mission on a journey we had made there the previous autumn. The meetings that took place behind closed doors were discreet and, judging by the expressions of the departing participants, somber. Now it all made sense; of course Milord's representatives

would be somber upon having to give up such a gem as
Saint-Etienne.

"Le Ferron should have put troops there instead.
His brother is man enough to keep watch over the doings
of the place, but certainly not to defend it. Of course, he
never expected such double dealing from Lord de Rais,
or he would not have left it so exposed."

One cannot imagine what a ludicrous scene this must
have been—Gilles de Rais, bold and armored atop his
huge mount, insulting and threatening this timid man
with bodily harm, but only after he had first been dragged
out in chains by the Marquis de Ceva and thrown to the
ground. A desperate and confounding move.

"But why would he part with Saint-Etienne?" I
fairly moaned. "He was baptized there."

"Apparently he, too, believes it was a mistake, Sister.
He has ruthlessly stolen it back. The sale was made in a
desperate attempt to raise funds because his expendi-
tures have so depleted his stores."

"Has his situation become that dire?"

"One sells what one can, Sister, when there is no
other means of bringing in gold. But—common brig-
andage?"

There would be reprisals, and they would be swift. I
tried for a short while to convince his Eminence that
caution ought to be exercised until we had more information on the matter—we had only the first reports, and
surely when all sides were heard, a less dastardly picture
would be painted of the entire affair. Or so I hoped.

Jean de Malestroit entertained no such ideas of for-
bearance. "I am certain of the truth of the report and absolutely outraged that such horrors should be done to an
unarmed brother in Christ, a man who was only performing his expected filial duty."

"You have but one report."

"A reliable one."

"Still, if you see for yourself, your mind will rest easier on the matter," I said.

"I think perhaps it is *your* mind that will rest."

I begged and pleaded, and finally he acquiesced. It was decided that we should depart in the early morn of the next day. For the rest of the day, as we made hasty preparations, the Bishop railed against Milord Gilles, cursing him for his sinful excesses. *The man knows no limits at all—none! He throws away gold as if he could pluck it off a tree. And when the fruit of that tree is gone, he simply steals another one. He makes traffic with the devil and takes pleasure in the company of alchemists.*

"Eminence!" I cried when I heard this. "These are grave accusations indeed—you are speaking of blasphemy."

"Yes," he said calmly.

"Surely you have not stooped to believing ... *hearsay.*"

"I have reason to think it is not hearsay but simply the despicable truth. I have heard it told by reliable witnesses that the man engages in the darkest sort of worship. I am coming to believe that it is true."

His expression became tender, almost sympathetic, for he knew the effect such news would have upon me. "I have had questions asked in the village of Machecoul," he said, "carefully and discreetly. Many of the day servants live there, some in the very shadows of the castle. There are no secrets that can be kept from these people— their lives are so plain and brutal that they must find their enjoyment in observing those who rule them. And there is plenty of talk. *Plenty.* It is said over and over again that Milord keeps constant company with this Italian Prelati and that together they practice the black arts."

I crossed myself in defense of the unthinkable. "But ... it is forbidden completely."

"All forbidden things are practiced in secret, Guillemette. They are forbidden because they are too sweet for the weak to resist and because they draw those who are otherwise innocent to their ruin. We forbid them as a means of protecting those who cannot protect themselves. Lord de Rais has been harboring this shaman Prelati since Eustache Blanchet brought him here."

He had been investigating Milord in depth without telling me his findings. Though this was his right—indeed, his responsibility—I felt hurt by having been left out of it. Even so, I must admit that I did not wish to hear what he was telling me. I squeezed my eyes shut, forgetting somehow that it is the ears, not the eyes, that do the task of hearing, as though if I could not see the speaker, the speech might by some miracle prove untrue.

"Blanchet himself almost never leaves Milord's company," he went on. "But not because he is so cherished. Rather, Milord will not permit it because he is afraid Blanchet will run away and speak of what he knows to one of his enemies." Then his tone went very hushed. "There is even talk of sodomy among the lot."

"Enough!" I nearly shouted. "You who hate gossip so, how can you say these things, especially to me?"

"You of all people know that I honor the truth," he said softly. "I would not make these assertions without some confidence in their authenticity. My inquiries have been very careful. I have learned many disturbing things."

Woe overtook me; tears poured down my cheeks, and with his free hand, Jean de Malestroit reached out and brushed them away, very tenderly.

"Guillemette," he whispered, "please do not weep."

I disobeyed him.

"Please," he said again. He put his hand on my chin and raised up my face. "Open your eyes. You must see the truth. I tell you these things because I know that you love this man like a son. It would be terrible for you to hear them from a stranger. I know you have already lost a son and do not want to lose another. But he has gone bad, Guillemette. He is not worthy to be your son. Not worthy of your tears."

"You do not understand ... you *cannot* ..."

"You are right," he soothed, "I cannot. I do not understand how such a vile beast can deserve your regard. When you wanted to undertake this task, I tried to discourage you, to protect you so your pain would not be revisited." He sighed, and took his hand from my face.

"You are a strong and determined woman, Sister, qualities I have long admired in you. You inspire me to be the same ofttimes when I cannot find inspiration in myself. When I feel I have nothing left within myself to give to my obligations, I remember that you have suffered greatly and yet you still give so much. You wanted to help these people who have lost sons. You could not have known where it would lead. . . ."

Of course he was wrong; deep within my heart, I had known all along, somehow. But the deeper implications of this knowledge had the power to take me to a dark place I did not think I could bear to go and would resist with all my soul.

Jean de Malestroit mistook the true meaning of the pained look on my face and tried desperately to console me. "I am sorry," he said with agonized sympathy. "So terribly sorry."

I reached out and took his hand in mine. "I know. And it comforts my tortured heart to hear it said. But there is much torture yet to come for me. Promise me," I begged, "that as this progresses, you will keep me by your side and fully informed."

"It may turn out that these are matters not suitable

for a woman's ears—there is much I have not told you yet."

"There is little more I can see or hear that will shock me."

"Guillemette," he pleaded quietly, "do not ask this."

"I am owed it, and much more."

Finally, he agreed.

chapter 12

LARRY WILDER'S MOTHER had every right to be just as much of a snarling doggie as Mrs. McKenzie had been, but instead she was pleasant and gracious about my request to see her at 1430. On the way to their home in a neighborhood just south of Brentwood, I stopped at the Third Street Promenade in Santa Monica to pick up some lunch. I used to really like to come here with my kids because there's only foot traffic and it seemed pretty safe—that is, until one of the narcs took me on a short cruise and pointed out the ne'er-do-wells, the vast majority of whom were camouflaged as law-abiding citizens. While my order was made up at a taco stand, I watched the young kids who frequented the area. There was one group of boys who all looked to be in the same age group as my victims— knowing what I know now, I'm of the opinion that they're too young to be here without their parents. They evinced that pack behavior so typical of young teenagers. When the leader moved, the rest followed in the choreographed manner of a flock of starlings. I always thought that being the prime mover in a group like that was an indication of real leadership qualities in a kid. But how would you state that on an employment application? *I ran a gang, kept everyone in line, so give me a fucking job already.*

No one had disappeared from the Promenade, at least not that I could recall, a surprising fact in view of the degenerate multitudes. The pack leaders weren't the ones who were going to get grabbed—it would be one of the less visible followers. If I were an abductor, what would I look for in a victim? I watched the group for a few moments, then focused my observation on one boy in particular, because my gut told me he would be the most vulnerable in the group.

I imagined him separating off from the pack for a few moments and myself sidling closer to him. *Hey, kid, what are you looking for? Smoke? Blow? Ecstasy?* Then I could draw him further from the rest of the group and *voilà*. He would be mine.

That was an exaggeration; it wouldn't be that easy. But it wouldn't be impossible either.

I enjoyed the chili on a bench as I watched more passersby, many of whom were burdened with shopping bags. Their leisure was enviable. Then it was a short ride to the Wilder home. Mrs. Wilder answered the door almost immediately. She had a very pleasant face with a friendly expression, but such sad eyes. Larry's mother looked older than I expected she would be, but an ordeal like the one she'd been through and was still experiencing can really age a person. We've all seen it too many times.

I was shoving out the badge when she said, "Detective Dunbar? Please come in."

What if I hadn't been Detective Dunbar? People are too loose about security. I didn't say anything—it would have been like salt in a wound. "Yes. Mrs. Wilder?"

"Come in, please." She offered a hand. "I'm glad to meet you," she said pleasantly. So gracious and polite. Once

I was in the living room, my eyes went straight to a family photograph on the small grand piano tucked into one corner. Mother and father, and four kids. The blond one, Larry, was the smallest, probably the youngest.

This mother, like all the others, would be heaping tons of guilt on herself for this—Larry was her baby, and we're all a lot looser on discipline and vigilance with our youngest children than with our oldest. Of course we mess up our oldest children with overkill, but by the time the youngest comes along, we're relaxed pros with all the right answers. She'd probably been more inclined to let Larry do things unsupervised than when she was a new parent.

I eased toward the piano and pointed at the photograph. "May I?"

"Please," she said.

My finger came to rest on Larry's chest. "He looks a little different here than in the photo you gave us."

"I know. That one was more accurate, though. He hates to have his picture taken, so he never looks quite like himself when we pose. That's why I gave Detective Donnolly the candid. It looks more like the real Larry."

"Ah. Typical of the age, I think."

"Yes," she said quietly. "And these are my other kids."

Her *surviving* kids, I thought. I berated myself for that negativity as she identified two boys and a girl, whose names I promptly forgot because I would never need to know them again. But their ages were of interest and potential value to me.

"Twenty, eighteen, and fifteen," she told me as she indicated each child.

We sat down; I reviewed the particulars of the case aloud as I had read them in Donnolly's file. The uncle was seen and identified by witnesses, but he had been at the firehouse at the time, in the presence of six other firefighters, all of whom gave trial-worthy testimony on his behalf. Mrs. Wilder had nothing new to add to the information

Donnolly had dug up. It was time to take out my own shovel.

"Did Larry have his own room?"

"Yes, he did."

"I wonder if it would be possible for me to take a look at it."

I saw her face sag; the room was probably a kind of shrine to her. She didn't even bother to answer, just sighed deeply, then motioned with her head for me to follow her.

We climbed the stairs and turned right down a long, well-lit hallway. The house was bright and open, with lots of windows. It didn't have the look of a home mired in mourning. The floor was carpeted with salmon plush so thick that I couldn't hear my own footsteps, and the walls were decorated with all sorts of photos of wild animals, each one framed in a different primary color. Kids would like the way it looked.

Larry's room, in contrast, was cluttered and messy. There were clothes strewn on the bed and shoes tossed casually on the floor. It looked as if she hadn't touched anything at all. I pretended to need balance as I worked my way through the piles of videotapes and comic books and put my palm down flat on the desk as if to support myself. What I really wanted to do was to check for dust without her seeing me. I snuck a look at my fingertips when Mrs. Wilder was looking away—they were clean. The disarray appeared to be of the genuine boy-sort. She had apparently just picked it all up, dusted the surfaces, and then put it back in place again.

According to what was strewn all over the room, I would guess that Larry Wilder had to have been something of a nerd. There was a lot of computer stuff, including a joystick.

"Did your son play a lot of video games?"

"On the computer, yes. But we don't have one of

those—oh, devices, I guess, I don't know what else to call them—that you can use to play on the TV."

She said that with a lot of triumph. I thought, *Good for you.*

"We limited the amount of time he could be on the Internet too. The modem goes through a timer. We were always afraid—"

She couldn't seem to finish the sentence, but I knew pretty much what she was going to say. Larry's parents had been afraid that some electronic mutant, some pedophile presenting himself as another teenager, would seduce their son into that unthinkable void. A prudent fear—we were constantly on the alert in our division for deviants employing the pedophile community's new favorite method of enticement, that being the on-line masquerade.

It was beginning to look like I had a masquerader on my hands, but he didn't seem to be contacting his victims through an Internet chat room. It was something of a relief to be thinking that way, because these guys are among the worst of the deliberate predators—they do so much damage to the kids they work over, not the least of which is to keep them away from other more beneficial activities during the seduction attempt, even if the kids don't bite fully.

But it was also something of a disappointment, because we have our own equal-and-opposite predators, cops who pose as young kids and play along with these creeps. We had a case in our division recently—one of those times when Escobar *did* have a bran muffin and was out of the head long enough to take a phone call—where a kid's father got suspicious when his ISP usage climbed sky-high one month. Before he said anything to the kid, though, the father went to the ISP and started talking about lawyers because the boy was a minor. For a few days after that, when the kid tried to sign into that chat room, he got a SITE UNDER REPAIR message, so he didn't realize he was actually being blocked. The father got the info to Escobar, who assumed the kid's on-line identity and managed to set up a meet with the perp inside a week. We took him down in the parking lot of a local fast-food restaurant. He screamed entrapment, but the judge laughed and held him over. Almost made me a believer again.

"A timer," I mused. "On the line itself?"

"Yes. Breaks the connection if he stays on the same site for more than a certain amount of time. Only his father and I know how to override it."

"That's a unique way of keeping control," I said. "I never heard of that before. But what a good idea."

"It worked beautifully. It was becoming such a problem. But after we set that up he knew just how much time he would have to do that stuff and planned his homework and other activities so we didn't have to fight about it."

"I'd love to try that with my own son. I think he spends way too much time on the computer."

She seemed very pleased. "I'll have my husband call you—he's really the one who knows the details. I got to be the main enforcer, though."

I smiled and said, "Isn't that always the way."

"It was tough at first," she told me, "but when everyone got used to the routine and the limits, we didn't have too many problems. We also had a site blocker on there, which we specifically set to keep him out of chat rooms. There was one his school sponsored, but you had to have a password to get in and it was randomly monitored."

Mrs. Wilder automatically wiped a bit of detritus from the tabletop in her son's room, but the determination in the sweep of her hand confirmed what I suspected, that the room had become sacred to her. It was so sad—this fastidious, well-groomed, educated woman on the verge of matronhood was trying to let me know that she had been a good and vigilant parent, an effort in which she would be hopelessly entangled for the rest of her life. She would unconsciously plead her case with just about anyone who

knew that her son had disappeared. If she could just convince herself, the rest of us probably wouldn't matter so
much to her.

"From what I could see in Detective Donnolly's
notes, he thought the probability of an Internet abduction
was pretty slim. I take it that you agreed it shouldn't be a
priority in the investigation."

"We did."

"Has your thinking on that matter changed at all?"

"No."

I pointed to Larry's bed. "May I sit down?"

"Please. Go ahead."

I lowered myself onto the edge of the mattress and
looked all around the wood floor. There was a carpet in
the center of the room with vacuum strokes all through it
and only one set of transgressing footprints: mine—she
would vacuum up her own footsteps as she retreated out
of the room. Then I let my gaze drift upward and examined the walls. They were a lighter shade of green than
the carpet, a color that used to be called hospital green
because it was theorized to be restful and calming. There
was a bulletin board with dozens of small notes pinned
to it and a calendar from the year before with the month
of Larry's disappearance still visible. There was a practice
schedule for soccer and a card for a dental appointment
and a couple of birthday cards with that telltale grand-
mother look. There was a math test with a big *A* in a circle.
Nothing beyond the expected norm.

But if the walls themselves were supposed to be restful, the things he'd hung on them were not. There were
two giant posters for *Star Trek* movies, one of Bruce Willis
all cut and bleeding from one of his *Die Hard* things, and
then an assortment of smaller posters with dinosaurs on
them. A couple of WrestleMania ads had been torn out of
magazines and taped up rather haphazardly, definitely not
by a parent.

No Farrahs or Britneys just yet.

But the poster that really caught my eye was for an Animatronic exhibit of prehistoric beasts at the La Brea Tar Pits Museum that had closed down the year before after a very long run. The big dark rectangle was positioned in the place of honor opposite the foot of the bed, where he could see it easily. Evan had gone to see that show with Jeff—I forget whose parents were with them—and he raved about the thing for weeks afterward. All sorts of special effects, he told me, with these incredible beasts from ten thousand years ago. The thing Evan liked best about it was that there were knights and warriors, like those in some of his fantasy games, he said, and they were riding the beasts. Science purists created this huge vicious controversy over the chronological inaccuracy; I remember being amused over that because I used to watch *The Flintstones* all the time when I was a kid. Hey, they *rode* dinosaurs! The important thing to me was that it piqued Evan's curiosity about what was really true.

Seeing the poster, I understood even better. It depicted a grotesque warty boar dripping with hideous slime, too purple to be normal blood, but something the artist probably wanted you to imagine as bestial blood. Upon this boar's back was a warrior-being in ornate, dark armor—the whole effect was intriguingly medieval. He had a short sword raised up and was holding the boar by the mane—it had a hairy ruff around its neck, almost like a lion might. The sword's angle and position made me think that this knight or warrior was going to kill the beast while he was still riding on its back. He would slay the demon, but in the process he would have to take a fall, maybe lose his own life. The compelling image disturbed me, but my eyes kept wanting to examine all the tiny details the artist had put in, the jewels on the sword hilt, the fancy impressed decorations on the armor, the flashing pointed rivets on the fingers of the metal gloves.

But despite all the minute detail everywhere else in the image, when you looked into the slit opening on the front of the helmet, there was no face.

"Hmm," I said as I stared at the poster.

"Yeah," Larry's mother said, almost inaudibly—an odd reaction. But I let it go.

I came away from the Wilder home with a better sense of the kid himself. It's so hard to put an image together from photographs and descriptions. What I really needed was an Animatronic boy. But hanging out in this kid's room, sitting on the edge of his bed, seeing the spot where his sneakers would land and his jeans would be tossed, looking at the things he liked to look at, I had come to the conclusion that he was a nice, normal kid, not a Promenade kid. I told his mother I would be in touch if I needed anything more and that I would keep her closely informed of any new developments when they arose. She knew that *when* really meant *if*; I could see it on her face as I left. But she was kind enough not to challenge me.

I would not get the same deference in the McKenzie house. My arrival there was delayed by a stop at the café near where Larry had been taken. I pulled into a loading zone and was confronted almost immediately by a frowning waiter, who invited me with obvious annoyance to move my car. My badge and assurances of a reasonably quick departure backed him off.

I walked up and down the sidewalk a couple of times while this waiter watched me impatiently. When I had a feel for the block, I walked right past him into the café and asked for the manager. She came out of the kitchen wearing a white jacket and a soiled apron, on which she wiped her hands before offering one in greeting. I guessed that she was probably the chef as well, maybe even the owner. She said she'd been there on the day of the grab but hadn't seen anything herself, then told me that the two other potential eyewitnesses were no longer employed at the café, so I'd have to contact them at their homes, if either of them still lived in the same place. She thought at least one of the two still lived in the neighborhood, because she stopped in from time to time and hadn't mentioned moving.

I thanked her, then went outside and annoyed the anxious waiter even further by smiling right at him and sitting down at one of the outdoor tables. He would actually have to pay attention to me, poor baby. As I did, a car pulled slowly down the street and came to a stop parallel to my own vehicle. The driver motioned to the waiter, who cast a nervous glance my way and shook his head slowly from side to side. The car pulled away slowly and headed down the street. A classic low-key wave-off, because the coast was not clear.

No wonder the little jerk didn't want anyone, especially a cop, taking up that loading zone. He was waiting for a drug delivery. Probably just for himself; he didn't look tough enough to be a dealer. I memorized the plate number on the departing vehicle and would pass it along later to someone in narcotics. If he wanted to be annoyed at me, I would be happy to give him a really good reason.

I got the feeling that Marcia McKenzie's peevishness was her natural state, even beyond her grief, just as Mrs. Wilder's natural state was to be gracious.

"I don't know why I have to go through all of this again," she whined when we finally got settled. Already I felt like an intruder; the house was so perfectly decorated that I felt underqualified to enter it. I could imagine plastic covers on the furniture when no one was going to be visiting for a few days. It scared me to walk across the Oriental rug in the family room; the thing probably cost a couple of months of my salary.

Sadly, this family's affluence hadn't protected them. Jared McKenzie's disappearance had landed on them like a ton of bricks and they were still digging out. People who don't expect to become crime victims feel angry, frustrated, unsafe, violated, and tremendously confused about how the world could become such a foreign place in one short tick of the clock. Marcia McKenzie was accustomed to complete deference but found herself having to scratch and claw her way through a cumbersome system that automatically defaulted in favor of an anonymous criminal. Everything she'd encountered in the process of trying to pin down some justice was in direct opposition to what she believed about how things ought to be. By rights, the system *should* have treated her better, but she didn't have to be so mean to me. There were at least a dozen times over the course of our interview when I just wanted to get up and walk out. If I heard the word *disgraceful* one more time—it was as if Terry Donnolly and I had been the direct cause of all her misery.

She went on and on. "A deplorable lack of response, a galling failure to acknowledge my family's needs ..."

Yes, I understand how you might feel that the ball was dropped while we are reorganizing Detective Donnolly's cases. But that's all going to improve now. I had to be careful; if I agreed too heartily, she would have unreasonable expectations, even more unreasonable than she already had. It took me almost an hour to cut through all this anger and get to Jared's room, and then—a blessing—the phone rang. She left me alone while she went to answer it in a room down the hallway.

She stayed away for a long time and I eventually got tired of standing, so I sat down on the bed, without permission. Unlike Larry Wilder's room, this room had been worked over by a very anxious mother who needed to maintain some control over a son who was no longer present. There was no better place to start than his private space, which might have been one of their battlegrounds before he disappeared. I was bolder in Jared's room; I touched things readily, picked them up and turned them over, examined them carefully. Larry Wilder's room seemed a place of respect, while Jared McKenzie's was a place of turmoil, tones set by their respective, or in the case of Marcia McKenzie, *disrespective,* mothers.

I started going through his drawers, expecting to find them neat and orderly. But to my delight, they were messy and boylike. Dried felt-tip pens, small rocks, bent paper clips, chewed pencils, broken shoelaces, trading cards, foreign coins, movie tickets—

And a pencil case, from the gift shop at the La Brea Tar Pits.

thirteen

THE HORSE I WAS GIVEN to ride to Saint-Etienne was a gentle bay, but even so, as the ride progressed I began to dread the morrow, when my legs and flanks would be so stiff that I would barely be able to walk. I had once loved to ride a horse, especially when Etienne took me and our sons out on excursions into the countryside. We would beg four mounts from the groom at Champtocé, who was not supposed to allow it but kindly obliged us, especially when the household was installed at Machecoul and would not know. Michel and young Gilles would often ride out alone, on horses much too big for them, to chase small beasts through the forest or play at falconry with the fledgling that Milord was training to his arm. They often stayed out for hours at a time, worrying not only myself but Jean de Craon, who had so much invested in the success of his grandson that a hair out of place would set him to raging at all those who gave care to the boy. Yet between the lot of us we could not always manage to inflict an escort upon them, for they often snuck out from under our noses.

I could only imagine the rage into which Jean de Craon would fly had he been told what I had yesterday been told about his grandson.

Now, as we neared Saint-Etienne, I could not imagine ever having loved this pounding torture. Adding to my physical discomfort was an ill sense of foreboding. There would be no encounter between us and Milord, at least not one that had been planned; we were a small party and unarmed, and his Eminence wanted only to observe the situation from a comfortable distance. We would not make ourselves known unless it became absolutely necessary, but rather we would quietly seek intelligence from witnesses to the taking of the castle. And we would wait, to see what developed. All this his Eminence had arranged to humor me. The night before, after the preparations were complete, Jean de Malestroit had had a small dinner brought to us, which we ate together in the privacy of his chamber. It was a pleasant evening under the circumstances, which soured somewhat when he argued once again that we should not make the journey.

Now I sat on a horse in the light of day, my senses honed to exquisite readiness, a state of mind I rarely knew, for such crafts are not often needed by a woman of God, unless she happens to be Jean d'Arc. I stared at the fortress of Saint-Etienne from behind the protective cover of a clump of trees, feeling what I imagined a warrior might feel on the verge of a surprise attack, though no such attack was imminent. I was excited, a bit afraid, imagining glory. I noticed everything: the foot soldiers well-armed and ready who stood around the perimeter of the castle near the ancient church, the mounted troops whose horses shifted under their armored weight. I recognized the Marquis de Ceva—a rank scoundrel if ever one walked the earth.

"Milord is nowhere to be seen. He must be inside the castle yet," I said to his Eminence.

He nodded gravely but could not cover his smile. My warrior state must have seemed humorous to him. To me it seemed a way to pass the time, for I was growing tired of staring into the distance while soldiers milled about the church entry in apparent confusion.

The sun had risen significantly in the sky. I scandalized the company by removing my veil and shaking out my hair but replaced it quickly when all heads turned in my direction. Jean de Malestroit let a quiet chuckle slip out and then arched his eyebrow. He leaned over and whispered, "You may take some comfort in knowing that a helmet is no less bothersome. You will be wanting your sword soon, I suppose."

What I wanted was a more accommodating seat—I was forced to shift my position on the horse every few minutes to keep from stiffening up. It was difficult to do so while wearing all that cumbersome drapery. But there was plenty to distract me in the small movements that catch one's eye when the vision is not keenly focused on one specific thing. Most riveting of all was a cat who could not seem to be banished; he—or she, I could not tell from that distance—would rub up against the legs of the horses and make them whinny, thus annoying their riders. Time and again, the Marquis de Ceva would shoo this pest away with the tip of his sword, but the cat always came back, as cats are wont to do, especially hungry ones.

This little game went on for a while, and then suddenly Milord Gilles himself appeared from the door of the church.

"Eminence," I whispered.

"I see him," he said to me.

We all sat at attention and watched as Milord, in his black armor, clanked angrily over wooden planks, brandishing his drawn sword at nothing in particular and everything all at once. He carried his helmet in the other hand and tossed it to one of his men, who caught it tenuously. I wondered, on seeing Milord's grim look, what price the man would have paid had the helmet been dented by a fall to the ground.

Perhaps Jean le Ferron was proving more defiant than expected. Milord stomped back and forth among his men for a few moments, ranting visibly, a scene all too familiar to me from his childhood. Then the cat got in his way, nearly causing him to topple in his ungainly metal suit; he raised his voice and let loose a string of foul language such as ladies seldom hear, though he had no idea that a lady was present to hear it.

I could have forgiven him that. Men, in particular those of the nobility, are expected to behave in that manner on occasion. But then he did the unforgivable before my disbelieving eyes—he grasped his sword with both hands, and with one clean slice cut the unwanted feline in half.

I have no great love of cats. But neither can I sanction their slaughter. The two parts lay twitching at the feet of the horses as Gilles de Rais's troops laughed at its misery. What remained of it would be stomped to a pulp before the day was through, of that I was convinced. All I could think of was Lady Marie's poor little dog, so cruelly hung.

I turned and heaved; the remnants of my breakfast, already churned to a slurry by the ride, now visited their bitterness upon my tongue. Precariously atilt, I clung to the horn of my saddle and spat out the residue as best I could. Jean de Malestroit, his face emotionless, took hold of my arm to keep me in balance. He said nothing, but out of the corner of my eye I saw him nod to *Frère* Demien, who quickly produced and passed over a flagon.

"Drink," his Eminence urged gently.

I was expecting water, but it turned out to be wine, of good quality. But its excellence was moot, since I could not bring myself to swallow; I swished the fruity stuff around in my mouth and then spat it out. It could not possibly be sweet enough to cleanse this bitter taste.

☙

Thereafter, *Frère* Demien took one of our escort and set out—by a circuitous route so as not to be seen—toward the village of Saint-Etienne, which lay off to the west. Jean de Malestroit had charged him with the task of questioning Le Ferron's parishioners about what had actually happened at the church. We remained behind with our diminished guard and watched the comings and goings outside the castle. When my stomach felt more settled, I brought out the bread and cheese I had stowed in my saddle pack and shared it with those in our entourage, reserving enough for those who had gone out in case they found no hospitality in the village. I had no real appetite myself. I wondered if my desire for food would ever return.

The sun was at the midpoint of its decline when the forayers returned. They slipped through the woods behind us and snuck in quietly from between the trees.

Demien wore a grim look on his face as he emerged from cover. Our tonsured brother in Christ Jean le Ferron had apparently been dragged out of the sanctuary, forced down on his knees in full view of everyone, and beaten with a stout stick.

"His hands and feet were chained," *Frère* Demien said. "They say he was then hauled, maimed and bloody, back inside his own church as a prisoner. Some of the witnesses wept as they told me. Some who had seen this unholiness could not bring themselves to speak at all."

"Outrageous," his Eminence hissed quietly. "That

this property should have been seized in this vile manner. There will be immediate action."

I could see the anger in his eyes, which rested steadily on the speaker; I have never known a man who paid such close attention to what was being told to him, nor one who could bring what was said forth again with more sting. *Knowledge is my weapon,* he would often say, *since I bear no sword.* But much as I admired, even loved the man—improper feelings under the best of circumstances—and agreed that anger was in order, I believed that he was angry for the wrong reason.

"Jean," I said, very softly. He turned to me quickly on hearing his given name.

"*Oui,* Guillemette?"

"Do you not find it regrettable, as I do, that when a castle disappears we pursue its purloiner with more vigor than we do the violator of our children?"

He looked away again and grunted noncommittally. My dissatisfaction was immense.

I prayed, as earnestly as my near-heathen conscience would allow, for the soul of Gilles de Rais and asked God to show me that he was not what he seemed to have become—a monster, a fiend, a worshiper of the Dark One himself. I begged God against all logic that we would somehow discover it was all untrue and that Milord, upon whom I'd had a mother's influence, would be proved blameless. Such an outcome seemed more unlikely with each new revelation about his character. But one thing I knew with surety: Duke Jean cared more for the castles of his comrades than for the children of the folk who lived in their shadows. And that was a matter deserving of someone's outrage.

♛

By mid-afternoon we had relaxed our vigilance a bit; there seemed little danger that we would be noticed in

our wooded hideaway. Gilles's men were far too preoccupied with their own business (and with greater mutila-
tion of the cat halves) to even glance in our direction.
Our horses, who were far more pleased with boredom
than were their riders, made no noise at all. The quiet
was stunning, yet no one heard the approach of a man
through the woods but I. It was only because I was pok-
ing through the contents of my saddle pack and therefore
turned slightly backward that I heard the small movement in the brush.

Keeping my wits about me, I finished my business in
the bag and turned back around again. Then I feigned a
slight swoon, at which point his Eminence leaned toward
me and reached out. I took advantage of this closeness to
whisper to him.

"A man lies in wait behind us. I could not see him
clearly, but I know he is there."

With equal retention of wit, the Bishop straightened
up again, slowly so as not to alarm our hidden observer,
and turned to face one of our escort. He looked pointedly
at the man's sword and nodded his head backward very
slightly.

"Behind, in the brush," I heard him say, though his
words were so soft that the intruder could not possibly
have heard them. The escort closed his eyes slowly, then
opened them again, indicating his understanding.

After a few seconds the man said, "By your leave,
Eminence ... might I stand down for a moment?"

Jean de Malestroit made an exaggerated nod and
said, "Of course."

The man got down off his horse and made to fool
with his breeches a bit, as if he were going to relieve himself, and headed toward the brush behind me. "Mother, I
beg your indulgence...."

"I shall not look," I said.

Into the brush he went, his hand supposedly near his

loin but closer instead to the hilt of his sword. I heard the scrape of the sword edge as it was pulled from the scabbard, and then a quiet scuffle. I turned around to see what transpired; all instinct told me to bolt out of the wood into the clearing, but that was not the action of a warrior who would remain undetected. So I sat on my mount, frightened, and watched the branches thrash about wildly. There was no shouting—instead, there was a rushed and low exchange of abrupt phrases, as if the intruder as well wished to remain undetected by Lord de Rais's men. And then the thrashing stopped.

All was quiet for a moment until the escort emerged, his charge ahead of him with hands lashed behind his back. He shoved his captive toward us. The man stumbled a bit, then found his balance just in front of his Eminence. He looked up at the Bishop's stern face and then bowed immediately.

It was a priest!

"Speak your business, Brother, and it had better have great import," Jean de Malestroit ordered, his voice still low.

Still bowing, the man said, "Forgive me, Eminence." His voice trembled slightly.

"First reveal your sin."

"My sins are many," the priest whispered in haste, "but I mean to say that I seek your forgiveness for surprising you thus. I did not want to reveal your position to Milord by walking through the clearing to speak with you."

"For that we are grateful," his Eminence said. "Now, how did you know we were here to be revealed?"

"I followed the young priest from the village."

"He was not aware of your presence?"

"No, Eminence."

Jean de Malestroit cast an unappreciative look in

Frère Demien's direction, then turned back to our petitioner. "What is your name?" he asked.

"La Roche," the man answered. "Guy."

"Well, Brother Guy, I must ask—why did you not speak directly to *Frère* Demien when he was in your village?"

"I had nothing to say on the matter of the church's capture, which I understood was his purpose. I serve a much smaller parish on the other side of the village and was not present when the atrocity took place. But one of our young men saw your entourage approach from far out."

"We saw no young men on our route."

A thin smile appeared on La Roche's lips. "Then I suppose he was well enough concealed after all. We wondered if that were so."

"A spy?"

The priest nodded. "We have placed men in the woods all around here." To the Bishop's curious look, he explained, "We dare not leave them unwatched. Demons are taking our children."

From Jean de Malestroit there was only silence. But the priest continued, "Our man told us that the Abbess was among you."

Not *an* abbess, but a specific one—myself. He looked at me as I looked all around in bewilderment.

Jean de Malestroit's gaze fell critically upon me. "It seems you have acquired a reputation, Sister," he said, very hushed.

"Indeed, my lord," I whispered back. "God forgive me."

He grunted his displeasure, then whispered, "We shall see."

The priest took a step closer to me. The escort reached out to pull him back, but a simple glance from Jean de Malestroit put an end to that.

"If I may speak, Mother."

I looked instinctively toward Jean de Malestroit, who left it entirely up to me by looking away.

"You may," I said. I sat taller in the saddle, for I was enjoying this moment of authority. "But make haste," I admonished, "for the light wanes."

"Word comes to us from Bourgneuf that you heard many tales of lost children there. We, too, have a tale to tell."

"We?" I asked.

"Yes. Others await me, well back in the woods." He pointed behind him and beckoned with a look.

"How many?" his Eminence asked warily.

"Seven," the priest answered.

Enough to overtake us. But why reveal the number if the intent was impure? Or perhaps he had understated it to gain our confidence, unwarranted. It was too confusing, this warrior business. I glanced in Jean de Malestroit's direction, but his face was unreadable. I made my own expression plain: *Please, might we hear what they have to say. . . .*

Finally he nodded. We turned our horses around and followed La Roche.

⚜

It quickly became clear that we had nothing to fear; among the seven were three women, one man who looked to be quite old, and, of course, the priest. The other two were strong-looking men, but neither was armed.

Bows and curtsies were made, and then his Eminence spoke. "You have come a good distance on foot to tell your tale," he said.

"We come in memory of a child. The distance does not seem long to us."

Jean de Malestroit regarded the group for a moment, then asked, "Is one of you the child's parent?"

"No," the priest said. "He was an orphan."

One of the women said, "His mother died in bearing him."

It was every woman's fear as her labors began. "What of the father?" I asked.

Again, La Roche spoke. "He died two years hence, of consumption. For a while he struggled to keep the boy, and he was doing well until his illness overtook him."

Another woman said, "The father was my step-brother, and when he knew that his own death was near, he asked me to look after the boy myself or to find a good family for him if I could not keep him. But I had no means to feed another mouth." She lowered her gaze in shame.

"Our whole parish looked after him," the priest said. "The child endeared himself to us. He was quick-witted and was beginning to take up Latin with great enthusiasm. I thought he might even do well in the priesthood himself. He was quite devout."

Jean de Malestroit seemed to ponder all of this but did not speak.

"So we have lost a son," La Roche said, "but God may also have lost a servant."

"We are all servants of God, Brother."

The priest looked at me when he continued. "I know this is most irregular for all of us to come forward, Mother, but he has no one else to speak for him."

"Then you must do so," I said.

They all began to speak, one atop the other.

He was a fine lad despite his disadvantages. Always a pleasure to those who knew him. A good boy, a worthy boy.

And the final line, spoken by a young woman: "We know that others have been taken. It can no longer be denied."

They eat small children there.

"What was his name?" the Bishop finally asked.

"Jacques, by Baptism," the priest told him. "But we called him Jamet out of affection. His father's name was Guillaume Brice."

"When was he lost?" he asked.

The priest looked back to me again, though it was the Bishop who had spoken. I wondered if Sister Claire had somehow let it be known that in me he would find a more sympathetic ear. "The last anyone saw of him was well more than a year ago," he said. "In February. He liked to bring something back to those of us who provided for him. Then one day he went out to beg for alms and never returned."

"Were inquiries made?"

The boy's half-aunt said, "All about the area, and beyond, Mother. He was the last of our line, and it was only through him that his father's name—also my father's—could be preserved. We do not want to let him fade away as the others have, when no one could find them. We wish to seek some justice over his loss."

It was the same bitter frustration I had heard in all the other complaints. But this time an entire community had come forward on behalf of a boy who was in truth no one's son. Their hopes and expectations hung in the air like a mist, enshrouding us.

"I will look into the matter," his Eminence finally said.

The boy's aunt stepped forward. "When will we hear from you?"

It seemed to catch Jean de Malestroit by surprise—he was not accustomed to such forthrightness in his petitioners. But the common outrage of the people was a force whose power he understood well. He answered, "There are other more urgent matters that have been given to me to tend, but you have my promise: I shall see to it in a timely manner."

The crowd murmured and nodded its gratitude.

Then La Roche said, "Eminence, please allow me to speak to my people for a moment, and then I would speak to you again."

"As you wish, Brother."

They conferred quietly among themselves for a few moments. Finally the priest emerged from the group and said, "We have our suspicions as to who might be the culprit in these disappearances."

"I am sure you do" was Jean de Malestroit's answer. Wisely, La Roche kept his silence. After a pause, the Bishop continued, "But I will come to my own conclusion through a fair inquiry. In time, if there is a trial, you will all know what I know."

It seemed to satisfy them. After a great flurry of appreciation, they bade us good-bye and disappeared into the woods again.

All through the journey back to Nantes, by the light of our torches, I mused quietly on the events of this long and exhausting day. As we passed through the forested area just before the city, I heard Jean de Malestroit's voice. He was directly next to me, but it sounded as if he were calling out from a long distance.

"There is finally reason to move against Lord de Rais."

I let that declaration hang between us for a time. It was a bitter truth that our lost children meant less to Duke Jean than the title to Saint-Etienne. Lord de Rais must have understood the folly of his attempt to regain the property—how long did he think it would be before Duke Jean sent out a larger, better-equipped force, with troops of greater loyalty, to stomp Milord into the Saint-Etienne mud?

Milord's true crime was that he considered himself to be an equal to Duke Jean. He saw that in his *grandpère,* who had more wealth, more property, more retainers, more cleverness, and certainly more audacity than the

Duke. It was a ludicrous blunder on Milord's part to assume that such equality passed automatically to him. Even more stunning were the insane accusations Gilles was reported to have made when he attacked: "You thieving scoundrels," he'd shouted at Jean le Ferron. "You have beaten my men and extorted money from them. Come outside the church or I'll lay you dead!"

No one believed for a moment that Jean or Geoffrey le Ferron had extorted anything. And none of us could fathom how a man who had shown such humility and piety at Pax might suddenly lose control of his own soul in the crazed manner of Gilles de Rais at Saint-Etienne. He had been heard, both in his brief penance at Pax and subsequently in other situations, speaking a sincere wish to make a pilgrimage to the Holy Land, to quit his evil life, and to beg for forgiveness. Yet only his confessor and perhaps Jean de Malestroit knew the nature of the sins that required absolution. And neither would speak of it.

Jean de Malestroit knew enough already to cripple Milord Gilles on Duke Jean's behalf. But had he not foolishly laid siege to a church, Gilles de Rais might never have been tried for anything, even after the pleas of so many parents.

You see, Milord was still too much one of us.

But he would not remain so much longer.

chapter 14

IN MY MINNESOTA LUTHERAN FAMILY we went to church for about eight hours on Sunday morning (at least it seemed that way to me) and then we had a big old comfortable dinner that lasted the rest of the day. I don't live like that anymore, but I couldn't bring myself to call any of the families of my seven documented cases on the minuscule chance that they might. I spent a quiet Sunday reading and rereading the case files, trying to formulate an overview.

It's a strange life being a snoop. Only three of these families knew that a complete stranger was busily absorbing the intimate details of their lives and that, even though this stranger was trying her best to maintain professional detachment, she would form opinions about them based on what she learned.

It is my opinion, Your Honor, based on my training and professional experience, that if the mother had just kept a closer eye on her kid, he might still be around.

Or, I came to the conclusion, based on the preponderance

*of evidence, that the boy's uncle really is a pervert, even if he
did have an alibi.*

You can't help it sometimes. I want to be kind and
give people the benefit of the doubt, but you see so
much—too much.

A slew of questions would emerge, chief among them:
Had the missing child been to the Tar Pits Museum within
recent times prior to his disappearance? And if so, with
whom?

And if there were such striking similarities between
the victims, might there not also be a pattern to be gleaned
in the intimates? So far the only visible common thread
between the initial suspects, all of whom had later been
cleared by alibis—including Garamond, though he wouldn't
admit it—was that they were closely associated with the
victim in some trustworthy way.

Hardly a breakthrough observation.

Few of the cases had progressed to the point where
there were photos of the intimates in the files, because
none of them had been booked, except Jesse Garamond,
who was really starting to make me mad. To rot in jail just
so he could protect his brother—it was like he was living
one of those Greek tragedies we had to read in high-school
drama class. Of the few photos I did have, one made me
feel terribly sad. The supposed perp—also an uncle—had
his arm around the victim; they were standing in front of a
baseball backstop and the kid was in uniform, all scruffed
up like he'd spent the whole day practicing his slides. A
loving amateur had to have taken the picture, because
there was way too much background and the whole thing
was slightly skewed. But the adoration was so obvious; the
kid was happy, the uncle was happy, the photographer
caught it all very honestly. I looked at this guy in the picture, and all I could think was, *no way.* I had no basis on
which to make that assessment, but I still couldn't shake it.
So much for professional detachment.

I don't think I was ever so happy to see my kids as I was when they came back that afternoon. It just made everything feel normal again. They'd obviously had a good time, because Kevin looked really beat when he dropped them off; that was always a good sign.

Believe it or not, one of my favorite things to do with them is laundry, because it's such a cooperative effort. Evan found a basket in that mess he calls his room, and we all sat down on the living-room floor around a mountain of socks, underwear, sports uniforms, and T-shirts and proceeded to attempt to make sense of it. Julia pulled out the whites, Frannie the light colors, and Evan the dark—he won't do the whites because Frannie's little bras are in there and he doesn't want to touch them.

"You're such a coward," she teased him. "Jules has to look at your stupid underwear, but you're afraid of a little bra."

"Yeah, little is right, Miss Flat-Chested," he taunted back.

A lot of screaming ensued. Suddenly, laundry was flying all around the room. Not to be left out of the fun, I picked up a towel and snapped it at my son, who laughed with his cracking voice and slipped nimbly out of the way.

"Insensitive lout," I said, barely containing my own laughter. "You better hope she doesn't grow up to be bigger than you."

"Yeah," Frannie chimed in. She flexed her biceps, Arnold-style. "You think it's dancing I do at that studio, you dumbhead. It's *karate*."

She chopped inexpertly and Evan grabbed her wrist. Squealing in delight, Julia entered the fray by jumping on Evan's back and starting a wrestling match, during which everyone's hair got really messed up. It wasn't long before we were all on our backs on the floor, grinning and panting.

Eventually we got all the laundry sorted and the first load in the machine. I put on a Beatles CD as part of an ongoing effort to pass on the reverence for sixties music that my older brother had imparted to me. It always made me feel good that my kids knew enough of the words to sing along to most of the songs. We checked the completion of everyone's homework and made grilled cheese sandwiches.

Julia and Frannie fell asleep in front of the TV. I hoisted Frannie over my shoulder. It wouldn't be too long before she got too heavy for this. As I was heading toward her bedroom, I had to stop for a moment and look back into the living room. There was my lovely son doing a wonderfully sensitive thing—he had picked up his baby sister, just as I had done with Frannie, and was following me down the hallway.

It was all I could do to keep from crying.

Of course I had to slime him with kisses when he went to bed himself a little while later. And naturally he was appalled by this excess of motherly appreciation. I didn't care. When everyone was asleep, I cleaned up the kitchen, because there is something unholy about waking up on Monday morning to Sunday night's grilled-cheese mess. That done, I stacked all my files and folders and shoved them into my thickening briefcase.

Erkinnen's book stared up at me from the bed table when I slipped between the sheets. I looked down at it and thought, *Enough already.* But I picked it up anyway and started to read. After a few minutes I started making notes. I woke up the next morning with page creases on my cheek. There were so many things I needed to know.

Two of the three remaining files showed up in my mailbox Monday morning. I wonder if I would have been so quick to give up control of something as these initiating detectives seemed to be. But careerwise it makes sense, because you hate to have too many unsolveds on the board. Taken individually, these cases were all going nowhere fast. Even with the recognition of their connectedness, I might not solve them. My closure rate would drop down to normal for the first time in my career.

I started calling the families of the victims to introduce myself. I explained the change in primaries as a matter of "workload readjustment." Most of the people I spoke to were very understanding and eager to cooperate. I managed to make an appointment for an interview with the mother of another one of the victims for late in the afternoon, after I dropped Frannie off at dance class. Most of the calls went well, considering the circumstances, but there was one very strained conversation that left me feeling depressed. The alleged perpetrator, the father of the boy who'd disappeared, had gone into a complete funk after being questioned as a suspect. His own alibi was probably the shakiest of all—he'd been traveling by himself for work. A whole month passed before anyone figured out that he'd been videotaped by a toll-booth security camera, one that had just been installed to try to catch toll evaders. The mother told me that the detectives had been pretty aggressive in their pursuit of this guy, which is what we are supposed to be, especially when there is strong evidence—in this case, an extremely reliable eyewitness—pointing to him. He committed suicide about three months after the incident, leaving his wife not only widowed but also potentially childless, because the missing boy was their only offspring.

I wanted this monster so bad. *So* bad.

"Round up all the known sex offenders in the area before you do anything more," Fred told me.

"Oh, come on, Fred, that's not going to go anywhere. Talk about spinning wheels ..."

"Cover your ass, Dunbar, because I'm your lieutenant and your ass is an extension of mine. If your perp—and I'm still not sure we're talking about just one guy here—turns out to be one of the knowns after all, there'll be some heavy-duty explaining to do when someone sees that you didn't drag them in right away."

He was right, of course; it was a professionally sound thing to do, and it gave us some political safety. But it seemed like such a waste of time; there are literally thousands of sex offenders in the Los Angeles area, and it would take forever to bring them all in for questioning.

"Can I at least try to narrow it down a little first?"

"How?"

I tried again. "How about a profiler?"

I should have known better.

"Stick with Erkinnen."

This time he took me out to lunch, to a rather nice little restaurant in West L.A., on the south side of Melrose. "They can't be reimbursing you," he said. "I know these folks."

"I took the first one out of petty cash," I told him. "The second one was on me. But I don't mind. You've been a tremendous help."

"Well, then, this one and the next will be mine."

We got settled; the place had a deliberate bistro atmosphere, complete with out-of-the-way corner booths. All it needed was a haze of cigarette smoke and we could have been in a forties black-and-white movie. It was a tony way to acquire privacy, but I didn't mind—there was a purpose, and the company was very pleasant.

Until he started talking about perverts, which, I had to remind myself, I'd asked him to do.

"Statistics conclusively show that sex offenders repeat their crimes at a rate significantly higher than the recidivism rate found in all other major crime categories. There have been several well-structured, scientifically sound studies that confirm this notion. Beyond that, the results of two meta-studies—"

"English, Doc."

"Sorry."

Then there was a bit of a pause. "You know, I'd like it very much if you would call me Errol."

I must have stared, because he added, "Please."

"Of course. That would be nice."

A truly stupid thing to say.

"So, Errol, a meta-study is . . ."

"Yes. Right. It's a study where we take statistics from a bunch of smaller studies and combine them to see if they reveal anything different from the original results of the small ones."

"Oh. Sounds like something you'd do if you had to get a paper done right away."

"That's how they come about sometimes—someone has to complete a Ph.D. and runs into a snag on the research. But they can be really useful because the samples are broader. Sometimes I think the little studies that get done are too narrowly designed. You have to understand that we are supposed to do original research when we get our grants, so we can't just do a better job of something someone's already done. The egg has to get sliced in a totally new way."

I thought I understood. "So instead of just doing research on the sleep habits of coffee drinkers, you have to do a study on the sleep habits of coffee drinkers who exclusively use Styrofoam cups."

"Very good, Detective."

"You know, I think I'd like it if you'd call me Lany."

"I'm sorry. Of course. I just didn't want to be rude.

Lany it is. Anyway, recidivism is studied quite regularly. Too regularly, a lot of us think. But hope is hard to kill."

His tone was a bit too pedantic for my liking, and I wondered if he was one of those professionals who think cops are too stupid to live. "We always hope for the disturbing truth to change, or for some factor that ameliorates the established trend to emerge so we can reasonably discount the credibility of that trend."

"Wait a minute there." Maybe all those folks were right about cop stupidity. "You lost me."

"We have treatments for this stuff. We want to be able to say they're successful, not only as a matter of pride, but to justify what it costs to treat and study these guys. I know that *I* would like to believe that our efforts to rehabilitate sex offenders can have some appreciable benefit. But I'm not so sure. The sad truth is that no matter how you read the statistics, the outcome is always the same: The recidivism rate for perpetrators of sexual crimes against children is disturbingly high. One study recently had it as high as fifty percent."

"I could probably have guessed that. We get the same perps all the time doing this stuff."

"Yeah. It's always the same sad story. But we're always trying to make it look better. I read an article in a forensic psych journal recently that argued for a new definition of recidivism. The author contended that fifty percent is falsely inflated because it represents the repeat rate for offenders who have been out of prison for ten years or more. They prefer the five-year statistic—a thirty percent repeat rate, which somehow seems more palatable."

I was trying, but failing, to understand how a thirty percent repeat rate could *ever* be acceptable.

"That's kind of a big disparity in only five years." It was all I could think to say. But Erkinnen was inspired.

"What it really says is that over time, the ability of the sexual offender to control his compulsion will eventually break down in more than half the cases, which in turn means that given enough years, the first-time offender is more likely than not to reoffend."

He leaned closer, though the waiter had long since left us to our meals and there was no one anywhere near us. "In truth, it's a lot sadder than that. The real unadjusted rate may be higher than fifty percent, because we are not taking into consideration those men who repeat their crimes but are not caught. The other thing you have to think about is something I touched on before—most of the studies are attempts to prove that treatment makes a difference in the reoffense rate of first-time offenders. Anyone who'd already repeated wouldn't be included. So the stats won't include their repeats. And it's an unfortunate truth that not all victims are brave enough to come forward to report a molestation, so those incidents won't be included."

It was so depressing to hear these things, because I would go home and *think* about them. "Is there any good news?" I asked.

"Oh, some, for sure. There are indications that sex offenders who receive treatment while incarcerated do have a lower repeat rate. Maybe *lower* isn't the right word. *Slower* is probably more accurate. Among those who do eventually repeat, which we already know is a lot, the interval between release after treatment and reoffense is longer."

"Well, that's a start," I said, almost sarcastically. "Paces the workload."

He chuckled quietly. "I suppose." Then he went serious on me again. "I'll tell you one thing, though, and I really believe this. We can throw all sorts of resources at these guys, and they're still probably going to repeat. I think most of the leading psychologists specializing in sexual-offender research would agree that these criminals can't ever really be cured of their compulsions. Sexual violence can be controlled to a reasonable degree with aggressive treatment and therapy, but the urge will always dwell within these men, and we can only hope to tamp it down. Sooner or later, though, it pops."

"Sweet Jesus. Why?"

"We don't have a clue. You've been reading that book, right?"

"Yeah."

"It goes into great depth in explaining why these guys do this stuff. Nature vs. nurture, biological factors, all that."

"Doesn't help me much. It's not like my perp *might* go active and I can stop him if I just know what to look for. He already has gone active, and now I'm just trying to play catch-up."

"Well, we can draw up a generalized profile like the FBI would, but I'd rather just tell you informally."

"I'd prefer that myself. And there's no time like the present."

"This won't take long," he said. "It's a lot simpler than what most people believe. In a nutshell, they're just wired wrong. Their souls are inside out."

"Their *souls*."

"Yeah. Or gone. Their souls have been stolen some-where along the line."

I was not accustomed to hearing that word in my work. "Well. That does complicate things."

"Yes, it does. It would be easier if there was a struc-tured, agreed-upon methodology for examining someone's soul, but there isn't. Not even for a sound, functional soul. And it appears that you're dealing with someone whose soul is unfathomably out of sync with the rest of the world."

"If you did manage to find out what was inside these guys, I'm guessing you wouldn't like it much."

"Probably not," he said to me.

We went back to his office and worked up a rough profile. My abductor would be male, as we had previously established, and he would also probably be white.

"I don't get that at all," I said when he told me.

"Neither does anyone else. But it's true that about ninety-five percent of serial pedophiles are white. There haven't been too many studies done on that issue, though."

"Gee. I wonder why."

"There's a lot of speculation, most of it understandably controversial. One prominent sociologist put out a theory that white males generally feel more empowered within our society than males of other races; I can see that there might be some validity to that point."

"You guys hold all the tickets."

"Don't go getting feminist on me, Detective. Oh, sorry, I mean Lany. I was just beginning to like you."

I was starting to like him too. We liked each other for a few embarrassing moments, then got back to the matter at hand.

"There is another theory that's been offered to explain the racial imbalance in serial killers. One rather extreme social theorist thinks that males of color do not get the chance to develop patterns of repeated homicide because they are more avidly pursued than whites by law-enforcement agencies."

"You mean to say that they don't get to develop their serial nature because they get caught more often?"

"Precisely."

"Oh, bullshit," I said, forgetting all my manners. "I don't know one cop of *any* color who would go after a white guy any less than a black guy if they thought he cut some kid's head off. What a stupid, stupid notion."

"Well, yes. I would agree with that. And just remember, on April fifteenth, that the development of this theory was probably funded by a federal grant."

"It's total crap, Doc. There are limits to protecting your own, even among the brotherhood."

"I always believed that, but I'm glad to hear you confirm it. That theory always seemed specious to me, even inflammatory."

"Well, if the guy wants someone to get inflamed, he succeeded with me," I said. "So I'm looking for a white male. How old?"

"Eighteen to forty," he said, "but the typical age of serial pedophiles is late twenties to early thirties."

"Not exactly dirty *old* men."

"You usually catch them by the time they get that old."

"We try."

"Now, another thing to remember is that your guy will be something of a loner. He'll keep to himself. He wants to remain anonymous because the limelight bothers him."

"But this abductor is making his grabs in broad daylight, right in front of witnesses."

Erkinnen pressed his point with a smile. "But he's not doing it as himself. Which fits," he said, "because these guys are all big time into fantasies."

"The book talked about that. A lot."

"Rightly. Every serial abductor or killer who's been deeply studied says he started out in fantasies and then progressed on to the real thing when the fantasies didn't do it for him anymore. When he finally does the act, it's usually triggered by some kind of event."

"Such as . . ."

"A loss, an accident, a move, sickness . . . anything that might be traumatic to the individual. Rejection and desertion are big on that list. And these guys are mostly smart—maybe not book smart, but very clever."

My head was beginning to spin. Smaller doses would be better for this type of information. And I was looking forward, rather consciously, to another visit with him. An excuse would make it easier. I stood up. "I have to get going, Errol. But thanks, both for the lunch and for the information. It's incredibly helpful."

"Oh, you're welcome. I'm enjoying this case. It's a real pleasure working on it with you."

Then there was one last moment of uneasy silence between us. "There was one other thing I wanted to say, though," he added.

Instead of the hoped-for dinner invitation, he issued a caveat. "The guy you're looking for hasn't been caught at this before. At least not around here."

I guess even shrinks don't know how to toss off a good closing line.

"How can he say that?" Fred asked me. "How can he know if this guy has been caught or not?"

"He can't, but he's making that guess based on what I've told him, what the evidence bears out."

"You don't have any evidence."

"I have patterns."

"They don't mean diddly-squat in court, you know that."

"It's a much better use of my time to try to find out who it is rather than who it's not. Erkinnen gave me some guidelines."

"Great. I can't wait to hear them."

"Well, for one thing, this guy is probably not smart. But clever. Maybe not the kind of student a teacher would remember, but survivor-type smart."

"You'd think if they're so smart," Fred said, "they'd figure out that we usually get them in the end."

"Yeah, but some of them really crave that attention. Bundy's a good example of that. He didn't achieve that spectacular notice in his normal life. He got close, but he never could quite grab the ring."

"Well, his brains must have lost out to his ego. Imagine trying to be your own defense attorney in a state like Florida. They love a good barbecue down there. And anyway, Bundy killed close to forty women, they say. We're not talking about that kind of numbers."

"Bundy was originally thought to have killed sixteen or seventeen. Those gaps in my perp's time line could be *unreporteds*."

"With all due respect, Lany, your guy is not going after throwaways. The kids he's taking are the kind who get reported."

"How many fourteen-year-olds run away every year?"

"Too many to count, but—"

"I think it's a safe bet that some of the ones who aren't reported are blond and angelic-looking. Practice, maybe, for the ones who *would* be missed."

Fred didn't have anything to say to that. I plunged ahead.

"Erkinnen says that this guy will be a big-time fantasizer. And that's why he impersonates the intimates—he's fantasizing about intimacy. He's creating an illusion of being someone else."

Vuska just sat there with steam rising off his head. Finally he said, "So? How are you going to round up all the fantasizers?"

"He has to have some skills to pull this off, right? He's creating illusions. That's where we need to start."

What a zoo the division room was—it was lousy with crazy white men who either made money at appearing to be something they weren't or wanted to make money that way. It probably goes without saying that there were varying degrees of success and effectiveness from one to the next. Some of them were pathetically bad—but the good ones could really make you smile.

We hauled in every known impersonator and magician in the Los Angeles area, at least those that weren't out on the road performing. A few I'd actually heard of or seen before, one on *The Tonight Show*. He was borderline famous, probably too high-profile to be my pervert. Someone with that much visibility would be too well scrutinized to pull off elaborate crimes without being noticed.

Or so I thought at the time.

It took three days to round everyone up and complete the interviews; the beat cops who actually had to hunt these guys down were talking about it nonstop. By the time it was all over, I was pretty much the laughingstock of the whole division. I came in on the third day and found a sign on my chair that said COMEDY CENTRAL. I couldn't argue that it was all very amusing. What didn't amuse anyone, myself especially, was the undeniable fact that in the long run it hadn't gone anywhere.

So just to be careful, I did what Vuska wanted and dragged in a few more of the local known perverts. I still couldn't shake the sense that it was a lot of wheel-spinning. Most of the guys in our area were molesters, anyway, not abductors or murderers. Not that molestation is an insignificant crime. But killing is a big, big step. The men I interviewed were icky and deviant, but not evil. Most of them were embarrassed and ashamed to be hauled in for that kind of questioning again. One guy pleaded with me to get everyone to leave him alone, said he'd been through this kind of thing seven or eight times before. I did feel kind of bad for him, for a few seconds. Then my sanity returned.

I was looking for a sociopath, someone incapable of genuine shame, and the local perverts that I interviewed were all ashamed to death, which took most of them out of *my* running. My guy probably wasn't a magician, but he morphed himself into someone each of his victims trusted, well enough to get the victim into a car without making a scene. The depth of his illusion-making had to be incredible, nearly flawless. He had to be connected to them; he couldn't pull this off without having a lot of firsthand observation. And the amount of research this perp was doing had to have been phenomenal, his preparation impeccable. Where would he find the time to do it so thoroughly? I couldn't figure out how someone could work at a job, have a life, and manage to devote so much time to this activity.

Unless the work and this activity had something to do with each other. Unless the work *was* his life.

There is a small group of young, hip undercover cops in Los Angeles whose job it is to stay in close contact with the street kids. They get hauled directly out of the academy to mingle with the little lost souls of the City of Angels at some of the more infamous street corners. The first uniform they wear is attitude. They run informants and gather information on the various drug scenes, with the vague and dismally unrealistic hope of trying to keep a street kid from pumping himself full of the bad drugs that inevitably come into town. They're tough to pin down, but Vuska got word to one of their sergeants and managed to arrange for me to get a call.

The young cop I talked to told me right away that what I wanted was a tall order and it might be a while before he got back to me. It surprised the hell out of me when he called me a few days later to say that four, maybe five, kids had abandoned their usual haunts without any advance word. Kids came and went in that scene all the time, he explained, but often if a kid were going to split, he'd generally talk about it first. These boys had all just stopped showing up very abruptly, all within the last year.

Estimates of the disappearance dates were predictably

loose. *The time when we had that big thunderstorm* was one of the offerings; *around the holidays, maybe Thanksgiving or Christmas* was another. It made me really sad to think that a child of roughly the same age as my own son could pass into nothingness without more notice than that.

My perp had been cruising. *Maybe someone saw something,* I said to the young cop. *Maybe one of the other kids— Don't hold your breath,* he replied.

It was all so demoralizing. Everywhere I turned, I found discouragement. Only Errol Erkinnen seemed to be investing himself in these disappearances, and he couldn't pull cops off the ever-increasing post–September 11 security details to go out and canvass neighborhoods where the grabs had been made, talk to friends of the missing boys, all the grunt work we do. In our daily interactions, Escobar and Frazee were oozing encouragement, but their caseloads and schedules were nearly debilitating. I didn't have the heart to take either of them up on their gracious offers of help. If my life were a movie, there would be some astonishing break, an unexpected bit of evidence, or maybe a glaring slip-up on the part of the abductor. It would take 120 minutes to solve the crimes, because that's about the time limit for audiences, who are notoriously fidgety after that amount of time. It was becoming plain to me that my best shot at finding the door to this new Bluebeard's world was to understand how he selected his victims. I made one of my famous charts, spent a lot of time sorting through ethnicity, socioeconomic status, health, all the highly visible qualities. Two of the kids had the same pediatrician, but so what? They lived in the same general area. Three of the families were vegetarian. Again, it was interesting and noticeable, but it meant nothing more than the possibility that the mothers might have shopped in a couple of the same markets or that they owned the same cookbooks. I was looking for a swap meet kind of connection. Were they all at the same flea market one day, and had he written down all the license plates?

Had they all gone to the La Brea Tar Pits on a day when he happened to be there?

I would have to reinterview *all* the families again, with a new focus. What a nasty job that would be—some of these families had lost their kids a long time ago and maybe, just maybe, their wounds were finally starting to heal.

But I was pleasantly surprised. Mrs. McKenzie was really the only one who gave me any trouble. The widow of the suicide was quiet but extremely cooperative. Most of the rest were eager to help and participated fully.

At first I thought it was a lucky coincidence that all of the families were still in the area, until I realized that while there was still hope a child might return, very few parents would move away from the homestead. Talk about having your life on hold; only two of the families had rearranged the missing child's bedroom to any serious extent. I went through all of the bedrooms again. I found myself traveling through a dizzying assortment of wall treatments, each reflecting what the decorating parent hoped and dreamed for the kid. The plaid wallpaper in one of the rooms had me a little concerned. This kid spent all his private time surrounded by infinite perpendicular lines in red and green, and that would be the last thing he saw when he went to sleep at night. What would he dream about?

There was one room where one wall was a floor-to-ceiling chalkboard, at the base of which was a tray of brightly colored chalks. The kid's last artistic opus was still there, untouched—a toothy monster that rose up the full height of the board and breathed some kind of beam out of its nose like an electronic dragon. It caught my attention because it bore a more than passing resemblance to the poster of the dark knight. The shaft of directed light was fiery red-orange and was aimed at some little beady-eyed bad guy who'd been relegated to the bottom two feet of the board. This diminutive ne'er-do-well was about to melt, if I understood the artist's intent correctly. Despite the goriness of the subject matter, it lifted my spirits to think of this kid standing there with all these colors in a bucket and his own permission to go wild on a blackboard. What a treat, even for an adult.

One boy's room, airbrushed blue with white clouds, reminded me of the little boy's room in the movie *Kramer vs. Kramer*. There was a stunning silence about that room, a sense of conflict, as if all were not well within the family when the abduction had taken place and the sense of having caused it had oozed out of the parents into the son's personal space. No Tar Pits souvenirs, though, which was a momentary disappointment. Maybe I was wrong about that connection.

Of all these missing children, only one had shared a room. I didn't spend a lot of time there; there didn't seem to be much of a point. The brother who still inhabited the room was older than his missing sib—seventeen, a miserable age at best. And he was a miserable kid with a slit-eyed look on his face that screamed *go away*. He answered my questions about his brother with clipped brevity. I thanked him for his help and I started out of the room, but just as I was crossing the threshold, he spoke again.

"Do you want to look at the box of his stuff?"

Stuff was what I craved. "Yes, if you don't mind letting me see it."

"You better ask my mom, though."

It turned out to be good advice. The mother became quite agitated, but in the end she allowed me to take it, with the understanding that I would inventory the contents and bring everything back when I was done examining it.

I experienced a sad letdown as I left that last house, box in hand. My next order of business would be to create another masterpiece, another perfectly organized layout of everything I knew about my victims and their personal habits, including each one's Tar Pits factor. What sign would they put on my desk when I got through with this one? MUSEUM ENTRANCE, maybe.

Ordinarily, this kind of task excited me, made me feel like I was on the verge of some wondrous revelation. Okay, so some of them had been to the Tar Pits Museum, but it didn't necessarily mean anything. There were other obvious commonalities: a shared disdain for clothes hangers, and a tendency to have more video games than books. Mismatched socks, candy wrappers, stained Popsicle sticks.

I got back to my desk, set the box down behind my chair. There were a dozen messages on my voice mail, one or two from lawyers, who I just bet had magicians and illusionists for clients. The thought of calling any of them back made me nearly nauseated. I chose instead to concentrate on the maddening question that torments every mother as Christmas approaches, in the hope that it would clarify a few things on this case.

What do adolescent boys like?

In total frustration, I rolled my chair away from my desk. I ran into the box and got jolted backward.

It would be just another dead end, so why bother? There wasn't going to be anything earth-shattering in there.

I opened it, Pandora again. Sneakers, baseball glove, a stack of comic books tethered by elastic bands. A tube of bright blue zinc oxide nose protector that was shoved into a baseball cap of the same color. Superhero cards in a plastic box. Three posters rolled up, one of a rock star, one of a famous wrestler—

The answer to the Christmas question came crashing through the haze: Adolescent boys like beasts. Monsters, gremlins, satyrs, gargoyles, centaurs, basilisks, chimeras, dragons, cyclopes, serpents, and werewolves—these were a few of their favorite things. The last poster I unrolled was the same one I'd seen before: the same beast, carrying the dark knight from the La Brea Tar Pits. The knight still had no face.

But I knew, I just *knew,* that he was the monster I was looking for.

fifteen

CHÈRE MAMAN,

June has begun gloriously, with blue skies, warm winds, and the air thick with the scent of jasmine. We are glad for its abundance this year, for there is a sister in one of the adjacent convents who can extract the scent from a potful of the blossoms as if she were a conjurer, a useful and welcome heresy if such can be said to exist. She uses it as a base on which to build more-complex fragrances, all of which enhance worship by inducing a state of calm and peace in the worshiper.

Three days ago his Holiness turned an ankle, which is said to have become quite blue and yellow in the aftermath of the injury, but he was otherwise unharmed. Of course it cannot be left at that; the cardinal who was with him at the time says that he simply collapsed, but a bishop who was also present says that he appeared to have caught the hem of his robe on the tip of one of his slippers. Now we have an intrigue between a cardinal and a bishop within the Pope's immediate circle; it does not require much imagination to know who will triumph

*in that test of might! Whisperings about the state of his
Holiness's health are due to begin by sunset.*

*I hope these bits of news will help to take your mind off
the terrible events by which you are now surrounded. None of
our paltry intrigues can approach your fare in Brittany. Take
heart, dear Mother, and be strong as always; God will do as
He will do, and we must accept His will as part of a plan, the
wisdom of which we may never understand but of which we
may be assured.*

What wisdom? There was none that I could see in
the unfolding of these events.

The jasmine of which Jean spoke so fondly had yet to
even bud in the north, but that was no bother to me, for I
always found its scent cloying, especially in perfumes;
better the stink of the body, in which there is admirable
honesty. The Brittany sunlight is always thinner than that
with which the fair south is blessed; the air is cooler and
the scents more muted. If we take comfort in any success
here, it is that of our orchards under *Frère* Demien's mas-
terful husbandry. The remnants of pear blossoms had
fallen to the ground on Brittany breezes like so much ill-
timed snow, and if the summer remained fair we would
have a bountiful harvest. I can almost taste the *pots des
fruits* that will grace our board when the yield comes in.

Cher *Jean,*

*Through your eyes and words I know the beauty of
Avignon, which helps to keep my woes at bay, if only for a
moment. When I travel there in the fall it will all seem so familiar to me. No doubt you will recall what June looks like
here, but this year the flowers and trees seem more wondrous
than ever to me, a bounty for which I am grateful, because I
feel so helpless in the wake of our discoveries. I feel as if the
very soul has been stolen from within me. This quest, begun by
me with such good intent, now seems to have all the breath
and blood and will required for self-perpetuation, regardless of
my wishes. I am so deeply torn; I both crave and despise the*

dark knowledge that Jean de Malestroit is uncovering and, as I made him promise, has shared with me. My desire to know the fate of the lost young ones is quickly being overshadowed by my fear of coming to know who has taken them. Each day a fresh arrow is shot into my breast, and through no amount of effort can I seem to pull out the barbs, which fester within and will poison me if I do not get them out soon.

The sharpest of those heart arrows was the growing certainty that Milord Gilles was not the man I believed him to be. Once he had been the veritable brother of my own son, flawed indeed but still a part of my family. He was one of the few remaining links I had to that lost child, and now I stood to see that destroyed.

Rumors of all this are spreading like a fresh plague, Jean de Malestroit told me one morning. *We must be discreet, so Milord does not get wind of all this unnecessarily. We need not upset him without due cause.*

What he meant to say was that he did not wish Milord to know that he was under suspicion. My bishop needn't have worried, as it turned out, for Milord was much preoccupied with his own affairs and could not be bothered with answering common rumors. He was far too busy fending off the considerable wrath of Duke Jean after the incident at Saint-Etienne-de-Mer-Morte.

⚜

"Fifty thousand *ecus? Mon Dieu!*"

The letter from Duke Jean authorizing that enormous fine lay on the table before Jean de Malestroit, whose look of satisfaction could barely be hidden.

"Almost impossible for anyone to pay," I said. "All the King's jewels would not cover it. Even at the height of his fortune, Lord Gilles would have struggled with that amount."

His Eminence did not need to speak to reveal his

pleasure in this new development. It adorned his face more visibly than a plume on a cat.

I moved toward the window, where the air was not so stale as that which seemed suddenly to surround me. The gray gloomy sky was no comfort. As I gazed outward, I heard Jean de Malestroit arise from his chair. He came up behind me and laid a hand upon my shoulder in what seemed to be an attempt at sympathy. "One is never truly pleased by another's fall from grace, Guillemette, but this time even you must admit that it is well deserved."

His comfort would have meant more to me if his glee had been less obvious. I could not reasonably argue that the fine was improper, but it gave rise to other concerns, among them the possibility of a violent reaction from Milord. "The man is a warrior," I said. "When you strike him a blow, he will surely respond with a goodly blow of his own."

My bishop managed to suppress a blossoming smile. "Without credit, the man is crippled, and with such a fine hanging over his head, no one will lend him a *sou*. We shall see how he reacts, when he has to pay the cost out of his own treasury."

⚜

Milord reacted as if there were no cost at all. There came yet another outburst from him, perhaps the most crazed to date. In what was described by those present as a fit of rage, Milord dragged the priest Le Ferron out of the castle at Saint-Etienne in chains and took him to the dungeon of his own castle at Tiffauges. There he subjected Le Ferron to torture and humiliation worse than he had perpetrated on his direst enemies, and word of it got back to Le Ferron's brother, Geoffrey, who was quite predictably outraged beyond reason.

"But why Tiffauges?" I fretted aloud.

"Because it is outside Duke Jean's authority," Jean

de Malestroit replied. "The only other place he might have brought him was Pouzages. He has lost Champtocé again."

His hold on Tiffauges and Pouzages was artificial, since they actually belonged to his wife, who had heretofore not allowed her desperate husband to sell them. I pitied Lady Catherine—we all did. She was a ghost of a woman, a formless thing without influence, always so silent and dour. Though Gilles had sired a daughter by her as was his duty, I am certain that they both had gritted their teeth through the entire act by which little Marie was conceived. Ironically, the little girl was a sweet and precious child and the closest thing that I would ever have to a grandchild. I often wondered how she could have been the product of such discord.

For discord there was, and plenty of it. Milord never spoke a kind word to his wife nor showed her any favor at all in the time I observed them; in the best of their days together, his treatment of her could not be described as anything beyond polite. More often he showed complete disdain for her, except in her appearance—he was always careful to see to her wardrobe so she would be a proper ornament for him. Had he treated her as most noble husbands treat their acquired wives, with distant courtesy and discretion in his philanderings, we would all have admired him more. But he tried to bully her into submission in property matters where her consent was required, almost always with the help of Jean de Craon. Often we heard the shouts of coercion ringing through the chambers and halls of Champtocé, and we all feared for her.

Once, perhaps a year earlier, Jean de Malestroit had asked, "Tell me, Guillemette, you would know—does he beat her?"

That question should not have surprised me as much as it did, occasioned as it had been by a discussion on the nature of marriage, that discourse itself having been prompted by a scandalous murder. A certain noble-woman had been subjected to one too many beatings and had answered her husband with the point of a dagger, well-placed and quite capably thrust. The vicious rogue died naked and writhing in his own bed with his wife standing equally naked over him, dripping with his hated blood. We had all seen the bruises on her from time to time and noted her shamed looks, though none of us would dare to interfere—such matters were between a husband and wife alone, unless the wife happened to have powerful kin. Hers were not powerful enough to save her from the gallows, but there was much discourse in the aftermath of the affair on what husbands and wives owe to each other and how they ought to conduct themselves. There was little agreement among the participants, but I could not help but think of the Wife of Bath, who cast her judgment on marriage of high estate with such precision: *As in a noble household, we are told, not every dish and vessel's made of gold. . . .*

"One must wonder what occurs between them," I replied diplomatically—I am certain now that he wanted verification from me and was disappointed with my response. "With a temper such as Milord possesses, there is surely a danger of him striking Lady Catherine from time to time."

"But you do not know for sure. . . ."

"No, Eminence," I said. I remember feeling slightly miffed at this pointed inquiry—I had been Milord's wet nurse, not his wife's chambermaid, which position might have afforded me a closer view but less dignity. "Such knowledge would have required me to be present in Lady Catherine's bedchamber. Milord himself was rarely there. And when he did make an appearance, I assure you, I was not invited."

But the man was a dogged inquisitor and would not

let the matter lay. "None of her own ladies spoke of it, not even in passing?"

I smiled very thinly but with great satisfaction. "Eminence, I am shocked," I told him. "Would you have me listening to such gossip?"

Thereafter he asked no more questions. But it set me to wondering on the matter myself, not that it was my business. Milord had, after all, abducted Lady Catherine into marriage against her own will and that of her family in an affair that very nearly prompted a war, then falsely wooed her with such fervor that she actually began to believe his avowals of love. By the time they stood before a priest (who was convinced by the tip of a sword to perform the ceremony against her family's orders), Lady Catherine de Thouars was willing to swear her loving devotion to Baron Gilles de Rais. Imagine her disappointment as the true nature of her marriage unfolded.

But if Milord had subjected her to ill treatment in this particular matter of property, it did not have the desired effect, for Pouzages and Tiffauges remained firmly in her control. Still, he must have done something to her in the wake of the Saint-Etienne affair. Or perhaps her shame was so great that she could no longer remain in Brittany. She fled to a cousin's hotel at Pouzages in France and took ten-year-old Marie with her, leaving Gilles de Rais alone and furious.

I could not help but wonder what Jean would think of these developments in the protected little kingdom of the Pope in Avignon. *I fear for Milord,* I wrote, *I fear for his soul. Has more news of this reached you from other sources,* I asked him, *and if so, what are they saying of it? We have tried to be discreet, but rumors do have wings. . . .*

When I went to Jean de Malestroit after Matins to give him this letter for conveyance to Avignon, I found him in a state of deep concentration of the sort usually reserved for important affairs of state or matters of deep faith. The page on the table before him was lumpy in quality and odd-shaped, as if it had been made by the writer himself. I would not have given it much attention except for the notice his Eminence paid it.

I waited in silence, as was required of me; when he finished reading, he set the page down and rubbed his eyes for a few moments. Then he covered his face with his hands and sighed through his fingers.

"Eminence?" I said quietly.

He did not lift his face. It remained buried in his hands. "Yes," came the muffled acknowledgment.

"You are troubled...."

He looked up at me. "You cannot find this a surprising condition in me right now."

He patted the parchment and indicated with a nod that I ought to look at it myself. He rose up from his chair and gestured for me to sit and read.

The writing was crude and there was no signature. But the descriptions were vivid and could not have been made up except by the most talented tale-spinner. Three accounts of witchcraft during which Milord was alleged to have tried to invoke the demon for his own purposes were revealed.

My hands trembled as I read the page.

They took candles and a few other things, as well as books of instruction, and, using the tomes to guide them, drew several large circles with the tip of Milord's sword. After the drawing was done and a torch lit, all but the conjurer and Milord left the room. They placed themselves in the middle of the circles, at a certain angle close to the wall, at which time the conjurer traced another character in the soil with burning coal that they had brought and poured upon it some magnetite and aromatics, whereafter a sweet intoxicating smoke arose....

The conjurer. I stood up when I finished and handed the rough parchment back to him. "Do you believe this?"

He hesitated slightly. "The incidents are so clearly described that one has reason to think it all possible."

The answer to the question I posed next was well known to me, but I asked anyway, hoping for better. "What is to be done now?"

He paced around the chamber, but his steps made no noise. "These allegations are grave enough that I am required, even if it were against my own will, to put them under official investigation. With the matter of heresy so credibly raised ... Duke Jean will require it of me to proceed against him."

"A charge of heresy must be prosecuted by a judge of the Inquisition," I said, as wetness welled up in my eyes. "Whether to proceed or not is yours to decide, and yours alone."

He would require it of himself, I had no doubt.

Uncontainable tears dripped down my cheeks. The deep anguish that flowed through my veins was bitter and hot and threatened to collapse me at any moment.

Jean de Malestroit put his arm around my shoulder and placed a small, brotherly kiss on my forehead.

"It is not mine to decide, Sister," he maintained, "but God's."

I whispered in a trembling voice, "I know only too well how *that* will go. God always decides in ways that do not favor me and mine."

"You must have more faith. God favors all His creatures, but we often do not recognize His favor when it comes our way. But none of us can hide—we must acquiesce with grace and acceptance."

There would be no grace or acceptance from Gilles de Rais for *this* act of God. Faced with the certainty of his own imminent ruin, Milord made the boldest move—if not bold, then surely lunatic. He went to see Duke Jean.

He was no stranger to boldness, certainly not to bravery; they say that when Jean d'Arc required it of him, he fought like Ariel, God's own lion. On the fourth day of May in the year 1429, young Lord de Rais arrived with Lord Dunois in Orléans with the reinforcements and supplies that the Maid's armies required, if there was to be any hope of victory at all. In a field outside the town, the maid Jean went forth to meet them in the company of many notable lords, among them Sainct Severe and the Baron de Coulonces, highly ransomable men whose capture would be a coup for any Englishman. Together with the Bastard Charles, these lords rode into the town of Orléans, passing directly in front of the English. It must be considered the greatest of her miracles that no sword was raised, no lance or arrow sent flying against them.

But that same day, Lord Dunois received an intelligence that the English captain John Fastolf was on his way to Orléans with fresh troops and supplies, and so the English failure to attack was explained—they had wisely held off in anticipation of greater numbers.

Dunois went straightaway to the Maid's lodgings to advise her of this disturbing turn of events, Etienne recounted to me. *He was fairly frothing with distress. She bade Dunois to let her know when Fastolf arrived and then, being completely exhausted, went to the bed she shared with her hostess. How can a warrior go to sleep with such an event impending? Soldiers do not behave so!*

That soldier was a young girl, I told my husband. *She required rest.*

We all thought it preposterous—foolish beyond imagining! That a warrior should not make ready when a battle looms. . . .

She would not rest long. No sooner had her pages

and hostess retired after settling her in than she came awake holding her head—fresh voices were screaming within her. She had seen and heard a vicious battle under way but swore on the Virgin that it was a vision, not a dream, so she sprang up from her bed and went outside with the purpose of ascertaining where that battle might be taking place. There again she was gripped by a new vision; she fell to the ground with her head clutched between her hands, crying, *Les voix, les voix!* The voices were commanding her, but she did not know what God wanted her to do. Should she intercept Fastolf, who had not made his presence known yet, or should she look for a different battle? Her clamorous wails of indecision woke everyone in her lodging and all those in the near surrounds.

But then Jean d'Arc rose above her own confusion; she threw on her white armor and rode out to the Burgoyne gate, where flames could be seen leaping into the sky. Faint sounds of battle came from that direction, and before anyone could stop her, she was riding toward it all. Her page sounded the alarm to the lords whose armies had been gathered in her support, among them Lord Gilles, who, according to Etienne ...

... *let loose a string of profanity sufficient to wilt the very leaves. Had the Maid heard him just then, she would have banished him from her side, for she had strictly forbidden such language among her troops. All would have been lost.*

I could only imagine the florid words that flowed off his tongue that day; Etienne would not repeat them verbatim, for he would not have them heard by any lady, least of all his own wife. But I knew—Milord had a distinct way with words. At a very early age he liked to shock me with profanity as vulgar as that which regularly poured out of his beastly grandfather.

I shudder to think that but for Jean d'Arc being out of earshot just then, France might have been lost, for it was Milord Gilles de Rais who rescued her from sure death that day. Had she sent him away, who knows what the outcome might have been!

At the gate she found citizens of the town engaged in a pitched and bloody battle—the fools had already begun an action against the despised English on their own. They didn't know how to fight and had no weapons beyond clubs and scythes, so when the Maid arrived, she found dead and wounded all about her in mud so saturated with blood that it fairly glowed red. She sat paralyzed on her horse for a time and wept as she regarded the legions of those who had fallen, according to the few who lived to speak of seeing her there. It is said that in that moment she was desperate to confess her sins, even before this day of grievous sinfulness had come to an end. But God interceded in her reverie—a miracle in and of itself—and prompted her to take command of those citizens who had survived.

But here God nearly deserted her. The English commander Talbot saw the opportunity and sent out troops to attack her from the rear. She was trapped between two enemy forces with no route available for retreat. When Milord learned of this terrible situation, he and the rogue warrior La Hire rode directly to Saint-Loup. They came up from the rear and began to attack the English forces with as much viciousness as they themselves had used in slaying the villagers over whom Jean had wept only an hour before. Jean then turned her own ragged troops against the English as well, and now the enemy was itself caught in the sort of trap they had set for her earlier.

Had Milord not come to her aid that day, the Bastard Charles would never have been crowned. We prevailed in battle despite great odds against us, largely on the shoulders of Gilles de Rais.

The trays of our supper lay before us on the table. After a small, polite belch, Jean de Malestroit surprised me with a revelation. "Milord told his servants that he went to Josselin to collect monies owed to him by the Duke. But no one will be fooled. Many of his servants have gone unpaid, and they are grumbling mightily."

"You must have spies among them."

Jean de Malestroit did not deny but instead deflected my charge. He wiped his mouth with a *serviette* and pushed the tray away. "The hour of Vespers approaches," he said. "We ought to be about our preparations."

I could do little more than lower my gaze and nod. We rose up together in a rustle of fabric. I followed him out of his chamber as dutifully as ever.

But when we were outside, I feigned exasperation and said, "Goodness, I almost forgot. Sister Élène asked me to find her before now; I think it may be about a housekeeping matter."

"Well, hurry, then. God does not like to be kept waiting."

I nodded. Then, after a quick bow, I turned away from him, just in time—skirts in hand, I flew down the dark hallway until I was far enough away so he could not hear my sobs.

⁂

The courtyard was dark and quiet; a small breeze brought relief from the heat of the day, which lingered oppressively. The mystery of the Mass remained with me still.

"I have just heard a tempting bit of news," *Frère* Demien said as we progressed slowly toward the abbey. "I have learned that Eustache Blanchet fled Machecoul some time ago."

"No," I said, "he would never."

"*Yes.* To Mortagne—they say he was attempting to leave Milord's service."

They say.

That would explain Blanchet's absence at Pax. "But why? He coveted his position as Milord's priest, and I cannot imagine him giving it up."

Frère Demien seemed equally confused, and shrugged. "One cannot say, Sister. It is indeed uncanny. Perhaps he did so under duress. Blanchet is back at Machecoul now, but there is apparently no peace between them."

The bold or desperate doings of an ordinary man are not always worthy of a crier's voice, but those of a priest draw particular attention, especially among his higher-ups. I wondered why Jean de Malestroit had kept it from me.

When I later heard Blanchet's private testimony, I understood.

Poitou and Henriet escorted François Prelati and myself from our lodging at Saint-Florent-le-Vieil in Tours to Milord's castle at Tiffauges. Now, in that period Lord Gilles sought the company of Prelati frequently—yes, I will confirm that he was intrigued by the Italian conjurer in many and diverse ways, and I have come to curse myself for bringing him into Milord's service. When Milord came to the room where I and some others were lodged, we all departed to another room in order that Prelati and Milord might be alone. The following night I saw them leave the lodging room and enter a low hall located directly behind us; they remained there for some time. I heard cries and pleadings to the effect of, "Come, Satan," or simply "Come!" I heard Prelati say also, "to our aid . . ." or a similar utterance of supplication. There were more words, none of which I could understand, and then Milord and Prelati stayed in the room for another half hour, with candles burning all about.

God have mercy, within a short time a cold wind rose up and blew wildly through the castle, making loud and unholy shrieks as it whirled around me, and I thought for sure that this gale must be the voice of the devil himself. I went to seek counsel with Robin Romulart, who was also at Tiffauges then. We were in accord that Milord and Prelati were invoking demons and that neither one of us wanted anything to do with it.

On the morrow at first light I took it upon myself to escape Tiffauges and that unholiness and went straightaway to Mortagne to the hotel of Bouchard-Menard. Seven weeks I remained there, during which time I received many letters from Milord asking me to come to him, saying that I would find myself in good standing with him and Prelati. I refused him time and again and eventually failed even to answer; I had no desire to be in his presence nor that of Prelati and his demons.

In the time I was lodged with Bouchard-Menard, there came another lodger, one Jean Mercier who was the castellan of La-Roche-sur-Yon in Luçon. Mercier told me that there was much public rumor in Nantes and elsewhere that Milord Gilles was writing a book in blood by his own hand and that he intended to use that book's power to tempt the devil into giving him as many fortresses as he desired. Thus he would restore himself to his proper state of Lordship and, when he did so, no one would ever be able to harm him again. I did not ask whence the blood for these writings came.

The very next day the goldsmith Petit came to l'hôtel Bouchard-Menard to see me on Milord's behalf. He told me that both Milord and Prelati were anxious about my welfare and conveyed their urgent request that I come to them. To which I said, in no event would I go to see him, because of the rumors I had heard. And I told Petit to say to Milord that if such whisperings were true, he had best cease his activities altogether and forthwith, for it is wrong to engage in such vile practices.

Petit must have conveyed this message from me to Milord and Prelati, for Milord immediately imprisoned the messenger in the castle at Saint-Etienne, which castle he later gave over

*to the Duke's Treasurer Le Ferron and then harshly took back.
He sent Poitou, Henriet, Gilles de Sille, and another manservant named Lebreton to seize me at Mortagne, against which I
was powerless. I suppose news of Petit's imprisonment ought
to have made me more wary—it would have been wise for
me to flee Mortagne at that time.*

*But I did not, though God alone knows why. Milord's men
then took me as far as Roche-Serviere, and it was there that
they told me I would also be imprisoned at Saint-Etienne
and that Milord would have me killed for spreading such gossip and rumor as I had. Whereupon I staunchly refused to go
further, for I had spread no rumors as he had accused me. I
made such threats of retribution as I could not possibly have
carried out, which for some uncanny reason had the desired effect upon my captors. I suppose all men believe that priests
have certain powers that others do not, though whatever Godly
power I might once have had has surely been destroyed by my
congress with men we have come to know as heretics. They did
not harm me but instead took me directly to Machecoul to see
Milord. I was lodged there against my will for two months.*

⚜

Gilles de Rais left Josselin unscathed, at least corporally.
What effect the audience might have had on his spirit I
could not say, but with his situation so desperate, I imagined that Milord must have been enraged by the unfa-
vorable outcome of the discussions between himself and
Duke Jean. If his Eminence knew anything, he was not
speaking. We went about our daily activities with what
looked to be calm on the surface, but underneath it lay a
seething cauldron of inquisitiveness.

Matins, Vespers, and all that lay between—that was
my life. I spent my time traversing the courtyard from
the abbey to the palace and back again, going from one
duty to the next. One night as I was abbey-bound I
heard a rider off in the distance. I had just entered the

arch-covered passageway that skirts the courtyard and leads directly to the convent and slipped into the protective shadows when the sound of fast hooves fell on my ears, faintly at first, then in an awesome crescendo, until the earth beneath my feet shook with the force of it well before its source—a rider who thundered in the courtyard—was revealed. From somewhere out of another shadow, a groom appeared to take control of the lathered animal as the rider leaped off.

My curiosity burned; a rider from Avignon would not travel with such urgency, unless the rumors about his Holiness's health were indeed true. But the sky had not yet fallen, so I assumed they were not.

I spent the night in wide-eyed speculation; what little sleep I managed was poor in quality. The next morning when I sought out the Bishop, I was as brittle as an icicle. The morning's customary politenesses, usually such a comforting ritual, suddenly seemed a bothersome overindulgence.

"The messenger," I said anxiously.

Jean de Malestroit seemed perplexed. "There has been nothing more from Avignon, save what I have already given you," he told me.

"No, Eminence, I mean the rider who came last night as I was retiring. . . ."

After a pause he said, "Ah. *That* messenger. I wondered if anyone had seen him."

"He came in like a thunderstorm. No one could have failed to *hear* him."

"Ah, yes . . . well, I shall have to make rules regarding the approach of riders so no one will be disturbed."

"Was he from Josselin?"

He nodded slowly and then began shuffling parchments, as if that might actually thwart my inquiries.

"Well, what had he to say?"

Suddenly Jean de Malestroit began to squirm, rather

uncomfortably. Finally he said, "I regret to tell you that Duke Jean has not revealed the details of what happened between them. He said nothing of import in the letter he sent beyond that Milord Gilles asked for his help and support in resolving the Saint-Etienne affair."

"Which, naturally, he did not receive, no matter what the enticement."

"No, he did not. And he has nothing more to offer in the way of enticements. No means by which he might bargain anymore."

I had not understood that his fortunes had diminished to that degree. "But . . ." I said, "surely he must have said more than that. . . ." I felt tongue-tied; I knew not how to extract from him the knowledge I craved. He was subtly avoiding all mention of how he had been told to proceed, which was an entirely separate matter from what had transpired at Josselin and would surely have been included in the urgent missive. He turned away from me again and started toward his study table, which was strewn from one end to the other with parchments. Once he lost himself in them, I would not be able to break through.

There was no recourse but to ask, "Are you to proceed against Milord?"

Again, he did not answer directly. "I have been told of Milord's movements," he said. "He has left the castle unharmed but has not yet returned to Machecoul; he settled yesterday into the place where he lodged on his last visit to Josselin, the house of a man named Lemoine outside the walls of Vannes."

"I know this house—it is a fine manor." I could easily imagine Milord seeking refuge in that elegant and sumptuous place. "But I wonder at his purpose for malingering."

"Buchet," his Eminence said.

We would hear later, from Poitou, of the influence Buchet had on Gilles de Rais.

Buchet brought a boy who looked to be age ten or thereabouts to Milord at Lemoine's house, where Milord had carnal knowledge of the child. He practiced his lust upon the boy in the same vile manner as he had with so many others before: First he caused his own member to become stiff by rubbing it in his own hands, and then he worked his stiffened member between the thighs of the boy, whereafter he used the boy's unnatural opening to achieve his release. All the while this boy was hung from a beam above us with ropes around his hands. I had rendered the boy silent with a gag stuffed into his mouth. Therefore he made no cries of protest, though his expression was full of terror and desperation.

When Milord was through with the boy, he ordered Henriet and me to kill him. But there was no place in Lemoine's house in which this might be done without attracting notice. So we led the child to the nearby house of a man named Boetden, where the squires who accompanied us on the journey were lodged. We knew that this landlord would leave us to our purposes there and reveal nothing of what he saw or heard. Milord seemed to have a retinue of such accomplices throughout the land, one in almost every parish we visited, though how he comes upon them and secures their cooperation I do not know.

In Boetden's house we severed the boy's head from his body. Either the knife was dull or the neck bones strong, but we had a miserable time of it. Milord became sorely frustrated and anxious, so we burned the head right there in the room where the killing had taken place. But how were we to get rid of the body without anyone beyond the landlord seeing us do so? Boetden's house was near the center of the village and quite exposed, so we could not do our work outside. It came to me finally that the child's body should be put into the latrine in this house, and when I spoke this idea aloud, the others agreed that it was a good one. So we secured the boy's own belt tightly around him and lowered him down the hole.

To my great dismay, the depth of the ordure was not sufficient to cover the body. It stuck up, a headless witness to what had been perpetrated upon him.

I was lowered, with much difficulty, into the latrine by Henriet and Buchet, who stayed above in order to better control my descent. There were moments as I hung suspended above the pit when I wondered if they would let me fall into it after I had done what was bidden of me. They insisted it must be me, for I was the originator of the reckless scheme, and they thought I ought to be the one to suffer because it had gone wrong.

After much strain and labor I managed to sink the body deeply enough into the slop that it could no longer be seen from above. I accomplished this by pushing it into the ooze with my own hands; despite my efforts it bobbed up twice and I had to push it under again until it stayed down without me holding it. And when I was pulled out of the pit I retched and retched until I thought my stomach would leap out of my body.

chapter 16

YOU'D EXPECT THE LA BREA TAR PITS to be in a more remote location, but there it is, plunked down in the middle of all those glass and steel behemoths in central Los Angeles. There's a grassy area around it, but with all the surrounding "civilization," it's easy to forget that the tar pits were there first. You smell them before you see them; makes you think someone is working on a roof in the hot sun. I almost like that smell if I'm just passing through it. But all day long? I don't think so.

When I remarked on that to the museum director, he just gave me this wild-eyed smile and took in a big long sniff. After that I expected to see him beat his chest and shriek, but somehow he managed to contain himself. Nice guy, completely unabashed in his love for the establishment he oversaw. I was expecting someone more academic, and I'd prepared myself to have to grapple with the pale-ontological equivalent of an art fart, which is what we run into when we have to go to the art museum. They all think cops are terminally uncultured meatheads, but they do

248 • Ann Benson

want our advice about their bothersome little security problems. Go figure.

But this guy genuinely adored his job. Several times I had to say, *That's very impressive, sir, and I hate to interrupt you, but I need to ask you some questions of a more specific nature....* He was always very apologetic about getting off track.

I described the poster I'd seen. He went to a drawer and pulled one out, rolled it open for my examination. "This one?"

Again, it made me shiver. "Yeah."

"A bit anachronistic," he said, "but what the heck—you have to have some fun every now and then."

So the poster had been his idea. My guess was that he'd spent a lot of time justifying its inaccuracy. "It's a great poster," I said. "I'll bet it got a lot of people in here who wouldn't otherwise have come."

"Oh, no question about it. That exhibit brought in the most diverse attendance we've ever had. People from all over the country—all over the world."

I thought, *And all over Los Angeles.*

He went into a drawer in his desk and produced a volume with the same image on the cover. "The book was also a huge success. It was very pricey because of all the color printing, but we sold a slew of them. A *slew*. A lot of money went into our endowment fund from that book."

"It must have been an exciting experience to be involved in it."

"Only the best of my career. Especially in the development stages. I got to work with some of the most talented people."

Then he let out a big sigh and shook his head.

"And to think that it almost didn't happen."

In the hope that he'd explain, I waited a few seconds before asking. "I don't remember reading anything in the press about it not happening...."

"Oh, you wouldn't have. We kept it very quiet. We notified the police, though, so I'm a little surprised you didn't know about it. We had a bomb threat."

"Really."

"Yes, really. I suppose it's good that you weren't aware of it, because we were trying to keep it quiet. One of the donors was very publicity-shy. We were afraid that he was going to pull out. Took some last-minute negotiations to keep him in. It turned out to be a hoax, but that donor—he was actually the creator of a large number of the Animatronic devices—insisted that we put a better security system in place."

"Probably not a bad idea, anyway."

"Well, it was quite expensive. He ended up funding some of it himself."

All very interesting, but probably not germane to my quest. "I'm working on a case," I said, "that involves several young boys. A number of them seem to have visited this exhibit. It's the only common thread I can establish so far, so I'd like to start looking into some of the people who worked on the exhibit."

He wore a hungry-to-know expression. "How ominous."

"Yes. Unfortunately, until I've developed my leads a little more, I can't tell you anything further."

"That's too bad, because I might be able to narrow it down a little for you. There were hundreds of people involved with that exhibit."

"I assume they weren't all museum employees."

"Very few. We contract out for a lot of the services like cleaning and supplies. The security system we were talking about—another company supplied the employees. We had our own cameras, of course, and the exhibitor set up the videotape system for us, complete with the blue screen—"

"The blue screen?"

"Yes. I thought everyone knew about that. It was almost as much of an attraction as the exhibit itself."

In response to my bewildered look, he said, "Do you have children?"

"Three."

"*Hmm.* I thought just about every kid in L.A. came to this exhibit."

"Their father did bring my kids with a group, and I think one of the other parents came too. But I don't remember hearing about a blue screen." They'd talked about the moving animals and knights but not the blue screen.

"The idea was to make the security system part of the fun, to keep it from becoming too much of a distraction. It was really quite a spectacular setup. We had a video system, broadcast quality, not like what you'd expect for a security camera. All the visitors were recorded as they passed through the waiting line. There was a fluoroscope to examine the backpacks and purses, but the visitors got to operate the machines themselves and examine their own bags as they passed through. Of course, a trained security person was there watching, but it made the visitors feel like they had a real stake in the security. It was all wonderfully interactive. But the highlight of the whole thing was this blue screen. It's what they use in film special effects when they want to insert people in backgrounds that have already been filmed. In our case, we encouraged visitors to clown around in front of the camera, and then as they moved down the line they could see themselves against a variety of different backgrounds. One was this sort of primordial ooze, another was a medieval forest with a boar that jumped out from behind a tree. Everyone loved it, and we got a good image of every person who passed through the line without seeming like Big Brother. It was very clever. The donor went to great lengths to make it really special."

It seemed a little excessive to me, but I didn't tell him

that. "So these people were taped. With their knowledge, of course."

"Yes. The whole thing was for fun, really. And they could buy copies of their segments if they wanted to. That offset a good portion of the cost."

"And were there security guards on the premises otherwise?"

"Yes, two roving, two who stayed in a booth to monitor the various cameras."

"Were the security tapes kept?"

"Not by us. The exhibit ended more than two years ago. We've copied over the tapes we had from our own internal system, many times by now, I'm sure. But I don't know about the blue-screen tapes."

"Who would have them, if they weren't destroyed?"

"The security company." Then he hesitated a moment. "Or perhaps the donor." .

The donor. Not the donor Mr. So and So, or a donor. Just *the donor*. "May I have this donor's name, please?"

Another little hesitation. "He likes to keep a low profile."

I thought, *Tough,* but said, "I'm sure he'd understand if you gave us his name, in view of the situation we're investigating."

"I won't be able to make that kind of determination unless I know the nature of the 'situation.' "

I could see that one hand would have to wash the other. "All I can tell you at this point is that we are looking into some incidents of pedophilia, possibly connected."

It would have been simpler to say *serial* pedophilia, but he gasped anyway. "Well. I guess that's pretty serious, then."

"It is." I handed him my notebook with a blank page. Maybe if he didn't say the name aloud, he wouldn't feel like he'd betrayed any kind of trust. "Now, if you'd write down the name of that donor, please, I'd be grateful."

He took the notebook and removed the pen I'd clipped to the right side. With a dramatic flourish, he clicked out the point and scribbled. Then he clipped the pen back on the pad, flipped the whole thing closed, and handed it to me.

I didn't look through the pages to see who it was. I didn't want to show inordinate surprise if the person was famous. "I'll also need the name of the company from whom you contracted the security guards. And the one that does your cleaning as well." I handed back the pad.

"Certainly," he said as he wrote. "Then will there be anything else I can help you with at the moment?"

"I'd be grateful if you would point me to your employment office. I'll need to look at some of the records for the exhibit period."

By then his posture had stiffened significantly. *The thrill is gone,* his expression said. I would have to come back another time to get anything more specific out of him. But I had my first new lead in weeks.

Wilbur Durand. He was a special-effects whiz kid who'd done an impressive amount of work in Hollywood, mostly on horror-type films. I began a search for information about him, which took a backseat to reinterviewing the families and the failed suspects, from which I didn't want to be distracted.

And then came the ultimate distraction: Five days before the two-month mark, a twelve-year-old boy was reported missing by his parents. But this time there was a stunning departure from the previous pattern: The boy was black, albeit relatively light-skinned. Everything else was right; he was a good kid, last seen with an older brother. The patrol cop who took the initial call had learned that there was some strife between the two brothers and passed that information on to me right away. Before going out to the home, I called and spoke with the parents. It didn't take long to establish the source of the strife: The biological father of the missing boy was the mother's second husband and stepfather to the older son, who acted out his jealousy by creating a chaotic household whenever possible. The missing child's mother told me that her own mother reported seeing the two brothers together, having words, not long before the disappearance.

So it fit, pretty nicely—there was just that one little problem of skin color.

The mother expressed shock and outrage at my telephone request that her older son submit to questioning in the matter.

Not him, she told me. *He's such a good, good boy, more like a father than a brother. They have their problems, but they love each other, I know they do.*

I had no choice but to insist. The mother eventually acquiesced and said she would bring him to the station. I wanted to go out and talk to him at the family home, but she was adamant that she bring him to me.

They got there pretty quickly, and the sergeant put them in an interview room for me. When I walked in, I stood there for a moment and just stared at them like a complete idiot. So much for all my diversity training.

Both the mother and the older brother were white.

It was like a pole vault—an epiphany. The appearance of the victims was roughly the same in all but one of the missing boys, but it wasn't the only determiner in the perp's selection process—I was absolutely sure of it. It was the skin color of the supposed abductors that matched.

Just to make it look good, I asked a number of relevant questions. They answered everything straight out, no hesitation, no shifty eyes, none of the classic signs that they were lying or withholding something important. When I asked the older brother if he'd be willing to take a polygraph test to verify his testimony, he didn't even flinch, just said yes right away. I thought his mother was going to smack him.

The last question I asked was the only one that mattered to me at that point.

"Were there any special events that you and your brother attended in the last couple of years?"

Both the mother and the brother looked completely bewildered. I know they wanted to hear questions that were relevant to the search for their lost kid. But the brother answered.

"A couple of ball games, a concert, that dinosaur thing at the Tar Pits Museum . . ."

In view of how they'd been investigated previously, there was no reason on earth why any of these people should be expected to answer more questions about where they'd been with their missing kids. I'd already spoken with most of them, ostensibly to bring myself up to speed on their individual cases, but in this round the questions would be more pointed. It took some world-class convincing and a good deal of apologizing, most of it for things I hadn't done myself. Imagine how humiliating and degrading it would be to go through something like that, to be suspected, nearly accused, of harming someone you loved, and then have the accuser say, *Never mind, we didn't really mean it.* Why hordes of lawyers hadn't descended on the LAPD in the aftermath of these initial investigations is unfathomable. The trauma of their experiences would stay with these people for a long time, and I had to be achingly careful that none of them thought they were under suspicion again.

I reassured everyone that the information would help me determine if some new theories about their kids' disappearances were workable, and this explanation was generally accepted. But they were all a little confused about the questions—what special events did you and your missing child attend? It would have been too leading to ask the question outright—did you and your kid attend the beasts exhibit? It needed to come out without being dragged out.

In every case, they mentioned the museum. I spoke to all of them over the course of three or four days, and I came away with a new conclusion: Most of these people were of early middle age, had heights between five eight and five eleven (including the three women), were of average or below average weight, and all were Caucasian.

It was a rough physical description of my suspect.

I needed a Doc fix, but on neutral territory. Being in his office made me feel like a student, and I didn't want to feel that way with him. The PD was always chaotic, so I asked him to suggest a place where we could meet. We ended up at the Santa Monica Pier, for a hot-dog lunch.

The seagulls were as loud as ever, but the noise didn't bother me. I love the pier, with all its activity and energy. The place can be lousy with bad guys sometimes—bad girls too, especially on Friday and Saturday nights. But in the mid-afternoon it was heaven. It was a place that my kids loved to visit, especially Evan, one of our special spots.

"All of the failed suspects are roughly the same height, average of five nine to five ten, and they're all on the thin side. So I'm assuming my suspect is like that too, since those qualities are pretty hard to fake."

"What about the facial appearance?"

I thought about the poster, with its black slit where the eyes ought to be. My mental image of the suspect had a bigger, darker hole where the face was supposed to be. "I don't have a clue what the guy's face looks like."

"So what did you want to get from me on this?"

"I want to talk about the psychological attributes again, if you don't mind beating it with a stick. I finally

found one thing that all the missing kids and failed suspects have in common. They all went to a certain exhibit at
the La Brea Tar Pits Museum—"

"The one with the animals?"

"Yeah. It went on for a long time and a whole slew of
people went through there. So I have to check out all the
people who worked there during that period or were associated with that particular exhibit, including the employees
of some of the contractors who provided services."

"Sounds like a lot of work."

"Yeah. It is. I'd like to separate out a reasonable number of suspects from among hundreds, and I need all the
help I can get."

"You're pretty sure this is where he finds his victims?"

"At this point it's still wishful thinking. Truth is, it
seems kind of far-fetched to me, but it's the only common
thread."

"Well, if it is someone who works at the museum or is
associated with it, then you probably have an organized
killer on your hands."

That already seemed obvious. "Well, the pickups don't
seem to be spontaneous. . . ."

"True, that's one determiner, but there are some subtle qualities that are worth reiterating. Organized killers
are generally rather quiet people who live in a fantasy
world that is highly developed, as opposed to the disorganized, random guys who are much more impulsive in their
fantasies and their acts. Your organized deviant will plan
his act down to the last detail as a form of fantasy and then
go out and, you'll forgive the word, execute that fantasy.
The disorganized guy will have untethered fantasies and
be triggered by something exterior to go out and pick up a
kid. What they do to that kid won't necessarily coordinate
with the fantasy that prompted the grab, except in a general way."

"When you say quiet, what do you mean? If you're

doing something like this, you have to be bold, I'd think. Bold and quiet seem sort of contradictory."

"It does require a certain kind of bravery, I'll give you that. But you could also call that quality compulsiveness. You probably won't see it on the exterior—few of the people who commit sexual crimes against children are so outwardly distorted that we would recognize them as such. You hear talk all the time of seeing it in their eyes, usually after the fact, but the truth is that if you put a suit and tie on one of these guys, he would blend in nicely on a commuter train. That runs contrary to the image that comes to mind; most of us immediately envision a Manson-type character—although Manson was actually more a spree killer than a serial killer—wild hair, unkempt clothing, crazy eyes, a discernible psychopathy to warn us away. In most of these cases the book's cover belies its contents; most of the men who commit serial murder or serial pedophilia exist inside external packages that are alarmingly normal. John Wayne Gacy is a perfect example of a guy who looked really good on the outside. He was a successful building contractor with a thriving business during the time when he committed his crimes. As his own boss, he had the freedom to take time away from work to attend to his compulsion, and the money to make it easier for himself. We could go right down the list of the most famous killers in history and find lots of normalcy, even some exceptionally attractive figures. What distinguishes these men from everyone else is far more internal than external."

A block or so down the pier, a workman tossed a bag of trash into an open Dumpster. The seagulls came screaming down in a swoop of wings. They attacked the top of the bag with their beaks; a few flew off with tidbits. The rest duked it out over the Dumpster.

"Survival of the fittest, I guess."

"It's a strong urge." Errol tossed a broken seashell onto the sand below the pier. "There's an anthropologist named Lyall Watson who theorizes that behaviors we consider to be evil often have real survival value, in genetic terms. He explains it in the context of Darwinian evolution, that the disruption of order in the world—specifically in population—contributes to the rise in evil deeds we've seen in the last couple of centuries. And that the reason serial killers are primarily men is that they are in competition to pass on their genetic material. Eliminate rivals, your genes have a better chance."

"Sounds a little far-fetched to me."

"His theories go a long way toward explaining why some people do the crazy things they do when there are no other obvious reasons. I have to admit I don't get a lot of it, and this is something I get paid to do."

"Well, I'm up a creek then."

"Maybe not. You're a very smart woman. But I might be able to save you a little bit of time. It's unlikely that he's an actual employee of the museum."

"Why?"

"Because it's highly unusual for an organized killer to soil his own nest."

"Gacy buried all his victims in his basement. Dahmer put them in his freezer."

"But, believe it or not, those are more exceptions than rules. They really put themselves at risk of being caught, and both were caught, *because* of that. An employee of the museum would put himself at immediate risk by picking his victims there. I would concentrate on people with outside associations instead. The contractors. The service people. And another thing too—the way these crimes are being done, it requires some resources."

"I know, I've been thinking about that. He has to get ready somewhere, has to be able to take these kids somewhere pretty remote...."

"And it costs money. He's doing disguises, acquiring vehicles, creating all these illusions. This guy has either been saving up for this big bang for a long time, or he's rich."

"The museum talked about one of the donors. Said the guy partially financed the security system because he wasn't happy with the one that was in place originally."

"What was the name?"

"Wilbur Durand."

Doc's jaw dropped neatly. "The special-effects guy?"

"Yeah."

"Well," he said. "I'll be damned."

Before I had a chance to ask him what he meant by that, my pager went off. The vibration at my belt line startled me. "Hold that thought," I said as I called in.

He would have to hold it for a while. We had a body.

seventeen

THE SUMMER WEATHER remained beautiful, as we had all hoped it would, and by virtue of this good fortune the apples and cherries began to form in great abundance. *Frère* Demien was strutting as pridefully as a rooster, while at the same time clucking like a protective mother hen over his pampered trees swollen with fruit. We did not see each other as much during this chaotic time as I would have liked; he was busy in the orchard and gardens, or so I told myself. But I came to believe eventually that even he was avoiding me at times because he did not wish to have his fine, light mood tainted by my ever-increasing darkness. He was as good and kind a friend to me as ever, but I could not help but notice the distance that had grown between us.

By the end of July, the harvest was assured, barring the wrath of God in weather. Now it was time to watch and wait in all things, the matter of Gilles de Rais included. Waiting is abhorrent to me; all who know me understand this. His Eminence had wisely left me alone during the time between Milord's departure from Josselin and the first official move against him. Though we spent as much time together as ever, most of it pleasant, our intimate conversations contained no mention of Gilles de Rais.

In keeping myself occupied, I drove the young sisters to new heights of cleanliness, as if to mimic Sister Claire's success in Bourgneuf. My bishop found me one afternoon in the courtyard engaged in a rare moment of leisure. Before me was a piece of fine linen stretched against a wood frame. I had sketched a floral spray on the woven fabric, which I was now embroidering in colorful silk threads. The late-afternoon summer light was perfect for this engrossing activity, one to which I often turned in times of trouble for the comfort it gave. My pleasure in it must have been quite obvious, for the Bishop commented on my absorption when he came upon me, almost apologetically.

"I had thought to invite you to sup with me," he said with a smile, "but you seem so taken by your work.... There is capon. Your favorite."

"You need not entice me," I told him. I secured my needle in the fabric and rose up from my chair.

The robes of the clergyman were upon him, but he behaved as the gallant diplomat he often was by offering his arm. The blush that rose up on my cheeks was maddening, but I was powerless to stop it. I put my hand upon him, and together we walked through the courtyard of the episcopal palace to his private dining room, wordless all the way.

Capon and carp and steamed onions—my palate was well-contented. But of course I understood there was a reason for this occasion.

"I have been ordered to prosecute him," the Bishop

finally said, "initially for his assault on Jean le Ferron. As that charge progresses, we will gather more evidence in support of a charge of murder." He hesitated, as if it would soften the hard words that followed.

"And there will be an Inquisition."

I sat back and contemplated for a moment the things that had come to pass. I squeezed my eyes tightly shut to ward off the swirling dark images that marched through my soul like an army of invaders. I had not dared tell anyone, but it was this onslaught of lunatic visions, ever increasing in their frequency and potency, that turned me into the dark brooding crone my young brother Demien seemed to want to shun. Were I to tell, they would shut me away, assured at last that I was no longer sane! Always it was the same: a dark and faceless monster, fully armored and wielding a bloody sword. He would ride in on a beast I could not name with his sword drawn high and charge forward to snatch an infant from my arms, carrying it off by the nape of the neck like a bird of prey. He would toss the infant into the air and, with one mighty swoop of the sword, lop off its head as it fell back to earth again.

I knew who it was behind that iron mask. But how could he so viciously slay that infant, who must have been himself?

I could barely whisper. "Can it not be avoided?"

Jean de Malestroit's hand came across the table. When our fingers interlocked, he said, "Even Christ could not avoid the cup that His Father presented to Him."

"What will happen now?"

From somewhere below the table, the Bishop produced a folio of parchments and handed them to me.

"This is a draft of what will be copied and published."

It was written in his own hand. He had been *un avocat,* after all, before he became a clergyman. Before me was the carefully crafted opening charge of the assault that would eventually bring Gilles de Rais to his knees. I had been offered the opportunity to read it before the requirement to make it public was fulfilled.

A bittersweet honor, indeed.

To those who may see the present letters, we, Jean, by divine permission and the grace of the Holy Apostolic See, Bishop of Nantes, give blessing in the name of Our Lord and require you to notice these present letters.

Let it be known by these letters that on visiting the parish of Saint-Marie in Nantes, wherein Gilles de Rais, mentioned below, often resides in the house commonly called La Suze and is a parishioner of the said church, and on visiting other church parishes, also mentioned below, frequent and public rumor first reached us, then complaints and declarations by good and discreet people.

The list that followed was long and painful to read, for I had met some of these people myself in the course of bringing this to light: Agathe, wife of Denis de Lemion; the widow of Regnaud Donete; Jeanne, widow of Guibelet Delit; Jean Hubert and his wife; Marthe, widow of Yvon Kerguen; Jeanne, wife of Jean Darel; Tiphaine, wife of Eonnet le Charpentier. All were parishioners of churches in the areas surrounding properties owned or formerly owned by Gilles de Rais; the churches were listed alongside the names of the witnesses.

We, visiting these same churches according to our office, have had the witnesses diligently examined and by their depositions have learned, among other things of which we have become certain, that the nobleman Milord Gilles de Rais, knight, lord and baron of the said place, our subject and under our jurisdiction, with certain accomplices, did cut the throats of, kill, and odiously massacre many young and innocent boys, that he did practice with these children unnatural lust and the vice of sodomy, often calls upon or causes others to practice the dreadful invocation of demons, did sacrifice to and make pacts with the latter and did perpetrate other enormous crimes within the limits of our jurisdiction; and we have learned by the investigations of our commissioners and procurators that the said Gilles had committed and perpetrated the abovementioned crimes and other debaucheries in our diocese as well as in several diverse outlying locations.

On the subject of which offenses, the said Gilles de Rais was and is still defamed among serious and honorable persons. In order to dispel any doubts in the matter, we have prescribed the present letters and put our seal upon them.

Given in Nantes, July 29, 1440 by mandate of the Lord Bishop of Nantes.

"When will it be delivered to Milord?"

"Tomorrow."

"And the posting?"

He looked down at his empty plate. "There is time yet," he said.

My own plate had disappeared, and a beautiful *crème* appeared before me as if by magic but in reality by the hand of a young novice so quiet one would hardly know she had entered the room. I could not recall seeing her at the convent, though she was assuredly installed there; she wore the same habit and wimple as all the other novices and was equally invisible.

I admired the beautiful dessert for a moment, but had no more appetite. Feeling suddenly watched, I looked up; Jean de Malestroit's eyes were upon me so intensely that I could feel the burn of them. On this night, I was not invisible.

⚜

Two days of rain kept us all indoors, but *Frère* Demien still watched carefully over his ripening fruit. From the safety of an upper window, I would see him from time to time shaking water off the heavy limbs, thus to keep the branches off the ground. There were dozens of trees, and hours worth of rain to be shaken off. An impossible task, except for those who are divinely inspired to success.

As the light was nearing its retirement for the day, I watched him walk back to the abbey for what I thought might be the last time before sunset. He was himself in need of a shaking, for he was drenched to the skin. On the road that passed between the orchard and the episcopal edifices, he crossed paths with a rider, one who must have known him, for the man stopped and spoke with the young brother for a few moments. When they parted in opposite directions, I thought I saw *Frère* Demien's pace pick up.

He came straight to me, breathless, still in his wet robes.

"There is news," he said, dripping and panting. "De Sille and de Briqueville are gone. They have left Lord Gilles's service and run off."

♔

Who could fault them, in truth? These scoundrels must have known that their master and cousin was no longer in a position to defend them. But what unholy ingrates—they had departed with some of his fortune. They had been responsible for the acquisition of building materials for his chapel, for the purchase of clothing and gifts for his victims, for the procurement of the supplies required for transporting a bloated entourage. Had these rogues added a *sou* or two to each item on a bill and presented it to Milord for payment with his own share added in? It was as certain as the rain that fell outside the window.

One hoped Milord was not dullard enough to expect better of them; if so, he was proving himself to be the duped fool I had begun to think him. These thoughts were troubling, but other notions regarding Milord Gilles—some even more disturbing—were slipping into my mind as well, one in particular that would not let go but at the same time refused to allow itself to be identified. Try as I might, I could not make it surface in my mind. In time I knew it would.

♔

Despite *Frère* Demien's efforts, the lower branches in our orchard were finally skimming the ground. Horrified, our good brother conscripted us all, from the lowest novice to myself. En masse, we went out into the still-wet grounds and tied the offending branches up with such ropes and cords as we could put our hands on quickly— in one case, a frayed cord from a monk's robe. We picked off all fruit that showed the potential for later imperfection and propped the lightened stems up on Y-shaped sticks gathered from the nearby woods. The necessity for this massive effort escaped more than one of us, but we adored our prodigious brother and tolerated his quirky anxieties with what amusement we could manage.

Toward the end of the morning, as I labored among my daughters in Christ, a movement in the far distance caught my eye. I came out of the shelter of the trees and peered into the west. An entourage of some sort approached. As the column advanced, I saw Duke Jean's familiar standard billowing in the wind. Mud rose up behind them like so much dust on the roads, and in what seemed less than a heartbeat the entire party disappeared through the gate into the courtyard. I excused myself, though I need not have done so, being the highest among the workers, and started in a trot toward the castle, rolling my sleeves down as I made my way through the garden and across the road. In the main courtyard I managed to untie my apron and tossed it into the kitchen as I passed, which elicited a look of surprise from the scullery maid, who was quick-witted enough to catch it. As I wound my way up the staircase, I tried to straighten my veil and cap.

All of which proved fruitless in the end, for the first

thing Jean de Malestroit said when he saw me was, "You are disheveled, Guillemette. One would think you had rushed here from someplace . . . *feral.*"

"The orchards," I explained. "*Frère* Demien—"

He sighed in resignation. "When does the young man manage to find time for his devotions?"

"Those *are* his devotions, Eminence," I said breathlessly. "But enough of this chatter. I saw Duke Jean's riders."

"Yes," he said. "They have just left me with his messages. Not a minute ago." He placed his hand on the sheaf of pages that lay on his table. "I have just begun to read them."

Uninvited, I sat, to wait.

"He would finish him with one swift blow," the Bishop said to me before he was completely done. "Take hold of all his properties, here and in France, to cripple him completely."

"But he cannot assume control of the estates in France. . . ."

"Not legally."

The pages landed with a soft *thwump* on the table where he tossed them. I ached to read them for myself but contained the urge.

"Duke Jean may do whatever he wishes to do," he mused, "but such a seizure will have consequences, one of which would no doubt be the loss of King Charles's favor. The King is in no way indebted to or enamored of Lord Gilles—more likely he would as soon be rid of him as the Duke is. But there is still rancor between Charles and the Duke in the wake of that failed rebellion, which the Duke supported—against my advice, of course."

Of course, I thought. "But surely that has been resolved between them."

"The King has a long memory, I fear."

"He seems to have a short memory for the support of those who put the crown on his head. Milord Gilles among them, lest you forget also."

I suppose it was for my benefit that he made himself look chastised. "No one forgets that, Guillemette. But these matters transcend the memory of Milord's bravery. He behaves as the worst of cowards now."

"Even a coward has rights where his own land is concerned."

"A coward who has committed unspeakable crimes may be forced to forfeit his rights. Now, if you will allow me . . ."

He went back to the pages; I watched him read. His concentration was intense and unbroken. After turning the last page over, he sat back in his chair, folded his hands together in his lap, and sat very still. He might have been in prayer. When he opened his eyes again, it seemed that he had reached a conclusion.

"I shall advise Duke Jean to proceed very carefully in these matters. Whatever trial takes place, whatever charges are brought, there must be no doubt of their fairness."

"Such perfection would require cooperation between Duke Jean and the King," I said, "for their interests are at odds with each other."

He paused and regarded me for a moment. "By all the saints, Guillemette, I believe you are wasted as an abbess. You should be a diplomat. Why have I not seen these qualities in you before?"

It was because they had only just begun to emerge.

♔

To me it seemed that fairness was the best Gilles de Rais could hope for, as exoneration in any form was no longer possible. To Jean de Malestroit, it was the means by which he could preserve the dignity of all the players in the legal battle as well as the integrity of its outcome. We spoke a bit longer of strategies toward the end of fair justice; I knew that his Eminence would have many such conversations with the men who would stand with him at the table of judges, and it occurred to me that he was practicing in our discourse for what would surely come.

"I am beginning to think it would be best," the Bishop concluded aloud in one of his musings, "for King Charles to give over control of Milord's properties in France to Duke Jean. But he will chafe at making so public a concession to his rival."

"Then a liaison might work, one who will shield both parties from embarrassment. Perhaps the Duke's brother Arthur," I offered. "He is Constable of France and as such is an intimate of the King."

"There is yet a childish rivalry between the Duke and Arthur. One hopes this brotherly intrigue will turn out better than that which transpired between Cain and Abel, should it be advanced."

I had my doubts. I wondered briefly if there would be such a rivalry between my sons now if Michel were still with us. There was nothing over which they might quarrel, really; no estate, no money or inheritance. The only thing they had in common was an alliance with Gilles de Rais—Michel as a child, Jean as a young man. Many times in my secret heart I have wondered why Gilles had gone out of his way to help Jean, to see him so well placed in Avignon. Perhaps it was because he needed some true brotherhood; his still-running rivalry with his own brother, René, had started when Jean de Craon bequeathed his sword to René, not Gilles as was expected. Thereafter it was all tit-for-tat between the blood brothers.

"Brotherhood is often a difficult state of kinship, though one would hope it might be otherwise," I said.

"Surely the Duke and Arthur can overcome their differences under the circumstances. With some guidance, of course."

"One hopes. It would be greatly beneficial to all concerned."

His Eminence conferred later that day with his advisers, who agreed that it was a brilliant course of action. A letter was composed suggesting to Duke Jean that he meet with his powerful *Frère* Arthur to discuss his intentions toward Milord.

If you are intent upon confiscating Tiffauges and Pouzages as settlement for the fine imposed upon Milord Gilles, you must first prevail upon your brother to convince the King to allow you to do so without interference. It is the wisest path for all involved.

Of course, all of this brilliance would go for naught should Charles suffer a sudden tumor of conscience over his debt to Gilles for his support of Jean the Maid, without whose victories he would not have been crowned. But it had been nearly a decade since the incurrence of that debt, nearly a decade since she had been put to death. Long memory or no, Charles would not pay his debt unless its repayment was directly solicited. It seemed to me that peasants always know when their debts are due, yet kings rely on their creditors to remind them.

We sat on our horses and regarded the fortress at Vannes. How many of these monstrous edifices had I encountered in my days on this earth? Far too many, I think. Often I think the lowborn can only imagine the intrigues that take place on the other side of the murky moats. As a woman mid-born, I had seen enough to know that too much of it was unholy.

Inside these walls, above which flew Duke Jean's standard, there occurred a meeting between brothers,

wherein an accord was reached under the guidance of
His Eminence Jean de Malestroit, by divine ordination
Bishop of Nantes. Arthur de Richemont, Constable of
France, friend and ally of King Charles, would occupy
Gilles de Rais's properties in France, including Tiffauges
and Pouzages. Duke Jean would be spared the embarrassment of doing so himself. King Charles would be
spared the appearance of acquiescence and the shame of
having his treachery regarding Gilles de Rais made public. In return for all this, de Richemont would receive
Milord's Breton estates when they could be legally confiscated.

We traveled from Vannes to Tiffauges, where de
Richemont met up with us. The confiscation of Tiffauges
was bloodless and quick. The priest Jean le Ferron, who
was still imprisoned there after his humiliation at Gilles's
hands in the assault on Saint-Etienne, was finally released into our safekeeping. The poor man still bore the
angry red scars of his beatings, though he rode over the
drawbridge with his head raised high in dignity and triumph. He spoke not a word as we escorted him back to
Nantes, where we gave him into the hands of his brother,
Geoffrey.

There could no longer be any doubt that Gilles de
Rais would tumble from his high wall of glory and that
he would not rise again, ever.

⚜

A chill wind from the west nipped at my ankles as I
stood on a wood platform and reached up into the
branches to retrieve the highest of the apples. Jean de
Malestroit was so preoccupied with preparations for
Milord's undoing that he required less of me, a situation
I either liked or disliked depending on my mood. Simple
harvest tasks brought me peace: I carried boxes for some
of my elderly sisters, whose willingness exceeded their

strength, and I was thereby blessed with an illusion of youth. I steadied ladders while young brothers climbed toward heaven to retrieve God's bounty. I consoled a novice who had unwittingly consumed half a worm by telling her that the slimy things had hidden medicinal benefits and were often disguised in elaborate potions— so a learned midwife had told me. In these small services I found the means to concentrate on the joys of the moment without dwelling on the terrors that surely lay ahead. But contentment will always be subject to God's whimsies, and so it was on this day. Up high on my picking box, I was the first to see the young monk who came out of the Bishop's palace and into the orchard. I watched with curiosity as the boy/priest approached *Frère* Demien, who listened for a few moments and then glanced in my direction.

I stepped down from my box and selected from my basket the most perfect apple I could find, then polished it vigorously on my sleeve. When *Frère* Demien arrived at my side, I presented it to him with inordinate ceremony.

"We are blessed this year, I think," he said as he accepted it.

"We are," I concurred. "I am enjoying these calm moments of bringing in this harvest."

"Then I fear I must interrupt your enjoyment. His Eminence wishes to speak with you."

⚜

"Ah, Guillemette," Jean de Malestroit said when I arrived. "What frown is this?"

"Does it not seem unnatural to be inside stone walls on such a glorious day?"

"Perhaps *Frère* Demien's excessive love of gardening has taken hold of you as well." He hesitated for a moment, as if he were rethinking something, then said, "Forgive me for taking you from your serenity. But I thought you might appreciate seeing this before it is seen by others."

He handed me a parchment inscribed in an unfamiliar hand. As I lowered myself into a chair, I skimmed over the greetings and salutations, as they were always the same in any legal document, which is to say confusing and plagued with frivolities. *In the name of, by the grace of, under the auspices of.* These words did nothing but delay my arrival at the only part of the missive that mattered:

We, not desiring that such crimes and heretical sickness, that grows like a canker unless it is torn out immediately, should be ignored in silence, by neglect or dissimulation, and further desiring to bring the required remedies with efficiency, in the name of these present, we request and require you, one and all, without any placing blame on the other or excusing himself at the expense of another, by this one binding edict, to cause to show yourself before us or our representative in Nantes, on the Monday that follows the Feast of the Exaltation of the Holy Cross, to whit, the 19th day of September, the nobleman Gilles de Rais, knight, our subject and under our jurisdiction, whom we summon accordingly by the terms of the present letters before Us as well as before the case prosecutor of Our court in Nantes, charged with proceeding in the affair, in order to answer for its protection in the name of faith, as well as law, and for this, it is Our wish that our present letters be duly executed by you or by another among you.

Given the preceding Tuesday, the 13th day of September, in the year of our Lord 1440.

Which day it happened to be, though early still, so the document could not yet have been delivered to its intended recipient. The page was transcribed by order of the Lord Bishop Jean Guiole, a man not ordinarily among our familiars. I set the parchment on my lap. "You did not sign it yourself."

"Others have the authority to do so."

Another legal notice would follow the next day:

I, Robin Guillaumet, cleric, notary public in the diocese of Nantes, was careful to render executory as intended these letters promulgated against the said Gilles, knight, Baron of Rais, named as principal in this same writ, and executed by me in my own right this September 14th, in the year 1440, according to the form and manner mandated by the same letters.

"Again, my Bishop, you did not sign."

"It is not required that the signature be mine," he said.

He would try to keep his distance.

⚜

Nor did Jean de Malestroit accompany the arresting party when they arrived in Machecoul two days later on the fifteenth of September—he sent another *avocat* in his stead to accompany Duke Jean's captain of arms. The party of legal representatives and soldiers presented themselves, well-mounted and heavily armed, at the gate of Milord's castle.

These were Gilles de Rais's peers and familiars, among them men who had gone to battle with him against the English at Orléans. I tried to imagine the hardness of spirit it would require to arrest one's own brother-in-arms. Somehow, in an act of incomprehensible manhood, Captain Jean Labbé, who once rode among Gilles's own forces, read the warrant of arrest and demanded that Gilles de Rais surrender to his party immediately.

We, Jean Labbé, captain of arms, acting in the name of my lord Jean V, Duke of Brittany, and Robin Guillaumet, Lawyer, acting in the name of Jean de Malestroit, Bishop of Nantes, enjoin Gilles, Comte de Brienne, Lord of Laval, Pouzages, Tiffauges and other such places, Marshall of France and Lieutenant-General of Brittany, to grant us immediate entry to his castle and to make himself our prisoner so that he may answer to charges of witchcraft, murder and sodomy.

As always, we removed ourselves from the chapel after Vespers and returned to the abbey. Jean de Malestroit was no master of verbiage that evening, nor I its mistress; we said barely a word to each other as we passed under the arches that surrounded the outer edge of the church.

But words that must escape will; Jean de Malestroit took my hand in his and brought me to a stop. "I have had a message from Captain Labbé," he said quietly. "They will arrive before morn. He will try to position their arrival so it will fall in the dead of night."

"Wisely," I said, in a voice I myself could barely hear.

"The capture went quietly," he said. "As did the journey from Machecoul—there were no difficulties. Labbé says that Milord gave himself into their hands with a pitiable lack of resistance, as did Prelati, Poitou, and Henriet."

So it was with the intent of watching the arrival in quiet privacy that I climbed the twisted staircase to the north tower of the abbey in the smallest hours of the morning. A torch flickered above me, held high by my aching arm, which had reached one too many times for apples in the past few days and now complained by trembling. I needed the light more than ever; the stones were worn from many centuries of footfalls, and there were only occasional slit windows to let in the moonlight. Round and round I went, slowly; it was a fair number of minutes before I reached the top and the parapet from which I would observe Gilles de Rais's shameful reentry into Nantes.

I stepped out onto the small landing and was amazed by the moonlight, which illuminated the night sky with visible shafts of gossamer gray through the intermittent clouds. Countless stars blazed above me, and for one brief moment I was transported away from my travails.

I set the torch into a crack I found in an ornamental stone beast whose vile expression seemed even more menacing in the flame glow. Below me was the city square, through which Labbé's entourage would have to pass to reach the Bishop's palace. It was a long way down, perhaps fifty meters, and as I looked over the edge, my gorge rose. I leaned back to recover.

Where would I find the sleep to replace that which I would sacrifice to watching this macabre parade? I wished for a hot cup of the sublime *thé* that Sister Claire had so graciously served me in Bourgneuf, or some energizing tonic from the chemist. Minutes passed, then half an hour, then an hour; the moon slipped lower in the sky and its light began to falter. Yet below me there was more light than I expected, for one by one, torches began to show themselves in the square.

They seemed to come out of nowhere, to slip in through the shadows. Their light shone down on the heads of those who held them up, and as the glow increased I could see that the people who were beginning to assemble there were clad in the garb of ordinary folk, not nobles or soldiers. The arrival of more and more of them captivated me so deeply that I did not hear the footfalls behind me. It was when someone called out my name that I knew I was no longer alone.

At first I did not recognize the voice, for the echoes of the passageway distorted all sound. Jean de Malestroit stepped out into the diminishing light, hatless and in a simple robe.

"You are not attired properly to greet a great lord," I observed.

He smiled. "I shall not be greeting him. Captain Labbé will take him directly into the palace. Rooms have been prepared for his accommodation."

"Ah," I said. "Rooms. By which you mean the dungeon."

"He is yet a man of the nobility, Guillemette; he will not lack for comfort, of that you may be certain."

I turned outward again to watch the gathering crowd. "It seems that news will not be contained."

"Not news of this sort."

Jean de Malestroit stood behind me for several minutes, and then I felt a hand upon my shoulder.

"I am sorry," he whispered.

"I know, Jean," I said.

We stood thus for the remainder of the time we were there, saying not one word to each other. Long before we saw the cart that bore Gilles de Rais and his accomplices we heard the distant creaking of the wheels. The crowd below—now perhaps a hundred strong—began to stir. From our perch above we saw their torches swirl about in a nervous rhythm, the tempo of which increased as the sound of the wheels grew louder. When horses began to appear in the square, the torches moved toward them in a wave of light. We heard the scrape of swords against their scabbards and watched Labbé's soldiers pressing the crowd back with sharp tips.

Somehow order was maintained, until the cart itself came into view, at which point the throng rushed it madly. Shouts and jeers rose up in an angry chorus; torches danced ghoulishly below us as if it were All Hallow's Eve, prompting soldiers to break out of formation to try to press the light-bearers back. In the glare that was cast upon the cart, I could just make out Gilles de Rais, who had slipped in between his accomplices and was using them as protection. The young men who had been taken prisoner with him were shields against the grasping hands of the crowd. We watched as this eerie scene unfolded below us, like some great dramatic tragedy, the ending of which would break my heart.

Henriet later spoke of their arrival in Nantes:

I am almost at a loss to describe my condition as they took us away. I should have run, but there seemed nowhere to go—how I wish that I had had the foresight of de Sille and de Briqueville. Milord Gilles would not respond to my entreaties— none of us could reach him, so deep was his self-containment. I have seen him thus before, but usually when these silences come upon him it is in truth a reverie, an enjoyment of something inside himself. He answered none of our frantic questions of what might become of us, but only stared outside the bars of the cart as it bumped along, muttering prayers for forgiveness, assurances of devotion to God, and vows of eternal penance, and yet more promises to travel to the Holy Land. I could not imagine that God was listening to him in that moment, else He would have shown some sign to comfort us. Milord's face was taut and tearful, and he looked very much afraid. And if God would not hear a great lord in his hour of greatest need, how could I, merely a page to that lord and guilty of many of the same crimes, expect that my own pleas would be heard? What hope I had of any salvation was joined firmly to that of Milord by a cord of undeniable complicity.

In that moment, had I a knife, I would have slit my own throat. But they had wisely taken all of our weapons from us, so I was forced to remain alive and face my fate, which could only be terrible.

chapter 18

THE TWELVE-YEAR-OLD VICTIM, Earl Jackson, was found at one corner of the parking lot in a complex of abandoned warehouses not too far from LAX. The scene was within the Los Angeles city limits, but not by much.

Erkinnen was still with me as I pulled up alongside the yellow tape. Four units surrounded the cordoned-off area, all with their lights flashing. Overkill—the nearest traffic was at least a hundred yards away. But procedures are procedures.

It wasn't at all what I'd imagined from an illusionist—no props or sets or accoutrements of torture. "I don't know about this," I said as we pulled up. "This doesn't seem to fit."

"Weren't you saying something about practice grabs?"

"All he could practice was the pickup itself."

"Well, he probably has the rest of it perfected. The pickup is probably his most vulnerable point. Everything else is completely under his control."

There seemed little point in arguing. "Have you ever seen a dead child before?"

"No."

"It might be gruesome."

"I don't doubt for one minute that you're right."

Funny thing is, I was the one who puked.

There's always a bottle of water in my car, and I was glad, because I could rinse the bile out of my mouth before getting down to the business of the scene. No one would fault me for that momentary show of emotion. When I finally took a serious look I saw that Earl, like the rest of the missing boys, was slightly built and young-looking for his age. He was left propped up against a Dumpster with his legs out in front of him. Both arms were behind his torso and were probably tied, though we wouldn't be able to determine that until we rolled him over. We were still a ways from that point. From the waist down, he was naked. His scrawny calves and thighs showed none of the increased musculature that comes after puberty. His genitals were partly tucked between his thighs and were only half-visible but appeared on first glance to be intact. The lower three buttons of a short-sleeved denim shirt were undone, as if the killer were planning to remove it.

But there were no signs of abrupt disrobing, such as missing buttons or ripped seams. "He was taking that shirt off pretty carefully," I said to Erkinnen.

"Ritualistically. Very organized."

A flow of dried brownish blood ran from somewhere under the shirt to the crotch area. I gloved my right hand and lifted the edge of the shirt. There was a clean-edged knife wound centered on his belly, from which a small section of entrails were beginning to protrude, similar to a hernia.

I was concentrating on the body, until I heard Doc's quiet voice. "Look at his face," he said.

Of course that would be where he would look first, the place where emotions show. I let the shirt hem fall and glanced at Earl Jackson's unblemished visage. On it I saw what had probably been his last emotion: terror. Stark, undisguised horror.

I could not comprehend being a twelve-year-old boy, propped against a Dumpster, with a knife about to enter my belly. No wonder he looked so tortured. "God, can you imagine ..."

"No," Doc said, "I can't."

I let my eyes drift away from his face to his neck area, which broke the grip of grief and moved me back toward outrage, a far more productive state of mind. The tissue under his chin was swollen and bruised.

"Looks like strangulation," I said. "The knife wound isn't that bad."

"His mouth is open," I heard Erkinnen say. "Wide and round. He was screaming. It was bad enough to cause that look."

"Well, yeah, it probably hurt like hell. But it didn't kill him."

"He was screaming. I can see it on his face."

It didn't matter. Only two people knew what Earl's last utterance might have been—he himself, and the person who killed him.

I stood up and walked over to one of the patrols. As I snapped off my latex gloves, I asked, "Who found him?"

"I did." The cop who answered me looked very young. From the ashen look on his face, I assumed that this was his first real body.

"How did you happen to find him?"

"I was just doing a routine check," he said. "If I'm not out on another call, I'm supposed to do this lot twice a day. I missed the morning run today because of a domestic," he said, lowering his head. "Jeez, I hope this didn't happen then...."

"Probably not," I said. "The blood's pretty dry. He's probably been dead all night." It was only a guess; the coroner would be able to say better. "When was your last pass through here before this one?"

"Last night. I did a switch with one of the other guys for the evening shift. I went through here about 2230."

"See anything untoward?"

"No. It was quiet. But I did a real quick scan because there was a lot going on. Usually I'm a little more thorough." He sighed heavily; he would carry this *what if* with him for a long time.

I took the name off his tag and wrote it in my notebook. "I'll be in touch to get your statement," I told him. He nodded gravely.

The coroner determined later that the time of death had been late evening of the previous day.

"Ten-thirty or eleven," he told me. "And that stab wound was not a violent thrust of the blade. It was very clean and very clinical."

"What about the entrails? That doesn't seem too clean to me."

"I think the killer was in the process of pulling them out. There are signs that the wound was spread open. It was probably made quite slowly and precisely."

"Would you say *surgically*?"

"Yes, you could say the wound was surgical in nature. But I wouldn't want this surgeon cutting me open."

The patrol car's approach had probably interrupted the act in progress. I wondered if it would have been any consolation to the young cop to know that his arrival had probably hastened Earl's inevitable death, thereby saving him an immense amount of pain.

He hadn't looked as if it would.

Fred arrived. If he told me to haul in all the known eviscerators in the Los Angeles area, I would punch him out. But he didn't. He took one look at what remained of Earl Jackson and quietly shook his head.

"Keep me posted," he said to me. Then he got back into the car without another word and escaped.

I thought once I had a body it would make Fred see things my way. But he didn't believe there was a connection, precisely because there *was* a body. It made the Jackson case different in his mind.

I had to admit that I had my own doubts, despite Erkinnen's apparent certainty that this was either a mistake or an escalation. In the end, I had little more to go on than what I'd had before the body was found. You'd think if the killer was interrupted, there would have been more evidence at the scene, that he would have had to beat it so fast that he'd leave things behind in his haste to escape. But there were no screaming tire tracks that any of us could find, no hairs or fibers. The surrounding cracked pavement was not conducive to picking up the longed-for shoeprint. No witnesses came forward to say they'd seen something related to the case. The only blood at the scene was Earl Jackson's.

It was my case, but I began to view it as something of a distraction from my real case, even though all I had was the name given to me by the museum director. I dove into an investigation of Wilbur Durand as if it were my last hope.

A talent of Hitchcockian magnitude in the horror genre. This hyperbolic rave was plastered across the opening page of a Web site that dealt extensively with horror films. A list of familiar classics was posted, all of which he'd had some hand in creating, unbeknownst to me. At the bottom of the list was his most recent oeuvre—Wilbur Durand was the writer, producer, and director of *They Eat Small Children There.*

It wasn't being promoted in conjunction with his name. According to the editor of this site (who was, I had to remind myself, promoting his own point of view and not necessarily that of his subject), *Small Children* was some kind of big deal to Durand personally, because he had complete creative and financial control over the project. Had Durand made statements to that effect in an interview? If so, I couldn't find it, at least not on the Web. There was plenty of information on his body of work, which was quite extensive. It wasn't at all difficult to get basic information on the projects he'd touched.

But his personal life was a complete blank. *People, Us,* and *Entertainment Weekly* had apparently all been unsuccessful in getting him to cooperate in feature articles. He was a shadowy recluse of the highest magnitude. Photos of the man were like hen's teeth; in the few I could find, he was wearing dark glasses and looked like an evil, twisted reincarnation of my hallowed angel Roy Orbison. Was he married? Did he like dogs, eat ice cream? No one knew. I looked on the OUT/LOUD Web site, but he wasn't mentioned on their annual list of Hollywood *prominentes* who were closet homosexuals, though that didn't mean that he wasn't, just that they hadn't fingered him yet, the bastards. My own gay detectors were picking up something, just from the photographs.

If he engaged in philanthropy like some other notable Hollywood whiz kids, he kept it very quiet.

We had our weekly division update meeting at lunch that day; they brought in pizza this time, which seems to have a peculiar tongue-loosening effect in our groups. When everyone else was finished talking about their cases, I gave a brief synopsis of the Jackson murder. I wasn't ready just yet to mention Durand—he was still too vague in my mind—but I did talk about the museum visit and let everyone know that I would be pursuing the subsequent leads with great vigor. Fred Vuska looked very uncomfortable when the others unexpectedly began to ask a lot of questions.

As soon as Fred left the room, Escobar and Frazee approached me together.

"Want some help?" Spence asked.

To my troubled look, Escobar said, "Fred doesn't have to know."

I glanced back and forth between the two of them. "You got time?"

In unison, they nodded—eagerly.

"You guys are terrific," I said. "I'm right in the middle of figuring out where to focus next, but I should be able to get with you both no later than tomorrow morning."

I had some visiting to do first.

Durand's house was in the Brentwood section of Los Angeles, goal of that infamous slow-speed chase that made it onto the all-time *where were you when* lists, but higher on the hillside than the Rockingham estate. Up there in the stratosphere the houses and yards are bigger, the fences heavier and higher, the aura of *do not enter* more oppressive. Durand's house—really an estate—was set fairly well back from the street on a heavily treed corner lot.

I couldn't see much in my first drive-by. There was a locked security gate in front, with a rectangular intercom mounted squarely in the middle. I turned the car around about a block down and parked it about thirty yards east of the gate. I took a long, slow walk along the front boundary and the adjacent side. A hungry-looking black-and-tan Rottweiler showed up about a minute into my stroll and paralleled me roughly ten feet in from the fence. He never barked once, never even snarled, but he let me know with a few well-timed chop licks that I looked tasty. I put my hand on the fence, and he curled his lip. That was enough for me.

The side of the garage was the closest edifice to my position on the perimeter. An extension that looked to be some kind of guest or servants' quarters was attached to the back of the garage, maybe a studio if this guy was such a creative genius. It was separate and set well back from the main house. There was another sixty or seventy feet of yard area between the attachment and the next property line—it must be nice to be so rich that you can have that kind of land right in L.A. I would have been growing something edible on it. Tomatoes and eggplant. Or lots of herbs.

I turned back at the end of his fence and walked the route in reverse, with the same Rottweiler keeping me in his sights. When I reached the gate again, though, a voice crackled out over a speaker that I didn't immediately see. I determined eventually that it was buried inside a finial ornament on one of the gate standards. Was this a clever detail that Durand, master of foolery, had conjured himself?

No one knows better than a detective that attention to detail is everything.

But they must have dug the speakers out of the rubble of the Malibu burger drive-through that slid down a hillside in the last big rain.

Cnn hlp you?

"No thanks."

Silence. Then, *Cnn uh help you?* It was more deliberate this time, but not a whole lot clearer.

"No. Really. But thanks again." If the sound came through the same on the other end, he probably hadn't heard my chuckle.

This was perhaps not the kind of response Durand's sentinel was accustomed to hearing from a fence-hanger. Tourists would skedaddle in embarrassment. Creeps would beat it so as not to be questioned for loitering, which was one of those neat crimes that permitted us a closer look and often led to a more serious arrest. But I was just walking along the sidewalk; like any other citizen, I had every right to be there on a public thoroughfare on this sunny California afternoon.

Then why did I feel so out of place? Probably because the only way I would ever get into a house like this was in the course of an investigation, or on the *Architectural Digest* Virtual Tour, which the recluse Durand would avoid like the plague.

I wanted a nice juicy steak to toss to the drooling canine who had placed himself at the gate in the direct line between me and Durand's front door. Not that it would have done me any good—fifty bucks says that this dog had been trained by the Son of Pavlov *not* to salivate over meat or any other kind of temptation. He'd probably been zapped but good every time someone other than his trainer or handler offered him something, to the point where the poor dog could probably only eat out of certain hands. Durand probably paid big bucks to rent this animal, who didn't have that *pet* look.

I stood there for a few moments, wavering back and forth between ringing the gate bell or just leaving them to wonder why I'd been there. What would I ask him if he was home and agreed to talk to me?

Mr. Durand, do you truly enjoy creating the illusion of gore? It would end up being something stupid like that, because I didn't have anything planned. I was just starting to hunt this guy; that isn't the way to bring someone in.

I walked nonchalantly back to the car, whistling, with my hands in my pockets. Somewhere inside that house, I was being scrutinized. My car was unmarked, a white Ford Taurus, Everywoman's vehicle. I didn't look like a cop, so I didn't think they'd made me for one.

Unless someone in there was already waiting for me to show up.

Frazee wanted to know what I was doing so intently at the computer that afternoon.

"Researching a suspect," I told him.

He practically leaped over the desk. "You have a suspect? Why didn't you say something at the meeting?"

"A potential suspect, I mean. He was involved with the museum exhibit."

He sat down at the chair next to me and stared at the screen for a few moments. "Any direct contact with the visitors?"

"None at all. But he has a strong connection—he was the creator of the beast exhibit. Every one of my victims went to it. And he designed the security system. Everyone who visited was taped."

Spence stayed quiet for a moment, then said, "I think I read that a million people went to that thing."

"The guy's an illusionist, Spence. I'm looking for someone who's really good at that. And Doc talked about a bunch of qualities that just fit this guy to a T."

"You've met him?"

"No."

"Then how can you say the qualities are right?"

"I've read about him. Enough to give me some strong hunches."

"Great," he said sarcastically. "The press is always a reliable source of information. We all know that. Let me know when you need some real help."

"I will."

After a long sigh and a worried shake of his head, he left me alone at the computer.

I was looking for a fan club. Spielberg, Lucas, Hitchcock, Industrial Light and Magic—all of them had devoted groups of fans who seemed to have nothing better to do than exchange e-mail about their heroes all day. Wil

Durand had nothing at all, which seemed completely non-sensical. People who are heavily into movies go all out to feel like they have some tangible association with their icons—it's a form of wannabe behavior that sometimes overlaps into stalking, to the point where we have to step in and straighten them out. Tragically, sometimes we're too late.

But no one was getting that kind of piece of Wilbur Durand. There wasn't one club, organization, or news group.

"How would you discourage someone from starting a fan club for you if they wanted to?"

"Have your lawyer write them a letter telling them to knock it off as soon as it starts," Escobar called out from across the room. "Or call them yourself. This guy is famous enough to have a fan club?"

"I don't know if *famous* is the right word. But he must have some kind of cult following—he works on horror movies."

"Ah."

"Erkinnen said the perp was likely to be a recluse, so he probably wouldn't contact fans himself. He'd probably use a lawyer. I think he's right about the reclusive part; there's nothing out there at all on my guy. Apparently he doesn't need the spin; he's so well-respected for his skills that he's in big demand by producers and directors who want him to work on their movies."

"Dunbar," Spence admonished, "this is Los Angeles. You can't say *movie* around here. You have to say *film*."

"No, I don't." I rolled my chair back from the desk and stood up. "Think I'll go run him now."

"I can do that for you," Spence offered.

After all that squawking about more help, I discovered to my own discomfort that I wasn't quite ready to let go of anything yet. "I'll do this myself," I told him. "I'll know by morning if I have any reason to move forward on this guy."

"Up to you," Spence said. He frowned slightly. "Just don't let it eat you up."

I guess it was already visible.

Durand had been granted driver's licenses in two states, California and Massachusetts. Three addresses came up on the California license; the first was in a tough neighborhood, probably where he'd lived in his salad days; the second was a better, safer area that attracted an artsy population with growing affluence. The third was his current address, where he'd lived for the past fifteen years. Three changes in twenty years of adulthood; not exactly a compulsive mover.

The Massachusetts address came up as D Street, in Boston itself. It showed up on a computerized map more specifically as South Boston. The license itself had expired when Durand was nineteen years old and was never renewed. The expiration date roughly coincided with the initiation date of his California license. Way back in his ill-defined youth, he'd had a number of speeding tickets and minor traffic infractions, more than most ordinary folks. A couple were for reckless driving. There was some rage there, perhaps, that he liked to let out behind the wheel. One of the citing officers reported that he was "belligerent and uncooperative," but Durand had apparently paid his fines quietly and without further protest. Back then we didn't make them go through road-rage programs, we just took their money and noted their skyrocketing insurance rates with vindictive amusement.

The violations stopped, about a year before he moved to his current residence. Had he gotten religion about driving? Probably not—these tendencies are statistically more likely to escalate than diminish. He might have found someone at traffic court who was willing to fix his little vehicular difficulties, which I could investigate. The more probable explanation was that he'd hired a driver.

Too bad. It would have been so sweet and poetic to have this guy get pulled over on a routine traffic violation with a backseat full of wigs and book bags.

But he wasn't going to be that careless.

Running the first California address brought up something more. In his second year there, he'd made several complaints about a loud cat that belonged to his neighbor.

"Hey, Spence," I said, barely stifling a laugh, "you gotta see this."

He took the printed complaint form from my hand and read its sergeantese aloud. "Wilbur Durand," he said, dwelling on the coveted name, "complaint, alleges that he has been frequently disturbed by howling from the male cat belonging to Edith Grandstrom, female of late middle age, who resides in the adjacent unit of the complainant's apartment complex. Mr. Durand claims that the cat's noisiness is disturbing both his sleep and his mental well-being. Officer T. L. Robison responded to the complainant's apartment and found the complainant in a state of agitation. The officer managed to calm Mr. Durand after several minutes of discussion and then advised him that since the cat was not making any noise at the moment, he was unable to take any action. He advised Mr. Durand to contact the police while the cat was in the actual process of disturbing him so the disturbance could be properly documented, or to document the disturbance on audio- or videotape. The complainant Durand wanted to know if there was anything else that could be done at the moment, to which Officer Robison replied that there was not."

He handed it back to me, grinning. "The complainant is your suspect?"

I nodded.

"I never heard of him."

"Apparently he's quite a muck-a-muck."

"Well, good for him. I gotta say, you don't see too many complaints like that. He must be some kind of nut."

"And a good driver, to boot." I handed him the print-out of traffic violations. "You want to help, you could look into these. See if there was anything fishy about them. They all disappeared pretty quietly."

"Which is what I would do right now, if I had any brains. Couldn't you have given me something juicier?"

We both laughed. The daily chuckle was such a necessity in our business. He walked away, page in hand, shaking his head.

But the next line down on the address search was no laughing matter. It was reported at the same building. But this time it wasn't Durand complaining about Edith Grandstrom, it was Edith Grandstrom complaining about Durand.

Her cat had suddenly disappeared. She wanted him arrested.

"Miss Grandstrom?"

All I saw as she opened the door cautiously were the gnarled fingers of one hand. She opened the door just wide enough to get a look at me. A stout-looking chain spanned the dark gap, taut enough that it would still be hooked into both ends. I saw bits of white hair and fear in the eyes.

I held up my badge and ID card in one hand. She squinted and read them.

"I'd like to speak with you for a few moments about a former neighbor of yours."

"Which one?" Her voice was high and thin. "They come and go all the time."

"Wilbur Durand. He lived here between the years—"

She couldn't seem to open the door fast enough. Chains clanked and bolts rattled in quick succession.

"Come in, Detective," she said.

The odor of cat urine assaulted me. I followed her into the living room, which was cluttered to capacity or slightly beyond. Miss Grandstrom clearly never met a cat statue she didn't like. And then there were the real cats— at least four in this room alone. The overall effect was very cloying and close.

"It's about time," she said. "I was wondering when someone would finally get somewhere with this investigation."

I purposefully said nothing, hoping she would continue. She did.

"He killed my Farfel, I just know it. That cat was as healthy as a horse, and he would *never* have run away from me."

For a couple of seconds I couldn't decide what to do. Should I explain that even though I was there about Durand, it was not really in connection with the old cat case, which had been put in the unsolvable file two decades before? Or should I play along and let her think I was working on that case, to keep her talking?

"I'm trying to clear up some old details," I finally told her. It wasn't exactly a lie, nor was it the whole truth. But it worked.

"Could you just refresh me about the incident?" I asked. "I know it was a long time ago, but I'm going to need to ask you to tell me whatever you can remember. I wasn't a detective when the original complaint was made."

My nose was already starting to itch. I wasn't actually allergic to cats, but I never did like what happened to my sinuses in their presence. There would certainly be more than the four; cats were like cockroaches—for every one you saw, there were a dozen hiding. One of them, a big double-pawed tabby, was purring like a Rolls-Royce against my leg. Miss Grandstrom reached down and pulled him away by the ruff.

"Now, Boris," she cooed, "leave our company alone. Not everyone likes pussycats."

She smiled and gave me the opportunity to express my personal adoration for cats, which I declined to do. But I did smile, which seemed to satisfy her.

"It was a very long time ago," she said. "But when you lose a loved one, you don't get over it all that quickly. At least I don't."

"I understand," I said. "Now, let me see ..." I flipped through the file until I found the printout of the incident report. "Previous to your cat's disappearance, Durand had complained about noise."

"That's right. But I really don't understand what he was upset about—Farfel did like to talk, but his voice was sweet and quiet. We had many fine conversations. Of course, he spoke human better than I spoke cat."

Mental illness can be so subtle and insidious. "It says in the report that the incidents of noise took place at night."

"I never woke up from any of my cats making noise," she insisted.

"Might you have slept through it?"

"Well, that's always possible, I'm a good sleeper...."

"Do you know how your cats behave at night?"

"I assume they don't behave any differently than they do in the daytime."

"But you don't know that for certain?"

"No, I don't."

"So you can't say specifically whether or not there was noise, then."

"No, if you want to get technical about it. But I still think Durand was making it up. He just didn't like me for some reason."

"It also says in the report that Mr. Durand worked at home at the time. Do you happen to know what kind of work he did?"

"Some kind of sculpting, as I recall, but I would think you'd ask him."

"I like to try to get the other party's impressions when I can. And I wanted to speak to you before speaking to him."

That pleased her; she started talking again. "He was always around, it seemed; he didn't go out much. The people who were in the apartment before him worked all the time and were hardly ever there. The people who've been there since—way too many to tell you about all of them, but none of them have been around all the time like Mr. Durand." She smirked when she said the name. "I went over there once with cookies to try to put a little peace between us, and he did let me inside, just for a few moments."

She gently pushed a cat off her leg. "Not the stockings, Maynard. You know better." She looked at me again. "It was a strange apartment. Hardly any furniture, just a few things up on the wall. But there was this one room I saw in the back, where my bedroom is—the door was open and I could see into it—must have been some kind of workroom. It was full of ... equipment, I guess you'd call it. Tools and materials; very cluttered. I don't know how a person could live like that—you can hardly walk around."

I wondered how long it had been since she'd taken a serious look at her own living room. Someday a lot of stuff would have to be moved out of the way before someone scraped Miss Grandstrom off the floor. Some poor unsuspecting patrol cop would walk in here expecting to find a simple natural-cause demise, only to be pounced upon by skinny, starving cats in survival mode.

"So when he first started making complaints, he came

directly to you, and you tried to respond to him. Tried to ameliorate the situation to his satisfaction."

"Well, as much as I could. I mean, they are cats, after all—they have a will of their own. I *sshed* them all day, but it never seemed to make much difference to them."

"How was Mr. Durand as a neighbor otherwise, Miss Grandstrom?"

"How do you mean?"

"Oh, personality-wise, I guess. Was he a nice guy outside of the cat difficulties?"

She leaned a little closer. "Do you want to know the truth?"

Well, duh. "Yes, please, if it doesn't make you too uncomfortable."

She was fairly frothing to speak. "He was a nut, if you ask me. A mean-spirited, animal-hating nut. He had no friends that I ever saw, except a couple of young men who came and went now and then. And no girlfriend." She sat up straighter, as if offended. "I thought that was quite unusual. After all, he was a good-looking young man. I don't know how he's aged, but he was handsome when all this happened. He must have had a very grating manner about him for the girls not to take to him."

"When you say mean-spirited, what do you mean?"

"Oh, he was very unfriendly. I was always trying to be nice to him, to make conversation. Our verandas were connected to each other by a common railing, you see, and I would try to talk to him when he was out there. He hung his laundry out to dry."

So every time Wil Durand would go out on his balcony with a basket of laundry, Edith Grandstrom would fly out there with a cat in her arms and talk at him in that high, shrill voice of hers. That would drive anyone over the edge. But to kill her cat? It was an overreaction.

"Tell me what happened when you made the discovery that your cat—uh, Farfel—had died."

She sighed heavily. "Oh, it was awful. I found him outside my storage bin in the cellar. We all have our own little locked places to put things. He'd been missing a couple of days and I was already frantic. I had to go downstairs to get something out of my bin, and when I turned on the light in that section, there he was. Hanging right in front of me."

"Hanging?" It wasn't in the report. "How?"

"His back legs were tied together with some kind of twine." Her voice began to waver and her eyes started to glisten. "He'd been cut in the stomach and his—his innards were hanging out."

Yuck. "I'm very sorry," I said. "It's too bad you had to see that."

"Yes." Her voice sounded lost and distant. "I have nightmares of it still."

"Was there anything specific that led you to conclude that Durand did this?"

"He hated me, and he hated my cats, especially that one."

It was logical. The placement of the carcass had been a message. But there was no other evidence that Durand had anything to do with it.

"Are you going to arrest him?"

I didn't have the heart to tell her that the statute of limitations had run out thirteen years earlier. "I can't do that based on what I have so far. And in the long run, that will be up to the prosecutor, not me. But I am going to go talk to him."

Pandora would require dynamite to blow the lid off the box that Wilbur Durand was hiding in. He was Nowhere Man.

I called the main number of his studio; for some strange

reason it was actually listed in the phone book. Someone's head had probably rolled for that oversight.

I'm sorry, Detective, but Mr. Durand is out of the country right now working on a film.

What film?

I'm afraid I can't talk about that just yet.

What country is he in?

I can't say for sure; there are a number of different locations and he could be in any one of them.

When is he expected to return?

We're not quite sure yet.

Roughly.

That depends on how the project progresses. Sometimes there are delays, so I can't say just yet when he'll get back. But I'll try to have him call you when he does, and perhaps you can set something up.

It was the first time I'd ever been penciled in for a phone call. There was no way to tell if he was really out of the country, because we don't require our citizens to present their passports when they leave; I would have to wait until he showed his passport to get back in.

"Detective Bureau. Moskal speaking."

I was jealous of his distinctive Boston accent. We don't have an accent in L.A., and my Midwestern nasality had disappeared long ago. "This is Detective Lorraine Dunbar calling from Los Angeles, the Crimes Against Children division. I know this is a stretch, but I'd like to speak to a detective who was on the force about twenty to twenty-five years ago. I'm working on a group of child-disappearance cases and I'm looking into a suspect who lives in L.A. now but lived in South Boston at that time. I was just wondering if there were any crimes that fit the description of the ones I'm working on. I thought maybe a detective could help me out."

"I'm the senior detective here, but I've only been in the division for about fifteen years. One of the retired guys might be able to help you, though."

A retired detective could speak from recall but would not have access to old files and case records. "Would you happen to know who's the most senior cop in your precinct?"

"Yeah, I know him."

There was a pause; I thought I heard a little chuckle.

"And could I have that person's name?"

"It's me."

"Oh. Well, that's convenient."

"Yeah, isn't it?"

"How long, if you don't mind me asking ..."

"Twenty-six years."

"Yikes," I said, disbelieving. "And you're not retired?"

"Go figure."

Some guys just can't ever leave. "I suppose I could talk to you, then."

"Well, if you're looking for an intelligent answer, you might want to try one of the younger guys. But go ahead," he said. "I'll do what I can."

"I have a bunch of young boys who have gone missing," I said. It took almost five minutes to relate the details, including my initial look at Wilbur Durand, during which the Southie detective remained attentively quiet.

"He came out to California for college," I told him.

Moskal figured the dates aloud. He was strangely silent for a moment before saying, "I know of one missing-kid case from about that time. We did find the body, about a week later. We never caught a killer, though."

I could feel my pulse speeding up. "So it's still officially unsolved?"

"Technically. No one's working on any of the old unsolveds right now, though. We just don't have the manpower. Oh, excuse me, the human resources."

I liked him.

"We don't either, but I took the call on the most recent one, which led to the others landing in my lap. Otherwise, they'd just be sitting there too. What about any kids who went missing and were never found—remember any of those?"

He laughed and then neatly sidestepped the question. "Detective Dunbar, with all due respect, at my age do you think I can remember what I had for breakfast?"

"Well . . ."

"I'm sorry. I'm the butt of all the geriatric jokes around here. We probably have dozens of missing kids who were never found. As you no doubt understand, that doesn't mean they came to a bad end. Why don't you give me a little time to take a look and get back to you. We're in the process of computerizing the old stuff, and some of it may already be in the database. If it is, it'll be easy to get. If nothing comes up, it might take a while. With a little luck I'll be able to get to it before the day is out."

I was making some notes in the files when he surprised me with a call an hour later.

"I don't know if any of this is going to be what you're looking for. I've got two dead boys and three missing in a two-year period about that time. They're all white, ages range from eleven to fourteen."

One of our service aides was from somewhere in New England.

"Hey, Donna, how long does it take to drive from New York to Boston?"

"About five hours, depending on traffic."

Damn.

"But they got a fast train now that does it in two and a half. And there's an air shuttle, takes forty-five minutes.

But by the time you get to the airport and all that, it's faster to take the train."

I went over the time line in my mind. It was doable.

"Fred," I said as casually as I could, "are there any slots left in that computer-training thing in New York?"

"I don't think so, Dunbar." He sat back in his chair and narrowed his eyes. "What's the matter, you running out of cases?"

"No. But I'm hitting some walls and I feel like I need to get my searching skills up a little. It's this weekend, so I wouldn't lose much investigation time...."

He looked decidedly unenthusiastic, but said, "I'll check for you. It was closed last time I looked. But, hey, you never know."

Half an hour later I knew that Jimmy Trainor's wife was having difficulties in mid-pregnancy, necessitating the young cop's withdrawal from the two-day course. "We already bought his airline ticket. Good news is that you can use it. You'd have to leave on Thursday night and come back on Sunday morning. Classes run all day Friday and Saturday."

I called Kevin. He would be happy to take the kids a day early. Fred had me booked into the course. Thursday was the day after tomorrow. I had some preparing to do.

nineteen

INQUIRY AND INQUEST toward proving, should such be possible, that Lord Gilles de Rais and his accomplices, followers, and devotees transported a certain number of children, small and otherwise, and had them struck down and killed to have their blood, heart, liver, or other parts, to make of those parts a sacrifice to the devil or to perform other conjurings with them, on which subject we have heard numerous complaints.

It was said without emotion, by Dominican cleric Jean de Touscheronde, without so much as a hint of the gravity that ought to accompany such accusations. Milord himself was not in attendance on this eighteenth day of September, but the purpose of this hearing was not to make him answer for their loss—that would come in time—but rather to legally document their taking, so that when his ecclesiastical trial began, Jean de Malestroit would have all the required mandates, from God and King, to tighten the noose of guilt directly around Milord's neck.

Among those who waited to give testimony were the same people we had encountered in Saint-Etienne, who had traveled the distance to Nantes so their memory of the child Guillaume Brice would not be carried off in the wind like the dust he himself had likely become. But in this rendition of their story, a new twist was added—an abductress.

A man from our village says that around last Saint John's Day he encountered an old woman with a rosy face, aged perhaps fifty to sixty; she wore a short linen tunic over her gown. Previously he had seen her passing through the woods of Saint-Etienne, heading in the direction of Nantes. On the same day that he saw her last, this man saw the child Guillaume Brice near the road where he saw the old woman. He says the location was an arrow's flight from the presbytery, near which there resided a man named Simon Lebreton, who is known to be an adherent of Milord Gilles de Rais. We complain on behalf of this child, with the hope that some means to explain his loss might be discovered. . . .

Oh, Michel, I thought that night as I knelt at my bedside, *you were so fortunate to have had a mother and father and brother to mourn you.* What fine ways this lost child must have had about him to be so well-remembered. He had taken clear shape in my mind as one of those children whose spirit was joyful, whose heart was pure, who always found the means to meet the challenges God laid before him despite his numerous disadvantages, which placed him squarely in the path of whatever evil might lurk in the forest shadows and made him want to trust that evil when it presented itself. One wonders if this old woman took the beautiful little boy by the hand and, with a reassuring smile, made him irresistible promises: decent clothing to replace his rags, a clean warm bed to sleep in, enough food to stop the constant grinding of his belly, shoes to keep his feet from bleeding in the winter. *All you need do is come with me to my master, who adores sweet little boys such as yourself and wishes very sincerely to meet you.*

His parents, both now in God's keeping, would never even know he was gone—perhaps that was a blessing. At least I knew what *might* have happened to my son. For me there was something tangible, a boar, for my hatred to settle on.

Why, then, did I suddenly feel so uncertain?

⚜

On Monday, the nineteenth day of September, Gilles de Rais was required to face his Eminence in the great hall of la Tour Neuve. None of those who stood to gain by Milord's imminent downfall were permitted to attend— Jean de Malestroit would not have it said of him that he eased their way, nor would he allow any one of them to enter the courtroom until the general public was admitted.

He very nearly did not allow *me* to be there. He entered the antechamber while I was seeing to his sacred vestments and announced, "Guillemette, I do not believe it is a good idea for you to be present in court today."

My voice went shrill in a heartbeat. "You gave me your promise that I would be present—for *all* of it— when I agreed to end my own inquiries in favor of yours."

"I made no specific promise."

"Eminence, this is shameful! Do you mean to separate me by trickery from that inquiry which I began without your help, which was well enough executed for you to find it fit to be taken up after me?"

He winced at my harshly delivered protests; Jean de Malestroit was not accustomed to hearing anyone shriek at him. Nor were his guards, who came running. He sent them off again with one quick look, and we were alone once more—me with my growing fury, he with his damnable patience.

"You cast this in such an unflattering light. I meant only to protect you from harm."

"You know me well, Brother; I am not delicate of constitution. God has worked enough of His whimsies upon me that I have grown strong."

"I would keep you from the whimsy He would work on you now. It may be considerable."

"You often remind me that our Lord did not refuse the bitter cup—now I shall remind you."

"I have it in my power to deny this to you. You know that."

It was a devastating betrayal. "Naturally, Eminence, you may do to me as you see fit while I am your hand-maid. But do not be surprised if I throw off this accursed veil and take myself out from under your power."

"You would not. You *could* not."

I yanked the veil off my head and threw it to the ground. "I have lived without this tent before and I will do so again if necessary. By whatever means."

For a few seconds he said nothing, just stared at me with an expression that seemed both sad and wishful at the same time.

"*You* may not care what becomes of you, Guillemette," he said finally, "but I assure you, I do. Greatly."

"Then you must keep the promise you made to me before God," I said. "Or I *shall* take myself away from here."

☙☙☙

And so when Jean de Malestroit set out for the secular court that morning, I was at his side. As we progressed through the palace, my mood was tainted by the jolt of what had just passed between us, so the huge angry crowd that greeted us in the square outside the palace was a jarring sight. As soon as they saw us, there rose up a shout, and then the multitude surged forward. These angry souls shouted in frustration, railing in complaint against the secrecy and slow pace of the proceedings. The intricacies of political retribution as nobles practiced it upon one another—that is to say, through gold and possessions—could not be appreciated by such folk. They wanted the same swift and simple justice that was practiced upon them.

But as I peered beyond the shields and the upraised swords of the guard, I saw among the crowd many whose attire betrayed far greater affluence, who I suspected were enticed by the promise of sordid intrigue—it is not often that a great lord and hero plummets so dramatically from grace.

We drew back hastily into the palace and were forced to make our way through a maze of damp, poorly lit tunnels that skirted the perimeter of the whole palace underground. We passed by the site where the English had once broken through, now repaired but still detectable after so much time, and emerged a good while later on the ground floor directly beneath the upper hall.

Light, illumination, air! I sucked in a nonfetid breath and shook the hem of my habit to dislodge any vermin invaders. We climbed hastily to the second-floor balcony and looked down at the crowd, perhaps five or six meters below. Though his Eminence stood back, we could not entirely avoid detection. A chorus of threats and damnation swelled upward and echoed off the flat stone walls.

Hang him! Let him suffer as our sons suffered! May he be damned to an eternity in hell!

Frère Demien found his way through the madness and came up behind us on the balcony. "The crowd," he gasped, "they are crazed...."

"More so every minute," his Eminence said. There was a rare hint of fear in his expression as he scanned the growing crowd. "The guard may be outnumbered," he said. "How diverse in composition they are—rich, poor, commonfolk and nobles."

Frère Demien was less generous in his assessment of their nature. "Charlatans, pickpockets, hawkers with their worthless trinkets ..."

He had a better eye for such things than I, but on closer observation it was plain that he was right. Easily noted from our high vantage point were the scoundrels and hucksters who would prey on those who had little enough to bring with them to Nantes but would depart with even less. Beyond the pickpockets and petty thieves there were dancers, jugglers, minstrels, and fools, gaily clad and in fantastic attire, all working the crowd for the few *sous* that might be pried loose. There was danger that these proceedings might be turned into some sort of entertainment, that the solemnity and seriousness of what was to come would be lessened by the sheer tawdriness of it all.

But the common desire of these people was unmistakable—they wanted Gilles de Rais. He had been housed temporarily in a suite of rooms in the brothers' section of the abbey and would be compelled to make his way through that throng in order to enter the palace, where the trial was being conducted.

They were waiting for him.

Not five minutes later, a lady's curtained litter appeared, borne on the shoulders of six strong porters instead of the usual four.

Something was clearly out of right. We all stared; *Frère* Demien finally managed to articulate our suspicions. "That is an excessively corpulent lady."

The crowd was no more fooled than he. They surged inward and began to tear at the curtains. The bearers increased their pace and gripped the carrying bars much more firmly, while their escorts pressed the crowd back.

"Surely he could enter through the passageways as we did," I said quietly.

"He shall enter in this manner," Jean de Malestroit said with quiet determination.

I stepped back and regarded him as he watched the scene below. It was not precisely enjoyment that I saw on his face, but an emotion more akin to satisfaction. He was giving these people what they wanted, which was the presence of Milord Gilles in their midst. Hence his concern for the guard, the need for which he might well have underestimated. I looked below and saw that they were managing, but just barely.

I turned to speak to the Bishop, but he had slipped away, seemingly in a breath.

The crowd reacted sharply when the Terce bell began to toll. The anger emanating from this mass of malcontents was vitriolic and hateful. Insults, curses, and threats were tossed off as if there were no consequences when a peasant maligned his sovereign. Before Milord's disgrace commenced, the crowd would have parted in deference to his position, as occurred at Pax when he came to make his confession. Today there was no deference, only sneering and jibes.

Soldiers of God attired in holy crimson were forced to turn their swords and lances toward the surrounding morass of humanity.

"They would tear him apart right here and now," I whispered to *Frère* Demien.

"There are those who would say that such an outcome is not undesirable."

Not I among them; there lived within me an unholy ache to hear him speak of what he had done.

Now more guards spewed forth from within the courtyard. The augmented force succeeded at last in parting the grasping crowd, and the litter surged forward once again, finally into the courtyard.

We left our balcony post hastily and proceeded toward the chapel. It lay across an open rotunda, through which the stairs rose up. As we circled around it, we heard urgent footsteps coming up the stairs. I looked down over the railing and saw Milord in the midst of his guard; the entire party was rushing up the stairs, as if in escape, though they were no longer pursued.

The handsome, charismatic Lord Gilles de Rais, brilliantly attired in royal blue, seemed dramatically out of place amid his crimson captors. Hearing my gasp, he looked up, and our eyes met. For the time it took him to climb the stairs, we remained locked in a mutual stare of bewilderment. I turned back time in my own mind and tried to imagine him entering under different circumstances, perhaps to receive some honor, and envisioned myself gaily clad in a gown, perhaps even with some cloth of gold upon it. By my side, whole and proud, would be Etienne, my adored and cherished husband, who would be bursting with pride at the accomplishments of his liege lord and partaking of a share in his own heart. A clarion would sound, and all who stood with us, many loyal retainers, would clap and shout praises. And in Milord's gaze I would see the regard and honor I wanted him to feel for me as a woman whose influence upon him made him worthy of the many accolades he might have received, had things gone differently.

Instead, I saw in his expression one brief moment of guilt, one flash of shame, before a hardness overtook it. And then, as if by some conjuring, the features of my once-beloved *fils de lait* began to melt away, until he was faceless in my eyes.

I heard his voice; he said, as if from a far distance, "*Mère* Guillemette ..." The sound was brittle and thoroughly without the tender regard that ought to have been there—

Had things gone differently.

What wits I had left I gathered to myself. "Milord," I said, as resolutely as I could manage. It sounded all too much like the plea it was. "I must speak to you, there is something I must ask you."

I extended my hand, but he was past me, out of my reach, beyond my grasp. But I knew as surely as I stood there that I would never entirely free myself of his.

☙❧

On this day, perhaps the most momentous in Jean de Malestroit's dual service, he looked every bit the patrician in his robes of deep-red velvet. Friar Blouyn, who sat at his side, was similarly decorated, though the effect was not nearly so breathtaking on him as it was on my bishop, who was the sacred and secular king of this courtroom realm for as long as it would take to accomplish the Duke's ends. Both of their names were solemnly invoked at the opening of the proceedings by the Duke's prosecutor Guillaume Chapeillon, who thereafter did most of the speaking.

Jean de Malestroit appeared stern-faced and impassive, but I knew the man too well to believe that dispassionate visage. His fascination was plainly evident to me, both in his expressions and in the excited posture of his body, which slanted slightly forward for better hearing. Not to be outdone, Milord Gilles appeared to be equally unfascinated, and more—he was diffident, unconcerned, seemingly bored by the tempest that was about to engulf him.

Frère Demien whispered to me, "I cannot fathom why he would indulge in such lunatic indifference."

"Nor can I," I said.

He might have been told by an advocate or legal adviser that a noble presentation would benefit him before the court. This was not the penitent man we saw at Pax, whose troubles drew down the very skin on his face, nor the man who had sliced a cat in half at Saint-Etienne, but rather something in the middle of those two. I watched him without interruption, my eyes fixed upon him as if my life depended on maintaining contact. He never looked directly at me again but stood silently as Chapeillon accused him of attacking Saint-Etienne, of taking a priest hostage. And lest it somehow be forgotten, of the sodomitic murder of many innocent children.

The scribes diligently made their record:

The Monday after the feast of the Exaltation of the Holy Cross, in trial before the most Reverend Father, the Lord Bishop of Nantes, sitting on the bench to administer the law in the great hall of la Tour Neuve in Nantes, personally appeared the honorable Guillaume Chapeillon, case prosecutor of the said court, who reproduced in fact the summons, with the published execution, on the one side, and the aforesaid Milord Gilles, knight and baron, the accused, on the other.

"Will you submit to an admission of doctrinal heresy?" Chapeillon asked.

I exchanged a glance of hopeful anticipation with *Frère* Demien that Milord would confess and save us all the agony of a protracted and controversial trial.

But Gilles de Rais would not acquiesce. "No, your Grace," he said, with surprising conviction, "I will not admit to this charge. Nor any of the others that have been made. It is my desire to appear personally before you, sir, and before any other judges or examiners of heresy, so I might clear myself of these accusations that have been brought against me so falsely."

The quills raced furiously across the scribe's pages as the incomprehensible words echoed in the chapel.

Which Milord Gilles, knight and baron, after numerous accusations on the part of said prosecutor against the said Milord Gilles, to ascertain whether he would admit to doctrinal heresy, insofar as the said prosecutor affirmed, stated a desire to show himself personally before the said Reverend Father, the Lord Bishop of Nantes, and before all other

ecclesiastical judges, as well as before whatsoever examiner of
heresy, to acquit himself of said charges.

It was no less a declaration of war to his Breton and
French judges than his raised sword had been to an
Englishman at Orléans. Few battles in history had such
an assured outcome as the one into which Gilles de Rais
seemed so ready to throw himself. But he had never been
a coward, so we ought not to have been caught as off
guard as we were. The disturbing challenge reverberated
throughout the hall, and for a few seconds after it finally
dissipated, the only sound that could be heard was the
whoosh of the parchments on which the charges had been
inscribed when they fell from the stunned Chapeillon's
hands. He, too, had been caught off guard.

When his Eminence spoke, his voice was firm but
whisper-quiet. "As you wish, Lord Gilles. That is your
right and it shall be arranged." Dagger-eyed looks of bald
disdain passed between the two. There was none of the
courtliness and civility that the scribe's formal record
would indicate. Certainly none of them would dare to
capture Jean de Malestroit's seething anger in words.
"Gilles de Rais, baron and knight," the bishop said, "you
are hereby ordered to appear in this court on the twenty-
eighth day of this month, September, in the year 1440,
before myself and the Reverend Friar Jean Blouyn, at
which time you will answer for such crimes and offenses
as have been enumerated in the prior statement of
Guillaume Chapeillon, who we appoint to continue his
able prosecution of this matter. In the name of God and
law, you shall answer for these evils."

And after a pause, he added, "May God have mercy
on your soul, if such may suit His purpose."

⚜

I sat on a stone bench situated outside a room that was
primarily used to receive guests of the abbey. Though

this edifice had many wonderful, less-visible hideaways where I might have had more privacy, this was my favorite spot. Here I could observe the comings and goings of visitors and petitioners, vendors, creditors, anyone who had business here, dignitaries included. But I was in my own small world at that moment, and the Holy Father himself could have passed by without my notice. When it became clear that they would not be admitted to the proceedings, the crowds of the early morning had all dispersed, leaving their detritus behind for laborers to pick up. I wondered with frank annoyance why it was necessary to leave behind such a mess, when the mess that was taking place within the walls was already so overpowering.

The weather was inexplicably glorious, and in a better frame of mind I would have wept for the joy of a purloined summer day before the cold set in again. There was a basket of bruised apples by my side and a bowl in my lap. With a small ivory knife, I denuded the fruits one after the next, removing their flaws so they might be made into *pâtisseries,* whose delicate texture stood to be ruined by the intrusion of a wayward bit of fruit skin or the slightest imperfection of the flesh itself.

I worked the knife; the skin fell away. I worked the knife harder; more skin dropped. I tossed the parings out into the dirt, for they were not of sufficient quality for further use. Ashes to ashes, dust to dust; all things that rise from the earth will be reclaimed by it in time.

As was my son, who rose and was returned far too quickly, or so I presumed.

On and on in dark rhythm I subjected the blameless fruit to the tumult I felt within. *Confutatis, maledictus, pergatorium.* If those qualities were reflected in our *pâtisserie,* it would be a bitter, inedible disaster. Truths I had taken to be unassailable seemed to be falling away one by one. I had always tried to believe it was God's whimsy that my son had been taken away from me, but Gilles de Rais had been with him that day—indeed, he was the last one to see him, as his servants had been the last ones seen with so many of the missing children.

I was in the high tower of Champtocé on that terrible day, mindlessly airing some linens, when a clamor arose outside. I rushed to the window and saw the castellan giving frantic orders to his men to raise the portcullis. When such a thing occurs, one naturally worries of an approaching force, and my son was out in the Champtocé woods with Milord, perhaps in their path. But when I saw the young Gilles come through the gate alone, my distress turned to genuine panic. I dropped my neatly folded linens, ran frantically down the stairs, skirts clutched high, and flew out into the courtyard.

Milord, all arms and legs, on the verge of manhood, was bent over with his hands on his knees with his head down. He was panting and wheezing from the exertion of his run. Those who stood around him, ready to attend to whatever need he might voice, were perplexed and confused and trying to make him speak.

He would speak to me: I was all the mother he had left, and he would speak to me, by all the saints. "Milord," I said urgently, "what of Michel?"

Pant, wheeze, pant, and then a look of sheer terror. "Madame," he cried, "the boar . . . we came upon him—I ran as fast as I could to escape, and I thought Michel was behind me, but when I turned around and he was nowhere to be seen—"

I cried out in anguish and swooned; the castellan Marcel caught me.

"Where did you last see him?" Marcel demanded of the boy.

He gasped for air. "I cannot say—"

The castellan shook him by the shoulders. *"Think— where did you last see him?"*

Cowed into submission, young Gilles blubbered, "West of the oak grove, fifty paces, in the ravine that leads down to the river."

"Is the boy harmed?"

"I . . . I do not know."

The castellan signaled for a horse. I grasped his arm in desperation. "The midwife—if Michel has been savaged she will be needed."

He looked to one of his men as he pried my fingers off him. "Find Madame Catherine," he said. "Bring her out to us."

I turned and started in the direction of the stable. Now it was his turn to grab me by the arm. "No," he said, "you must not go."

"He is my son!" I pleaded.

"No," he said again, even more firmly. By then all of his company had gathered around, so there were plenty of men to do his bidding. "Hold Madame la Drappiere here," he ordered, and one of them promptly stepped forward to do just that.

I struggled futilely against his grip. There was so much pity on the castellan's face; I thought if only I pleaded more, he would let me go. Wisely, he looked away, and said to another of his men, "Find Etienne and bring him out to the grove." And then he mounted the horse that had been brought for him and rode off, bringing the animal to great speed almost immediately.

I choked and gagged on the dust that flew up as they rode off. All these memories now choked me anew. A hand came to rest on my shoulder, startling me.

"Guillemette," Jean de Malestroit said, "you are torturing those apples."

The fruit whose skin was giving way to my savagery fell out of my hands. Together we watched as it rolled into the dirt.

I wiped my hands on my robe, which was an unusually

slovenly act for me, for I treasure fastidiousness. "You possess a discerning eye, Eminence," I said.

He seemed to want to sit; he had no need to ask my permission, and in truth, I ought to have stood when he appeared. But we were well past such silliness. I inclined my head slightly toward the open bench beside me, and he rustled down onto it, his judicial robes gathered in.

"I will hear your confession, if you wish, and thus relieve you of whatever burden it is that causes you such distress as I see in you now."

I pushed back a wayward strand of hair and looked in his direction. My expression must have shown additional unease, because he quickly said, "Have no fear—I will not assign you a difficult penance."

"As you wish, then. *Pater, ignosca me, ob malo dissipavi.*"

Jean de Malestroit made a small chuckle. "God may not be overly concerned with the waste of an apple just at this moment," he assured me. "But He would know, as would I, what *does* burden you."

A weary breath escaped my lips. I looked him straight in the eye and saw there a willingness to receive me in my graceless condition. But it was not yet time to tell him what thoughts were in my mind. So I told him something that was certain to appease him. "That which haunts all of us these days is what troubles me," I said.

"Ah." He sat back and considered my answer for a moment. "It is only natural, I suppose, for all of us to be troubled by the things we have begun to hear. It is all so lamentable! But others are making adequate lamentations, Sister—yours are not required just now."

"Nevertheless, Brother, I am troubled, and I cannot help but voice it. Look what he has become. I once thought I knew him. *Well.* But it appears that I did not know him at all."

"The Dark One takes many forms, Sister. He will

slip into the world wherever he finds the slightest crack. He changes form to suit the opening and will enter without being noticed unless we are eternally vigilant against him."

"Are we truly so ignorant, that such a ... a ... *thing* could walk on this earth without attracting our attention?"

"It would seem that we are."

"So many complained; why did we not listen?"

"These were mostly poor children, many of them all but forgotten—"

"They were not all poor. And some had parents who wailed loudly at their loss."

"Not loudly enough, it appears."

I did not remind him that his own ears were among those closed to the wails initially and that he had only reluctantly allowed me to pursue what I had heard. "Dear God," I said after a brief lull, "how could this have happened?"

"Likely this evil has taken place subtly over time and has remained unrecognized until now." He shifted slightly on the bench to fend off the stiffness that would settle in if he remained stationary for too long. "I have given much thought to the nature of evil, for God has charged me with its elimination. I will confess, that task has always seemed impossible. I struggle with my failures every day."

He shifted again, this time with a little grunt. "You like this bench better than I," he said.

I forgot my upset for a moment. "God gave me the ampleness of girth by which to tolerate it."

"So I have noticed. God is very liberal with His gifts." Then his expression sobered a bit. "But we must not lose sight of the fact that evil can be one of God's greatest gifts."

I stared at him. "How can that be?"

"Consider its many forms: wars, pestilence, the shaking of the earth, and the falling of the sky—indeed, the darkness. God put evil in this world with purpose and intent. He would help us to recognize, by virtue of comparison, that which we should take to be good. We loathe the darkness and celebrate the light, because we have an understanding that one represents evil and the other good. But dark and light have always existed; since God made them, they have not *become* anything different than what they were. They were revealed in stages, perhaps, but they were always in this world. I suspect, Sister, that Gilles de Rais has always been something unholy and that we are just now coming to see his true nature."

He had given voice to thoughts I simply could not speak myself, as if he knew somehow that I had them and that they would poison me if they went unspoken.

"I think there is yet more to be revealed," he said quietly.

I understood then that he knew more than he was telling me. I could not fault him for that. Bad news should sometimes be given in small portions, so as not to entirely cripple the hearer. I picked up another apple and began to peel it. "Time will tell, Eminence, as it always does."

I worked the knife; the skin fell away. He watched me in silence for a time, then said, "I fear that we will know much more than we want to when all is told."

I nodded. "I think you are right," I said. But, oh, how I wished he would be wrong.

⚜

It was three days before I could make myself ask his Eminence the question that had been poisoning me. I could no longer hold it in.

"You have questioned those with whom he did his evil, Poitou and Henriet."

He was a chancellor at the moment and brusquely busy with neglected affairs of state. "I have," he said. He seemed annoyed at the interruption, though he did look up at me, which he did not always do.

"Thoroughly?"

"Thoroughly enough to know that they are his accomplices in evil and should suffer whatever fate may befall their master."

"So they knew the manner of death for these innocents, then."

Jean de Malestroit evinced a bit of discomfort. "Not all were innocent, Guillemette. There were some who appeared to have sought out Lord de Rais's company to take advantage of his position. One cannot say those young men were entirely blameless."

I did not wish to waste time arguing that point, for my resolve was waning. "But those who were younger—you know the manner in which they died."

"I do." He set his reading down and leaned back in his chair, perplexed. "Is there something specific you would ask, Sister?"

"Yes," I answered. "There is."

"Then speak it, if you will be so kind; there is work before me and I would like to resume it."

"The younger ones," I asked, "say, ten, eleven years old—how were they killed?"

"Cruelly," he answered. "How else?"

"No, I mean what were the exact methods he used to end their lives—"

"Guillemette—"

"Tell me."

He paused before speaking. "Some were killed by having their blood drained. Others were slit at the throat and then decapitated."

For a stunned moment, I was quiet.

In the name of God . . .

I was almost relieved, because it was not what I'd expected to hear. But true relief would not come until the final answer had been given.

"Were any slit up the belly?"

He looked directly into my eyes. "Yes. Most. Now, why do you wish to know these gruesome details?"

I ignored the question completely. "Eminence, I would go on another journey. But this one will be longer than the last. I would like your permission to take *Frère* Demien with me."

He set aside his work. "That is impossible. You cannot be spared just now."

"Ask Sister Élène to take my place."

"And *Frère* Demien is needed as well—"

"The harvest is well in hand. We can both be spared."

"But where now? We have already—"

I raised my hand, and he allowed himself to be silenced.

"There are things I would know," I said.

chapter 20

THE PLANE WENT UP like a rocket out of John Wayne Airport and lurched quickly to altitude, but the rest of the flight was decent, and it seemed shorter in duration than the interminable security checks we went through prior to getting on board. We set down in Newark; it was my first in-person look at the diminished cityscape. Everyone on the plane was silent as we taxied to the gate. It seemed only proper.

The five of us went in a shuttle to our mediocre hotel. Being the only girl, I had a room to myself, whereas the guys were doubled up. It would work out perfectly. I actually learned some stuff in the class that Friday. It was too bad that I would have to miss the next day—the instructor had talked about covering some topics that sounded really interesting. Search engines that were specifically designed for investigative work, pay-as-you-go services, some similar to Lexus Nexus, that focused on bad guys. But I had things to do. Saturday morning I snuck out of the hotel at 0600 while everyone else was asleep. I hung the DO NOT

DISTURB sign on the door handle and tucked a note under one of the guy's doors to the effect that I'd been up all night with female troubles and wanted to sleep. Big strong cops could face guns without flinching, but a tampon is a whole other matter.

Detective Peter Moskal would be waiting for me at South Station, which he assured me was very convenient to Southie itself. I told him I would be happy to take a cab, but he insisted on picking me up.

I recognized him right away by the gold shield hanging off the pocket of his leather jacket, but he was not the shabbily dressed, worn-down donut depository I expected to see. Moskal was Clint Eastwood-handsome, right down to the cragginess. He had great hair, neatly cut and styled. He was trim and tall and had a friendly ease about the way he moved. Not a bit of gray, though he had to be in his late forties at least.

No wedding band.

"I guess they start cops real young here," I said.

Big smile. "Yep. I was four when I went into the academy. But I'm ready to retire, at least according to my wife."

Damn. The good ones are always taken.

"I want to thank you for giving up part of your Saturday for me."

"It's okay. None of my kids had anything going on but homework, so it wasn't a problem. I can't help them with their math anymore anyway."

He gave me a melting smile.

"So," I said, all business, "you have the files?"

"Sitting on my desk. I thought we'd go there and take a look at them—there's a lot of material. Then if you want I can take you around to the scenes. But they're not the same as they were back then. I hope you're not expecting to find anything new after two decades."

"I'm glad that the buildings are still there. Cripes, in

L.A. it seems like buildings go up and down every year. I just really want to see where these things happened. I'm starting to develop a sense of who this Durand is; I want to see if I can place him there. And if there's time, I'd like to talk to anyone who might have been involved in the original investigation."

"You're going to be disappointed about that. The lead detective is—well, let's just say he's a pretty serious alkie. He can barely talk anymore. The sergeant who first came on the scene retired about three years ago with a nice pension. Found out he had cancer not long after that and died last year."

"Damn. I hope he took the spousal benefit."

"He wasn't married."

"Well, at least he didn't leave an impoverished widow."

"No. Sean O'Reilly came from a pretty comfortable family. In fact, he was Wil Durand's uncle."

"Cut it out. No way."

Buildings whizzed by as he nodded. "It's true. I grew up right here in Southie and I actually knew his family. We all know each other here, at least by reputation."

The shock of this revelation took a moment to settle in. "Forgive me if I'm making false assumptions," I said. "But isn't Moskal a ... *European* name? I thought Southie was a pretty tight community of Irish-Americans."

"Well-put, Detective," Moskal said with a laugh. "It's Polish. I guess they give you diversity training out there too."

"Once a year, whether we need it or not."

"My mother's maiden name was O'Shaughnessy. They let her back in even though she married a Pole."

"Oh, well. There you go."

There we went, into his car, which he'd left in a loading zone—no one was going to give him a ticket. We worked our way southeast through the Boston waterfront, an area marred by stalled transitional construction. Gradually, over the course of a quarter mile, industrial gray cinder block gave way to pastel yellow and green row houses. The city's glacierlike push into the residential neighborhood was unmistakable. I wondered how hard the neighborhood was pushing back, or if the ice had already settled in.

"Durand's got two sisters alive, and his mother—Sean was her brother. They live in a real nice house on the beach. I would definitely suggest that you talk to someone in the family; they're an interesting bunch."

"How so?"

"Well, for starters, Wilbur Durand's sister is Sheila Carmichael. Half sister, I mean."

She was one of those lawyers with a high Dershowitz factor and a national reputation for making prosecutors jump off bridges. I'd seen her on television many times, as a talking head for some client whose right to commit mayhem was in danger of being abridged by the unsympathetic lackeys of the taxpayers, myself among them. Her defining feature was a barely tamed mass of deep red hair with a Bonnie Raitt–style white streak. A formidable woman, all steel, all the time.

"I guess he won't have any trouble getting an attorney, then, if he turns out to be the guy I'm looking for."

"Probably not. The family is lace-curtain Irish, though they're not Kennedy-rich, just comfortable. Jim Durand was his mother's second husband. The first one, Brian Carmichael, died young. Left her with a bunch of kids. You'll want to talk to someone in the family."

He kept saying that. I was aching to ask why, but it felt too soon.

The South Boston precinct had no lot of its own; blue-and-whites were parked in layers along the front of the building. Moskal pulled the car into the first available space.

"And I thought we had parking problems."

"Your streets this narrow?"

"No."

"Then you haven't lived."

"I'll bet our traffic jams are worse than yours."

He gave me a big broad smile and melted my heart. "Take the southeast distressway at four o'clock on a snowy Friday afternoon. Then you'll know what a traffic jam is."

It was an odd little game of one-upsmanship, but fun, and it took the edge off. As soon as we entered the dilapidated building, I knew he would win the bad-office contest hands-down. Moskal's desk was crammed into the corner of a room with a stained ceiling and rusting heat pipes.

"Welcome to my domain," he said. "Such as it is."

The files were right there, neatly stacked and squared up to the edge of the initial-scarred desktop. He picked up the pile and handed it to me. "This should keep you busy for a while. I'm about to make a coffee run. You want anything? I go to the Dunkie right down the street. They have bagels and muffins and all that."

I asked for coffee and a blueberry muffin and tried to give him money. He refused it and left me there with the files. They were heavy in my lap, so I set them back on the desk again and took the first one separately. I dove into the written report.

The first boy who disappeared in South Boston—Michael Patrick Gallagher—was thirteen years old but young-looking for his age, the classic "good boy" who did well in school and never got into trouble. He was last seen in mid-afternoon at a South Boston corner store, where he emptied his pockets of pennies and nickels to buy two candy bars and some gum. He parted ways with a small group of his regular companions at that corner. His arrival time at home should have been around 3:30 P.M., but it was a Friday afternoon, when it was not unusual for Michael to stay out later if he had little or no homework. When

7:00 P.M. rolled around and he had not yet made an appearance, his mother made several nervous phone calls to his immediate group of friends, which proved futile. His father called the police at 7:20 P.M. A patrol unit was sent via radio call to the Gallagher home. The police officer who took the call on this disappearance began the investigation with the standard questions to the parents: Did they have any reason to think he might have run away based on how things were for him at home and at school? Did they in fact know how things were going in school for him? Had there been any recent noticeable change in the boy's behavior? No to all.

The officer searched the home to eliminate any possibility that Michael might have come in unnoticed and fallen asleep somewhere or, worse, might be unconscious and unable to hear his parents calling. He was satisfied within a short time that the boy was not in the house and that the parents were being truthful with him, that this was probably not a case of a runaway teenager whose family didn't realize there was trouble in his life. Michael had a favorite television show that appeared in reruns on Friday afternoon at 5:00 P.M., but he had not come home to see it. His mother stated that she was very surprised he had missed it.

A description and photograph of the missing boy had been sent out on Teletype and distributed to all patrol officers within the city of Boston. The case was then assigned to a detective in the South Boston district. The initial incident report was signed by the patrol cop, one Peter Moskal.

I was just starting to read the other detective's last overview of the case, a bitter chronicle of frustration, as Moskal set my coffee and muffin down on the desk.

"Why didn't you tell me you were the first one on the scene?"

He got very philosophical on me. "It seemed like way too much of a coincidence. I don't know, I guess I felt a little spooked. But when I heard what you were asking about, I was really glad. I didn't think I'd ever get a chance to work on this one. I asked to reopen this case a number of times over the years, but they would never let me do it without new evidence."

I sat back and regarded him. There was excitement in his expression, to replace the previous troubled look, and fire in his eyes. "Well, Detective, looks like you're going to get another trip to the plate on this one."

"Let's just hope I don't get thrown a curve. This whole thing always felt so unfinished to me. But there wasn't anything I could do about it, until now. I should thank you."

"Well, it's my pleasure," I said. "I think. But speaking of unfinished, I have to get back to New York *tonight*. So prioritize my day for me, if you wouldn't mind, based on what you know."

He reached over and took the remaining files off the desk and dropped them on top of a nearby cabinet. "Forget these," he said. "Or at least put them aside for now. The Gallagher kid's case is the most complete of all of them, and if you're going to pick up anything, it'll be there. We'll go to the scene first—it's not far. And then I would talk to the Gallagher family. His father and a couple of brothers still live in the neighborhood. If there's any time left, there's someone I think you should definitely talk to. A real nice woman—knew Durand's family pretty well, but sort of from the side, so she doesn't have any kind of protective loyalty. Lady by the name of Kelly McGrath. Her sister Maggie was a caretaker in the Durand house for a while—she's gone now, though, from cancer too."

"It's an epidemic, isn't it?"

"I'll say. Hope it doesn't get me."

"Ditto."

Moskal made three calls for me before we set out for the scene where the Gallagher boy was found. Sheila

Carmichael's answering service said that she was out of town and would not be returning calls until Monday; he left no message, but wrote the number down for me so I could at least call her when I got back to L.A. Patrick Gallagher, Michael's father, said he would love to talk to me; according to Moskal, he even sounded eager. And Kelly McGrath would be happy to have me over around teatime. We would go straight from her home back to the train station. It would be a grueling little tour.

"I could try to find the detective who did all the follow-up on this case if you want, but I have to tell you, the guy won't be much help."

"Right now I have too much to do and not enough time. But I could call him from L.A."

"I don't know if he has a phone anymore."

"He's that bad?"

"Worse."

He drove; I read. The interviews conducted by the now-alcoholic were complete and beautifully done; I hated to think about that kind of skill going down the tubes. There was a discernible chronological escalation of the man's anxiety in each report he wrote, much like I'd seen in Terry Donnolly's work. When the shutdown finally came, it was one of those whimper-not-bang situations. The investigation just sort of burned itself out, taking with it a previously fine police officer.

He had rounded up all the known pedophiles in the area, as I had, at the request of his supervisor, also as I had. Three suspects, all white men in their thirties, were questioned beyond the initial interviews but later released because no evidence could be found to link any one of them to the boy's disappearance.

He had extensively interviewed all of Michael Gallagher's buddies, none of whom recalled anything unusual or disturbing about the afternoon's events or the boy's demeanor. Michael had bade them all a smiling good-bye, according to the transcripts, and then headed in the expected direction toward home with a half-eaten chocolate bar in his hand. One of the friends recalled watching Michael unwrap the rest of the bar as he turned a familiar corner, after which he could no longer see him.

That was the last reported sighting of Michael Gallagher until his body was found the following Monday morning.

The car came to a stop in an alley behind what appeared to be an abandoned building. It was a narrow triple-decker house with railed porches off the back. Clotheslines extended from each porch to a utility pole across the alley. It was altogether depressing, even a little scary.

"Here we are," Moskal said. We got out of the car and he led me straight to the bottom porch. He pointed to the lattice that enclosed the porch base to cover the support posts.

I pushed on one of the panels; it gave slightly but wouldn't open more than a couple of inches.

To my great surprise, Moskal kicked it in with one vicious thrust of his foot, disturbing whatever lay within.

"Nice place for a kid to die, huh?"

It was dank and smelly and filled with cobwebs. God alone knew how much rat shit had been deposited onto the dirt floor, how many skeletons of mice had been left behind by stray cats, how many skunks had shot off their glands in there, how many winos had escaped the rain. All of their leavings would have been worked further into the dirt during the assault on Michael Gallagher, probably by downward pressure from his belly as he was raped from behind.

The boards below the porch were suffering from terminal dry rot along the bottom edges. "Looks empty," I said quietly.

"It is. Been through a number of owners. None of them could seem to make the dollars work."

"Was it empty back then?"

"No, but the first floor was vacant, that I do know. The second-floor tenants were in the process of moving out."

"Who found him?"

"A work crew. They were replacing some split shingles on the outside of the house. The owner had told them they could put their equipment in there over the weekend. They quit around three on Friday afternoon. Michael was last seen around three-thirty. Monday morning these guys show up and—*whammo*—they get hit with the smell. One of the crew puked right where you're standing. Gathering the evidence for this homicide was a really nasty job, let me tell you."

The remnants of a hasp were rusting in place on the hatch. "It wasn't locked?"

"The padlock had been broken, but the killer repositioned it so that it looked to be intact at a glance. Unfortunately, whatever prints there might have been on the padlock itself got messed up by the man who opened it on Monday. The hatch door was open when I got there; they didn't close it again. First thing I did was call my patrol supervisor. Sergeant Sean O'Reilly."

Durand's uncle.

"Damn."

"Right. He came out in a flash and had me cordon off the area. He stepped over the puke and went into the space himself. All alone."

"Damn again."

"Yeah. And he was in there for a long time, maybe five minutes. I don't know how the hell he stood it, but he did. He had me call in for evidence teams after he came out."

"Not during?"

"No. He kept me busy with other stuff. Getting

names from the work crew, things the detectives probably should have done. But he had me do it anyway."

The report stated that Michael Gallagher had been strangled with a nylon stocking—not panty hose, but an open-top thigh-high stocking that required a garter belt or panty girdle—as he was attacked. Totally anachronistic, even twenty years ago. Both of the boy's own socks had been stuffed into his mouth, probably to stifle his screams. He'd been bound at the wrists and ankles, also with stockings, and flipped over so his belly was on the ground. He had been sodomized viciously, to the point where the ground beneath his groin was soaked with his blood. No traces of semen were found in the anus.

But there were traces of latex discovered during the postmortem.

"They never found a wrapper or a used condom anywhere?"

"Nope. The guy must have taken them away with him."

This was a careful killer, at least about those details. An organized killer. "He picked a good spot to stash the body."

"Except that it was getting warm and the stink was going to ooze out in just a couple more days anyway."

"He probably wanted it to be found," I said, "but not too soon."

The photos I'd seen in the file showed a carefully bound body in a tortured position. "I'll bet this kid put up a fight."

"Probably."

"Which means that the killer would have been rushed. Maybe the reason you didn't find any semen at all was that he didn't finish the act."

"No way to tell, unfortunately. The only thing we can say for sure is that Michael Gallagher didn't participate willingly. His hands and arms were all bruised and cut,

God bless him. The guy who did this would be covered with bruises, if we got him fast enough. Trouble with bruises as evidence is that they fade."

"How was Sean O'Reilly during all of this? I mean, did he seem nervous, or anything like that?"

"He just kept repeating what a shame this was, what a terrible shame, how the boy's mother shouldn't see him like that, all white with the blood having come out of him. And I remember thinking that he looked a little peaked himself, that he was pretty shook up. Sean was a real veteran; something like this shouldn't have gotten to him to that degree. I'll admit it was a bad scene, but I'd seen much worse and so had he—we had that train and bus collision a couple of years before, and there were body parts all over the place. He didn't flinch for that. I did ask him if he was okay, and he said something about having had the flu."

Moskal went quiet for a moment and looked at his feet.

"What else?"

The tall detective sighed. He was deeply troubled and made no effort to hide it. "Sean came out of the shed with blood on his hands, which he kept trying to wipe off on a white handkerchief—we didn't all carry gloves back in those days. We're like a bunch of old hockey players: no helmets, if we grandfather the mandate. I asked him how it got there and he said he was just determining for himself that the Gallagher boy was really dead. Like there was any possibility that he wasn't. We usually do that by pressing a finger on one of the pulse points. His hands were tied together, so Sean would have had to go for the neck. There was no blood on Michael Gallagher's neck. According to the M.E., he bled out through the anus."

"Which meant that he was alive long enough after being sodomized for that to happen."

"Yeah. I hate to tell you how many times that thought

has plowed through my brain in the middle of the night. I always wanted to know what part of him Sean O'Reilly touched. He probably messed up some evidence in there."

None of this was in any of the reports.

"And another thing—the stockings. I mean, they were just not a Southie item. I remember when panty hose first came out, my mother and sister tossed all their stockings and garter belts right away. I hate to think how many years ago that was. For someone to be using them had to have some significance."

I flipped through the evidence photographs until I came upon the shot of the stockings. They were laid out lengthwise but lapped back in the middle once to accommodate the shape of the photographic field. Fully laid out, the photograph would have been unclear. The table surface showed through the beige gossamer.

"Were they silk or nylon?"

He stared at me. "I don't know."

I studied the photograph again; something about the stockings was tweaking me.

There was a dark line along the shaped back of the leg.

"They have seams," I said aloud.

"What?"

"Seams. Up the back. Very fifties. Betty Grable, remember? There were a couple of famous photographs of her wearing seamed stockings."

"So?"

"So they went out of ordinary fashion in the very early sixties. Nurses and hookers still wore them, but that was about it. This guy would have had to go to some lengths to find them. Probably an exclusive hosiery store."

"Or a costume place."

"He was creating an illusion," I said softly. Then, louder, I asked, "Do you happen to know what school Wilbur Durand went to when this took place?"

"We had bussing then, so I can't say right off the top of my head, but he would have been in high school. I honestly don't know—you'd have to contact the school department. Good luck. You'll need it."

There was nothing more to see. I'd soaked up the ambience of the scene. It was bright and sunny and there was a warm breeze that blew little strands of my hair into my face. But I was chilled to the bone.

Patrick Gallagher invited us into the living room of his narrow row house and offered us coffee. Pete Moskal accepted; I declined.

It had been twenty years, but still this man bore the emotional scars. I expressed my heartfelt condolences. He wanted to know why I, a Los Angeles cop, had an interest in a murder that took place twenty years prior, an entire nation away from my home turf.

"I have a suspect in a child disappearance case in Los Angeles who once lived here."

"And you're hoping to establish a link between them."

I nodded.

"It's Durand, isn't it?"

Pete Moskal got as far as saying *We're not at liberty* when I overrode him with a firm *yes*. Everyone stared at everyone else for a few moments, until Gallagher finally said, "I knew it. That son of a bitch, I knew it." He pointed a finger at Moskal. "Didn't I tell you? I told you he had something to do with it."

I leaped in. "Mr. Gallagher, I don't know for sure that Durand is the man I'm looking for at this point. Please don't jump to conclusions here. I told you that only because I need your total cooperation. I also need your discretion, at least until I have enough to arrest him. Otherwise he may get away. Now, if you wouldn't mind, I'd appreciate it if you'd tell me what makes you think that Wilbur Durand killed your son."

"Because he was a pervert to begin with."

"A pervert."

"Yeah. He was a complete fag. And he had a motive."

"Which was ..."

"To get even with Aiden."

I looked at Moskal. "I don't know who that is."

"Michael's older brother," Gallagher answered. "Durand took a shine to him in high school. Tried to talk him into doing all sorts of disgusting stuff. Aiden told him to shove off, even beat him up a couple of times."

"Mr. Gallagher, why didn't you mention this when the police looked into your son's death?"

"Because Aiden didn't tell me until a couple of years ago."

I was imagining the scene between father and son, the disappointment and the letdown, the terrible shock of being told something so dreadful. "May I ask why it came up then, after all that time?"

Gallagher's shoulders slumped. Moskal finally spoke. "Aiden was a firefighter. That building that collapsed in Boston, where so many guys were badly burned ..."

I remembered it. The story had made the national news. It always does when a firefighter is burned and later dies.

Moskal and I were both drained and white-faced when we left the Gallagher house. There were things hanging unsaid like a fetid stench in the air, awful things that ought not to be vocalized by human beings. New wheels had been set in motion by Patrick Gallagher; it was up to Moskal and me to keep them rolling.

"Kelly McGrath is expecting us in half an hour.

It's only a two-minute drive. You want to go back to the station?"

"No," I said. "I think we have some things to talk about. Let's get to it."

"Okay," he said. He brought the car to a stop at the curb. There was a small park—an empty lot that had been rejuvenated. I wondered if a house had been there, maybe one that had burned down. Kids on a roundabout were screaming with the carefree joy of childhood.

I went first. "This is enough new evidence to reopen the Gallagher case."

"It is."

"And you're going to go for it."

"I am."

"I need a little more time to gather evidence in Los Angeles. I'd like to ask you to wait, if you can see your way clear to that."

"I thought you might."

"I've got thirteen missing children. Maybe one of them is alive still."

"You know better than that."

I did but denied it. "There's always hope."

The volume of the children's voices went up suddenly. We both turned to look and saw that two of the kids, older boys, had jumped off and were pushing the roundabout as fast as they could. The little ones loved it.

"Oh, to turn back time," I said.

"Yeah." He was clearly not thinking of that but aching to rush it forward. "I could wait, but if he gets wind of you coming after him and takes off on me, I'm really gonna have a hard time with that."

"I can't say for sure that he won't. I can promise you that I'll move as quickly as I can and I'll be as discreet as possible. I've already called his studio looking for him. Someone may have told him that there were inquiries. For all I know, he may already have skipped town."

"If he has, I'll retire right now and find him."

I believed he would.

We reached a tentative agreement: I would have one week to get what I could, and then Moskal and I would talk again to assess the situation. If he was unsatisfied with my progress, he would move forward on his end. But until then he wouldn't do anything official. At five minutes before teatime, we pulled up in front of Kelly McGrath's row house.

She wasn't as elderly as I expected her to be. Early sixties maybe, petite, colored her hair dark auburn, kept herself trim and neat. We were seated in the parlor immediately; a tea service was already out on the coffee table with cups and spoons and lump sugar. Cream, but no lemon. On the piano were photographs of Kelly and a slightly older woman who might have been her twin.

"Is that your sister, Maggie?" I asked as she passed a cup and saucer to me.

"Yes," she answered, crossing herself with a free hand. "Rest in peace."

"How long has she been gone?"

"Oh, a very long time. Thirty-three years now."

She had died when Wilbur was seven years old. "Your sister was a governess in the Durand household?"

She looked puzzled for a moment, then said, "Oh, yes, the little boy's name was Durand, wasn't it? I forgot. I always think of it as the Carmichael house. Well, they did too, that's why. They never did like it that Patricia married that Frenchman. I mean, he was a Catholic and all, I just don't understand how some people could be so narrow-minded. It seems to come with money if you ask me. So does cheapness, imagine that. Things might have gone better for her if her family had helped out a bit more."

I never asked another question.

"Patricia wasn't right, you know. She had a rough time of it with his birth, and the new marriage wasn't working out to begin with. She got this terrible infection and had to have her womanly parts removed—you'll forgive me for speaking like this in front of you, Detective Moskal. After that, her husband didn't pay any attention to her at all. Pretty much left her on her own. He moved her to Brookline right after the baby was born because he said it was an up-and-coming place and a good investment. Well, Patricia hated it. She had no friends there, the church wasn't as welcoming, and she just took to drinking to drown her troubles. The Carmichael kids—Sheila, Eileen, and Cullen—didn't have as rough a time of it because they'd had her when she was right, and their father had been wonderful, God rest his soul. What a shame he died so young.

"But Patricia just neglected poor little Wil something terrible. Maggie used to go by trolley out there every day to make sure Wilbur was getting fed and clothed decently—stayed over sometimes if the missus was sopped. We finally had to get a phone because Mrs. O'Day downstairs was getting a little bit tired of relaying her messages to me. Lots of times she would find his sheets soaked when she got there, and he'd have no clean clothes if she didn't do the laundry. She would sometimes have to sober the missus up to take her to the bank so she could get money for groceries. Once or twice she bought groceries with her own money. But I put a stop to that. Bring the lad here, I told her, and we'll give him a proper upbringing. But she didn't want to interfere in a private family situation. She was like that.

"No matter what she did, he was still a strange little boy. So quiet most of the time, but when he got his Irish up he was something to behold. His mother never disciplined him at all, and his father was gone by then. It was heartbreaking. But Maggie was keeping things decent for the boy—until she got sick, that is. He was six when she found the first lump. She didn't go right away to the doctor, claimed it was nothing, but I think she was scared. By the time she went, it was really too late, though they took both her breasts anyway, I think to give her hope. It did buy her some time, but not much.

"Wil's granddad—Patricia and Sean's father—he was the devil incarnate. Hated Maggie for what he said was interference in his daughter's affairs. He should have been on his knees every day thanking her, for my money. The old bastard got absolutely livid if anyone said anything against Sean, though we all knew what sort he was. Never married, always around little boys; the granddad wouldn't hear a word of it, that Sean ought not to be allowed to have kids alone. He was a police officer and all, and I guess that made him a saint in his father's eyes. Maggie would take Wil to see his gran and granddad because she thought it was only right that he should know them, even if his mother didn't make the effort. Told me that he called her 'that bloody wench' right in front of the boy. 'That bloody wench is ruining you,' he would say, as if Maggie weren't there. 'That bloody wench is too soft on you.'

"In all the time that Maggie took care of the boy, the grandma never tried to intercede against the granddad. I guess she was scared of him, with good reason. They say he knocked her around a time or two. Well, Maggie got herself all dressed up one day and called on the old lady at teatime, just like you're doing right now, and told her everything that had been going on. Pleaded with her to take the children in. Eventually she talked her into it.

"Maggie died about two months later, shortly after Wil and the other children were moved into the house by the beach. Wil didn't do too well after that, I'm told—he lost the only person who loved him for himself. And after that, we used to see him with Sean a lot. It wasn't right. Not at all."

All of this was spinning through my head as the train rattled and shook its way back to New York. High speed, maybe, but the ride could have been smoother. Nevertheless, I was happy to be on my way back. I had a lot of work to do; I had to find those museum tapes if I had any hope of nailing this guy. I needed a warrant to search his premises, both personal and professional. The report would have to be seamless. It would all be circumstantial, but it would have to do.

On Sunday next I would have to call Detective Moskal again. If he was busy with his family that day, I might be able to stretch it to Monday. If I didn't have what I needed, I was hoping he would listen to reason.

Standing on the platform at South Station, Moskal had said to me, "I've always thought that Sean O'Reilly found something in that shed to implicate someone and that he took it out of there. If I'd been more insistent on following procedures, maybe all these kids wouldn't be missing."

"He was your superior officer," I offered gently. "What else were you supposed to do?"

"He had a superior officer too—I could have made a report. But I had little kids and a wife to support and I couldn't afford to lose my job."

"You can't blame yourself," I told him. "Things like this are never within our control, no matter how much we'd like them to be."

The train showed up just about then. "I'll call you next Monday morning," I said.

"Whatever."

The landscape flashed by in a blur. I wanted to work on my notes, but there was too much motion. Instead, I lowered the seat and tried to think through all the new information I'd gotten.

Uncle Sean had diddled Wilbur—I would bet my badge on it. Wilbur had started to diddle little boys himself when he got old enough and big enough. One of them had probably threatened to talk, and he had killed him. He liked what it did for him, all that power. Michael Gallagher's murder, so carefully planned and precisely executed, was probably his first, and the catalyst for all that followed. Erkinnen was going to love this.

The only love Wilbur Durand got as a child was labeled "bloody" by a powerful authority figure. Bloody love was what he knew, what he would try to re-create. Over and over and over again.

But he wasn't going to do it anymore.

twenty-one

IT WAS A STOUT RIDE to Champtocé, a full day—
longer if the trip was made in a muddy season—along
the precarious edge of the river, where bare tree roots
were all that held the cliff in place. It made no sense that
this road should have developed in such proximity to the
river and not farther into the forest, where the ground
was firmer—that is, until one stopped and looked southeast on a clear day. The beauty of the view over the Loire
could take the breath away. I knew from journeys between Champtocé and Machecoul in my younger days
that there was always a danger of the road sliding along
this route after a hard rain, but today the weather was
fine.

We traveled intently and made good progress, but
even the most stalwart journeyer must stop now and
then. As *Frère* Demien tended to his own requirements at
the edge of the vista, I slipped into the woods so I might
discreetly see to my own. As I moved away from the road,
the twigs cracked under my feet; insects buzzed and birds

called out their warnings to one another of my approach.
A shaft of sunlight angled through the canopy; it was all
too familiar, and I found myself quite unexpectedly
flooded with memories of my life before the veil.
Sensations and images of previous times in these woods
overwhelmed me with stunning swiftness and power. I
could not hold myself upright but slumped to my knees.

His hand on mine, pulling me, coaxing, all smiles
and laughter and mischief ...

*Come, Guillemette, my pretty bride, and I will show you
a new trick, one you are sure to enjoy.* We were so young,
Etienne and I, just newly wed and so sweetly captivated
by our mutual desire. Willingly I had complied with this
bold request, but not until after a moment of blushing
pretense at resistance. I swear it was on that occasion, in
these very woods, on moss so soft as to put a feather bed
to shame, that his seed entered my womb and became
Jean, our first son.

I smile now to think of our excesses.

Alas, that ever love was sin.... My Wife of Bath
knew too well how sweet it could be.

Most often we would go to Machecoul in those days,
but sometimes we journeyed to l'Hôtel de la Suze, on the
other side of Nantes. It was as comfortable as any of
Milord's estates, more so in winter; it was, in defiance of
explanation, a good deal less drafty than most of his
other holdings in the short frigid days of January.

The journey back to Champtocé, however, was always far more pleasing because Etienne and I came to
view it as our home. My greatest joys and most terrible
sorrows had all been visited upon me there. What folly it
was for me to have let the place make such a claim on me,
when I had no such claim on the place itself.

Just after noon *Frère* Demien and I passed through
the village of Champtoceaux. There was a tavern there,
where I had often stopped with my husband, who would

listen to any musician, no matter how awful, for hours on end. Often he would grasp me at the waist and twirl me around to the rhythm of the drumming; my skirts would fly out behind me in a most vulgar manner, but he never seemed to care—he loved the revelry and would lose himself in it.

I had a sudden ache to be inside the place again. "There might be stories here," I said aloud.

"There are stories everywhere."

"Brother, let us take some refreshment."

He made no objection. We tethered our mounts outside the venerable establishment, whose wooden sign, saying simply TAVERN, hung slightly askew on a wrought-iron standard, as it had the first time I walked under it.

The moment we walked in the door, I saw that nothing had changed, not the landlord nor his plump wife, who still strutted about the place as if she were the mistress of the finest hotel. Their girth had increased—by some two beings, to be plain.

We removed our cloaks and settled at benches on opposite sides of a long table. The landlord came round to serve us; he looked me squarely in the eye but did not recognize me, though I could hardly have been called a regular since I did not live in Champtoceaux itself. Still, there was a pang of regret within me and a brief moment of wonder at whether we ought to have stopped here at all.

"God's blessings on you, Mother," he said, bowing slightly in my direction. "And on you too, Brother," he said, acknowledging *Frère* Demien. "How can I serve you today?"

"A flagon," *Frère* Demien said.

I added, "And then a word."

"What word would you be seeking, now?"

"What passes in these parts," I said. "I have not

come through this way in a good long time, where once I did more often."

The man smiled mischievously and then left us for a moment. I looked around at the other guests; in one corner, there was an elderly man whose full face I could not see. There was something familiar about him, but I could not place him in my mind's history. The man himself was large and shockingly white-haired, but what struck me most intensely was the size of his hands, which dwarfed the knife he held to whittle at a small block of wood. His fingers moved with expert delicacy, and I was inordinately curious about what he might be shaping. A pile of chips and shavings lay on the board before him. Every now and then as she passed, the mistress would swoop in with one hand and banish the offending chips to the dirt floor, where they would serve to sop up any spilled ale.

Her husband returned with a large flagon of ale and two mugs, which he placed beneath our noses.

We drank; he spoke. "Let me see now, what has transpired ..." He rattled off a short list of banal events: the birth of a cow, the purchase of a loom, a blight on a cherry crop, a bit of gossip about a corpulent wife pounding her fists on a scrawny husband in a fit of pique over some imagined infidelity. And then he looked me in the eye again and said, "But of course there is no need to tell you that more of our children have disappeared."

I was filled with inexplicable joy that he knew me, though it stung somewhat to realize that it was by reputation for my inquiries rather than a fondly recalled visitor from older times.

To my momentary speechlessness he said, "Are you not the Mother Abbess?"

"I am," I admitted.

He seemed to be expecting something from me. I tried not to disappoint.

"Well, then, how many have gone missing here?"

He shook his head and said softly, "We have lost count."

When *Frère* Demien tried to pay the bill, he would not accept our money. For a few moments after he left us, I could do little more than stare at the wood boards of the table. When I looked up again, my eyes sought out the white-haired old man. He had slipped away.

⚜

By the time we reached Ancenis—the last real town we would encounter before crossing into the bounds of Champtocé—I had worked myself into a nearly feverish state of anticipation. So many memories dwelled there for me. Why I felt so compelled to tear the scab from a wound that was as healed as it would ever be was something I had tried but failed to understand. Jean de Malestroit, the one person in this world who might have dissuaded me, had not been up to the task.

We approached the fortress along the main road, which cut through a wide, flat meadow. Anyone standing watch along the heights of the fortress walls would see us—we were as helpless and exposed as a mouse to an owl. But we heard no warnings, no shouts to identify ourselves. I suppose the warrior on the wall felt completely uncowed by the sight of a nun and a priest, one of whom was riding a donkey. One after the next, the familiar details came into view. First I saw the row of narrow archer's windows that encircled the south tower just below the parapet. Then I saw the standard waving in the breeze—it would not be Milord's at present. God alone knew who owned the place at the moment, so often had it changed hands of late, although we had been told that René de la Suze had managed to wrestle the title back from his brother's mortgager, whoever that fool might be. There was perhaps more greenery around the base of the wall than there had been the last time I was there; in

general the grounds outside the moat looked overgrown
and untended, a predictable ill effect of mutable owner-
ship. A number of stones were missing or misaligned in
the massive outer wall, and the whole place looked sadly
neglected.

But it was no less magnificent for its flaws. Finally,
one of the sentries signaled to us; we waved back to indicate our friendliness. The portcullis began to rise as we
neared the drawbridge. How well I remembered each
creak of the pulley wheel as the ropes heaved the massive
door upward. My heart was flooded with elation, terror,
uncertainty, hope, and many more emotions, most of
which I would never be able to name.

Would I find what I hoped to find?

It seemed so unlikely after so much time.

Frère Demien saw my anxiety. "Do not fret so,
Sister," he reassured me. "He will still be there."

On what basis other than his own optimism he made
this questionable claim I cannot say, but I tried to let myself feel comforted. "I covet your confidence, Brother."

"This man was a fine castellan, or so you have said."

"But unrelated to any member of the nobility and
therefore at risk for uprooting, as I well know."

"What fool of a lord would get rid of an exceptional
castellan to install someone who knows nothing of the
property's intricacies, merely for the sake of employing
one of his allies?"

"There are many lords who are complete fools, *mon
frère,* and allegiance is a powerful force."

"Not so powerful as it once was, *ma soeur,* nor will it
ever be as attractive as wisdom for which one does not
have to pay."

The mantles worn by the gatesmen bore the coat of arms of
René de la Suze, as had been rumored. And the influence

of wisdom had prevailed in his tenancy of Champtocé, at least in part, because the castellan Marcel still resided on the premises.

"I should have made a wager with you," *Frère* Demien said with a smile.

"You would not have won decisively," I said.

"But the result would have merited some payment, you must admit."

"But not full payment. We were neither of us fully right."

Marcel was indeed still in residence, though his official duties had been assigned to a younger man of René de la Suze's choosing. But Gilles de Rais's sensible younger brother had appointed the older man to a permanent post as an adviser to his inexperienced ally, who would benefit greatly from the advocacy. At the same time, the elder castellan was rewarded for his loyal service, which was only fitting and right.

The vibrant man of middle years that Guy Marcel had been while I resided in Champtocé was still quite visible in the old man he had become. His eyes still shone with *joie de vivre;* his stride was still purposeful, if abbreviated. There was the same pride in his carriage that I remembered so fondly. Still present, too, were his courteous mannerisms, especially to travelers.

"*Bonjour, mon frère,*" he said to *Frère* Demien when he approached us. "*À votre service.*"

"*Merci bien,* but it is my sister in Christ who seeks you, not I," the young monk said.

Guy Marcel turned toward me and regarded my face without recognition. He did not stare rudely, as a less polite man might have done. Instead, he said, "I am pleased to meet you, Sister."

I laughed quietly. "Ah, *Monsieur,* has it been that much time?"

"*Pardon?*"

"You once called me Madame la Drappiere," I said.

He nearly gasped. "*Mon Dieu,* Madame, you have returned!"

I knew he might not have been told of what had been done with me after Etienne died. The women would likely have known, for the same fate might have happened to any one of them. But I had not been friendly with the man's wife while we both resided here—she was a sorry shrew and always ornery, so I had avoided her, as I suspect he often did himself. I wondered if she was still alive.

He came closer to me, his arms outstretched in welcome. "Madame," he said warmly, "it is truly wonderful to see you here again after so many years."

I introduced *Frère* Demien and then inquired politely after the disagreeable wife. He told me she had gone to her eternal rest some years before. All this chatter took place before we had even dismounted. "Let me summon a steward for your—uh, animals," Marcel said. He offered me a helping hand, which eased what would have been an otherwise ungainly descent. As our beasts were led away, we two-legged beings were shown to the same quarters near the outer gate that Monsieur Marcel had occupied in those earlier days. The new castellan had chosen to live deeper within the fortress, perhaps for safety's sake, which was understandable; the first edifice to be attacked in an assault would be that one, so close and vulnerable, the white underbelly in any castle, or so Etienne had said. But the old man was probably accustomed to that danger and might have missed it had he been moved.

He made us comfortable at a long table and offered refreshments, which we heartily accepted. We faced one another over glasses of hippocras and a plate of blushing ripe pears, freshly plucked from the tree. *Frère* Demien turned one over in his hands and sighed out his admiration. *"Très belle,"* he cooed at the fruit. *"Magnifique!"*

Guy Marcel smiled pleasantly. "I take no credit for their perfection. We have an excellent gardener who sees to all our trees. I know nothing of these things save how to enjoy the fruits of another's wisdom and labor. But I am told that the soil here is by some miracle ideal for pears, and therein lies the secret."

"I should like to see the orchard and sample the soil, if I might," *Frère* Demien said.

"I shall arrange it," Marcel said. Then he turned to me. "And, Madame, what of you these days?" He gestured toward the cross that hung on my chest. "You are in service to God, I see...."

I told the old gentleman of my life since I had departed Champtocé, which telling sadly required only three or four breaths to complete. He was kind enough to show interest and congratulated me on my apparent good fortune.

"It is a fine thing to have the confidence of one's master, I think."

"You would know this well, if anyone."

"And what of your son, Madame? If God had not taken so much of my memory, I would recall his name...."

"Jean," I said. "He serves his Holiness in Avignon. I am forced to do constant penance for my excessive pride over the matter."

We all laughed for a moment. Then there was no further reason to delay.

"I would ask you some questions, *Monsieur,* about my other son. Michel."

When I spoke my son's name, Guy Marcel seemed to shrink back a bit. "Madame," he protested, "it was so many years ago that the tragedy happened...."

"I myself am subject to the whims of memory these days. I will not fault you for an incomplete recollection."

"You are far too youthful yet to be having such difficulties," he said with a kind smile. "Let us speak of other things."

His compliments did not lessen my resolve, nor did his sweet attempt to change the subject deter me from my chosen path. But I did not wish to make him uncomfortable, so we sat in silence for a moment or two; the pause in the discourse seemed somehow to honor my long-gone son. I waited patiently until the time seemed right to press him again.

"I simply want to ask you to recall as much as you can of what happened."

The poor man squirmed. "Madame, what more is there to be known? The boy simply disappeared—we know not why. Perhaps it was a result of the boar's villainy, as Milord Gilles told us. But no one can say." He glanced back and forth between me and my young brother and then took a long pull on his glass of hippocras. "It is my sincere wish that God cradles your boy in His arms, as I hope for myself one day. Not too long from now, I suspect."

"When Milord came back here that day, what was it exactly that he said to you?"

"Madame, please—I cannot recall such details after so many years."

Though it had been more than a decade since Etienne had died, I could recall the sight of his festering leg with such clarity that I longed to cast it out of my mind, if only such a miraculous thing could be done. I had tried desperately over the years to relieve myself of the image of his blackened limb, which rotted progressively until it took his life. No matter how sincere my efforts, I failed: It persists in my memory like a stone of such weight that it cannot be hefted and thrown. Buried in Guy Marcel's mind somewhere was the remembrance of what Gilles de Rais had said on his return from the outing that took my son from me. I would have those words drawn out again.

I told him so, unequivocally. "*Monsieur,* such things as you heard said that day cannot be erased from one's memory. You need only give a moment to thought, and it will come clear to you. I am certain of it."

He stood up and paced around, fretting quite openly, then sat back down again and took hold of my hand. "Madame, please." He patted my fingers. "I am *old.* I cannot recall what happened so far in the past."

I removed my fingers from within his and patted the back of his hand. "I respectfully put forth, sir, that you are not too much older than I. And I must remind you that it was yourself who caused me to be held away from Milord, so I must depend on your recollections of the matter. Now, please, for the sake of my heart's rest, try."

Guy Marcel had seen many men wounded and maimed in battles and wars; he had regarded Guy de Laval's belly wound firsthand. He had managed to maintain uncanny steadiness in those instances. Now, when asked to recall mere words, he was unnerved. I did not think he was disturbed by any lack of ability to remember but rather by the nature of the memory itself.

He rubbed his forehead as if it ached. "Very well," he said wearily. "I shall try."

Something dark seemed to take hold of him as he began to speak. "The sentries heard shouts from a distance, so I sent more watchers into the tower right away. When Milord Gilles came into view we saw that he was running hard, in obvious distress. I ordered the gate opened immediately. He came through alone and fell into my arms. At first he was panting so hard that he could barely speak. When he regained his voice he said that the boar had come back again, and that he himself had turned and run. And that he thought Michel was directly behind him. But when he looked back, there was no one there."

I had heard all this before, on the day of this terrible event. I wanted more. "He said nothing beyond that? He must have been terribly upset."

"He said nothing to *me*. His grandfather took him away immediately, so the boy might be composed and then more thoroughly questioned, he said. I had no more words with Milord Gilles or Jean de Craon on the matter. Nor did anyone else after that, of whom I know."

The castellan looked down at his hands, which were placed flat on the wood planks of the table as if he would anchor himself to it. "He was panting, Madame. He said very little beyond recounting his discovery of your son's absence. So I cannot say, exactly, what his state of mind was at that point. But Jean de Craon seemed to think that he was *quite* upset."

By the look on Marcel's face I could see that he had other thoughts lurking in the depths of his soul. There was something he wanted to say but could not.

"*Monsieur,* you may speak frankly to me. My allegiance no longer lies with Milord Gilles, but with God and his Eminence. Do not fear that I will betray you."

"Madame—" he said.

"You shall not be held accountable, no matter what you tell me."

He gazed into some blank place in front of himself for a few silent moments and then turned again to face me.

"Madame, forgive me, but I thought I saw Milord *smile* for the briefest moment."

"Smile? How do you mean *smile*?"

"As if he were . . . happy, or satisfied in some way."

This was a detail I had never known; my grief and fear at that time were so all-encompassing.

I heard the castellan say, "I remember two thoughts I had that day. Both gave me pause. The first was that it seemed odd Milord could turn about and see neither boy nor boar. One would think he would see one or the other. But *nothing* . . . it seemed so unlikely."

"And the second?"

He cleared his throat nervously. "I remember also thinking throughout the whole ordeal that Milord seemed more . . . *excited* than upset. It fit with his smile, I daresay."

I took out my *mouchoir* and, unashamed, dabbed away the tears that filled the corners of my eyes. "Was any blood to be seen on Milord?"

He paused to search his memory. In a few moments he said, "There was. On his mantle, in the midsection. But his clothing was disheveled; I assumed he had fallen and cut himself and then perhaps wiped his hands on his garments. There was some blood on his hands, but they were cut and bruised. He said he had hurt them running through the forest, when he pushed the branches aside. It seemed a reasonable explanation. He offered this information himself."

When I first saw his hands at close range several days later, the palms were all scabs. The midwife had applied ointments and salves to help the healing, but it was difficult for Milord to make a fist at first because of one particularly deep cut across the palm of his right hand. He would never open his fist so I might see the wounds more closely; he said that to do so was painful. In my grief, I could not find the will to press him further.

I sat back for a moment and tried to remember what he had worn that day, a detail that was buried deep in my own memory. The image of a dark blue mantle and yellow tunic struggled to the surface. Both would have been given away to some lesser relation if the blood could not be entirely removed. None of the laundry maids had made comments. I wondered if either garment had ever reached their hands.

"And none of the woodsmen who were about that day heard any untoward noises in their travels through the forest. All of them knew what had transpired in the woods, but none came forward."

I had not heard of any woodsmen about. My son had been a brave lad for his tender years, adventuresome and spirited—not a boy who would have let a boar overtake him without running, screaming, doing whatever he could to fend off the attack. He would not have died instantly; surely he would have screamed and shouted for help. Someone would have heard him.

Had Milord heard his cries and abandoned him to his fate?

"*Monsieur,* do boars often eat their prey?"

The man would not meet my gaze.

"*Monsieur?*"

"No, Madame, they do not. They are angry beasts, but when they kill it is usually in defense of their own survival."

For the thousandth time, I asked myself the question that had plagued me since that awful day. When it had made its way through me, I let it escape my lips in a low moan. "Then why, oh, *why,* was Michel's *corpus* never found?"

"It remains a confounding mystery, Madame."

The search party had gone out immediately, Etienne included. Every horse in the stable was given a rider; among those riders was our midwife Madame Catherine Karle, who would see to my son's wounds should he be found injured.

They were gone until the light finally dissipated. All returned in an apparent state of agitation. But Madame Karle, a woman enamored of the sound of her own voice, had been uncharacteristically wordless, even to me, and remained so for nearly a fortnight.

When I commented on the oddity of this to the castellan, he said, "I do recall that she seemed rather sullen for a time."

⚜

When our troubling conversation could go no further, it died a natural death. We tried to mend our spirits with a fine repast of quail and *escargot,* with turnips and fresh crusty bread to complement the various meats. Hippocras flowed like water from the decanter he set on the table, and I think we may have drunk the dregs themselves in our zeal to see it empty. The old man was only too happy to speak of the adventures he had known in the years since I had last seen him, and our hearts eased to hear tales that did not concern the sudden inexplicable loss of a child.

Our journey back to Nantes would be a long one; it was expected that we would stay the night at Champtocé, and we were graciously accommodated by our host within his own quarters. It was a good thing, I thought, and perhaps he had realized it as well: There were many ghosts for me in the main living quarters of the castle, and I did not really want to present myself to them for haunting nor to the occupants for scrutiny, both of which were sure to occur should I set foot within those halls. Our every wish was satisfied, and more, and I went to bed quite gratefully drunk, without saying my prayers.

In answer to my prayerlessness, God visited monstrous dreams upon me throughout the night and then a thundering headache in the morning, which the cold water of the basin would not banish. Nor would the pressing of *Frère* Demien's warm hands upon my aching brow do much good either, though he added an ornate and effusive blessing for good measure. With an understanding smile and some odd mutterings about the hair of the dog, our venerable host made me drink another cup of hippocras, which effected a near-miraculous cure. Even more miraculously, it did not make me drunk.

"But now that you have restored me," I said, "I have another favor to ask of you."

He did not seem pleased, but he was nonetheless polite. "*Oui,* Madame."

"When we go out to the orchards, I would like it as well if you would take us to the ravine where Milord said he last saw Michel."

The request did not seem to sit well with him, for he frowned slightly. "What is there to be gained, Madame?" he asked.

"I don't know. But I am compelled to return there."

There was no decent reason to refuse, and so he acquiesced. We packed our few belongings and strapped them to our mounts, then headed out in the direction of the orchards, during which time *Frère* Demien spoke continuously on the subject of husbanding fruit trees. The desired handful of earth was scooped up and carefully examined by my young traveling companion, who smelled it, tasted it, crumbled it between his fingers, blended his own spittle into it, all in the name of discovering its secrets. His final comment, after all that, was simply, *Hmm.* It left me wondering, but I did not press him, for my thoughts were elsewhere.

On leaving the orchard, we turned onto a westward path and rode for a short distance. Soon we reached the landmark grove of oaks and there turned onto a new path, which we followed for an even shorter distance, until the ground began to fall away sharply.

Just a slight bit down the crest of the hill, perhaps the length of a man's body, was the small white cross Etienne had pounded into the ground to mark the place where our sorrow had begun, although we could never say exactly where it was. He had taken me to see it not long after he'd put it in place, and I remember wondering if that cross would be my son's entire legacy, rather than the legends and tales of valor we had hoped for.

I stared at the symbol of his remembrance, so white and brilliant against all the green and brown that surrounded it. Though it had stood many years unprotected in this spot, its appearance was remarkably fresh.

"Someone has been attending to it."

"*Oui,* Madame," Marcel said quietly. "We come out once in a while with the whitewash."

I could barely speak my gratitude. In the reverent silence, the gurgling of the stream that ran at the base of the ravine seemed an unholy jollity.

Finally I said, "Does this stream rise much in the spring?"

"Quite a good bit."

"And in the fall—does it run dry?"

"I have never known it to, Madame. We have had little rain this month, and this is the driest season normally, so it will not get much lower than what you see now."

I watched the clear ripples dance over the stones. It was more than adequate for washing away blood.

♔

On the road that skirted the meadow outside the castle, we said our good-byes to Guy Marcel; we would travel west toward Nantes, and he in the opposite direction to his home in the fortress. *Frère* Demien offered respectful wishes for Godspeed to our host, but I could summon up only tender melancholy—the castellan was one of my few remaining links to Champtocé, and God alone knew if we would remeet before one or the other of us went to the grave. There was in the old man's eyes a bit of the same longing for the years to roll back, for a return to the old glory we had once known, a notion made no less alluring by its impossibility.

We were perhaps a hundred paces apart in opposite directions when I heard the castellan call out, "Madame! Wait."

I halted my donkey and turned back to face him. The mighty fortress loomed large in the background, dwarfing him in its fading grandeur.

"*Oui, Monsieur?*"

He urged his horse a few steps forward so as not to shout at me. "The midwife, Madame Karle . . ." he began. Then he waited a moment before continuing, as if he were considering the advisability of what he was about to say. "She herself could not still be alive, but her son may yet walk this earth."

I remembered him well. "Guillaume," I said.

"*Oui,* the same." He told us where the man lived, well near to our return route. "Perhaps you should seek him out."

chapter 22

I NEEDED A CONFIDANT on this case. Frazee and Escobar were buddies and coworkers, but I needed a friend. Errol Erkinnen was making himself extremely available, for which I was grateful, on more than one level.

"I submitted a warrant application this morning to search Wilbur Durand's house and studio. I need those tapes to go any further with this. I'm almost salivating over the thought of going through his stuff; he's got to have a stocking drawer somewhere—"

"A *what*?" Erkinnen said.

"Sorry," I said. "It's the place where girls keep their most-secret stuff. My ex had a top drawer in his desk like that."

"Ah. For me it's the toolbox. But I get really cranky when anyone but me goes into it. What a job you have, looking through people's most intimate things."

"You go through people's brains."

"Point," he acceded.

"I swear, sometimes I think we're all just as sick as the guys we're trying to haul in."

"Oh, I don't think so. Some of them are way beyond sick. But this is an acceleration—you must have learned something more about him."

"Yeah. A *lot*."

He listened with attention as I told him about my side trip to Southie, about Detective Pete Moskal, the Gallagher family, the strange lack of evidence in their son's murder, and about what Kelly McGrath had revealed to me.

"Jeez," he said when I was through, "I don't know if you could write a better script for a serial killer."

"Abductor."

He went somber. "You know there's a real probability that all these kids are dead."

"No bodies, Doc, except the Jackson boy, and we all agree that at best he's practice. The only one who's even legally dead is the nephew of Jesse Garamond. And that's only because the uncle was convicted of killing him, so the law assumes a body, somewhere. But it was never found."

"I wonder what he's doing with them."

Doc voiced that question in a bemused tone; his clinical detachment was such that it almost made me angry. My voice sounded harsh even to myself when I said, "We'll probably find out sometime in the near future. *If* we don't get sidetracked. Keep talking about the script thing."

"Right. Sorry. What I mean is that it's the classic profile. Lack of maternal bonding, weak or absent father, a male authority figure who intervenes in a negative, dominant fashion—in Durand's case, two: both his uncle and his grandfather. Loss of an important support person—the housekeeper—at a critical age."

"The uncle is the one I'd like to strangle. He really worked him over. I mean, to be in a position of trust like that with a child and then use him for sex—"

"Do we know for sure that he did?"

"No, not absolutely. But based on what I found out in Boston, I think there's good reason to believe that it happened. The uncle is dead, so I can't confront him. Too bad. Well, maybe it's not too bad—about the dead part, I mean—after what he did."

"Be careful here, Detective. Keep your emotions out of this. I've heard of cops getting involved sympathetically with the victims of crime, and that's a tough enough situation. But it's really a bad idea for you to get involved with a criminal in that way."

I didn't respond immediately, because I needed to think for a moment—what was I really feeling toward Wilbur Durand? A strange blend of contradictions—I despised him and was fascinated by him, sometimes all in one thought.

"You're right," I said, "and I know it. I hate this—here I am feeling bad for this guy for all the nasty things that happened to him when he was little, and I'm almost positive in my heart that he's a monster of the worst kind. How pathetic is that."

"It's not pathetic at all. It's only natural to feel sympathy for someone who's been through as much as this guy has. If he hadn't turned out to be a pedophile, if he'd ended up being a plumber or something, you'd be patting him on the back for turning his life around. For surviving at all. The irony is that if he'd turned out to be an ordinary man, at least on the surface, we would probably never know what he'd been through as a child."

"How could he go through all that and *not* blow up?"

"People do. They develop the most incredible coping mechanisms."

"Then why didn't Durand?"

"Maybe he did. Maybe he isn't as much of a fiend as he might have been. Look, I understand how you're feeling. I always see these people and think to myself how lucky I am that my own life didn't go that way. But these are killers. Cold-blooded, unfettered killers. The things that happened to them are tragic, but their acts are still inexcusable."

I knew that the moment a lawyer got up and started talking about all this, I would want to rip his or her throat out. A good jury would ignore that lawyer if there was sufficient evidence; in this case there wasn't, at least not yet.

"Sheila Carmichael will find a defense psychologist who'll testify that someone should have seen it coming and done something and that he can't be held responsible for his own behavior because no one helped him when it would have meant something," said Doc.

"Not if I shoot her first."

"Lany. This is new."

"I know, I'm sorry. I didn't really mean it."

He did not look convinced.

I said, "Why didn't *she* see it? She's his sister."

"She'll say she was already out of the house."

"Well, she pretty much was—there's a ten-year difference in their ages."

"And besides, it's not like we haven't heard it before," he said. "You know, psychology still gets a bad rap for being an inexact science. Some people don't even think it's a science at all, just a lot of manipulative mumbo jumbo."

"Let me guess—the paranoids."

He laughed, sort of. "And the bipolars. But society still wants us to predict who's going to crack." He patted his hand on the folder of notes he'd accumulated in the course of our visits. "Everything that we believe will predict a serial pedophile is *right here*. We could have saved a lot of heartache if we'd been able to poke and prod Wilbur Durand when he was young and make the unequivocal assessment that he should be locked up for the rest of his life as a matter of public safety. But imagine the effort and cost of screening every child for predictors of later pedophilia, the hue and cry from civil-rights advocates. It's completely impractical—we can't round up all the guys who are fixated on child pornography because they might graduate to the next level."

If I was right, Wilbur Durand had graduated long before and was picking up real children and killing them. All notions of sympathy evaporated in that realization. I stood up and paced around. "There must be some barren island in the north Atlantic where we can ship them all for a while to see if it really makes a difference in the rate of pedophilia. Or some archipelago out near Siberia."

Doc heard the deep bitterness in my voice. "You're more than a little frustrated with this case, aren't you?"

"I'm running out of time. And he's not."

God bless the judge. God bless the prosecutor. The search warrant for the museum tapes was issued that afternoon.

And Fred Vuska finally agreed to give me some help. He really had no choice, with the judge showing enough confidence in the case to officially sanction an action against the suspect. And I couldn't search two premises by myself at the same time—the whole point was to show up, shove the warrant under someone's nose, and toss both places before anything could be moved or hidden from either location.

We would hit both the house and the studio at the same time. I would lead one of the teams, Escobar the other. There was no way to predict which place harbored Durand's stocking drawer, but I couldn't shake the notion that this was all a creative process for him and that his main place to be creative was the studio. Love and work, right? The two things that really drive people. This was a guy who combined them in an exquisitely perverted way.

The studio was located on the far end of a back lot at

Apogee Studios, well outside the route of the guided tram tour. I'd seen blurry photos of the place in a couple of tabloid spreads, which reported that black magic and occult rituals were the normal fare at the studio, along with visits from space aliens, whose pointy-headed pictures were obviously pasted in, with laughable ineptitude.

It was all starting to sound possible to me.

The building was a big, square, flat-roofed eyesore completely surrounded by a desert of asphalt. As it came into view, my excitement gave way to nervousness. It was so stark and barren, devoid of all welcome. There was no landscaping around this fortress, Wilbur's kingdom, which he was certain to defend. I imagined pots of boiling oil stationed at twenty-foot intervals all along the roofline, and warriors with no faces poised and ready to spill hot death onto anyone who happened along.

The outer offices were equally foreboding—not that Durand had to impress anyone to attract business. We'd come in through a heavy glass door, which looked to be the only entry. That surprised me; most of these studio buildings have big sliding doors, and often they're wide open so you can see inside. But not Durand's—it was literally encased in metal and concrete.

We walked right in with our badges out and the warrant in hand.

"We're looking for Wilbur Durand," I said.

Cold stares from a young male assistant. "I'm sorry, but he's not here."

We blew right by him; Spence was actually chuckling. He was reaching for a phone as we went through the door into the work space itself, at which point we all came to a halt.

"Holy mother of God," Spence said, glancing around.

It was Disney World, a museum, a scene from *Alice in Wonderland,* all rolled into one. Hanging from every bit of space on the walls were masks and body doubles for all these characters we all knew. Reproductions of the heads and mangled necks of several famed actors were mounted in a display case just inside the door. Suspended from the ceilings were plastic aliens, mutilated arms, bloody-stump legs and arms.

It was an overwhelming array of stuff, and we were going to dig through it all. Finally Spence said, "This guy must be in love with his own handiwork."

"I think that's what this case is all about."

There were false faces everywhere, masks with transitional hair attached at the forehead and temples, meant to blend into the actor's real hair. A headhunter's dream. Boxes under a long counter, filled with items that you wouldn't think anyone would bother to collect. Shoelaces, gloves, belts, and umbrellas, all beautifully organized even by my own compulsive standards—bins full of toupees and hairpieces, Harpo hair, Marilyn hair, Moe hair. I picked up one of the hanks and gave it a good long sniff—it didn't smell like real hair, but it was definitely not the shiny vinyl stuff they use on dolls. There was bank after bank of shelving, which brought to mind a series of enormous spice racks, only the racks were loaded with makeup, hundreds of little bottles, each with a different color. And big globs of clay—I guess it was clay, it sure looked like it—on each of the tables. It could have been something like Play-Doh, from the way it smelled. He had every skin color you could imagine, in varying shades.

We photographed everything. The search warrant didn't specify that we could take photographs, and there have been some recent cases where unwarranted photos were disallowed as evidence, but I didn't care. If we could use the photos in court, great; if not, so be it. At least we would have a record beyond our own memories. I was desperate not to miss anything.

Stacks and stacks of boxes, so much stuff to wade through—I was starting to wonder if we could get through it all before Durand's lawyer managed to pry us out of there. There was so much to see that I had to remind myself and everyone else that we were there specifically for those tapes. We could take other clearly incriminating evidence, but there were no real crimes hanging on these walls, only illusions thereof. We didn't know what to look for, beyond the videos.

About thirty minutes into the search, one of the other guys called me to look at a box he'd found in a closet at the back of the studio. It had been tightly taped, but when he opened it, he found it stuffed full of videotapes marked with the name of one of Durand's movies, more cassettes than it seemed he'd need for one movie. I picked one up and read the label—it was marked with a date from the beginning of the exhibit's run. I picked up a few more, selecting them randomly from different sections of the box—they were all within the right time frame.

My heart felt like it would thump right out of my chest.

I started to count them, because we would have to do an inventory of what we took out of there and because I literally couldn't think of anything else to do with all the energy that had flooded through me. At number twenty-nine, I became aware that a new player had entered: a plaid-breeched and deeply perturbed lawyer, who'd obviously been pulled off the golf course.

He launched into an immediate rant about how he was going to get an injunction against us using anything that we seized.

I walked right up to him and said, quite politely, "Go right ahead." I showed him the warrant. "We have very clear authorization to seize those security tapes and anything else that might implicate your client in a series of child disappearances."

He was unimpressed by my declaration of authority.

"These are not security tapes," he sneered. "Look at the markings."

"It's my belief that they have been deliberately mismarked. Your client can have them back when we're done with them, and we will be very careful not to damage them in any way, but they are warranted evidence and we are going to walk out of here with them whether you like it or not."

I got a cold, nasty stare for my trouble. Out came a cell phone. The lawyer turned and walked away as he dialed.

I wanted so badly for Wilbur Durand to come in while we were there; I wanted to see and hear this guy for myself, to get a sense of him beyond the blurry pictures. Who could it be but him on the phone with the lawyer? I made note of the time.

I was guessing that the call would turn out to be local when we subpoenaed the phone bill.

Even though I had what I'd wanted, I wasn't ready to leave the studio just yet; there was something more there, I could feel it in my bones. Words from the book Doc gave me to read kept haunting me:

There is an almost universal tendency to keep souvenirs from each victim.

God alone knew what horrible things he might keep. Fingers, toes, ears? He had hundreds of fakes digits and limbs there, but the real ones would eventually give off a smell that we were all very good at recognizing. It might be an article of clothing or a student ID card—even elementary kids get them these days. A lock of hair, tossed in among all those wigs.

"We need to buy some time," I said to Spence. "I have to figure something out."

"We can start dumping out boxes and inventorying things as if we were going to take them."

"That'll do for a little while."

One of the guys put the box of tapes in the back of my car. I screeched out of the parking lot and went right back to division.

The first thing Fred said when I told him I had some tapes was "Good. Now you can get out of there."

"But we aren't done yet—just on a rough count, there aren't enough here to cover the entire time period of the exhibit. A couple of the guys are still there looking for the rest."

As the tapes were being carried out for me, I'd looked back at the slow-motion scene; you never saw people pull stuff out of boxes so deliberately. *One ringie-dingie, two ringie-dingies,* or *ninety-nine bottles of beer,* just paced and regular and slow. Going through the door, I instructed the others, with deliberately excessive volume, to make sure they took their time and did a thorough job of cataloging everything, in earshot of both the lawyer and the assistant. The lawyer was in outrage overdrive, screaming about the Supreme Court. Our guys were all grinning up a storm as if they were getting away with something. They were.

In one of our utility closets there was a hand truck that we'd seized in a raid and never auctioned. I used it to bring the tapes into one of the interview rooms. While I waited for the specialized machine required to view them, I pulled out all the cassettes that roughly corresponded to the times the families had told me they'd been to the exhibit. Their memories weren't perfect, naturally. When the machine finally arrived, I was already frazzled, but my frustration got worse, because in a couple of the cases I had to speed through several days worth of tapes to find the boy in question. They look so different in motion; all I had was still photos. But they'd all typed in their names, supposedly as part of the fun. Each time I found one I was just elated; it made it seem as if they were still alive.

I copied off the segment for each boy so when I was finally through I had one tape with everyone. I shuddered to think what a nightmare it would be to have to notify thousands and thousands of families if we didn't manage to stop Durand in the near future.

"Lany."

I almost jumped through the ceiling. Fred was standing in the doorway of the interview room.

"How much longer? I'm gonna catch hell on all this overtime."

"A couple more hours. Tops."

"We're supposed to be *diligent* in our search practices, in case you forgot."

God forbid we should keep a pervert out of his work space.

"There's something more there, Fred, but I can't put my finger on it yet. I just need a little more time."

"I got this lawyer calling me every five minutes with a new threat."

What could I say? "I'm sorry, Fred, we're going as fast as we can over there."

Clearly dissatisfied, he left me alone with my best hope—the tapes themselves. I knew that if I sat down and just watched the loop of what I'd copied out, something would jump out at me. I viewed it over and over and over again.

Escobar was back from the house.

"Anything?"

"*Nada.*"

"Hey, do you have a couple of minutes?" I asked.

"It usually takes me longer than that."

I laughed. "I'll keep that in mind. Could you just look at these tapes and tell me what you see?"

He sat and watched. "They're all blond," he said.

"I figured that out already."

"They're all young."

"I got that too."

"They all look like really nice kids."

Innocence, we decided together, was the attracting factor.

"Doesn't have much evidentiary value," Escobar said.

He was right. I could already imagine what Doc would say, that these qualities represented everything the abductor would like to have been and that, in his own eyes, he was the original victim—a sweet little boy who got hurt over and over again. He would be angry about having his childhood stolen, about having his own innocence destroyed, to the point that he made it his personal mission to make sure he would not be the only little boy to whom it happened. Wilbur himself was well past the age where the scars and bruises of childhood could simply be cast off to clear the way for that precious state of mind. He recognized the trusting quality in each of his victims and tried to acquire it for himself.

But that conclusion wasn't going to get me an arrest warrant. Neither would anything that they'd found in the house. No lawyers there, but Escobar went on and on about a very annoying houseboy who'd trailed them around from one room to the next, gesticulating wildly and swearing in some foreign language over the mess they were making.

"He went ballistic over the things that were left around," Escobar said. "But this toss was a lot cleaner than most because there just wasn't all that much to toss—everything was positioned like it meant something. It *was* a mess compared to what it was when we started. And this houseboy got crazy about it."

The lack of a lawyer was one of those glaring omissions that just shouted to be noticed. Why not send a lawyer to both places if he had nothing to hide in either?

A guy like Wil Durand would have a lawyer with underlings available. So the fact that he didn't dispatch one to his house while it was being searched had to mean that he had nothing there to cover.

The pretoss Polaroids showed clearly that Escobar was right—the place was as spare as a shrine, the enclave of a high-intensity control freak. The master bedroom was the most unwelcoming place I've ever seen. The bed was all ebony, very dark, with no ornamentation of any kind on the headboard or footboard. Probably cost as much as my car. There were bed stands, but there was almost nothing on either of them, just these little sculptures or whatever— I don't really know what to call them—they looked like some kind of Buddhist meditation rock things. Useless except to be dusted. On my bed stand I have books and moisture cream and a glass of water, K-Y in case I get lucky, all sorts of other stuff.

But what really got me was what he had on the wall above the bed—a print for his movie *They Eat Small Children There*.

"Where was the casket?"

Escobar didn't get it.

"The one he probably sleeps in," I said.

Escobar rose up, grumbling. "You're starting to come apart. Time to leave."

I went back to the Polaroids of the studio. The wreckage of innocence was visible everywhere in the artificial body parts and fluids, the plastic but real-looking swords and knives, the jolting vinyl wounds with muscle and sinew and putrefaction, so perfectly formed and painted. I tried to superimpose the images from the photographs with the images on the tapes. And then I superimposed all that on what I remembered of the kids' rooms.

It was there, so close, I could almost touch it.

Whatever it was.

I found Spence at his desk. "I need to go back to the studio right now. I just need to look at everything again."

He didn't question me. "I'll drive," he said. We were almost through the door when my pager went off.

Oh, yes—I had children, who needed to be fed, driven, and comforted on occasion. In all of this craziness, I had almost forgotten. "What now," I said, "did Evan forget his shin pads again?"

Not this time. It was the desk sergeant. I had a visitor.

twenty~three

THOSE WHO CHEAT DEATH by living to extreme old age often take on mythical status, whether or not such reverence is merited by noteworthy character or accomplishments—we know of one woman from Saint-Etienne who managed to see one hundred two springs; she was mean-spirited and rather slow, a veritable shrew in her middle years, yet people would travel from very long distances to touch her, in the hope of absorbing some of her longevity. If Madame Catherine Karle had reached that milestone, we surely would have heard of it, for she was a truly remarkable woman. It was said by those who knew her at Champtocé that she could work miracles with rocks and stones and a handful of dirt, and I could find no reason to disbelieve any of it.

Her son Guillaume was a good strong man with a kind and understanding nature, one who would have been the best of husbands had he married. It always seemed to me that he ought to have occupied a higher station; there was something about him that set him apart from the rest of us. He kept to himself but had no airs of snobbery; nevertheless, there was an indefinable quality of "highness" about him, a regency of carriage that could not be overlooked. It was expressed in good works and deeds, of which I myself was once the beneficiary. Toward the very end of my husband's ordeal, when I could not manage to roll him over, Guillaume was always willing to lend his strong arms and his good heart to the task of caring for a dying man.

I was a much younger woman then, more attuned to the demands and possibilities of life. At that time Guillaume might have been near sixty years of age, but he was as handsome a man as I had ever seen, tall, straight, slender, and well-built, with sky-blue eyes and a beautiful smile. I am ashamed to admit that in my Etienne's final days, I looked upon Guillaume with some longing. I had not known my husband's strength since before he went to Orléans, and I missed his caresses terribly. I have since managed to forgive myself for those shameful thoughts, though I doubt that God is ready to do so just yet, and were Jean de Malestroit to know, well, there would be no telling how much penance would be required of me for my human frailty.

We were to pass through Champtoceaux anyway, I told myself; *surely even his Eminence cannot object to a further small delay in our return.* And Guillaume Karle was easy enough to find: To a one, the folks of whom we asked directions knew him, and all spoke with great admiration for the aging *gentilhomme.* Still, one never knew what lay behind a door, and my diligent escort would not allow me to make the initial approach alone. *For your own protection, Sister, Frère* Demien had said, so seriously. How I managed to remain unscathed through the years without his guardianship, I was forced to wonder—it must have been through some unseen, mysterious angel whose powers were reserved specifically for traveling abbesses. Indeed.

I watched as the door was opened inward, and when the occupant appeared, there stood the man we had seen in the tavern. My shock was matched only by the shock of snow-white hair he himself sported. There was a stirring of pleasure in me that I wanted to banish, but it persisted—yea, increased—as I regarded him after so much time. I saw surprise and perhaps a bit of pleasure in his face as well; he turned toward me and shaded his eyes with one hand, and with the other waved an enthusiastic greeting. I could not suppress my smile of response.

He walked with astounding firmness through the small garden at the front of his house and came up to me, and though I was still on my mount, I was not much higher than he.

"Madame," he said, with genuine warmth. "Or perhaps I should call you Mother."

"*Mais, non, Monsieur,* no one but your own remarkable *maman* should have that honor from you."

"How kind of you to speak so well of her. And how truly wonderful of you to call upon me. It has been a very long time, has it not?"

I was smiling very broadly by then. "It has indeed, *Monsieur,* too long."

We sparred with admiring protests for a few moments until he said, "Perhaps we ought to go inside and speak of other things."

He offered a hand to me and I allowed him to help me climb down from my beast. When one is wearing a nun's robes and attempting to remove oneself from the back of a donkey, there is little hope of achieving grace. Somehow I landed on the ground without stumbling.

I found a measure of welcome inside the house that I did not often feel in unfamiliar places. The air was warm but fresh and smelled of oiled wood. No wonder—

the furnishings were handsome and well-made, their fineness beyond what one would expect from the son of a midwife. The presence of a woman seemed almost palpable—perhaps he had taken a wife after all. There was a richness to his world that made me feel inexplicably happy.

I had no idea how Guillaume Karle made his living other than helping his mother in her work, but I imagined that it must have been substantial for him to afford the niceties he had accumulated.

"How lovely your furnishings are," I said.

"Ah, thank you," he said. "Most of them I made myself."

That said, it was all too obvious: He was a maker of furniture. I should have gleaned that from the whittling. But there were tapestries and weavings all about, again of a quality that one finds only in noble households. I laid my hand on a finely woven cloth that ran along the top of a handsome chest. Guillaume Karle noted my interest. "Mother always complained that she rarely had time to do these things. She was taught her skills as a very young child."

The ability to produce such finery is not granted to the daughters of lesser families. There had always been rumors of intriguing origin, that Madame Karle was by birth a duchess or princess who had run away and would not allow herself to be found. I had never given any credence to this gossip—Madame was far too practical, far too versed in the natural world to have had such an upbringing. And I had been told by the woman herself that her father was a physician. In the long run, it mattered little to me where she had come from. She was a good woman who had raised a very fine son; both would have my admiration forever.

I could not keep myself from looking around the room. My eyes came to rest on a very small portrait of a young dame, rendered in ink on parchment and displayed in a carved ivory frame. I requested permission to touch it with a look in Guillaume's direction, to which he responded with a nod.

I picked it up with great tenderness.

The woman in the portrait wore a slight smile, an expression I recalled on the face of the midwife on occasion. "Madame herself?" I asked.

"None other."

It must have been a good likeness, because I was able to envision the old woman who had brought my children out of me as a young matron in her prime. Though it had been rendered without color, I could see that her hair had been very light in shade; in her late years it was silver with dashes of the original gold in it. There was great dignity in her expression and fire in her eyes, both of which were qualities I remembered from my personal contact with her. I set the portrait back down on the chest.

"Now you will tell me that she is still alive, and I shall not be shocked to hear it."

"I wish I could," her son said, "but she was called to God at the age of ninety-nine. Or so we think. She recalled having survived the Black Death, and that is how we came to that conclusion." He smiled with a bit of sadness. "But even she could not resist the final summons. No one can, our greatest hopes notwithstanding."

It had not been all that many years ago. "I am truly sorry," I said. "I will always be grateful for what she did for my husband. And yourself as well."

Frère Demien's silent presence reminded me that we had best be about the business that had brought us here.

"Well," I said with a wistful sigh, "this day's light will fade before we know it. Perhaps *Frère* Demien already told you at the door—we have just come from

Champtocé. We had a visit with the old castellan from my time there, who still lives on the premises."

"Ah," Guillaume said, "*Monsieur* Marcel."

"The very one."

"A good man if ever one lived. How goes it with him? I often think of him, but it has been a long time since I ventured into that place."

His tone of voice gave me the notion that he was happy to have been absent. "He is in good health and sound spirits," I said. "And things there look much the same, except for a bit of neglect one hopes due to time more than intent," I said. "But, of course, things cannot really be the same within the walls, the place having changed hands so often."

"All for the better, I say." He paused and then added, "There finally came a point when *Mère* would no longer go there, not for any reason. She always said there were evil doings therein. She could feel it in her bones, she told me."

♔

Her bones were correct. We would later hear from Poitou:

When Milord Gilles had once again recovered the castle at Champtocé from his brother René, Lord de la Suze, we went there, but our purpose was merely to hand it over yet again, this time to the Lord Duke of Brittany. Milord had sold it to him, though I suspect that he would not have relinquished the place had there been any means to avoid it. I do not know the intricacies of the arrangement between them, only that Milord was sorely unhappy about it and had enacted the transfer under some duress.

It was on that occasion that Milord Gilles first made me swear a vow of secrecy. He said, "Poitou, you must never betray my confidences. To anyone." I did not understand in that moment what he wanted me to keep secret, but in my devotion, I swore anyway.

It was with this vow that my shame began in earnest.

Milord ordered us—Henriet, his cousin Gilles de Sille, two servants, Robin Romulart and Hicquet de Brémont, and myself—to go to the tower, where he said we would find the bodies and bones of many dead children. He wanted to make sure that Duke Jean would not discover them when he took possession of Champtocé. I did not believe him at first. But the others verified the truth of it all, and I began to fear for my soul. We were to take these remains and put them in a coffer, and then convey them secretly to the castle at Machecoul. He did not say how many there were, but when we went there we found the remains of either thirty-six or forty-six children, though I cannot recall which is the correct number right now; we counted the skulls to determine it at the time.

We took these "bodies"—none was intact—to Milord's own chamber at Machecoul. We traveled under cover of darkness, each of us riding alongside the cart in which the remains themselves were drawn. There, with the help of Jean Rossignol and André Buchet, we burned the bodies in the great hearth under Milord's personal direction. And when the ashes were cold the next morning, we threw them into the moats and latrine pits of Machecoul. It was not a difficult thing to do, and we might have done it at Champtocé had there been time—but the Lord Duke would arrive too soon, or in his stead his emissary the Bishop Jean de Malestroit, we knew not which to expect.

I cannot say who killed these children; I do know that Milord's cousins called frequently upon him wherever he resided there and that there was great intimacy between them, sometimes of a sodomitic nature, as often occurs between Milord and myself. I know that they led children to him, as I also did on many later occasions, to satisfy his enormous lust. Between us, perhaps there were forty brought to him over time. More than I care to recall, may God save me.

Which He surely will not do.

After Michel's disappearance I was so steeped in grief that if evil began to sneak into the fortress at Champtocé, I could not have seen it myself. Catherine Karle, however, had none of my devotion to that fortress—she had come in and out of it over many decades, had witnessed its rise and fall without visible emotion.

"Your mother possessed wondrous powers of observation," I said to Guillaume, "so I will have to accept that what you are telling me is truth, though I myself did not notice it." For a brief moment I paused to reflect on my own shortcomings as an observer. "I suppose I ought to have seen it," I said woefully, "since Champtocé was my home for many years."

"Do not fault yourself for that, Madame. No one wishes to see such things."

"You would be surprised, *Monsieur,* at the flaws one can find within, given time for consideration, of which I have had plenty. But enough of these regrets." I laid my purpose before him unabashedly. "We are here in the hope of learning something more about my son's disappearance."

He drew back a bit and crossed himself. There was no need to remind this man of what had happened to Michel, which was a relief—I had once foolishly thought that each retelling of my sorrow would lessen it. "Marcel thought that there might be something more you could recall. We did not speak of it, you and I, at the time, nor did your mother and I. So now I am asking you to speak."

He reached out and picked up the portrait of Madame Catherine and regarded it for a moment. After replacing it reverently he said, "How will you benefit by my recollections? They are sure to be woeful and nothing will be changed."

"I cannot say, *Monsieur,* until I hear them said. But do not hesitate to speak plainly, for nothing you could say to me will cause me to suffer any more than I already have."

For a moment I thought he would offer a counterargument, but instead he said, "Very well, Madame. If it is your sincere wish that I should do so, I will. But first let us sit. My bones ache all of a sudden."

The chair into which I lowered my saddle-worn body was so comfortable that had the sun already slipped out of sight, I might have settled back in sleep at once, without a thought for the devotions that were expected of me before closing my eyes. But I sat full upright on the edge of the cushion—I wanted to see his face clearly as he spoke. Already there was anguish to be seen there.

"*Mère* did not speak for many hours after she came back from the initial search," he said, "for someone who was so fond of chatter. I tried to cajole her into speaking, but she was nearly silent, as if she were struggling with some great confusion. She would respond only to the most critical medical inquiries." He rubbed his palms together slowly; when his nervousness abated, he continued. "*Mère* was a strong woman with a very hardy soul; she had seen many grievous wounds and injuries in her life, suffered many trials, lived through some difficult times. I thought she had become immune to pain and shock. But there was such anger in her then ... surely your husband must have told you what she said to him."

I sat back in shock. "He never told of speaking with her."

"He did not tell you of the time he met up with us in the oak grove?"

I replied with a shake of my head. I felt betrayed, somehow, more so because I could not simply turn to my husband and ask him.

Guillaume Karle must have perceived my discomfort, for he said, "Do not fret, Madame. Were I your husband, I might keep such distressing things from you as well. But I will tell you what I remember of that day. Etienne was working through a stand of brush, moving the foliage around with the tip of his sword. When he saw us, he looked almost as if he had been caught in something sinful. But he did call out a greeting, and for a brief time we spoke. Had he inquired about our business, Mère would have told him that we were in search of medicinal herbs, but he did not. He was rather caught up in what he was doing."

When Etienne returned from those searches—always alone—his mood was dark and distant. "He went out so many times, he would have come upon numerous people, I suppose."

"We did not see many people. I think after Guy de Laval's goring and your son's disappearance, no one who lived thereabouts wanted to venture into that area. As happened in Paris, when the wolves were about."

"Ah, yes. May God save us all."

For a week last autumn, an evil wolf, who acquired the name Courtaut by chewing off his own tail to escape a hunter's trap, had boldly led a troupe of his brothers and sisters through the streets of Paris. Together they attacked and maimed dozens of people between Montmartre and the Porte Saint Antoine. They hid in the vineyards and the swamps and came out at night to stalk the terrified citizens who lived within the city's walls. If they came upon a flock of sheep, their natural prey, they would leave the beasts alone and take the shepherd. When he was finally caught on Saint Martin's Eve, Courtaut was paraded through the streets of the city in a barrow, his gaping jaw wide open to expose his bloody teeth.

"Then, if it was so dangerous, why did you and your mother go into the woods?"

"She and I were separated for several years after my birth, so she knew only too well the pain of losing one's child. Before we were reunited, she came close many times to losing hope, or so she says."

My eyes began to moisten. These were things I had not known. I would have offered comfort had she told me, but perhaps she had not wanted comfort—Catherine Karle was a woman whose shoulders seemed limitless in their ability to bear a burden. I lowered my gaze and said quietly, "One never loses hope. I half-expect to see Michel come walking up to me one day. My greatest fear is that if that happens, I will fail to recognize him."

Guillaume Karle was quiet for a time, as was *Frère* Demien. The only sound that could be heard was our combined breathing, until Karle spoke again.

"Madame," he whispered.

I did not look up.

He reached out and enfolded both of my hands in his. "Madame," he said again, "I regret to tell you that your son is not going to come back."

"One never loses hope," I repeated, "at least not until all hope is gone."

He squeezed my hands. "All hope *is* gone."

I looked up and saw terrible sadness in his eyes.

"You see, Madame—we found him."

♔

It was late in the day, the light fading, and we had been out since before noontime. Our horses were beginning to fidget by virtue of whatever unspoken urge it is that compels all beasts to chafe at riders near to that hour. Perhaps they sense the impending darkness and would seek cover before its full fall. One never knows, in the woods, what might cause a horse to become restless. My beast was even more unsettled than Mère's, for though she was a woman of statuesque height, she had little meat on her bones, whereas I, whom she claimed favored my father, was far more weighty and burdensome than she.

Let us water the beasts, she'd offered, for perhaps they will be gentled by the comfort of a drink, which seemed a worthy idea to me, so I took the lead in our duet and led my horse through the stand of oaks, where we had been searching for your son. As fortune would have it, we did come upon a substantial crop of mistletoe in the oaks, which Mère and I gathered to the full extent of what we could carry in our satchels. We were still congratulating ourselves on the treasure we had found when we came upon the stream at the center of the ravine.

The rains had been hard that year, and early, and the stream was as mighty and forceful as I had ever seen it. Silt and grit and leaves marked the height on the banks to which it had risen. By this time, the waters had receded again and were then a good forearm's length below their fullest height. Seeing this, we were careful along the edges of the stream, for the mud would be treacherous in some places and wet enough to suck in the foot and ankle of a horse, perhaps deeply enough that even the sturdiest beast might not succeed in retracting his appendage. So naturally we paid close attention to the rocks and sticks that lay there, and caused our horses to tread slowly among them.

In the course of this careful passage along the muddy banks of the stream, we came upon a strange arrangement of rocks, a cairn that looked so deliberate that it could not have been laid down by nature's hand.

We tethered our beasts to a low tree and stepped to the edge of the water, and almost immediately our feet were dragged down into the muck. I had hold of a strong branch and managed to extricate myself, and thereafter I pulled Mère back to the safety of a firmer footing. But neither of us had or would put a foot upon that cairn by the water's edge, for there could be no doubt that it was a grave.

"Madame," I heard Guillaume say. The words floated through the air but sounded as if they had come from under the waters of the distant stream by which they had found the remains. "Madame—shall I cease the telling?"

I managed to reach the surface somehow. "No," I said. So contained and taut was my grief that I could barely speak. "For the love of all that is sacred," I whispered, "*no*. Tell me *all* of it."

Suddenly the age from which he had previously looked so immune seemed to settle upon him with great weight, and I saw before me an old man who had carried a burden on his soul for many years.

♔

Again we were careful, but once we had established ourselves in firm footing, we began to remove the rocks from the top of the cairn. Soon there appeared the shape of arms and legs and a torso and, as we worked our way outward, a head. And by its size and shape we knew it to be a young man or a boy. By then the larger stones had given way to pebbles; whoever laid your son to rest had first covered him with sand and smallish stones and then layered over it the more substantial rocks. We proceeded with great care, so as not to disturb his rest, and at one point I said to Mère, let us just uncover the face, that we might know who it is.

She agreed that it must be done, so we worked around the head, scooping away the compacted sand until our fingers finally met the flesh. It felt spongy and tough at the same time under my fingers, and though nature had had her way somewhat with the lad's face, enough of the features remained that we knew it was Michel. A sash of cloth was tied about his neck.

We rested for a moment, and then my mother began to pray—aloud, an act of rarity for her. She was always very private in her devotions, very sure that God would listen to her and therefore unconcerned with creating an impression of piety. She prayed to God and the Virgin for the repose of your son's soul. And when she had finished her prayers, she sat quietly for a moment. Then she turned to me and said that God had given her a notion that the boy ought to be absolved of his sins, and that if it were done, the boy would be received in heaven as was merited by his sweetness in life.

When I protested that this must be done by a priest, she laughed. I have seen the Black Death, she reminded me, and in those times there was not a priest to be had for any price, for the pest would gallop through a monastery as if conveyed by the fastest steed. There were not enough living to bury the dead, and we had to make do with what we had. Many a time the last of the living would be the only one left to see to the souls of those who had perished before him. And though the last of the living might be writhing in death's cold hand, he would see to the absolution of those who went before him. Surely you cannot say that all those souls entered Satan's minions for lack of God's grace.

Te absolve, she said over your son. And I have always believed that those words had the needed effect.

⚜

She had been such a good woman, so pure in spirit and good in her heart. I had to believe that her words effected salvation for Michel.

"Well," I said as the tears poured out of me, "I am comforted to know that he did not remain unshriven. But I cannot rest until ... I simply must know ... how in God's name did he meet his death?"

⚜

Let us uncover more of him, she said.

But we must not do this, I told her. We must let him rest in peace.

No, she insisted, there is a mystery to be solved here. A boy does not lay down on the ground and then bury himself so exquisitely in preparation for a death he knows will surely come. He was yet three score of years from his natural end.

So we removed all the sand and silt from his corpse, and through the layer of grit that remained we saw the wound that must have taken him down. For his shirt was torn up the center and his entrails had been drawn out.

⚜

Tears poured down my cheeks and onto the breast of my habit, and from there onto my lap. All spirit had deserted me, and through my blood vessels ran not my own dear blood but harsh and poisonous quicksilver, which chilled me to the very core of my soul. He had died in pain, then.

⚜

We sat back for a moment and regarded what we had uncovered. Mère swore a vile oath under her breath and then bade me uncover the rest of his arms. She always carried a knife in her stocking—a habit she says was formed at the insistence of Grandpère—and so many times it was an expedient thing to have. She used it to cut away the front of the boy's shirt, which she then folded carefully and tucked into her apron pocket.

The better to see the wound, she said. I would not have it obscured just now.

We regarded the gash in the abdomen more closely. She touched it carefully with her fingertips and moved bits of the entrails around to see the place from which they had been pulled. And then she swore again. We shall have to do something now, she told me. He cannot be left here.

It is blasphemy to unearth the dead, I told her. 'Twas the cause of all your father's troubles, was it not? We shall surely be hanged if we are caught.

We shall surely rot in hell if we do nothing, she insisted. This wound was not the work of a boar. It will be upon our souls for all eternity if we do nothing. There is quite enough on my soul already.

All my protests and admonitions went unheeded. But I did manage to bring her to some accord, that being that we should go back to our home, therein to take rest and to consider the proper course of action without undue duress. This having been decided, we began to recover the body. By this time Mère was quite stiff, for she had been upon her knees a good stretch of time, and her knees were not those of a young woman; she was, I believe, well past seventy by then. I bade her stand to ease the pain in her joints while I finished the covering myself. When fully erect she turned about to look behind us. I heard her gasp and looked up in the direction of her stare. Up on the crest of the hill I saw a figure on horseback. It was the grandfather, Jean de Craon.

She had rarely spoken of her family, and then it was only to say that her *père* had been a master physician. He had served kings and princes alike and had studied under the greatest of teachers, from whom he had benefited sublimely. But in the course of his studies and subsequent practice of *cyrurgerie,* he had exhumed and dissected dead bodies, which was strictly forbidden by the church. But the man was long dead, well out of punishment's reach.

"Did Jean de Craon know about her father's history?"

"Enough of it, I suppose."

"But there was nothing he could do to harm her then; her father's crimes were not her own."

"Milord Jean would probably disagree with that."

"He is free to do so from his perch in hell, but I cannot understand how any judge would hold the daughter responsible for the sins of the father."

"God holds us all accountable for the sins of our fathers."

"Yes, yes," I said impatiently, "but this is an entirely different matter—the sins with which we come into this world, not the sins we undertake to create on our own."

"My mother had sins of her own to answer for," he said quietly. "Milord Jean had the means to silence her. There were secrets she had to keep about herself. Otherwise, I assure you, she would have come forward with what she thought to be the truth in the matter of your son."

I was almost afraid to press him. But I had come this far and saw no gain in retreating—there was difficulty in any direction I chose.

"I would know this truth."

"*Je regrette,* Madame, it will not be easy to hear."

"Speak."

"Very well, then. My mother was of the opinion that your son's belly was opened not by the tusk of a boar, but by a knife. Whoever did it, she said later, was clever enough to try to make the wound look as if it were beast-made, with the dirt and some ripping. But he must have thought better of his efforts and buried Michel in the end. Even so, had someone else found him, what she noticed might have been missed."

I was silent, staring at my folded hands, which lay in my lap, clutching my mother's *mouchoir* with desperate fierceness. I could not even recall having taken it out of my sleeve. But there it was, contorted into a mass of wrinkles—the object of all my contained rage.

My thoughts, which ought to have been focused on what Guillaume Karle had just revealed, drifted instead to Madame Catherine and her father. In view of her bastardy, it was a delicate subject on which to query her son, but something in her past had kept her from revealing what she had known of my son's fate, and I felt compelled to know what it was that had delayed the passage of that knowledge to me. Above all, I did not want to provoke this man into deeper silence on the matter by assaulting him with discomfiting demands for revelations. I finally settled on a question that seemed safe enough. "Do you remember your mother's father well?"

"Oh, very well," he told me. "As if he were my own. By the time I was born, my own father had already died. And *Grandpère* took care of me when I was separated from *Maman*."

"Perhaps, *Monsieur,* you will favor me with a history of your remarkable family."

He smiled, but would not answer directly. "It would take a good amount of time." He pointed toward the window, through which the light outside was visibly dimmer. "Now the sun descends, and you need to reach Nantes. But I would be honored if you would accept a quick refreshment before you depart. Some wine, a bit of cheese and bread. And I have some fine apples, if you like."

I glanced at *Frère* Demien, who nodded his acceptance of the offer. "How very kind of you to share your board with us," I said. "But I myself have no stomach for food at the moment."

"Ah, Madame," he said, "then your company shall suffice."

As he rose up from his chair, there was a brief moment when he seemed a bit unsteady, perhaps owing to the stiffness that follows sitting still in those of venerable age. I wanted to reach out to lend him a hand for balance, but refrained, and he managed on his own.

"You have given me much to think about, *Monsieur,*" I told him as we mounted our beasts a short while later. "I am grateful for your candor."

He touched my hand with true warmth. "Such things are not pleasant matter for thought."

"But must be considered, nevertheless."

His eyes said what his lips would not speak: that some things are best left alone, and that these were dangerous woods I was about to enter.

But enter I would. Let the wolves of Paris and the boars of Champtocé come for me. I would be ready to greet them.

chapter 24

I'D GUESSED RIGHT—Wilbur Durand wasn't out of the country. He was so close that if I reached out far enough with my arm, I'd be able to touch him. He breathed in and out, as did I and everyone else in the room; I could see his chest rise and fall as he stood there on the other side of the reception desk. Otherwise, he was like a statue, completely motionless in monochrome.

I stepped aside to draw him out of the cover of the countertop so I could get a better view of him. He didn't move from the spot, only changed his angle slightly to follow me. I couldn't help but stare for a moment. *Oh please please please,* I silently beseeched this dark demon, *do something stupid—pull out a knife or lunge at me suddenly so I can yank out my piece and put a bullet right into that twisted brain.*

But he would have had to go through security to get up here, including a trip through the metal detector, so he would be weapon-free. Still, he was not unarmed, not by a long shot—if he took off the dark glasses that covered his eyes and prevented me from reading him, laser beams would fire up and burn a hole right through my forehead.

"Mr. Durand," I said stupidly, "I'm Detective Lany Dunbar."

What an idiot I am—he knew who I was. He sniffed in disdain and ignored my extended hand.

"Thank you for coming in," I said, bumbling out each word.

I felt freeze-dried and crystalline; one quick move and I would shatter into a million jagged pieces, never to be repaired. My senses hadn't completely deserted me, though; I took him in, burned his image into my forebrain like a photograph, measured him in every way I could. Durand was of average height, very slightly built, pasty white where his skin was even visible. He dressed entirely in black, as in the few photos I had been able to find of him. He had dark straight hair on the longish side, very neatly cut. Heavy dark glasses shielded his eyes from view. His posture was ramrod stiff, his spine rigid. Before me was a walking caricature, but of precisely what I couldn't be sure.

Despite all that affectation, he was terribly nondescript—I would have had a hard time picking him out in a crowd. Durand was the type of person who could easily make himself look small and unimportant. He could probably make himself look like just about anything. But when he suddenly spoke, he scared the hell out of me.

"Give me back my studio."

Not "how do you do" or some other standard greeting. His voice surprised me; I expected it to have a spellbinding quality, along the lines of Vincent Price or Will Lyman. But instead of the rich, commanding voice I anticipated, he put out a series of high-pitched utterances that coalesced, against all odds, into a demand.

An alto, if he was a singer—not a man's voice at all, but not really a woman's either. If he'd called me on the phone, I wouldn't have been able to tell what sex he was.

His voice almost had a fake quality to it, as if he were speaking through some distortion device or from underwater; every word felt like metal scraped on metal. He didn't say, *Hello, I'm Wilbur Durand, I understand that you are interested in speaking with me.* He spoke just one command: *Give me back my studio.*

That studio was his weakness.

It was jarring to realize how poorly my phantom image of Wilbur Durand jibed with the reality. I was expecting a bigger voice, a bigger body, a more substantial presence. He was so innocuous that under different circumstances, I wouldn't have given him a second look. But I knew what I knew and it made me shake to be in the same room with him, this cat killer, this child stealer, this probable murderer. I was praying that he wouldn't notice it. But of course, he did.

When the desk sergeant had told me who was waiting, I flipped down the picture of my kids that I kept on my desk, so he wouldn't see it if I managed to get him back into the division room for a chat. I didn't want him to touch any part of my private life.

It would have been reasonable for someone like Durand to have an entourage of goons, but he was alone. One insane question kept running through my brain: What kind of balls does it take to show up at the police station when there's good reason to think you're a suspect in a capital crime, perhaps several? There had to be one of two blatantly antithetical psychological conditions at work in him: fearless confidence in the acceptance of the surrounding world when one pushes the envelope, or a sociopathic state where the limits of advisable behavior are unrecognized and consequently ignored. Maybe both; in any event, he managed to unnerve me, and I'm sure he knew it.

He gave me an icy sneer that said, *Gotcha.* And he

had—I was pretty much speechless as a challenging little smile spread onto his face.

By then Spence was at my side. He remembered how mouths work long before I did. "Your studio is under legal subpoena, Mr. Durand. We won't be releasing it back to you until we finish our inventory of the potential evidence we found there."

Durand ignored Spence completely and addressed his response to me. "I have not committed a crime. Therefore, there can be no evidence." The corners of his lips twitched almost imperceptibly, while every other muscle on his face remained still. "Whatever you think is real evidence in there is merely an illusion of evidence."

My voice returned, but it must have sounded shaky. "Mr. Durand," I said, "we will determine the evidentiary value of what we find as soon as we can. We won't inconvenience you any longer than absolutely necessary. But in the meantime, there are serious liability issues regarding your possessions—we have to be very certain that we do everything right, both for our protection and yours. Because of the possible historical and fine art value of the things you have in there, our legal counsel has advised us to exercise extreme care with them."

He knew what it all really meant, that we would be in there until we were kicked out by legal maneuvering. I sucked up all my courage and pushed him even further. "If you have a few moments, I wonder if you'd come with me to one of the interview rooms. We could speak more privately."

"No."

That was all he said. He could have started in about what his lawyer was going to do to us, but he didn't; he could have ranted and raved and cursed at me, but he remained silent. He wouldn't engage with me at all. No back and forth, no negotiation where I say something and then he says something and we come to a conclusion, with or without agreement. He made no threats, either vague or specific. He simply stood there, frowned, and then turned around to depart.

The reception area was dead silent as the door Wilbur Durand walked through finally *whooshed* to a close. I looked around the room; every face was drained of color. When the air conditioner kicked in with a sudden thrum, we all jumped.

"Jeez, Louise," the desk sergeant finally said, "what the hell was *that*?"

"I don't know," I breathed. "I think scientists are working on it."

"Good luck to them," Spence said.

The unmarked unit crawled through the sweltering city with Spence at the wheel. I sat in the passenger seat, still numb. The traffic was loud and tangled, and my head was pounding with images of Earl Jackson's small muti-lated body. All I wanted to do on this earth was to get Wilbur Durand.

"God, Spence, he was right there. All I had to do was pull out my handcuffs...."

"I know the feeling. But not yet. This is one you don't want to screw up with a mistake."

It would also have meant that I had to touch him. I couldn't bring myself to touch him, no way.

The photos of the studio were in my lap. Heat shim-mered up off the pavement as we crawled along. Once again, I worked my way through the images of Durand's bizarre world, craving the spark, just that one small spark of insight. Instead, I was confronted with heads, arms, teeth, wigs, ears, blood and guts—all of it incomprehensi-ble to a regular person.

"Look at this," I said. I held a photo out. Spence glanced quickly at it as he drove.

His forehead wrinkled. "What the heck is it?"

"A whole container of fake boogers—that stringy rubber stuff that you'd put into an actor's nose so it hangs down and looks like snot."

"I hope that's not why we're going back there."

Who could say what would get him in the end? "It's got to be something ordinary. I just don't know what it is yet."

We entered through the same reception area and were challenged by the same underling. Once again, we ignored him.

"He'll get used to us," I joked. But as soon as we were back inside, all levity ended. I fell into a sort of focused trance, letting my eyes go from box to box, from shelf to shelf, resting for a few moments on everything. I put my brain into scan mode and did the mental equivalent of channel-surfing, hoping that something, anything, would tweak my attention.

I thought about my own kids; what would they have that could be kept in this room without causing too much notice? The place was full of film memorabilia-in-waiting, things that might someday be as famous as Dorothy's ruby—

Slippers.

Footwear props. The box had been emptied on the floor and the contents were strewn all over the place. A detective from one of the other divisions was counting shoes methodically. It was like I was staring at my own living room—sneakers everywhere. Kids wear sneakers. There were way too many pairs of adolescent footwear compared to other kinds of shoes in that box.

Why did he have so many sneakers?

There was a glaringly empty sneaker box in Nathan Leeds's room.

The lawyer came back in. He stood in the doorway

with the assistant, who had probably summoned him the moment I reappeared.

"Shoot. Let's put the shoes back in the box," I said quietly to the counting cops. "We're going to take it with us."

They must have thought I was nuts. One of them gave me a look.

"Don't do anything that will ruffle the little twerp over there."

When we carried the box out—Spence on one side, me on the other—the lawyer went berserk. "What are you doing? Where do you think you're going with that? Your warrant doesn't say anything about my client's personal property—" He was hovering around me, shouting threats and covering me with angry spittle, even though he was still clutching the warrant in one hand.

"Shut up!" I commanded, and to my eternal amazement, he did. As we stood near the door holding the box, I calmly repeated my initial statement to him. "We have a warrant to remove materials as evidence in the investigation of several crimes."

He started shouting again. But his shouting didn't stop us.

Two burly patrolmen carried the box up from the garage and dropped it on the floor just past the division reception desk. I dragged it by myself into one of the interview rooms despite myriad offers of assistance—now that I had it, I didn't want anyone else touching it until I could examine every single shoe myself.

Nike, New Balance, Adidas, Puma—every brand imaginable. All hiding in plain sight. I started calling parents to make appointments for the viewings, half an hour apart, all evening long and then again in the morning.

I wondered when my ex would start asking me to pay him child support, instead of the other way around. He might have been right to accuse me of being a bad mother.

That's how it was beginning to feel to me. But at least my kids were safe.

The parents and guardians arrived as requested. Some were eager and arrived early; they had to wait. Nervous impatience permeated the air as family members of missing children abided ticks of the clock in uncomfortable bright-orange plastic chairs, knowing there was the chance that a beloved child's death might be confirmed at long last by evidence.

Two large tables dominated the center of the interview room, each one covered with rows of neatly paired sneakers. Escobar had rushed home and gathered up several sets of his own kids' old sneakers, marked by hidden stickers on the underside of each shoe's tongue. I set coworkers to digging through the depths of their lockers for forgotten pairs. It was like putting photos of cops in street clothes into a picture lineup with an actual suspect; the validity of the hoped-for positive identification was bolstered by having known negatives in the mix and having them passed over by the identifier in favor of the real thing. *We deliberately tried to steer this witness off track, Your Honor, just to be certain that he was positive about the identification, but he went right back to the defendant's picture no matter how many others we introduced to him.*

Fred Vuska, Spence, Escobar, and I watched through the two-way mirrored glass as a uniformed officer brought these apprehensive adults into the room and led them through the strange exhibit. I'd instructed the parents and relatives specifically not to touch the items to prevent contamination, but it was a sure bet that someone would try. It didn't take long; one of the fathers put his hand out, then pulled it back again, then looked toward the mirror—he was smart enough to know we were watching—

and just nodded. His shoulders slumped and he started to cry.

I went directly into the room and retrieved the pair of size sevens from among its peers. I held them out in my gloved hands and asked the father, "Are you certain that these shoes belong to your son?"

He managed to whisper "Yes" through his tears. He pointed to a faint paint mark on one toe. "We were painting the front porch last Father's Day and Jamie dripped paint onto his sneaker. I got most of it off, but there was some on the end I couldn't get."

I took a closer look at it, and saw that in the grooves of one toe there were bits of green visible against the gray-white of the rubber.

If there was any doubt about the identification of the sneaker as belonging to that child, we could make a paint comparison—sneaker to porch—to confirm it.

By that time, the evidence technician I'd sent out had returned from Ellen Leeds's apartment with the sneaker box nicely bagged and labeled. I had him put it in the evidence locker. I looked back through the glass just in time to see another man—an uncle of a victim—turn away, buckle at the knees, and vomit. I rushed in to help him. After wiping his mouth on his sleeve, he pointed to a pair of Disney World laces he'd bought for his nephew on a business trip to Florida. The ends had been cut off because they were too long and the boy was tripping on them all the time. He identified them positively by the dab of Duco cement he'd put on the cut edges to keep them from fraying.

And so it went, with several more positives. When all the evening's parents were gone, we were left alone to acknowledge our sad victory.

The weight of our new discovery seemed to land on all of us at once. Finally Fred turned to me and said, "I guess you got your man. You know that all hell is gonna break loose once this gets out."

He was right; it would be mayhem. Suddenly I was more tired than I'd felt in my entire life. And now that I had Wilbur Durand in my trap, I was struck with the odd realization that I wasn't quite ready to haul him in. My life had to be cleared out before I gave it over to him.

"I need a day to take care of a couple of things before we go out with it," I said.

Fred stared in disbelief. "What things?"

"*Things,* Fred. Details. I have to write all this up and get it into the files, and I need to get some sleep before doing any of that. All I need is one day."

"Is there any risk to any more kids if we wait?"

Now he asks.

"I can't say one way or the other, you know that. I know he needs to prepare for what he's doing if he keeps doing it the same way, and we've been in his face, so he's probably not ready for another one."

"I hate *probably.*"

We all did. "One day," I said quietly.

It was a Tuesday evening when all this took place. Fred gave me until Thursday morning to clean up the details of the case and organize everything so that a proper arrest could be made.

We actually shook on it. Maybe he was shaking my hand in congratulations, I don't know, but it felt like we were sealing a gentlemen's agreement. I had a little bit of time, assuming this didn't get out in some way. I'd already told all the parents that we were preparing an arrest warrant but couldn't say who the suspect was yet—we wanted to make it right, so we needed their cooperation in keeping things quiet. It was hard to do; they all pressed me pretty vigorously for information. I didn't give anything away, and it killed me.

It was close to midnight before I was through with

everything. When no one was looking, I slipped into one of the interview rooms, pulled the blinds over the two-way glass so no one could look in, and flopped down into a chair, where I crashed and burned with a vengeance. These would probably be my last moments of privacy and solitude for a while; there were mountains to climb still. Arrest warrant, the actual arrest, arraignment, indictment, trial, sentencing if we won . . .

Please, God, don't let there be a trial, don't let there be a chance for anyone to screw this up. . . . Make him plead to something so we won't all have to get dragged through all that legal muck. . . .

But did I really want that? Sure it was easier, but for that ease there was always a trade-off. If the state accepted a plea, the state would have to trade life in prison for the possibility of death.

Did I really want that? There was no sense dwelling on it for the moment. My whole life was about to change—more for the worse than the better. If we won this thing, there would be some accolades and maybe a promotion, but for the foreseeable future it was going to be sheer hell. My kids' lives would change too. There would be no quiet evenings of homework or TV. No trips to the Santa Monica Pier. They would be spending a lot more time with their father, not that that was so terrible. They would be hounded by classmates and friends.

I stood up finally and went to get Nathan's shoe box. I found the pair that had to be his from the mix, and laid the shoes gently into the box; like Cinderella's glass slipper, they slipped into place easily. I'd left them until last because it would have tainted something to know ahead of time if his sneakers were in there. Everything after that would have seemed like just a confirmation, and I didn't want to deceive the parents who were putting themselves through renewed pain to look through all those shoes. It just didn't seem fair.

The application for the arrest warrant was my career masterpiece, as clear and succinct as any piece of police writing I'd ever produced. I wanted the prosecutor to be so engaged in this thing that he would go to the mat for it if the need should arise.

Fred was busy handpicking the group who would bring in our bizarre suspect. When he briefed the incredulous brass, I was required to be there to explain when necessary. Fred was extremely careful to phrase his statements so they wouldn't think we'd missed this one. The whole thing made me sick to my stomach, not to mention angry.

And they say police work isn't creative.

I was enjoying a brief moment of amusement, thinking of Fred in his schlumpy suit in the middle of all those fancy uniforms, when the phone rang on my desk.

Pandora heard trouble in that electronic trill, but she picked up the phone anyway, fool that she is.

A twelve-year-old boy had been approached by what he thought was a family friend as he was walking home from after-school soccer practice. The supposed friend pulled up alongside him in a car and announced that his mother had asked him to pick the boy up because she needed him home sooner. The incident occurred on a side street where traffic was relatively light, with two witnesses. One was a bad-attitude, drugged-out little teenage tramp who was just about as unhelpful as she could be.

The other, miraculously, was the boy himself, who got away.

His name was Carl Thorsen, and unlike the junkie-in-waiting, who had to wipe her nose after every other slurred word, he spoke so fast that I had to ask him to repeat just about everything he said.

"The car pulled up alongside me real close to the sidewalk I slowed down because I thought it was Jake's car the passenger door came open so I stopped walking and

looked inside but there were shadows and I couldn't really
see whoever was inside very clear but I thought it was Jake
at first because it was the right kind of car and it sorta
looked like him so I figured what the heck of course it's
him but there was something about the voice that bothered
me it didn't sound right because it was too high so I got real
scared and stepped back but before I could get completely
out of his reach he grabbed my sleeve and started to pull on
me so I really struggled a lot and I got loose again and then
I ran as fast as I could away from there."

Carl swore that he screamed, but there was no one
around except the girl, who said she didn't hear a scream
and also claimed she couldn't have read the plate number
on the car from that distance. I regretted not hauling her
in to division for a little governmental inconvenience.
Maybe it's just as well that she wasn't cooperative; junkies
make lousy witnesses.

I put Carl in a patrol car and sent him off to division,
where they'd call his parents and get the wheels of justice
rolling. Escobar and I got the evidence crew started on the
abduction site and then canvassed the neighborhood while
they did their work. One of the people who lived on the
street told us that she thought she might have heard a boy
scream, but she didn't look outside to see what was going
on. No one else heard or saw a thing.

God, I would love tō have had the plate number from
that car.

When I got back to the station I asked Carl to give
me his shirt. There wasn't much of a chance that we'd
find fingerprints, but I was praying that we'd get lucky—
good fortune seemed to be out and about that day, especially in the world of Carl Thorsen. The shirt looked
awfully clean and unwrinkled for having been involved in
a "struggle"—no rips, abrasions, or stretched areas that I
could see.

The mother arrived; I let her spend a few minutes

alone with her son before I went in to see the two of them together.

"I'll need your friend Jake's phone number and address."

She seemed more than eager to cooperate on behalf of her friend. "I have his cell phone number," she said. "Call him right now. He didn't do this, I know he didn't."

I knew that too, but I couldn't say it just yet.

Jake had been alone in his car at the time the incident occurred and therefore had no witnesses as to his whereabouts, except one who turned out to be rather fortuitous: the state trooper who gave him a speeding ticket four minutes after the precise time of the abduction attempt, in a location more than twenty miles as the crow flies from where that attempt was made.

You're getting sloppy, Wilbur.

I advised the horrified Jake to come directly to the station; he arrived in less than fifteen minutes, in a complete state of hysteria. We established his alibi right away, and I let him know that he was not a suspect. Then I jumped right into asking him what I really wanted to know.

"Have you and Carl gone anywhere that you might have been seen together publicly within the last two years?"

You should have seen the look on his face. "Of course we have. All sorts of places. He's like my own kid."

I'll admit it's not the first question you'd expect under the circumstances. But I didn't want it said later that I had directed him in any way to the La Brea exhibit. I wanted him just to mention it on his own without prompting. So I asked him to be more specific about the events they'd attended. He got pretty flustered, then recited a list of movies, ball games, meetings, and entertainment events—

And an exhibit.

I couldn't help myself. I grinned like a Cheshire cat. I

didn't even try to hide it. I actually almost shouted I was so happy.

What did he think of the tapes that people were making as they waited to get in?

They were cool, a really great idea; he and Carl had clowned around and hammed it up for the camera. He said it was almost as much fun as the exhibit itself.

"What on earth does any of this have to do with Carl being abducted?"

I let the question hang in the air unanswered. "If you wouldn't mind, Detective Escobar is just going to ask you a few more things, and then we'll take you to see Carl and his mother."

Escobar wrote down what Jake revealed about the nature of his relationship with the boy and why he spent so much time with him, as well as a few more details about his schedule that afternoon so the alibi would be unassailable. Never in the history of crime have cops gone so far to bolster someone's alibi—usually we're bending over backward to tear it apart. It was overkill—all we really had to do was photocopy the speeding citation and get an ID from the highway patrolman.

Even Johnnie Cochran couldn't make *that* glove too small.

The whole squad room burst into activity after this incident. *One guy,* I kept saying to everyone. *It's one guy.* No one disagreed. It was a thrill to watch all these supervisors tripping over themselves to make it look like they'd been supporting my theory all along. Time flew by as we worked it all over; when I looked up at the clock, it was almost five. I had to call Kevin pretty quickly and ask him to get our two younger kids from swim practice at five-thirty. There was no way I was going to make it. For the first time since I'd started working on these disappearances, I wasn't worried—even Wilbur couldn't put another grab together that quickly.

twenty-five

"SWEAR!"

"I shall not."

"Brother, I shall make your life more miserable than you can imagine if you do not. You must tell no one of the things we learned."

It took a threat of condemnation to make him agree, albeit reluctantly. "Such things as this must be given their due," he said, "or they will fester within and harm you. I would not have your spirit infected with a malaise whose cure is simple release."

The matter was closed by my words: "That shall be my worry."

And that is precisely what it became. I bore my painful new knowledge in solitary silence. I did not write to my son nor confide in any of my sisters, who whispered behind my back with increasing frequency as I became more distant from them. While the activities of our convent took place with reasonable consistency, I gave the place only cursory attention at best, for my interest lay elsewhere. My daily life began to feel like a wet-robed slog through a swamp. One foot before the next, I plodded heavily through my obligations as if there were no heart beating inside my chest.

Even more significantly, I did not speak to Jean de Malestroit of the horror I had uncovered in Champtocé. It was to him that I would have made my confession, should absolution have been required of me for the guilty knowledge I had acquired. My bishop noticed the changes in me, the dark moods and spontaneous tears, and asked many times if I required unburdening.

"I am as holy as possible," I assured him, "under the circumstances." I considered it a true blessing that he did not press me further. He had other matters to consider.

All this being true, I must still confess that September passed with frightening rapidity. On the morning of the twenty-eighth, we gathered very early in the chapel/courtroom, well before Terce. Additional chairs had been brought in to supplement the rows of hard wooden pews that ran along the central path. A dais with witness bar stood front and center before the judges' table, at which Jean de Malestroit and Friar Jean Blouyn would sit as the case unfolded before them. All of this somehow banished the sense of sanctity that usually permeated the space.

The day had started out alive with the anticipation of forward progress, so long delayed, but as hour after hour passed without the arrival of Lord Gilles de Rais, a nervous grumbling set in. From my seat near the end of the front-most pew, I sat in stiff silence and watched the shadows shorten as the sun made its way to apex. The morning songs of the birds gave way to those customarily sung as the day progressed. *Frère* Demien fidgeted next to me like a ten-year-old boy; for all his desire to see these events unfold, he deplored the waste of a day when he might have been in the orchards.

His displeasure was such that he loosed a rare disparagement. "I had not thought Milord to be such a coward. He should be dragged out of his hiding place and thrust before these judges."

"Members of the nobility are not dragged out of anywhere, Brother. They must come to their humiliations with the appearance of consent."

His "hiding" place was a sumptuous suite of rooms in the Bishop's own palace. There would be no escape from that confinement, but neither was it precisely an imprisonment. He could receive visitors—not that any had been reported—and live in a manner that suited his station.

As the hours passed in waiting, I daydreamed of apples and pears and walnuts, of fine embroidery and colorful glass beads that might be added to enhance its beauty. A brief distraction was provided when a man and woman bowed their way into the chapel in apologetic haste—yet more witnesses, who had arrived well beyond the appointed hour.

"They need not have hurried," *Frère* Demien observed.

His Eminence had been eager to proceed and had taken his place of honor at the judges' table that morning with almost visible excitement. Now he was forced to preserve what dignity he could by stifling yawns with increasing frequency. Father Jean Blouyn, a stern-looking man of short stature, pendulous jowls, and a large, pitted nose, sat, equally bored, to his Eminence's right. I had often wondered if he came by his red face by some more natural means than the rumored excessive drink, such as having been scalded by steam over a pot. The Lord Inquisitor did not have the look of a fellow who had ever cooked for himself, so I settled on drink as the reason. He was an otherwise remarkable man, quite learned and devout, who possessed all the necessary qualities for these proceedings and was well-suited to the task of determining heresy, for he was as righteous a man as could be found in these parts, drink or no.

I was accustomed to seeing Friar Blouyn in his clerical garb, or occasionally attired as a teacher, but today he wore the robes of a judge and a squared-off hat of rich red velvet, which seemed on first glance a bit large for his head. He seemed to think so too, for he held it in place with one hand when he leaned toward Jean de Malestroit. On this particular occasion of incline, a tassel slipped down in front of his nose and swung back and forth, which he brushed away with his other hand, rendering himself completely unable to cover his words.

"So many witnesses," I heard—or rather saw—him say. "Shall more scribes be brought in?"

Those who were there had been selected for the strength and passion of their testimony, which would be recorded by the four scribes assigned to the task, who sat before and below the judges. Their ink-stained fingers all struggled for something to occupy the hours; one patted the table, another picked at a hanging bit of skin on his nails, yet another whittled away at the points of his quills to sharpen them.

There would be a trial and conviction to record, after all.

Strategy, cleverness, and legal maneuverings were the weapons they would use against Gilles de Rais, not the swords and arrows against which he could fight back. Jean de Malestroit and Friar Blouyn would cut him down like a sapling when the time was right. The witnesses—the peasants and tradesmen who would comprise their ammunition—fidgeted nervously in the pews like children themselves, each one anticipating his turn at the bar with probable dread. Few of these people would dare to even speak to a nobleman, let alone besmirch him in the presence of the King's intimates. Yet here they were, full of ready anger. It made me admire Madame le Barbier's courage all the more. I wondered now if she'd had some understanding of the maelstrom her visit to the Bishop would unleash.

The bailiff's voice crashed unexpectedly through the quiet with the invocation. I nearly jumped in my seat.

They would begin without him.

There followed a state of silence so complete that even our breathing seemed an affront. The bailiff then continued, speaking the words that demanded an answer from Gilles de Rais, even *in absentia*.

"On this Wednesday, the twenty-eighth day of September, 1440, in the tenth year of the reign of our Pontiff the Most Holy Father Monsignor Eugène, by God's grace Pope, being the fourth such of that name, during this the general council of Basel, before our Reverend Father of God Jean de Malestroit, by God's grace and that of the Holy Apostolic See, Bishop of Nantes, and before the male religious Friar Jean Blouyn of the order of Dominicans, bachelor of the Holy Writ and Vicar of the male religious, Friar Guillaume Merici, of the abovesaid Dominican Order, professor of theology, Inquisitor into Heresy in the kingdom of France, delegated by the authority of the same Friar Guillaume and specially appointed to the position of Inquisitor in the diocese and city of Nantes, now seated in the chapel of the episcopal palace of Nantes, and in the presence of scribes and notaries, Jean Delaunay, Jean Petit, Nicolas Géraud, and Guillaume Lesné ..."

The said scribes and notaries bent to their parchment and scribbled furiously, recording every word with intense diligence.

"... expected to write truthfully before these same Lords Bishop and Vice-Inquisitor on each and all of the things that occur in the cases before us, and finally, charged with and entrusted to draw this up in a public manner, to which task they deputized each and every one of us present."

Ad infinitum, ad nauseam. I understood Jean de Malestroit's desire for caution in establishing the authority of the court as it was comprised, but it was a tedious recitation. Immediately thereafter, the witnesses were called to give evidence in support of the charges. A few raised not only their voices but their tempers as well, and those who did were admonished to remember themselves.

Agathe, wife of Denis de Lemion; the widow of Regnaud Donete; Jeanne, wife of Guibelet Delit; Jean Hubert and his wife; the widow of Yvon Kerguen; Tiphaine, wife of Eonnet le Charpentier. I watched numbly as each one was called, arose, was sworn, and then gave witness. All spoke bitterly and at length against the accused and his accomplices; the stories varied little from one to the next. Poitou had led the child away; the old woman had appeared on the forest road and enticed their children with promises of food and other blessings; de Sille and de Briqueville had spoken of benefits. Positions in noble households were offered, clothing suitable to such honors given. Then nothing more would be heard, not a word, not a letter, not a shred of evidence that these good, devoted sons had either come to an end or had vanished for some other reason.

But one among the witnesses painted a different picture. She had not willingly given her son away in return for promises of benefit. She was small and thin and looked terribly frail in her dusty dress; I wanted to put my arms around her and speak solace, to catch her tears as they fell, which I was certain they had, bitterly and often. But she held her head high as she spoke, belying any frailty; never once was his Eminence forced to ask her to speak up.

"I am Jeanne, wife of Jean Darel. On the feast of Saint Peter and Paul last, I was returning home with my son. We had gone from our home in the parish of Saint-Similien to Nantes, where I had a few errands to do, and we took this opportunity to visit with my sister Angelique, who lives not far from this palace in which we are now gathered. I was also of a mind to visit Notre Dame de Nantes to make an offering there for the soul of my departed mother, which I knew would please my sister greatly.

"We are a poor family, Milords, and have no mounts. It is a fair distance, but the weather was fine and it seemed a pleasant day for walking. We made our pilgrimage to the cathedral and then had a sweet visit with my sister; she is dear to me and is a devoted aunt, so my son never complained of the walk to her home, which to a boy of his age must have seemed very long. And as sometimes happens when the time passed is joyful, Milords, the hours got away from us and we had to make a choice as to whether we would stay the night or go back to Saint-Similien. As we had not mentioned the likelihood of staying in Nantes, I thought we might be missed, which would cause alarm in our household. So we made our good-byes and left as the sun neared the horizon.

"My son was hungry by then, so I gave him a crust of bread to eat as we made our way. He ate a bit of it but did not finish, though what he did eat seemed to satisfy him for the moment. But by now my little boy was tired as well, for the day had been a long one for a child of such tender years. Often when we would travel I would play small games of hide-and-seek with him to keep him from fussing out of boredom. He would secret himself behind a tree and I would look for him. It gave him great joy to do this; he was not yet clever enough to hide himself completely every time, and it would make me smile to think he thought himself hidden from my sight. But there were times when he was maddeningly successful, enough to cause me concern. In these moments he would not reveal himself despite my pleas.

"The last I saw of him that night was his little hand sticking out from behind a tree, still clutching the remains of his crust of bread. I pretended not to see him and turned back in the direction we were headed, relieved once again to know that he was safely with me.

"I was aware of his continuous presence during our little game, until one moment when a cold shudder overtook me and I became very frightened for no reason I could understand. I turned to look for my boy, but I could not see him anywhere. He had not cried out to me, so I did not think him in harm's way, only perhaps a bit lost or hiding too well. If such an unnameable fear had gone through me, might it not have done so to him as well, and might he not have reacted by hiding farther into the woods? I called his name and offered reassurances, but he did not appear. I worked my way backward along the road looking for him, then rushed forward again when I could not find him. He never reappeared, and I have no idea of what might have happened to him, only that whoever took him has kept him away from me for all of this time."

I heard but little of what was said by those who followed her. Her son had disappeared without so much as a whisper of distress into the velvet darkness, while she herself was nearby, and had never been seen nor heard from again.

What is there to fear more than this? In one moment, everything is as it ought to be. But in the next, nothing that one has previously taken for God's truth seems viable any longer. All is lost, all is shattered, naught remains to grasp for safety.

Had he come upon *La Meffraye,* that old woman who prowled the woods and paths looking for lost little ones, who would show herself as kind and sweet and appear to be no threat? *Godspeed, my child,* the hag might have whispered from behind a tree in the darkness. *I see that you have a bit of bread to eat, but here is a softer crust, not so hard on your little teeth. Yes, reach out to take it, put your small hand within my grasp, let me lead you to where there are treats beyond imagining. . . . Oh, no, do not call out to your mother, you must not alarm her, for she will be angry with you if you do. . . . I will return you to her and soothe her anger later, so you need not fear her wrath. . . .*

Little ones want to trust, especially those whom they have been taught to revere.

The last I saw of him that night was his little hand sticking out from behind a tree, still clutching the remains of his crust of bread.

We stayed in the chapel until all who were summoned to speak that day had indeed spoken. The witnesses were told that they could go, but few rose up to depart, for there were further proceedings. Inquisitive whispers rose when a sheaf of papers was introduced into evidence; I recognized this handsome folio, uniquely bound with a gilt leather strap, as one I had seen in Jean de Malestroit's chamber.

I could almost feel the evil oozing off it. Contained within its pages was the initial testimony of Henriet and Poitou. Blessedly, it was not read aloud.

⚜

We adjourned for a while in order to refresh ourselves. When we returned to the chapel later, Jean de Touscheronde would make a few simple declarations to transform this court from ecclesiastical to secular. Gilles de Rais would be required to answer to Duke

Jean V, much as he would answer to God before Jean de Malestroit and Friar Blouyn in the same room.

But there was time before the transformation was to begin for *Frère* Demien and I to slip away to the kitchen, where we were almost certain to find soup and bread and, if the cook was in a pleasant mood, a sweet of some sort. On the way we were forced to pass through a crowd that had gathered outside the palace, hoping for news of the proceedings. I stopped and stood still for a moment within the milling throng, which had gripped my attention. *Frère* Demien went a few paces farther before he noticed I had stopped.

"Mother?" he called to me. "It is best to come along." He reached for my hand and began to guide me forward.

"Go ahead," I told him. "I will find you."

He sighed, shook his head, and left me there.

The crowd's number had grown dramatically since we had entered in the morning. The square outside the palace was a place where people gathered for all manner of reasons; usually they gathered to watch a bit of entertainment such as a juggler or minstrel, or sometimes it would be the crying of some important bit of news. With details of the morning's testimony no doubt spreading, there had grown quite a throng. The sight of them gathered as they were, the agitated hum of their words, the sharp sounds of their activities—altogether it was enough to make me pay attention.

I was not the only one engaged in observation; many eyes were upon me, as palpably as the touch of hands. I had come out of the great chapel, which hinted of higher knowledge of what had transpired within. But my flowing black drapes protected me. People who were staring at me would look away as soon as my eyes met theirs, until finally only one person's gaze was still fixed upon me. I could not help but look back, and when I did I was filled

with unanticipated gladness, for there before me stood
Madame le Barbier.

She nodded respectfully; I nodded back, and smiled
very slightly. It was a tempting notion to go to her and
share an exchange of comradeship. But neither of us
moved; there was really nothing that could be said to enhance the moment. Eventually our eyes parted, and I
made my way to the kitchen, where Cook obliged me
with a measure of soup for lunch, as there was no time
for a larger repast. But I did not mind; Madame had
given me all the refreshment I would need.

⚜

With Jean de Malestroit sitting behind him at the jurists'
table, de Touscheronde seemed almost diminutive. In
truth, his entire being was "slight." There was a soft, almost feminine quality to his voice, but that worked to the
prosecutor's advantage—we were all forced to listen carefully, and there was absolute quiet in the chapel when he
spoke. He handily persuaded a number of upset and agitated people to speak lucidly of unspeakable things while
under the stares of powerful strangers.

"And tell me, Madame, if you would be so kind, of
what transpired after you gave your son over to this fellow Poitou...."

Or, "*Monsieur,* as clearly as you can in view of your
visible distress, please tell this court what you believe
happened to young Bernard...."

They recounted everything to him, confessed freely
as though he were a saint, though they were not the sinners but instead those upon whom grievous sins had
been perpetrated. They told him when their losses were
first noticed, where the disappearances occurred, who
made the initial complaints, why Lord de Rais was suspected; a more commanding inquisitor might not have

managed that depth of revelation from witnesses as humble as these.

A man named André Barbé spoke of the disappearance of Madame le Barbier's son.

"I saw him behind Rondeau's house picking apples, and I have not seen him since.... Gone are many more as well: the sons of Guillaume Jeudon, Alexander Chastelier, and Guillaume Hilairet.... We would have come forward sooner, but none of us dared speak for fear of the rogues in Lord de Rais's chapel, or others who followed him, for they threatened us with imprisonment, or injury, or other ill-treatment should our suspicions be reported to the Magistrate, and the Magistrate himself seemed hardened to what we said when one of us found the courage to come forward."

Then, to my surprise, Madame le Barbier herself rose. "Your honor, if you please," she said, "there is something more I would add to the words of my good neighbor."

Displeasure and hesitancy were all over de Touscheronde's face. "Very well," he demurred, "but be brief, please."

She shocked us all by moving past the witness's stand and approaching the table where the judges were seated. Guards stiffened to readiness as Madame extended a clenched fist in front of her and began to shake it rhythmically. She seemed to be pumping determination and courage straight out of the air. "I curse Lord Gilles de Rais for all eternity," she said. "May his soul descend to the depths of hell for what he has done to me and these other good people. May the demon claim him for his own and chain him to a burning stake for all time."

Shouts and cheers of accord rose up. Jean de Malestroit stood partway up at the table and called out loudly for order, but it did no good: Inspired by her curses, the crowd would have its say. Mixed in with the excited sounds of triumph were wails of anguish from those who had suffered, and then more curses were hurled out. In the presence of a bishop it was a scandalous, nearly heretical thing to denounce one's sovereign. And though it seemed fair enough to me that those whom Milord had wronged ought to have a say in whatever pronouncement was eventually made against him, the shouts and jeers were little more than a gesture: The final word would be God's, spoken through His servant Jean de Malestroit.

Surrounded by guards, Madame stood her ground and stared accusingly at Jean de Malestroit, the man who had tried to spurn her initial complaint; her look seemed to say, *I curse you similarly for ignoring my plea, and all the saints know that you well deserve it.*

He became like a stone, expressionless and plain, as if there were no thoughts within. When the guards tried to close in, he motioned them away. He cleared his throat lightly and said, "You may step back, Madame, if you have said your piece."

Her eyes still locked onto him, Madame le Barbier picked up her skirt and stepped backward. As she blended into the assembly of witnesses, the room suddenly and without apparent cause grew hotter, as if all the fresh air had been sucked out by some giant creature who had just emerged from the depths of a lake. Men began to loosen their collars; women fanned themselves to ward off swoons. Jean de Malestroit rose halfway up from his judge's chair and gestured emphatically for the window to be opened. Metal hinges screamed in protest as the seldom-used window was pulled inward by the bailiff.

In rushed a cold wind, every bit as extreme as the oppressive heat. Before Madame had the chance to resume her seat, a large blue-black crow fluttered through the opening and hovered over the assembly. He stared down malevolently with his tiny yellow eyes and flapped his wings wide. A great cry of alarm went up in the room. One woman stood in a panic, then slumped back in a complete faint against her companion. The confused bird headed for the highest perch, which at that moment was Madame le Barbier's head. He clutched with sharp claws at her hair in a frantic attempt to gain purchase.

She screamed and reeled around, her arms flailing as she tried to pull the talons out of her hair. People shrank away in terror. One man stood up and shook an accusing finger at the black interloper, crying, "It is the devil himself."

It was then that the true wailing began. People rose to escape but were trapped within the clamoring mass. Fully standing now, his Eminence pounded on the table with his stout gavel again and again in an attempt to regain control of the proceedings.

I stood and ran forward to help my suffering cohort. With my face inclined away from the black feathery mess, I reached in and began to pull the bird upward. He went at my hand with his sharp beak—blood poured forth in a flood from the gash he tore in me. Others finally rushed in to give assistance, and we managed to untangle the bird from his screaming victim. Freed at last, the bird *whooshed* up to the heights of the chapel, where he flurried around in a state of wicked agitation. En masse, we cowered in fear as the black devil swooped low again, his claws outstretched and searching. It seemed an eternity before the wails of the people frightened it through the opening, back to the freedom of the sky.

De Touscheronde nearly hurtled to the window and shoved it against the frame with such thunderous, clanging force that I thought surely it would disintegrate, but somehow the iron framing held, and all the colored glass—so artfully joined with molten lead—remained intact.

How my mother would have wept to see the delicate white handkerchief soaked red in her daughter's blood. I clutched at my wounded hand as people all around me moaned aloud and embraced one another for comfort. Men and women alike prayed and crossed themselves, some quite furiously, to purge the evil spirit that flew in on those dark wings.

Had Lord de Rais sent this demon to torment Madame le Barbier and, along with her, the rest of us? Or was its sudden appearance only a coincidental event? We were not, any of us, certain of the truth.

But we were, all of us, terrified.

The crow was long gone, but the uproar continued, negating any possibility of moving forward—Madame le Barbier would be the last witness of the afternoon. His Eminence brought the day's business to a close with the shrieking of a few authoritative Latin declarations over the noise of the crowd, and the scribes hastened to put the words to parchment. Jean de Malestroit then nodded to the captain of the court guard, who gave a quick signal to those who served under him. As one, they began to pound the ends of their spears on the stone floor, but rather than lessening, the turmoil began to increase both in tempo and intensity. Soon the shouts were accompanied by clapping of the hands, which slipped into synchrony with the pounding of spears.

It was madness and mayhem. I saw Jean de Malestroit give another signal to his captain, who bade his guards cease their pounding. Then those spears were turned to the task of prodding the citizenry out of the chapel. The rhythmic noise finally began to dissipate as people grumbled their way out of the room toward the stairway.

The protests from those who had yet to be heard were strident and loud, as if each petitioner had the notion that his own tale would convince the judges of Milord's guilt. I felt great sympathy for these disappointed ones, though I could not fathom how one more recitation would make a difference in view of what had already been revealed.

I looked in Jean de Malestroit's direction; he questioned me with a quick glance on the severity of my injury, to which I responded with a small shrug. It would pain me on the morrow, but as yet it did not. That worry settled, the expression on his face became one of complete exasperation. Within his heart, he would be chastising himself for allowing this disruption to occur, though it was clearly God's work, or the devil's. Certainly he was not to blame. But blame himself he would nonetheless. I watched as he departed through a side door, his robes billowing out behind him in the haste of his exit.

Frère Demien and I exited with the rest of those who had been in the chapel. We moved along at a good pace; among the witnesses there seemed a great eagerness to reach the square, for there was news to be told. The throng that awaited all of us looked to have nearly doubled again since our last respite. Already a dark tale of sorcery—borne on the wings of a crow—was being thrown about, and I could hear exaggerations as it was passed from person to person.

His wings were as wide as a stork's.

The eyes—they were so human!

When he opened his beak, he spoke in tongues!

The embellishments would continue until the crow became a winged dragon with bloody talons, green scales, and demonic yellow eyes that could pierce the very soul with just one glance. It would be said that he bore some blood on his beak, which I knew to be my own. That usurper bird flew off with more than that—he took with him all of my hope that the trial and eventual punishment of Gilles de Rais might be accomplished in a smooth and orderly fashion and that we might all be spared the mayhem that threatened to cloud it. But there was too much of the devil in it now for godliness or sanity to prevail.

chapter 26

CARL THORSEN WAS A GORGEOUS blond angel, like most of his predecessors. Carl was not a small kid—he had some height to him, but he was slender and fine-boned. I had one advantage in assessing him that I hadn't had before: I got to see his live movements. Photos just don't cut it and even videos are weak when it comes to conveying a complete sense of the victim. Carl was athletic and a lot more graceful than you'd have expected; certainly he moved a lot less jerkily than most young boys of his age, my own included. He became an instant icon to me, an amalgam of all the lost boys. I watched him interact with those around him, in particular his mother. Of the others, I had nothing more than the hope-stained recollections their loved ones were willing to provide to help me understand the essence of the kid. Not so with Carl and his mother—they engaged in an exquisite little dance of familial intimacy. He floated back and forth between child closeness and adolescent diffidence. She was choked with anger at first, an emotion that she hid pretty well until it finally transformed itself into profound relief.

We'd put them in the best interview room, the one we generally reserve for nonviolent, cooperative witnesses or victims in distress. The chairs are cushioned and the lighting is soft. I let them get settled, and when they both seemed reasonably calm, we talked for a little while, mostly about how lucky Carl was to have escaped. Escobar came in—we'd prearranged a "casual" entry—and began to focus his attentions on Carl. As soon as he had the boy engaged in conversation, I took the mother aside and asked her if she'd be willing to step out of the room for a few minutes so I could ask her a few housekeeping-type questions to complete some paperwork. What I really wanted was to get Jake and Carl alone in the same room, to see how Carl reacted to his mother's friend without her influence.

He ran forward and leaped into the man's arms, repeating his name over and over again.

I knew it wasn't you, Jake, I just knew you wouldn't try to hurt me.

The whole scene really disturbed me. All these kids, wherever they might be and in whatever condition, had had their faith in a trusted adult shattered—that crushes a kid like you can't believe—and then they were assaulted by a stranger.

I brought the mother back into the room after just a few minutes. With Jake's reassuring arm around his shoulder, Carl Thorsen relaxed enough to start to crash; he'd probably been running on adrenaline, but the shock was catching up with him. He stopped every now and then to compose himself as he told his story again, but this time, with more detail.

"I could hear the car when it pulled around the corner. I turned my head to the left and sort of glanced over my shoulder. It looked a little like Jake's car, but his is a lot like a bunch of other cars, light color, not an SUV. But after a couple of seconds I heard it slow down; you know how you can hear tires crunching more slowly over the stuff on the street. I could hear that. It made me a little nervous.

"The car pulled up right next to the sidewalk so the wheels were almost touching and slowed so it was going the same speed as I was. Then it pulled a few feet ahead of me. The passenger door opened—the guy must have reached across the seat and opened it with his other hand. I stepped back a little. He called my name—but the voice wasn't familiar. When I looked in the car I saw a guy who I thought was Jake, so I went closer. I asked what was wrong with his voice, and he cleared his throat real loud and said he had a cold. Then the guy said that I should get into the car because my mom needed me to come home right now.

"I figured something must be wrong at home and I almost got in the car. But I just didn't believe it was Jake. The guy must have figured out what I was thinking because he grabbed my arm. I pulled it away. He yanked the car door closed really hard—I was afraid he caught my shirt in it and I was gonna get dragged. But he didn't. He took off really fast and just left me there. I started to cry."

Which is precisely what he did in the interview room as he neared the end of his account. I thought that was a good thing. He might as well get all this stuff out in a place where he knew he wouldn't be hurt.

I was heading out the door to get the boy a Coke and his mother some coffee when Spence came flying down the hallway with a very bad look on his face.

"There's been another one. Also failed."

"Looks like your *one guy* turned out to be twins," Vuska snarled.

Shouting was the only way to be heard, so I did, though I hated the sound of my own voice at that moment. "It could still be only one perp doing this," I shrieked over the chaos.

Frazee and Escobar were quiet and stayed off to one side.

"Wait a minute, think about this," I pleaded to everyone. "He hasn't failed before this that we know of. He's gotten pretty much every kid he decided to get. He let these two kids go to throw us off track. Don't you see? *He's dicking us around.*"

Dicks do not like to be dicked around. But it was plain that perps don't like it much either—at least Wil Durand did not. It was as if we'd turned on the electricity in Frankenstein's laboratory when we began to look into him openly. "We have to stay on this guy right now because he's really giving us the opportunity, and we may not get it again," I put forth. "Up to now, he's been almost invisible. He's letting us see him, getting in our faces. Challenging us, because this son of a bitch thinks he's smarter than we are."

My head began to pound and my palms were sweating. But I could see a shift in attitude as the briefing disbanded.

Carl Thorsen and his mother were still in the interview room. I corralled one of the PSAs and said, "Would you go tell them that I'm going to be detained for a short while because of another case?"

Through a look of annoyance, the PSA nodded.

"Tell them I'll be back as soon as possible. Get them some dinner from one of the authorized menus if they want it, and if there isn't enough petty cash, I'll pay for it myself."

I went back to my desk, knowing that I was about to start another round of Durand madness, feeling completely exhausted. The eyes of my fellow detectives were all on me. Fred and a few brass were back in his office, knocking the new development around, when the next call came in.

He'd done it again, not an hour after the last time.

No one knew what to say or what to do, least of all our supposed superiors.

"It's a message," I pleaded. No one seemed to be listening except Spence and Escobar.

"He's saying, *Catch me if you can.*"

Which was just what I planned to do, with or without help. *If* I was still a detective.

Although I had Errol Erkinnen's pager number, I'd never used it before. But this was an emergency. He responded to my page almost instantly.

"I have three kids who got away from this guy, all here at division right now."

"Wait a minute," he said, as if he'd misheard me. "They *all* got away?"

"Yeah. All three of them, believe it or not."

"This is a real escalation in his behavior—he's playing with you, making a statement."

It was so sweet to have someone's faith. "*I* get that, but no one else seems to. I'm beginning to think that this whole deal has turned into something between him and me. It's not about the boys anymore."

"You're probably right. He's gone out of pattern and he's communicating with you through that variation. It's a pretty sure bet that he wants you to respond."

"And I will, trust me. But right now I have to interview these kids. I want to talk to all three of them together because I think if they talk to each other they'll open up and reveal more than they would otherwise. I need your help because the lieutenant wants me to have 'someone medical' present."

"I'm not medical."

"They call you Doc, don't they? That's good enough for these purposes."

"Okay," he said. "I'll be right there. But don't allow

yourself to be sidetracked by this little deviation of his. You know he's going to do it for real again, and probably soon."

"I'm gonna have him in jail before then."

"You think so."

"I *know* so."

True to his word, Doc arrived about fifteen minutes later.

We had each of the three groups in a separate holding room. The PSAs were complaining about having to bring in drinks and food for the kids and their family members, which I, the insensitive detective, had brazenly offered for their comfort. *The place is turning into a damned Holiday Inn,* I overheard one of them say.

What if it had been her son?

Before we went into the individual rooms, Doc took me aside. "They should be as comfortable as possible when we do this," he said. "Do any of them need to be cleaned up?"

I didn't understand.

"Did any of them have a physical reaction to the abduction attempt, like soiling or wetting himself?"

"Not that I could tell when they first came in."

"Good. That bodes well."

We introduced ourselves and spoke to each child separately for a few moments. I arrived back at my desk feeling like I'd been talking to stone walls.

"They're not saying much," I observed, quite unhappily.

"They're probably clamming up because their parents are there. We'll have to talk to them without the parents," Doc said.

"Is that wise right now? They've all been through a

lot. You'd think that it would make them feel more safe with their parents there to support them."

"They'll all have an extreme sense of vulnerability right now, not too different from posttraumatic stress syndrome. These kids aren't big strong soldiers. They don't have nearly the coping mechanisms that adults do."

"Then why should we get them away from something that makes them feel safe? Won't they be even worse without the parents there?"

"Maybe. I can't say for sure. But one thing I'm certain of is that they're all assuming their parents are angry with them over this. How many times do you think each one of them has heard *Don't talk to strangers*? Probably about a hundred times. And how did this whole thing develop? A stranger."

He was right. Evan would be mortified if he'd fallen prey to something I'd warned him about over and over again; he would shut right down on me.

"They're all too young to have survivor guilt, though," he went on. "They might later, but now I don't think it will be a factor. Often there are delayed effects; sometimes they don't show up for years. Of course, there are treatments—"

I reined him back in. "Teach me later, Errol. Right now I need you to stay with me on this, let me lead. I could use some suggestions as to how we can put all this theory into practice."

A bit cowed, he said, "Maybe we should just start out with all three of them in one room, no parents, and see how it goes. We have to be careful not to make them feel like they're being interrogated."

None of the parents objected, but it didn't go as well with the boys themselves as we would have liked. All three fidgeted like they had frogs in their pockets; their legs dangled and jerked. They pouted like this was some sort of group punishment.

Erkinnen guided me to the far corner of the room and whispered, "We have to get rid of this classroom aura. This may sound a bit perverse, but we need to make this fun for them."

What did boys like other than beasts?

Cars.

"Stay right here," I told him. "I think I may have the fix."

Spence borrowed a hat from one of the patrol cops and pretended to be the chauffeur. Doc and I got into the passenger area with the three boys. The confiscated Mercedes limo, a shiny black behemoth that floated down the street like a hydrofoil, was our vehicle for a motor tour of the sites of all three failed abductions.

There was a moment of nervous hesitancy until I patted the gun in my shoulder holster.

They settled down nicely after only a few minutes. There was a VCR and a PlayStation and a phone and all the latest technological gizmos in this fantasy car, which was about to go on the auction block as required by law. We cruised around through the forest of neon, and made a group decision that it was best to go chronologically, which pleased me because I got to see what Wilbur would have had to go through to get from one site to the next. In all three locations, after some initial quiet, the conversations became animated and descriptive. *I was standing right there and he pulled up, and then the door opened, and ...*

In the safety of common experience, their near-tragedies became more like items brought to show-and-tell. Only the boy involved could specifically address what had happened at each site, but just as I hoped, the others responded with enthusiastic comparisons to their own events. There were times when all three were out of the car, comparing notes and engaging in one-upsmanship.

The tour ended with a trip to a famous ice cream parlor in Santa Monica and a brief stint on the pier to run off the energy left over from sitting and sweets. Doc and I leaned on a railing and watched them as they pranced around on the beach to the north of the pier. All three of these boys had narrowly escaped becoming photos on my victim board, but there they were, alive and running in the sand, just like my own son would have if he were here. I considered the possibility that there is, after all, a God.

"All young and pretty," I observed.

"Yes, indeed. His fetish, naked and exposed," Doc said. "It's not uncommon in serial situations for a predator to be driven by forces he doesn't understand to choose victims with certain characteristics. When we get this guy, I'm going to want to ask him about it. Those qualities can have deep significance."

When we get this guy. It was such a pretty dream, but we were getting closer. I wondered if there would be a signed arrest warrant for Wilbur Durand on my desk when I returned.

Seagulls screamed above the sound of the surf. The western sky was still bright orange over the gray ocean, though the sun had already set. It was gorgeous. "Look at that sky," I said with a sigh of wonderment. "How can something so ugly as Wilbur Durand exist in such a beautiful world?"

Doc put a hand on my shoulder. It was warm and comforting. "I thought we went over this," he said, quite sympathetically. "Survival of the fittest. The last one standing breeds the most, and if that takes evil, then evil is what will happen. I'm not sure we're really equipped to understand it."

"He's not going to get the chance to breed."

They pranced, they ran, they threw sand at one another. Eventually they'd all come crashing back to reality, but now they were characters in a narrow-escape movie with a good ending. "Look at them. All that wonderful early adolescent springiness."

"Yeah. Very enviable." He looked directly into my eyes. "Someone must have stolen that part of Durand's life from him. He's trying to recover it by stealing it back again. And look at them—practically clones. He's patterning his victims after someone specific."

Michael Gallagher's older brother Aiden. I would be calling Moskal sooner than I thought, for another photograph. I wished I'd asked for one when we were at the Gallagher house.

"We should take them back," I said. "Their parents are probably going nuts by now."

"Yeah. I know. But I hate to leave. This is the calmest I've felt in weeks."

"Me too."

He whistled through two fingers. All three boys turned in our direction and came running in response to his waving hand. The universal dad, a safe haven.

"And by the way," he said, "nice job."

I went back inside the station just long enough to deliver the boys back into the custody of their anxious parents. I arranged for follow-up with all three families, but I knew it would be a while before I got to it—there was so much else to be done. But before I did anything else at all, I needed to go home. There would be sanity there, of the sort that can only be found in a good stint of mothering. Kevin was more than agreeable to bringing them back, saving me the effort of going out to his place; he did have his moments.

I needed so badly to wallow in the sweet, warm, chaotic normalcy of my two daughters and son. They knew about my work and the effect it could have on me sometimes; I'd come home so many nights with the world's badness just plastered all over me. They'd tiptoed around me when I slipped into a funk following the arrest of some juvenile for a crime that most adults could barely conceive of, an event that happened all too often.

Frannie, my perceptive one, was the first to ask about the underlying distress.

"You all right, Mom?"

I brushed a few errant strands of hair back from her forehead. She was growing out bangs and it had become a little routine between us.

"All things considered, honey, I'm doing okay."

She was not convinced. "Things are busy at work?"

"There's no fooling you, is there?"

"Why would you need to fool me?"

Why, indeed—to save her from things she shouldn't have to understand. "Unfortunately," I told her, "it's going to get worse before it gets better."

"I can help with the housework," she offered sweetly. There was genuine sympathy in her voice.

I hated the thought that my job stress made her feel she needed to take on adult responsibilities while she was still a child.

"No homework tonight," I told them all. "I'll write notes to your teachers. Tonight we play."

Squeals of glee ensued. Video games, popcorn, ice cream, loud music, pillow fights; we did everything that represented decadence to those who are simply too innocent to know what it really is. My sullen son, who could be so distant when the mood came over him, was inexplicably friendly.

The girls went to bed around ten. Evan seemed to want to stay up and hang out with me, for which I was almost tearfully grateful. We popped in *Apollo 13*, fast-forwarded to the good parts, and listened to Frannie and Julie giggling in the background through the closed door of the room they shared. Sometimes I thought Evan felt chromosomally excluded. Tonight, it didn't seem to affect him. He had a parent all to himself.

I could barely believe it when he snuggled up against me during the dramatic reentry scene.

"Mom," he said tentatively.

"Yeah, honey ..."

I felt his shoulders tense. He didn't like to be called honey. I squeezed him to me briefly and said, "I'm sorry, Evan. I forget when I get distracted. What is it?"

"You're not home much anymore."

A knife to the heart. "I know, and I'm sorry. I have a case right now that's keeping me at work a lot more than I want to be."

He was all curiosity. "What is it?"

I wasn't sure if I should tell him. There was no way to predict how my revelations might make him feel. I decided to be as general as I could about it. "It's a bad one, son. Some kids are missing. Boys about your age. Some of them have been gone for a long time and I'm afraid they may be dead."

He was very pensive for a moment, and then asked, "So how is it going?"

It surprised me, but I answered him the way I would have spoken to an adult. "It's very frustrating," I told him. "Sometimes that happens in my job, though. I've had a suspect for a while, but I didn't have enough evidence to arrest him until recently. I'm waiting to hear on a warrant for this suspect, and I have no idea whether or not it will be issued. It's not like I can just call up a judge and say, *I think this is my guy.* I have to have what they call probable cause. And probable cause is different from judge to judge. Sometimes the same judge will give me a warrant on one case and then not give me one on a similar case. There's no explaining it."

"That sucks."

Way too adult. But I didn't correct him—that could

wait for some other time, when we weren't in the middle of a "moment." "Yeah, it does suck. My advice to you, if you don't want to get frustrated, is not to be a cop."

"I think your job is cool, Mom. I brag to my friends all the time about it."

I wanted to cry. "Evan, that's so sweet. I had no idea."

"I like that you're a cop. I like that you get bad guys."

I'd always hoped I could raise children who understood the value of meaningful work. Apparently I had.

For the first time in what felt like years, I actually tucked my son away and shut off the light in his room. In the solitude that remained to me, I went to my computer and wrote the report of that afternoon's meaningful work while the events were still fresh in my mind. It was another careful bit of writing, designed to bolster a position I'd already taken on this case: Wilbur Durand was the one perpetrator who had abducted all these boys. There was also the small matter of an unauthorized joyride in a confiscated vehicle that now belonged to the taxpayers, which required justification.

All three boys were accosted by a man disguised as a trusted intimate of each victim. The attempts occurred at approximately one-hour intervals; in the course of our re-creation of the events, we confirmed that the routes taken between sites could easily be negotiated in less than fifteen minutes, even considering traffic, which allowed adequate time for one perpetrator to change disguises if they were created with speed of change in mind. All three boys were of similar height, weight, coloring, and age, in keeping with a victim pattern previously established in multiple cases suspected also to be the perpetrator's work.

My professional training and experience have led me to the conclusion that the abductor is very aware that we are pursuing him vigorously and that he wanted all three of these victims to escape as a means of confusing the investigator(s) and throwing the case off track. The attempts were made at sites where witnesses were not likely to be present, though in one case there was a witness, who has been uncooperative and might be deemed unreliable. None of the victims were of sufficient strength to resist a truly determined abductor, but all managed to slip out of the perpetrator's grip with relative ease and very little struggle, which supports a theory of staged failures.

He would have gotten at least one of them if he'd really wanted to—if he was using only a mask and wig as his disguises, there would be plenty of time. The boys all agreed that they were pulled, but not hard enough to yank them into the car, and that it had felt to them like the man in the car was acting at the abductions rather than really trying to complete them.

I wished I'd been able to include this in the warrant application.

When I got into the squad room the next morning, I discovered that it wouldn't have mattered. Spence and Escobar were standing on either side of my desk, both grinning as wide as a mile.

I got the good judge again.

"We're good to go," Spence said.

"I guess we are," I said, in some disbelief. "Only question now is, *where?*"

twenty—seven

JEAN DE MALESTROIT SENT PRIVATE WORD to me that he would spend that evening in the company of de Touscheronde and Friar Blouyn as they conspired on the morrow's proceedings. I took my dinner with other ladies of the convent, who fussed over my pecked hand like a bevy of physicians. Though there was much I would have liked to discuss with his Eminence of the day's events, I confess that the company of women was a pleasant change from the masculine congress in which I had been immersed of late. We assembled around the long table in the main room of our convent. I had never seen such rapid crossing in all of my years here: a touch on the forehead, *swipe swipe* across the chest, and then the whispering over the day's intrigues began. But there was none of the desperation in their gossip that I had heard in the square, the absence of which was as nourishing to me as the meal that had been set before us. I retired to my own chamber refreshed thereafter and found the additional blessing of solitude.

Solitude; thought. One naturally followed the other. And what else would I think of than the things I had learned in Champtocé? What ought to be revealed, if anything, and to whom? I had not written to my son in Avignon in a fortnight, though I had had two letters from him in that time, both full of warm sentiments for me and great curiosity about our growing intrigue. I wanted to answer with a history of what had transpired in the proceedings so far, but I did not know how I could put quill to parchment without telling him that I now knew the fate of his brother and that a terrible suspicion had invaded my soul.

Beloved Son, We have had a visit from the devil himself in the form of a crow. And your brother was eviscerated, though not by a boar. . . .

I could not achieve a satisfying start. After a time I surrendered to my own illiteracy and took up embroidery, at the great expense of several candles. But as each thread went through the cloth and was pulled into position, I came a stitch closer to resolution. When I slipped between the linens to sleep, there was determination, if not peace, in my heart.

In the morning it all commenced again. De Touscheronde started the day's session with another witness whose child had been taken.

Frère Demien whispered to me, "These stories bring more yawns now than tears. How many more must we hear?"

I shrugged; the weeping woman resumed her seat. De Touscheronde went to the bench, where there took place much grave whispering as he, Jean de Malestroit, and Friar Blouyn worried over some point of law. After nods of accord, de Touscheronde turned back to the court again. He called out the name Perrine Rondeau. A woman I recalled having seen in the previous day's crowd rose up from her seat near the front of the chapel.

My husband has been sick for many years on and off, and during one period when he was particularly ill I took lodgers into my house to help meet expenses. It was a great source of shame to him, but of course I would not hear of him working. The Marquis de Ceva and Monsieur François Prelati were lodged in the upper floor for a while; I myself slept up there, though usually in a lesser room. I was so upset one night in thinking that I would lose my husband that my nurse installed me in the room where Prelati and the Marquis were lodged— she thought the good beds would benefit me. The gentlemen had gone to Machecoul and we all thought they would stay the night there. But the Marquis and Monsieur Prelati did return sometime later in the evening, both quite stupid with drink. When they discovered me in the better room, to which they had laid a claim whether justified or not, they were sorely agitated.

I was in a state, I will admit; nevertheless, they had no right to treat me as they did. First they cursed me vilely, and then they grabbed hold of me, one taking my feet and the other my hands, and tried to throw me down to the first floor. Had my nurse not reached out, I would have gone straight over the railing and fallen, perhaps to my death! Then who would have cared for my husband? Surely not the Marquis or Monsieur Prelati.

While I lay there on the second floor, they both kicked me squarely in the back, many times with their pointed boots, and I have not been the same since.

Later that same night, I overheard the Marquis de Ceva telling Prelati that he had found a handsome young page for him in Dieppe. Monsieur Prelati seemed greatly delighted, and a number of days later a very beautiful young boy arrived, claiming himself to be of a very good family from the Dieppe region. He resided with Monsieur François for about a fortnight, and in that time I saw him on many occasions, always in Prelati's company. Then suddenly he seemed to vanish—his master came and went without him. So I inquired after him. Monsieur *François became very agitated and claimed that for all his supposed good breeding, the boy had cheated him royally, departing with two gold crowns. Good riddance to the young scoundrel,* Prelati said.

I was confused by this assertion; the boy had made a good impression on me and had seemed an honest sort. And I am not often wrong in my impressions of people.

Not long afterward, Monsieur Prelati and Master Eustache Blanchet *left my house and went to Machecoul to stay there. I heard it said that they forced a man named Cahu out of his house, relieving him of the keys most ignobly and with great force. I knew this house already, having been to Machecoul many times with my husband. The house was far from other houses, on a street outside of the town; it had its own well, but despite this blessing, the place was dilapidated and careworn; certainly no one would take it to be a proper lodging for honorable men.*

The Marquis de Ceva continued to lodge with me; I believe he found my accommodations more suitable for a gentleman. He demanded much of me, even during times when I was clearly distressed by my husband's failing health, but he was always slow to pay what sums were owed, and when he did pay, the coins were not handed over until there had been long, distressing negotiations about what was actually owed, or rude comments about how he might have been cheated. François Prelati *and* Eustache Blanchet *frequently came from their pitiful little lodgings in Machecoul to visit the Marquis and often stayed with him in my upper rooms, but they did not quit the wreck in which they themselves were lodging. Instead, they left their pages there to retain possession of it. With good reason, I have come to realize.*

It happened that I was required to be in Machecoul for a number of days while my husband consulted with a healer, just before the time of Lord Gilles's arrest—rumors of his impending difficulties were already flying about in great number, so I was curious to see what passed around Cahu's house. On a few occasions I hid myself in some close bushes and observed the comings and goings of these men and their servants, who all appeared quite nervous.

One day while I was watching they removed a great barrowful of ashes from Cahu's house. It was overflowing with gray powder, and the young man—a girlish slip of a thing—had some trouble in keeping it balanced. Some of it spilled out on the ground. Where they took what remained I cannot say, but as soon as the opportunity presented itself, I went to the spill. There was a greasiness about it when I rubbed it between my fingers, and the smell—mon Dieu, it was unlike any cooked animal that I had ever known. I separated out some gritty shards and blew the dust off them. They were white and had the feel of bone when I tested them with my teeth.

And then I realized what I had in my hand, and then in my mouth, and I was sick to the very pit of my stomach. God save me, I thought to myself, these are human bones—perhaps those of the beautiful young page. And I spat and spat until every last bit of the taste was gone from my mouth.

She began to spit in demonstration right in the chapel, but quite suddenly she began to shake and tremble as if in the grip of the falling sickness. Only the whites of her eyes showed as she convulsed pathetically.

Once again Jean de Malestroit began to stand, but before he was fully erect, she had regained herself.

"Oh, my lords, forgive me—I suffer from the fits, and when I am distressed it seems to come upon me more frequently."

Suspicion and concern blended on Jean de Malestroit's face. "Can you continue, Madame?"

"Indeed, my lord."

Not long after that I detected the approach of the returning servants, so I returned to my hiding place in the thick brush. I was frightened to be so close, but there were no other hiding places. I was perhaps only two good paces from Monsieur Prelati when he came out of the house with several

*items in his arms, all of which I could see quite clearly. Among
them was a shirt so small it can only have come from a child.
It was covered with damp blood and other detritus. He held it
out as far as he could, and no wonder, for even in the brush I
could smell it—a horrible and putrid smell, and I thought once
again that I would be sick. But I kept down the bile that
wanted to leap out of my throat and looked hard at the shirt as
Prelati walked past my hiding place. I was glad that shirt
could not speak for itself—I would not have wanted to know
how so neat a slit came to be in its belly, surrounded by blood.*

I heard nothing more of what the witnesses said that day.

Jean de Malestroit was alone in his study when I
found him later, staring into the light of a single candle—
no brilliant diplomat but a simple man of God in near
darkness who looked to be aching over some deep matter
of faith. He held his head in his two hands; in place of his
usually regular breathing, I heard deep, pained sighs.

I cleared my throat very lightly to get his attention.
It was a few heartbeats before he unfurrowed his brow
and brought his eyes to meet my gaze.

"Guillemette," he sighed. There was a measure of affection in it, a bit of relief as well.

"Do I disturb you, Eminence?"

"I am already sore disturbed."

"Perhaps you will wish to remain alone ..."

"No, please—truth be told, I was about to send for
you. I am tired of my own thoughts and I crave the
sound of another voice. The diversion of your company
would be most pleasant right now. I am sick to death of
the people with whom I am forced to spend these days,
myself among them."

He spent his hours with wailing witnesses, all repeating the same story, and calculating lawyers, each one hoping to please Duke Jean more than the next. Stiff-backed

scribes who hung on every word that was uttered in the chapel were his constant companions. Advocates and prosecutors and dignitaries surrounded him, all with a stake in the outcome of this trial. He was charged with the daunting mission of bringing it all to conclusion on God's behalf. His disturbance was more than understandable.

But we both knew that it might have been far worse. "Imagine how much more distressing these last two days would have been had Milord graced us with his presence," I said.

Small consolation. "One cannot," he said quietly. "And in time he will have to appear again. I do not know how I shall keep order then."

More witnesses were due to be heard on the morrow, and it was a comfortable wager that Milord would not show himself then either. In some ways, it made the entire mess easier to weather, because Gilles de Rais, sodomite, murderer, conjurer of demons, was still Gilles de Rais, Marshal of France, hero, baron, and knight. It was far easier to think him a hideous monster in his pale absence than his splendid presence.

"More charges will grow out of these testimonies," Jean de Malestroit said. "If he refuses to appear, then I suppose we shall have to drag him into the court by force. But I suspect he will show himself before coercion becomes necessary." He put a hand gently on top of mine. "Are you prepared for that?"

Gilles de Rais would not just meekly appear in court, there to sit quietly while grievous accusations were hurled against him—he would be faithful to his bellicose nature and stage a majestic fight.

I said, "I think the more germane concern might be for Milord's preparation. But as for myself, I suppose I *am* as ready as I shall ever be."

It was not an entirely truthful statement—there was

indeed some preparation needed on my part, but it had nothing to do with seeing Milord in court. And on that matter I cautiously approached Jean de Malestroit. "Perrine Rondeau's revelations were intriguing, were they not?"

He was still distracted. "In their difference from what the other witnesses had to say, yes. Quite."

"She was bold to watch those goings-on."

"Quite bold."

"I cannot imagine placing myself in such a position, no matter what I stood to gain. But I am wondering," I said carefully, "if anyone knows what became of the things that were brought out of Cahu's house by Prelati and the others, beyond the ashes that Perrine described."

He gave me an odd look. "Why should any of that interest you?"

"I would like to examine them."

"God in heaven, why?"

"Because I think something might be learned."

"What more can be learned from these items? They are the work of the devil, and to be disdained."

"The devil's works reveal the devil," I countered.

His frown was accompanied by frank disapproval. "It will be gruesome stuff—bloody and malodorous, hardly suitable items for any woman to examine, especially a woman of your station. What is this sudden morbid fascination?"

It was an elegantly phrased refusal, its content mindful of my supposed delicacy, a condition he attributed to my "station," the nature of which I could hardly define anymore. "I simply thought—that is, I wondered if something might be learned by examining the items associated with these crimes, that is all."

"To what end is this learning required?"

To an end I cannot speak of just presently. "As proof, of

course," I said. "Proof of the crimes with which Milord is charged."

"Proof will not be required."

I had not expected *that* response. "But ... how shall he be convicted without proof?"

"He will confess."

My first thought, undistilled, was, *Never*. "Gilles de Rais will not confess," I told him. "His pride will not allow it."

"He will, I assure you. He will answer to God for his crimes, and he will do so of his own accord. Even if we have to torture him first. And if it is required, then it shall be done."

"Nevertheless," I said, my voice almost pleading, "I would see the proof for myself. I ... I *need* to see it, to settle my heart." I placed my hands over my face and began to weep quietly, which led further to heaving of the chest and, finally, to full-blown sobbing.

I would regret this splendid performance on the morrow and repent fervently, for my bishop is a good man, unworthy of this vile sort of deceit. Sister Claire's prophetic words about the predictable sameness of men, even the mighty, rang in my ears. Only the hardest of the hard, such as the monstrous Jean de Craon, could escape the influence of a woman's heartfelt tears. And truth be told, my tears were not so terribly false.

Jean de Malestroit was already wincing when he said, "Oh, very well, if it means that much to you, I shall inquire of the whereabouts of these things. But do not hope too greatly. It is likely that they have been discarded or lost."

I knew that my dear bishop was probably right—there was little realistic hope that the shirt, ghastly as it was, had been retained by anyone, and certainly it would not have been kept by any of those scoundrels whose guilt it would affirm! Where could it be put, lest it despoil all that surrounded it?

François Prelati would know what had become of it, but he was a cur who would try to barter that sort of information for some sort of judicial advantage. I had no chips with which to seduce him. My only recourse was to seek out Perrine Rondeau. I knew that she had traveled to Nantes for this trial along with many others, all of whom now made their temporary homes on the periphery of the city. Great encampments of such pilgrims had risen up close to the river. I had only to walk from one campfire to the next and inquire in order to find her—she had made herself known among the crowd by the heft of her character.

When I came upon her the next morning before trial began, Perrine Rondeau's jovial temperament spoke of complete recovery from the strain of her previous day's testimony. But, then, she had said her piece and was done with the matter. Unlike so many others, with whom the pain of testimony would linger, she had not lost a child.

A stout stone fireplace had years ago been erected near the river, where fishermen often cooked the fish they brought out of the silty waters. A sturdy pole of very green wood had been laid across the stones, and from it Madame Rondeau had suspended a pot by its handle. There she stood, humming as she stirred porridge over the fire, her roundish hips swaying with the circular motion of her arm. At her feet, resting on a cloth, was a large flat river rock, washed clean, on which the gruel would be poured when cooked. When it had cooled, it would be broken into glutinous hunks to be eaten in hand. It was bland and unpalatable, but it would fill the bellies of the hungry people who waited nearby, none of whom were likely to possess the bowls and utensils to eat it properly. How accustomed I had become to such blessings—

a bowl, a board, a spoon, abundant food that could be eaten hot and with dignity. Mere habits to me, but great treasures to a pauper. God's arbitrary bestowal of fortune was always so puzzling.

But He had blessed Perrine Rondeau with a wonderful heartiness, which she now used to the benefit of those who lacked such substance. The steam that rose up from the pot caused little ringlets to form on the side of her hair, which was pulled back and tied with a cloth. She wore a great apron over her frock, the sleeves of which had been rolled up slightly.

She regarded my habit and reacted with a respectful nod. "Good morning, Mother," she said.

"Good morning. You are Madame Rondeau?"

"I am."

"God's blessings on you, Madame. You were in my prayers last night after your testimony; I hope you have recovered from the sudden malady that overtook you."

"I have, indeed. And I thank you for your words to God. They come and go, the shaking fits. I always regain my senses in time."

"You are a brave woman; tenacious in your inquiries as well."

"Ah," she said, "some would say that I am just too curious."

"I shall not judge your behavior, Madame, but your curiosity, as it turns out, was quite beneficial."

" 'Tis not always the case." She smiled rather mischievously. "But if the prosecutor's cause was advanced by what I said, then I am glad for that. And I am none the worse for having spoken," she said. "I pity those who have lost children. Especially the woman who spoke the day before, when court was suspended."

She lifted the wooden stirrer out of the pot and tapped the clinging clumps of porridge back into the slurry, then laid the stirrer across the top of the pot. Once her hands were free, she folded them together and muttered a prayer. She crossed herself, then recommenced stirring, her previous rhythm barely broken.

"And what happened to her in the chapel ... and yourself ..."

I hid my bandaged hand inside my sleeve. "I will be none the worse for wear. And Madame le Barbier is a resilient woman. I am sure she will fully recover from what the crow—"

She quickly cut me off. "Mother, forgive my impertinence, for I mean no disrespect," Perrine Rondeau said, "but that was not a crow. It was the demon himself, disguised and sent by Gilles de Rais, to punish her for speaking harsh words against him."

How powerful this witchcraft was to all God's children. "If so, Madame, then we are all surely doomed, for there are few kind words being said of late."

She went through another round of tapping, praying, and crossing. "God will take care of us," she said, lifting the stirrer to accentuate her point. A glob of porridge slipped off and fell back into the pot. "Well, 'tis not royal fare, but it will fill many bellies. Will you eat with us, Mother? There is plenty."

"You are too kind, Madame; I have already broken my fast. But if you can spare me the time, I would ask you about something specific, something you mentioned yesterday—the shirt. You said you saw Prelati taking it out of Cahu's house around the time of Milord's arrest."

She looked down into her porridge and frowned. "It was unspeakable to see, unbearable to smell. Stained all along the front with blood and ordure. Why, the odor reached me through the leaves and branches—only my fear of discovery kept me from gagging."

She gestured with a nod of her head in the direction of a man asleep on the ground nearby. "The distance was no more than that which is between him and me. Probably less."

Two to three paces at most. "So you must have been able to see the shirt very clearly, then."

"Oh, quite. *Monsieur* Prelati had it out at arm's length, two-handed, to keep it away from himself. It was practically beneath my very nose."

"You spoke of a tear in the middle of it. . . ."

"It was not a tear but a straight cut—it had to have been knife-slit," she said, answering a question I had not yet spoken.

The morbid fascination of which Jean de Malestroit had spoken was beginning to overtake me and I began to feel very unholy. "If you recall, Madame—where on the shirt was this cut?"

"From the hem almost to the neck. On either side of the slit, the cloth was soaked with dark blood, so heavily that the edges of the fabric did not ravel. But I did notice that the lower part of the cut was jagged."

I saw in my head what she described. I imagined the knife entering the soft flesh of the child's belly, and I swooned momentarily. I put a hand on Madame Rondeau to steady myself, which brought a look of concern. "It is only a bit of dizziness," I reassured her. "It will pass."

Before it did, several other grisly images had paraded naked before my mind's eye. I restored myself with a deep breath. "It seems impossible to conclude anything but that the knife slit both the shirt and the child at the same time."

"*Oui, Mère.* Whatever child wore this shirt was slaughtered like a lamb."

A jagged but unraveled cut near the hem; I tried to envision it. "Madame," I said, "in which direction did the bloodstain appear to spread?"

For the next few moments she stared into the porridge, stirring it rhythmically as her eyes darted back and forth without focus. She rested the spoon on the side of the pot again before she spoke. "There was a great deal of blood collected around the neck hole. So it must have spread upward." She gave me a troubled look. "But how can that be?"

The child had been hung upside down.

I felt my own previously eaten porridge rising in my gorge. When my nausea subsided, I asked her, "Of what age would you say the child who wore this shirt might be?"

"Oh, very young. A child so small cannot have been more than seven or eight years of age."

Michel at age seven appeared in my consciousness. He climbed up into the lap of my memory and wrapped his small arms around my neck.

"Beasts," I whispered. "Unholy beasts."

"Aye, Mother," Perrine said.

I thanked her as politely as I could for the information she had given me, then turned and walked through the encampment. The unjagged hem of my habit dragged in the dust of the ground. There were even more people there than when I had arrived earlier; each and every one of them seemed to be staring at me.

⚜

By the time I returned to the palace itself, Jean de Malestroit had already left his private chambers to go to the chapel, so I would not have to explain my whereabouts until later. Except to *Frère* Demien, who came out of the chambers as I was leaving.

"Where have you been?" he demanded. "You have had me worried! His Eminence was asking after you as well. And we shall be late to the proceedings."

And thereby miss yet another outpouring of misery. I tried to feel some disappointment, but could not. "I went into the encampments to find Perrine Rondeau," I told him.

As if I had been tainted, the young priest crossed himself and whispered a hurried blessing. "But why?"

"There were questions I wished to ask her, Brother. I wanted to know about the shirt she saw."

There was no need to explain why that interested me; *Frère* Demien had heard the story from Guillaume Karle. Instead, he commenced a disturbing harangue against the poor woman. "She has the shaking sickness, Sister, and the demon's influence might still be upon her—why, she shook like a Romani during her testimony yesterday."

"I think she has managed to purge herself of whatever evil might have o'ertaken her yesterday. When I found her, she was doing something that our Savior Christ Jesus once did—feeding the gathered multitudes."

"The demon can trick you with false goodness. He will show you light and then lead you into darkness. He will intoxicate you with false promises and persuade you to believe—"

"Enough," I said. I crossed my arms over my chest. "One would think you were practicing for the miter, Brother."

"One need not be a bishop to speak on the evils of the demon."

"But it is surely not a disadvantage. Have no fear for my soul," I said. "I have come back unscathed."

"Well, I hope you found some satisfaction in her answers."

"As much as can be had for the moment, I suspect." But as often happens, the answers she gave me led only to more questions. I would have to go elsewhere to find satisfaction for them.

News of what was being told in court spread through the encampments and surrounding villages as if there were some invisible cord on which the words were transported. No one spoke of anything else, but that is how it always happens—we fail to sniff out God's roses when there is ordure to entice us. The afternoon before, I had heard above me the *whoosh* of beating wings and looked upward to see a small flock of pigeons circling one of the towers. They flapped around in confusion for a few moments before flying off, each in a separate direction, but as soon as those birds were gone, another bevy was released. All over France and Brittany, royals, nobles, and churchmen would soon be reading these small bits of *papier* on which the crucial messages were written. By the next day, the birds would surely be in Avignon, and my son, whose written words of affection I had shamefully failed to requite, would know the progress of things.

"Duke Jean must be anxious for word," *Frère* Demien said to me as the birds grew smaller and smaller and finally disappeared from view.

"He is eager for Milord's downfall," I responded, "though it seems to be proceeding apace without regard for his enthusiasm. I am wondering when he will show his own face. He would wash his hands of the whole thing but reap the benefits nevertheless. It seems positively un-Christian of him. But, then, he has many men who are willing to be Christian on his behalf."

The news was cried out in the great square of Nantes outside the Bishop's palace by the same speaker at the end of each day. Always there was a great crowd present to hear his lurid words, and coins fairly flew into his upturned hat, for he was a most excellent teller of tales. The listeners would gasp and moan and then shake their fists in condemnation when shock turned to anger. As the number of reports of lost children rose, so rose the wrath of the populace against their sovereign lord.

He told of more abominations and related new stories of intimidation by Gilles de Rais's men:

"About six months previous to now, a charwoman who labored in the palace told me of seeing a small bloody footprint. She went to summon the housekeeper, but when they returned it had already been expunged. She lost her position for speaking out...."

And tales of foolhardy bravery:

"It was a dark and moonless night as I waited on the castle wall at Machecoul. It seemed only fitting that these culprits should have their vile activities laid bare. If another was taken on this night, I would not hesitate to call up the men of the surrounding villages to the cause of taking Lord de Rais to the proper authorities.

"Alas, sleep claimed me, and it could not have been too long before I was awakened by a man of slight build who surprised me with a dagger under my chin. I cried out, but he laughed and said, 'Scream if you like! No one will save you. You are a dead man!'

"I was sure he meant to kill me. I pleaded for my life. By God's grace this fellow took pity on me and left me to ponder the encounter, but by then I had no stomach to stay—I hurried down the stones of the outer wall and made my way to the road, and though it was deeply dark, I ran and ran until I thought I was far enough away from that evil place to stop and breathe. And the next day, as I was traveling back to my house, I encountered Lord de Rais himself, riding from the direction of Boin. He looked to be a giant up on his horse, even more so in view of my previous night's activities against him! He glared down at me with great malevolence and put a hand on the hilt of his sword. I closed my eyes and waited for the scrape of metal, but he only snickered in disdain. He rode on, but his fellows stayed round me a moment and boxed me in. None spoke, but their expressions said,

We know what you have been about, and you best be done with it!"

⚜

That was the last of the horrors I heard that day. Back in court, there was a lull in the proceedings, which I welcomed despite my illogical compulsion to hear what was being said. As we waited, I worked the cool, smooth beads of the rosary between my fingers for the sheer distraction of doing so, without saying the requisite prayers, while Jean de Malestroit consulted with Friar Blouyn and the prosecutor de Touscheronde. The three conferred with heads together in voices so low that even the scribes, though seated quite close, would not be able to hear them.

It did not matter, for Jean de Malestroit did the writing this time. With accord from his cohorts, he drafted a brief statement, which he handed to one of the scribes with a whispered instruction. The man immediately began to sort through his own parchments, then rose and recounted the basic testimonies, saying who had given them first and summarizing what that witness had said.

When he was done, the scribe looked back at his Eminence, who nodded grave approval for the recitation of a coda:

"Which complaints having been made known to the Lords Jean, Reverend Father in God, Bishop of Nantes, and Friar Jean Blouyn, Vice-Inquisitor, the same Lords Bishop and Vicar having thus been informed, insisting that these crimes should not go unpunished, hereby decree and mandate all clerics to summon the aforesaid Gilles de Rais on Saturday, October eighth, to respond as required by law to the aforesaid Lords Bishop and Vice-Inquisitor of the faith, and for whatever objection and defense he might have to be made, as well as to the prosecutor duly appointed in this case and in other cases of this order."

☿

Air too warm for October streamed in the open window of the upper chamber. We had gathered there because the threat of uprising had become too great in the chapel below. The upper chamber was commodious, unlike the lower hall and the chapel, but its most endearing feature at the moment was that the simple placement of guards at the foot of the stairs rendered the room unapproachable. Admission to this court would be at the sole pleasure of the man whose orders the guard obeyed.

Even though our safety seemed assured, there was much confused milling as we all resettled ourselves into the business at hand. New faces began to show themselves, some of them known to me. The appearance of Pierre l'Hôpital, president of Brittany under Duke Jean and an intimate adviser and confidant of my bishop, was a noteworthy arrival.

"I see that the Duke has sent his watchdog," *Frère* Demien said.

"De Touscheronde will surely take umbrage," I answered.

"Tsk, tsk," *Frère* Demien said.

"It is a fair bit of fortune for all of us that he is more lawyer than politician in his service to our Lord Duke," I added. "Elsewise we should always be in a state of diplomatic crisis."

Footsteps echoed in the last passageway. *Frère* Demien looked back. "Guillaume Chapeillon," he said.

The honey-tongued Chapeillon was a good counterweight to the petulant l'Hôpital. He would speak for and answer exclusively to Jean de Malestroit. He appeared dressed in his finest robes of advocacy with great billowing sleeves—I wondered with some envy how many treasures might be hidden within those copious folds. A troop of scribes and notaries followed Chapeillon like ducklings. Each had black-stained fingers and gripped a clutch of quills, most of which would be worn down before it all came to conclusion.

These workmen and officials eventually found their places at the front of the court, though I was not inspired to confidence in observing the confusion that occurred before they finally settled down. Removed though we were, a residue of fear lingered. I sat in one of the high-backed chairs that had been brought out in a rush of accommodation and went through a quiet routine of small personal attendances: fretting over the hem of my robe until it was straight, tucking in stray hairs and fussing with my veil, and other such distractions as I could come up with. When at last I was perfectly arranged, I closed my eyes and thought of the beautiful apples that had been stowed in the cold cellar and how delightful it would be to sink my teeth into one of them in January's bleak darkness. My breath evened, and I began to feel calm.

But no sooner had I found my breath again than it was taken away from me by the sudden arrival, against all expectations, of Milord Gilles de Rais.

chapter 28

I WAS A FEW DAYS EARLY in calling Moskal.

"I didn't expect to hear from you until Monday," he said, his Boston accent as thick as ever.

"I nailed him," I said, beaming through the phone.

"Wow."

He said it quietly, as if he were actually disappointed. I could understand this completely; he wanted him as badly as I did.

"Yeah. I got a warrant for the bastard."

"Good for you. And fast."

Could he hear me grinning? "We're about to head out to pick him up. The warrant is for felony abduction of a minor child, several counts. I just wanted to call you and let you know."

"Not homicide?" He sounded even more disappointed.

"Not yet. But we might have a body. I don't know if it makes your local papers—"

"You can't really call the *Globe* local," he said, "but I've been picking up the *Los Angeles Times* too."

"So you saw it, then."

"I did. But I'm confused. The victim was black, which doesn't fit your pattern."

"We are proceeding on the basis that he was a practice grab."

"Sweet Jesus. Hasn't he had enough practice?"

"And then there were three failed grabs in one day. He was teasing me."

"Ah," he said. "Well, that makes more sense, then. Now that you have a body, I guess you can go for murder when you get all the evidence organized."

"We can. And we will."

"Okay, then."

By the resigned tone in his voice, I guessed that Moskal knew he would have to ask very nicely to get Durand back to the Bay State, which would not happen until the Golden State had completed the process of ripping his lungs out, God willing.

"How'd you finally get him?"

"Sneakers," I said. "He kept all their sneakers."

I could almost hear his jaw hitting the floor. The line seemed to go dead.

"Pete? You there?"

"Yeah," he said, nearly in a whisper. "Hang on a sec. I'm going to put you on hold. But don't go away."

He was gone and I was left chained to my desk by a spiral cord with a nagging thought swirling through my head. *You're keeping me from getting the bad guy....*

It seemed like a week before he came back. The two copies of the arrest warrant I clutched tightly in my hand were rumpled and sweaty, but they felt hot enough to burst into flames. Out of the corner of my eye I could see my five comrades checking their weapons, getting into their vests, making sure their radios had fresh batteries. The tribal prehunt ritual was under way, and I would have to play catch-up. I was growing impatient as hell.

"Sorry," Moskal said when he came back on the line again. "That took longer than I thought it would. I had to check on something."

"What, for God's sake?"

The fax machine suddenly whirred to life on the stand next to my desk. The first few millimeters of a transmission emerged from the slot.

"Is that fax coming from you?"

"Yeah. I'll hold on if you want to check it out."

After a two-minute labor the page was born. I pulled it free almost desperately; it was the stark, high-intensity fax version of one of the photos I'd seen in the South Boston case jacket.

The shoeless feet were circled.

"Son of a gun," I whispered into the phone.

"When you pick him up, if you wouldn't mind looking for a pair of black high-tops with a Boston Celtics logo ..."

It would be my pleasure.

Each of the two teams of three took a car. I rode with Spence and one other guy in the first car going to the studio. I was grateful for the company, because I was nervous—this was the biggest case I'd ever worked, and it goes without saying that I hoped it would go smoothly. There are so many things that can go wrong when you try to take someone down.

I didn't take Wilbur Durand for the skittish type; when he'd stopped in for his little visit, he was about the coolest customer that ever sauntered into a police station. He must have known that we couldn't do anything to him on the spot. He had to have talked to a lawyer before showing up. Not the corporate-type we'd dragged off the golf course in our warranted search, but probably his renowned sister, the Wicked Witch of the Right Coast. No doubt Sheila Carmichael had heard it all, but still, imagine announcing to another human being—your own flesh and blood, no less—*I'm a suspect in a series of kidnappings of adolescents.* Silence would follow, because the person you were confiding in would know better than to ask if you actually did what you were suspected of doing. Then imagine hearing back, *Let's brainstorm on some things we can do to keep this from landing on you too hard.*

And lawyers wonder why *people* equate them with sharks.

Shortly we would barge into Wil Durand's closed-circuit existence and try to blow it wide open, lawyers be damned. He would have been prepared ahead of time to say nothing if he was taken into custody, of that I was certain. The postarrest interview would be among the most challenging that any of us, Frazee included, would ever face—the subject would be prepped and counseled and rehearsed.

And cold as ice.

"You okay?" Spence asked.

It must have just been oozing out of me. "Yeah. No. Maybe. Ask me when he's cuffed and stuffed."

He made a little chuckle. "You did range practice recently, right?"

"Yeah."

"Good. I don't want you shooting me."

"No one's going to shoot anyone. Durand doesn't have a gun permit that I could dig up."

"That doesn't mean he doesn't have a gun. Or that he doesn't have five or six big goons with guns *and* permits who get paid to make his messes for him."

"Not his style. This is going to go smooth as silk."

"Yeah. Just like it always does."

We were trained to be ready for anything, to expect the unexpected. Unless I was dead wrong, Wilbur Durand would not go for a big-bang confrontation. His bullets were made of gray matter. If he shot us with that, we might never know what hit us.

There were two cars parked at the front of the studio vestibule. One was a late-model Mercedes, sleek and shiny, black with tinted windows, the other a VW Jetta maybe five or six years old, also black. I radioed in the plate numbers. While we waited for the response, I checked my gun, just in case.

The reply came back that neither vehicle belonged to Durand, which was a disappointment. The Mercedes turned out to be leased, which momentarily restored a bit of hope, until the dispatcher added that the lessee was a big downtown legal firm. I scribbled the numbers in my notebook and then unbuckled my seat belt.

"Neither one belongs to him or his company."

"He might still be here."

He wasn't. Mr. GolfPants and the Skankmeister assistant were there waiting for us. Both insisted that Wilbur Durand was once again out of the country.

"So he just flew in from wherever he was for the day to come pay me a visit and then went right back out again?"

"I can't speculate about my client's motives for going where he goes," the lawyer whined. He looked much more authoritative wearing non-golf clothes, but he didn't sound any better. "Mr. Durand is still quite distraught over your commandeering of his studio. He has a schedule to meet and now he has to work very hard not to miss his deadlines."

"He wasn't working here when we arrived."

"He might have been working on location somewhere; I don't know. But I do know that he can't work in his studio with that kind of disruption."

"All he had to do was ask us to leave."

"And you would have vacated the premises?"

He was deliberately leading me off track, and I was falling for it.

"Where is he?" I demanded.

"I have no idea."

"But you've been in communication with Mr. Durand."

"That's privileged information, Detective."

I could feel the frustration building in myself; it wouldn't be long before I popped and started shouting. Spence must have sensed it, because he poked me in the elbow and saved me by asking, "Do you mind if we have another look around?"

"I mind very much."

"When he comes back," I said, "please tell your client that I'd like to have a word with him. Oh, and you might add that we have a warrant for his arrest."

The lawyer never asked for what crime.

We went back outside and radioed the crew that had gone to Durand's house. All they had to report was the same gibberish-spewing houseboy, with no Durand.

We had no choice but to leave. We went back out into the late-afternoon sun with its piercing, low-angled rays, the ones that make everything look decrepit.

"So, what's plan B?" Spence asked.

"There is no plan B," I said. "There was barely a plan A."

He stared at me in near disbelief. "Come on, Lany, you have a plan B for when you lose your nail file."

"I'm not kidding, Spence. No plan B."

"So what do we do now, all dressed up with no one to pinch?"

"I don't know."

"I think we should flush him."

"How?" Fred said. "You said yourself the guy's a human disappearing act. And we can't put that out yet."

A couple of brass and a few detectives from the division

were in on this emergency meeting. I was in the hot seat again, and I had to come up with something fast.

"I know someone at the *Times*," I offered. "I haven't worked with her in a while, but we used to have a pretty solid relationship. If we offer her something in exchange, we might be able to get her to put it out for us that Durand is somehow involved, although we could stay short of calling him an actual suspect. She could refer to *anonymous police-department sources* so no one's ass will get kicked by anyone upstairs."

"You trust her?"

"Yeah. I think so. As I said, it's been a while, but she was always a very decent person."

I expected more resistance from Fred, but he seemed ready to try just about anything. "It might be worth a shot. But before it goes to press, I'd like to get a look at whatever it is she's going to say."

What was he *thinking*? "I don't know, Fred, she'd probably object to that. Editorial autonomy."

"I'm not gonna correct her grammar, Dunbar. I just want to make sure that the gist of it is what we want it to be."

"She'll probably want something exclusive when it breaks for that kind of cooperation."

"First interview with you, how's that?"

"What if I don't want to do any interviews?"

"Tough."

Well. There I had it.

It was a tender negotiation, but we managed to work out a reasonable deal, just the two of us, no brass, no Fred, no editors. She agreed to plant the article in exchange for immediate access to the process when it was under way, regardless of how the rest of the press was being handled. And I would sit down with her for one hour as soon as I managed to break away from the arrest paperwork, during which time we would speak freely about the case and how it had developed.

The next morning, the shit hit the fan.

Anonymous police sources have revealed that Hollywood special-effects and makeup genius Wilbur Durand, whose stellar career has included work on some of the top-grossing horror-genre films of all time, is under investigation in connection with a series of disappearances of young boys in the Los Angeles area. His recently released motion picture, They Eat Small Children There, *by all accounts a spectacular success, was the first effort of his own production company, Angel Films. Durand, 40, is considered by many Hollywood stars to be the best makeup artist of his generation, though that title hardly encompasses his range of skills. One actress, who wishes to remain unnamed, is quoted as saying, "He could make me look really young again like no one else could."*

After what one investigator describes as a "long and thorough investigation," Durand is being sought for questioning in connection with the separate disappearances of three young boys, two age 13 and one 12, all of whom were abducted from western sections of Los Angeles. One has been missing for approximately two years, another for about one year, and the third for about two months. Items thought to belong to each of the three missing boys were found hidden in Durand's work studio and were later positively identified by relatives of the boys. He is also under investigation for possible involvement in the death of Earl Jackson, age 12, whose body was found in an abandoned parking area near the airport last week.

Durand himself has not been seen by authorities since shortly before the evidentiary items were discovered, at which time he came to the Crimes Against Children division and confronted investigators over what he felt was harassment in the search of his work premises. He demanded that his work space be released back to him. As a result of information gathered in the temporary seizure and search of Durand's premises, a multiyear series of disappearances of young boys, previously considered to be the work of separate abductors, is now being treated as potentially the work of one individual.

Durand has apparently been suspected of involvement in these disappearances for some time, but police sources say that information regarding him has been difficult to develop. They cite his well-known reclusive tendencies as an obstacle to the investigation.

Additionally, one unnamed police officer close to the investigation claims that Durand's exalted position in the film community has sheltered him somewhat, similar to the deference accorded to O. J. Simpson at the beginning of his legal troubles. According to that officer, it's not unusual for well-known members of the Los Angeles film community to be given special consideration when they have difficulties. "Cops are no different than any other people—they want to rub elbows with the stars. What better way than to be an ally when a star has trouble." When asked to comment, Los Angeles police spokeswoman Heather Maroney refuted these assertions vehemently, calling them "irresponsible and unsubstantiated."

A nationwide search is under way for Durand, whose whereabouts remain unknown. He is not thought to be carrying a weapon but should be considered extremely dangerous, especially to children. His spokesman says he has been "out of the country"

working on a film, a claim that has not been verified.
Because of his facility in creating alternative appear-
ances, it is unlikely that Durand is traveling as him-
self. Los Angeles police have set up a toll-free number
that may be called by people who think they have
seen him. Those calling the tip line may remain
anonymous if they wish to, but anyone giving infor-
mation that leads to Durand's arrest may receive all
or part of any future reward(s).

Three minutes after the paper arrived on Fred's desk,
I was summoned to his office.

"I didn't see any of this 'deference' stuff in the copy I
read." He whacked the article hard with one hand; it had
to have hurt. "What is this shit, anyway?"

"I told you, they have editors. My friend didn't want
to tell her editor that this was all arranged, so she couldn't
keep the extra stuff out."

"Bullshit. That was *you* putting that in there."

He was right—it was me. I slipped it in between
Fred's reading and the editor's final run-through. It hadn't
been axed. But the truth would never surface. "No, Fred,"
I lied, "it wasn't me. I gave her the okay on what she originally wrote and the rest of it just sort of got worked in.
Don't forget, these people get paid to have big imagina-
tions and to stretch the truth."

"Well, guess what, now that this is out, my neck is
gonna get stretched if we don't find this guy *fast*. Yours
too."

Pictures of the nondescript Wilbur Durand were emblazoned on the front page of every newspaper in the
country. Mexico and Canada were on high alert to look
for the fugitive genius, as were the European nations. His

story prompted international headlines, quite predictably: It was dripping with the juice that none of us can seem to resist, though very few of us will admit it.

I'm not ashamed. I have to confess that I'm just as much of a sucker for this kind of intrigue as anyone is. I suppose that irresistibility is a good part of why I became a cop; I did my time on the street, but I always knew I would end up a detective—there are some things I just have to know. I got some of the answers in Boston, but it wasn't enough.

Like how it is that a man with such immense wealth and power, such incomprehensible genius, such enviable talent can become what he became. If I had his money and his brains, I would sure as hell rule the world, because that's what you can do when you have what he has.

And the next thing I'd want to know is how parents with that kind of child can fail to recognize and nurture his strengths. That's bad enough, but to take it a step further and actually damage him, well, that has to be some kind of crime.

Finally, someone needs to tell me why it is that the deepest part of my heart feels some sympathy for this monster, while my brain is screaming, *Fry the bastard, now.*

Everyone seemed to want to touch the ring after the story broke. We had every psychic, every forensic psychologist, every profiler in the country begging to take part. This case would be a cash cow to anyone with the proper tools to milk it, and they were lining up, pushing and shoving each other in a battle for a position already occupied by one Errol Erkinnen, who had paid his dues early on this one.

Calls came in to the tip line by the thousands. We went nuts following them up.

I saw him at the drugstore, you know, the one next to the Ultra Mart gas station. . . . He was in front of me at the movie theater line. I was seeing They Eat Small Children There, *so it had to have been him, since that was his own movie. . . .*

We saw him at the airport. He was dressed up like Greta Garbo, fur coat and all. In this weather, imagine wearing a fur coat—no one does that unless they have to, so it had to be him. . . .

He was trying to get into the locker room at the baseball stadium. He had this old, beat-up glove with him.

Or the ultimate impersonation: *He was in uniform. I saw him hanging out with a couple of other cops. They didn't figure it out, but I did. I knew it was him. . . .*

The press frenzy neared the Simpson Line. Every day as I came in and out of the station, they were there with their truck-mounted disks and shoulder cameras and radio microphones. Women coiffed and made up at that hour of the morning, men Armanified before sunrise—what could motivate someone to do that? Of course it was the hope of a shot at the one serendipitous sound bite that would propel the lucky personality into the stratosphere of recognizability. This was one way to get the required Nielsen numbers.

I guess all jobs have their "numbers."

I felt oddly insulated from all of it, courtesy of the anonymity that Fred insisted I maintain until we had a better handle on things. For once, I agreed with him. Before we identified Durand, there were good reasons to keep the public out. Now that we knew it was him, we needed the public's help without its interference, a delicate state of affairs that is achieved only by careful public relations. For the first time in my career as a cop, I understood what Heather Maroney really did as spokeswoman—she was the front line in the battle with civilians. There was very little chance that someone from within the department would give me up, unless I had some unknown enemy within the ranks—and that seemed unlikely to me because I'd made a point not to step on anyone's toes. Fred was more worried that someone from Durand's organization would reveal my identity.

I did get given up, but not by anyone from the department, and not by anyone in the press. It was Wilbur Durand himself who finally let the world know who I was.

twenty-nine

IN THE CORE OF MY SOUL I now understood that Gilles de Rais was a monster, the demon himself, and in defining him so I hoped to disarm him so he would lose his power to affect me. Gone was the *mater* in me, the woman who had wiped away the boy's tears and gentled him to sleep when his own mother would not do so. I could no longer bring myself to care for his anguish, his suffering, the terrible horrors that had happened to him at the hands of his grandfather, from whom no one—not I, not his absent parents, nor anyone—could protect him.

Hush, child—she is gone with your father to Pouzages. But take comfort, little one, they will return in less than a fortnight to Champtocé and you shall be reunited.

Of course, my young charge could not help but notice that Milord Guy and Lady Marie would often take René when they rode out, most often to Machecoul. I always suspected that the sickly younger brother, nearly lost in her labor, had a stronger hold on his mother's heartstrings. Invariably there would be trouble when this

occurred—perhaps not at the moment of their departure, but at the next occasion of disappointment, always
quite unrelated to his perceived abandonment. On the
slightest provocation he would strike out at me with his
little fists and throw himself into a fit of temper. Sometimes when I tried to contain him he would thrust his
arms up straight and propel himself downward through
my grasp like a slithering snake, and when he landed on
the floor he would kick his feet until the stones shuddered. I was forbidden by his parents to punish him for
these dreadful tantrums when they were not present,
even though he ought to have been harshly corrected.
And when they were present their own discipline of the
boy could best be described as timid and ineffectual.

Once, at wit's end over this abhorrent behavior, I
made a grave mistake, the consequences of which have
haunted me ever since. I went to Jean de Craon, interrupted him at his accounting. When I explained my
quandary, he set down his quill, cursed aloud, and declared that the child was being spoiled to a state of femi-
ninity. I waited patiently during the diatribe, hoping he
would stop so I could ask him what I ought to do. His
obscene declarations escalated until he exploded in a fit
of swearing so vile as to sicken the very saints and angels.

He headed straightaway to the nursery, with me following close behind, pleading as we rushed along for him
to be gentle in his corrections. We found the boy in the
care of the nursery maid with whom I had left him. They
were talking quietly and he seemed calm enough, which
surprised me—he had been so upset when I put him into
the girl's arms. Jean de Craon, believing I had disturbed
him without cause, gave me the most withering look I
had ever received.

*Please forgive me, Milord Jean, but this is a complete
turnabout—a blessing, of course, but quite surprising since the
boy was in a very agitated state when I left him and—*

Without waiting for me to finish my plea for pardon, Jean de Craon turned and headed for the door, muttering vague curses as he departed. But no sooner was his grandfather's back to us than Gilles started up again. He whined and sniveled for the benefit of the old man, who was about to abandon him as his *mère* and *père* had done.

What strange aberration was this, what departure from normalcy, wherein the child seeks out punitive attention, merely for the sake of having it when the more pleasant sort of attention is not available?

However deviant its nature, the performance was immensely successful, for on hearing the child's wails, Jean de Craon turned back to us, his face contorted in anger, and headed directly toward him. Gilles performed magnificently; he stretched his body out on the floor and slammed his feet into the stones for all he was worth. The enraged old man lifted my little charge by the back of his collar and dropped him on the stones, then pummeled the lad with hardened fists as I stood by screaming for him to stop. The terrified maid dashed out, leaving me alone to defend the child against his brutal grandfather, who brushed off my attempt at intercession with far more ease than I would have expected from a man his age. He lifted a hand to me and would have beaten me as well, though I was not his own wife, had a concerned guard not knocked on the nursery door.

While the grandfather was distracted in dismissing the guard, I scooped up Gilles and ran, beseeching God to make my husband or someone else who might help me appear. Little Gilles lay like a whimpering rag in my arms as I escaped into the narrow passageway between the nursery and the chambers of Lady Marie. I knew the hiding places well enough, for every one of her ladies had been forced to disappear within her apartment at one time or another when Guy de Laval presented himself without notice in expectation of receiving Milady's

amorous attentions. On such occasions there was no time
to depart gracefully, for he was a demanding lout who did
not care to be kept waiting. He would take her on the
spot, on a bench, against the wall, even standing, without
waiting for all the rest of us to leave. So we slunk into
hiding and waited in silence for Milord Guy to finish his
business, which he usually did with brisk efficiency.

Such events, agonizing then, seemed mild in comparison to my distress of that moment, but the knowledge of the suite's hiding places served me well in my
immediate situation. As I passed through Lady Marie's
door, I whirled around to see Jean de Craon surging forward almost drunkenly in his rage to quarry us. Gilles
was clinging and squirming, but I managed to free one
hand and push the door shut. It *whooshed* against the lin-
tel, wood echoing on wood. I gave the bolt a violent shove
just as he was about to fall upon us. To my inexpressible
relief, the bolt found home in its wild slide, and the door
held. The vicious old brute slammed against it with such
force that the planks began to bulge and splinter. With
the child clinging to my breast, I dashed to a closet, while
Jean de Craon pounded with impotent rage on the unyielding wood.

It was some time before he wore himself down
enough to abandon his battery of the door. I quivered
in mortal fear inside the closet until I was certain he
had departed. By the time we emerged from our stifling
tomb, my bodice was stained with my own tears and
those of the child. And the stink in the closet was unbearable, for as his grandfather had pursued us, my terrified
little charge had soiled himself in every way possible. The
shame I saw on his face as we reentered the light was
heartbreaking.

Some hours later, when the child was safely tucked
into bed, I slipped into the great hall to find my husband.
He had been gone all day and I wanted desperately to tell

him what had happened. He was taking his evening meal at the long table with the rest of the fellows. Within this jovial group was the wicked old man who had terrorized me and his grandson earlier; his mood seemed hale and convivial as he swayed drunkenly to his feet.

For a moment I stood paralyzed with my back against the wall. It was impossible to avoid an encounter should he take it upon his drunken self to confront me. My only hope was that he had imbibed enough hippocras to cross his eyes, and when I saw his first lurching attempt to walk, I began to think it might be realized.

As he teetered toward me, I summoned up my courage and slipped past him with my eyes lowered. I felt his eyes upon me, though I did not look up. He dismissed me with a small, disgusted grunt and then said nothing more; he did not try to stop me or even speak to me. It was as if the entire ugly incident that took place in the nursery had never occurred.

I wish I could say that my husband was horrified when I recounted the afternoon's events to him, but he disappointed me: *Young Master Gilles is the first son of a noble house and he must learn to accept his role as a ruler. That will require fortitude.*

I countered with conviction: *He will get violence from what is being done to him.*

Violence is what will be required of him. And it is not your place to decide these things.

That was the end of the matter. I was miserably dissatisfied.

Gilles de Rais did not present himself to the private court that day as an unchecked child in need of sympathetic discipline, nor did he appear to be *un grand grotesquerie* worthy of shunning. Instead, he showed himself as precisely what the people he had wronged thought him to be before this all started: a wealthy and powerful man in his physical prime, a great lord with the power to squash his accusers—like so many insects—on a mere whim. He wore his position with glaring aplomb; one doubted that he even knew what modesty meant. He was garbed as a minor god that day in the finest red velvet mantle, all encrusted along the front with costly jewels and glittering gold. The fabric moved with indescribable fluidity, so pleasing to the eye.

"God forgive me, but he is a splendid sight to behold," *Frère* Demien breathed.

And he was. Gilles de Rais required no beauty to fulfill his mandated role in this world, for his wealth alone would have assured success, had he not squandered it. But he had been blessed with beauty nevertheless and wore it on this day like a ruby on a maiden's throat— one's eyes will come to rest on it, even against the will. But something inside this man was broken to the point of inhumanity, though his potions and powders and kohl had heretofore been quite effective in disguising it. In view of the dreadful deformities that were surfacing in his character, I was doubly glad that Jean de Craon's wicked schemes for Milord's ascendancy had not come to fruition.

Despite his difficulties, Gilles de Rais's stride was sure and his air privileged. But his presence was unnerving. The longer the court carried on without him, the more comfortably theoretical his existence had become, as if he were an idea of evil and not a man who had given himself over entirely to its influence. His jolting magnificence rendered it nearly impossible to fathom that Gilles de Rais was the defendant in these matters. He looked instead to be the equal of those who sat in judgment of him.

He stood there in silent challenge to those men. Jean de Malestroit responded first, as was proper; he cleared his throat once, then called out, "Gilles de Rais, knight, baron, lord, and Marshal of France."

The tales of woe, the endless Latin proofs of jurisdiction, the weeping mothers, all that went before this moment seemed suddenly insignificant. Milord stepped up to the witness stand, his chin raised high. He placed a gloved hand on the hilt of his sword and stood there in lofty silence as the charges against him were read by God's prosecutor.

"...that you have taken or caused to be taken by your adherents and accomplices a large number of children ..."

Their names were read. I prayed for another hundred nameless sons long gone and grievously missed.

"...that you have abused them sodomitically and practiced upon them the grave and mortal sin of sodomy ..."

In a dream state I recalled the words that Henriet had said when questioned on arrest: *And Milord disdained the natural chamber of the girls, but instead would know his pleasure with children of both sexes by placing his member between their thighs, thereupon to work it rhythmically until his lust was satisfied.*

"... that you and your adherents have called upon evil spirits and offered tribute to those same spirits, and have committed many other crimes against God, too numerous to name."

Now Prelati's confessions rang in my memory: *The words of convocation we used were as follows: I conjure you, Barron, Satan, Beelzebub, by the Father, the Son, and the Holy Ghost, by the Virgin mother of God and all the saints in heaven, to appear among us in person and speak with us and do our will.*

"You will be given a written copy of these charges as soon as one can be made," Jean de Malestroit said to the defendant. "Do you understand the accusations that have been made against you by these many citizens?"

Gilles's voice was unnaturally calm, almost quiet. He lifted his chin slightly and said, "I refute these charges and appeal for their dismissal."

Along with everyone else, I gasped, *"Mon Dieu."* No one had anticipated a simple refusal to be tried. The judges and prosecutors gathered into a hasty têtes-à-têtes. When they broke away again, Jean de Malestroit stared at the defendant with unswerving disgust and said, "These allegations are not made lightly, Milord. Nor have they been brought forward by simpletons. There is considerable evidence, some of which appears to be beyond denial, that you are guilty of those crimes with which you have been charged."

"Falsehoods and slander!" Gilles professed loudly. "I swear it on my soul!"

"Guard your oaths, sir, lest you put your soul in jeopardy."

"The devil, you say! These charges are completely unfounded."

Another unison gasp ran through us all. His Eminence regained command of the situation by saying, "The court thinks not, sir. The court will entertain the possibility that there is truth contained in the allegations. Moreover, in view of the nature of this case and the weight of the evidence against you, this court finds your appeal to be quite frivolous and wasteful of our time. And *furthermore,*" he added, "your appeal has not been presented in writing."

Gilles himself was caught unprepared and appeared flustered by this declaration. "But . . ." he sputtered, ". . . I have not been given opportunity to do so!" He turned his palms up, demonstrating his lack of parchment and quill.

"The law requires that any appeal be presented in writing, sir."

"This is preposterous!"

"Indeed not, Milord," Jean de Malestroit said with a barely visible smile. "It is a law of many years' duration."

"Then it shall all be written!" the defendant cried. "By my own hand, if necessary! I beg materials of you."

All of the judges were quiet for a moment. Finally his Eminence said, "I would advise you to retain the services of an advocate for such a writing, should you pursue this course. But I should further advise you that this will be wasteful of your time, for we shall not entertain an appeal, no matter how eloquently inscribed."

"This is *unacceptable* to me!"

Jean de Malestroit rose up slowly; in his hands I saw a slight shaking, which disappeared when he placed them firmly on the table. His voice was harsh. "It need not be acceptable to you," he said. "It need only be acceptable to God and our lord Duke." After a pause, he offered something of an explanation, perhaps an appeasement, in a more reasonable voice. "Rest assured, Milord, we do not overrule you out of malice or disregard—we do so because both faith and reason demand us to continue diligently on the path we have begun."

"But these are lies, blasphemies all—there is no cause to proceed. This is a plot by those who would destroy my reputation before God and my king. These fiends would take my property."

It was the simple truth, though it would never be acknowledged by any of the judges. Milord Gilles appeared ready to burst. His face reddened, and one trembling hand slipped toward the *braquemard* sheathed at his waist, to which gesture the guards all reacted as one by putting hands on their swords.

"I deny the competence of this court," he nearly shouted, "and I withdraw all my previous statements, except my avowal of Christian Baptism, which cannot be

denied and gives me the right to be properly judged before God!"

De Touscheronde rose up in anger and threw back
the disdain that Milord had shown him. "Your judgment
will be proper, Milord. And truthful. I swear on my hope
of salvation that everything alleged in these charges is
based on true testimony. Now swear by the same hope of
eternal reward, sir, that your own words shall be true."

He was answered only by silence.

"Swear, I say!"

"I shall *not*. I do not recognize this court's jurisdiction over me."

"Swear!"

"Never!"

"Under threat of excommunication, you are ordered
to swear!"

Gilles de Rais's silence rang as loud as a bell.

Jean de Malestroit rose up out of his seat and banged
the gavel down hard on the board. Through its reverbera-
tions he said, "This court shall be adjourned until
Tuesday next, the date being October eleventh, at which
time *you,* sir, shall be required to swear an oath of truth-
fulness, or else all hope of eternal salvation shall be taken
from you."

He pointed directly at Gilles de Rais, who responded
only with a noble sneer. Guards came forward and took
him away to his private suite, therein to contemplate his
increasingly untenable position.

👑

The news of this confrontation roared like a wildfire
through the encampments. Talk arose among the aggrieved of taking matters into their own hands, prompting Chapeillon to send out several hasty messages to
Duke Jean, advising him of the possibility of an insurrec-
tion. There were endless meetings and discussions between

his Eminence and a veritable legion of advisers over the course of the next few days; I and my sisters spent much of Monday in supplying whatever they required so their scheming for the next day's proceedings might be completed in time and in comfort.

Yet for all their effort—which must have been considerable for all the nourishment they required—they seemed to have accomplished little or nothing. On Tuesday next, when court was supposed to have reconvened, we gathered together again, anticipating the perhaps even more shocking drama that would unfold. Instead, we were surprised to hear this announcement by one of the scribes:

"This court will be adjourned until Thursday, October thirteenth, at the hour of Terce, at which time we shall proceed in this case and the cases of this order, as required by law."

As we waited for the crowd to dissipate, I looked down from our lofty vantage point and saw their grasping upraised hands and their open, shouting mouths.

It would swallow us all.

꧁꧂

When I brought Jean de Malestroit his supper that evening, our conversation was drowned out by the continued chanting, which had not abated in the least. The drapes and tapestries on the windows barely reduced the noise, even at this great height.

I pulled one bit of a drape aside and stared down into the milling throng below. "They put me to mind of the crowd that gathered for the Maid."

His Eminence came alongside me and looked as well. "One would like to have all that pass out of memory."

There was no hope of that, of course. Mistakes will always remain in memory, whereas the pleasures are chased off by woes and cares. Thank God her execution was not Jean de Malestroit's personal error. Nevertheless, he could not escape a common regret shared with other clerics of authority over how badly it had gone. I was only four years in his Eminence's service then, too fresh to have the responsibilities I now have. In me Jean de Malestroit seemed to find the kind of compliant retainer he needed to assist him in the small tasks of his office, and I was nothing if not compliant then. And so on that terrible day in 1431 I found myself in a place that I ought never have been allowed, with a view generally reserved for the mighty.

My pain over the death of Etienne was still almost constantly in my heart and mind then, but the trial and execution of Jean d'Arc took me out of it, at least for a time. His Eminence swears that there was good and substantial reason to believe she had indeed engaged in the heresy of witchcraft. I am certain that this belief springs from a need for absolution from complicity in the matter. His sin, perhaps still unconfessed, was his inaction.

But to what end had she engaged with the devil? Certainly not to obtain riches or power, nor to part some man from his property or, worse, steal his soul. If witch she was, it was warrior witch, who beat back the English and elevated the bastard Charles to the throne. We were all still smarting from Agincourt, wherein our Gallic heart was ripped from our breast by the arrogant English and stomped to a pulp like that poor cat in Saint-Etienne. If God had not supplied the Maid with the means to win, then it was fitting and right that the devil should have done so. Too many souls had already been sacrificed to that cause, including that of my own husband.

And despite their legendary companionship, Milord was not there to save her when they tied her to that stake. Many who stood by and watched in horror as this young woman was destroyed retained the hope, as I did until the straw beneath her was finally lit, that Milord would come forward and whisk her off to safety. There has always been talk that he was conspiring to do so, for he had been in nearby Louviers and he had bought a horse, tack, and weaponry. We all took that purchase and his proximity as signs of preparation for a rescue. But it never materialized, and if a conspiracy had been formed and then thwarted, we shall never know, for no one has spoken of it since. Perhaps Milord had come to believe as many had that she was insane, and that her voices were nothing more than the rantings a lunatic heard inside her head, repeated with credible fervor on ears too willing to hear.

Jean de Malestroit and I watched her demise from above, out of harm's way should the crowd turn ugly. I shall never forget the swarming huddle of humanity. People slithered around the cordoned immolation platform, climbing over one another like so many ants. Dust rose up like steam from a hot cauldron. As the death cart was brought through the crowd, the chanting began: *witch, heretic, sorceress.* Without her stunning white armor, she looked small and so pathetically frail. Wave after wave of people parted to let her through, many of them reaching out to touch her as she passed. At the hour of her death, she was not a warrior but a child, one who understood she was about to die.

Inside myself I screamed at God, asking how He could let this happen. This treasure, the force behind our unification, was about to be consumed in flames by the will of His servants and in His name. I wanted to shout out that we were killing the best among us, only to make it possible for the men whose hides she had preserved with her bravery to appear unassailably strong and wise.

But God showed Himself that day—as the flames took hold of her clothing, as her flesh began to blacken and sizzle and split, as her eyes squeezed shut and her mouth tightened in exquisite pain, He brought forth a white dove to take her place at the stake. It sprang up out of the flames and flew off into the sky with its wings furiously beating the air above the empty platform.

It was not until much later that his Eminence and I found the means by which we might speak of what we had each seen and hardly dared believe.

The wails of the gathered multitude were indescribable and deafening—but were they crying in terror for their own souls in having sent Jean to her death or shrieking in joy that God had claimed her as His own?

The crowds that milled about in the courtyard below me now, though smaller, looked much the same, with everyone shouting and crying. God's power and influence were nowhere to be seen among them. Perhaps they were pleading with Him to allow the excitement of Milord's ordeal to continue, just for a little longer, and He was angry with them for that deplorable wish.

Even so, it would be granted.

⚜

His appeals, though painfully impassioned, did nothing to sway his stern judges. Gilles de Rais had simply gone too far. We gathered at the morning hour of nine in the upper hall of la Tour Neuve on Thursday, October 13, in the year 1440, the thirty-seventh year of Gilles de Rais's life, certainly the last.

Though it was disruptive, observers were once again permitted in the court. Jean de Malestroit knew well the political wisdom of allowing his own judicial impeccability to be witnessed and whispered. Guards were posted every few feet along the edge of the room to maintain order, creating a complete surround through which those entering had to pass. When the room was comfortably full, no more were let in.

As if it were some entertainment to which they had

been invited, the lords and ladies of Brittany turned out in force, handsomely clad in the most admirable finery, almost to rival Milord himself, who had attired his person to the utmost for the opening hour of his final judgment. I gaped shamelessly at the jewels and beautiful embroideries worn by men and women alike; I had never been draped in such things, even on the day of my wedding.

"You are staring," *Frère* Demien observed quietly.

"Please allow me to have my moment of sin undisturbed."

Frère Demien sighed and shook his head but said nothing more of my base-minded preoccupation. Shortly our attention was drawn back to the proceedings by the sound of a new voice, that of Jacques de Pencoëdic, venerable doctor of law. He would serve on this day as the prosecutor, by agreement of all parties; he was an experienced man with an unassailable reputation for crisp justice, an excellent choice. He had a way of turning the most confounding matter into something pure and simple.

The air was thick with the rich sound of his words, and the drama of it all was consuming—great lords and beautiful ladies craned their necks to listen, even to the long and tortuous legal description of the court's authority.

But the crowd's fascination rose further when the descriptions of the crimes began in earnest.

"... that these same boys and girls were abducted by the said Gilles de Rais, the accused, and by his adherents ... that by them these children had their throats cut and had been killed and dismembered and burned and in other manners shamefully tormented. That the same Milord Gilles de Rais, the accused, had sacrificed the bodies of these children to demons in a damnable manner, that by many other reports the said Gilles de Rais invoked demons and evil spirits and sacrificed the said children to them, sometimes after they were dead, sometimes as they were dying; that the aforesaid accused also horribly and ignobly exercised the sin of sodomy on these children, disdaining the girls' natural vessel ... that the said Gilles de Rais, filled with evil spirits, bypassing all hope of salvation, took, killed, and butchered many children, as many by himself as by the aforesaid accomplices. That he caused and ordered the bodies of these children to be burned, reduced or converted to ashes, and thrown into hiding places ... that during the said fourteen years he also held discourse with conjurers and heretics, that he solicited their aid numerous times to carry out his purposes, that he communicated and collaborated with them, hearing their dogmas, studying and reading their books concerning the forbidden arts of alchemy and witchcraft ..."

In all, forty-five articles of indictment were read aloud—by their finish, several of the ladies were in near faint. The crowd of observers, at once aghast and intrigued, had grown quiet during the repeated recitations of horror upon horror and seemed now to be completely numbed by it all. But two among them seemed to dwell on every word, ladies both, *Mesdames* Jarville and Thomin d'Araguin, who looked as if they wanted more horrors when the readings were done. They were fixed upon Milord as a believer fixes on the image of a saint, hoping for some saintliness to rub off.

"Scandalous," *Frère* Demien said when he saw me staring. "I have heard it said that Poitou brought these two into Champtocé and allowed them to watch some of the killings from a secluded place. That they were extremely desirous to watch such activities again."

I sat back, shocked; how any woman, even one whose womb had not brought forth life, could watch the destruction of a child was beyond understanding. And then, to say nothing—

De Pencoëtdic's voice rescued me from my melancholy; he called out Milord's name and bade him stand to face the court. Gilles de Rais came to his full height and faced the panel of judges at the front of the court.

"You will respond, sir," de Pencoëtdic said with gravity, "to these ponderous charges. You will do so under oath and in the French language to each and every article of these indictments."

The defendant surveyed the great hall, now and then catching the eye of one of his peers. Only his two female admirers would return his glance for more than a flash of time. The implications of holding the gaze of such a man were dire indeed.

"Do you intend to respond, sir?" de Pencoëtdic asked again.

The courtroom was so silent that we could hear flies buzzing, and remained so, because Milord said nothing at all to the prosecutor's request. All eyes were steadied upon the great Marshal of France. The next sound we heard was de Pencoëtdic's sigh of disappointment, which drew the eyes of the assembled to him instead. Slowly, in keeping with the stiffness of his age, he turned to face his Eminence and Friar Blouyn. He gave the slightest nod, some sort of prearranged signal, then sat down in the velvet-cushioned seat from which he had previously risen, a voiceless old man once again.

Jean de Malestroit inclined himself forward slightly and said, "You will respond, Milord."

Why he would reply to his Eminence, an enemy of many years, but not to de Pencoëtdic, who bore him no enmity, I cannot say. But that is precisely what he did. Gilles de Rais looked directly at Jean de Malestroit and said, with pronounced haughtiness, "I will not."

The crowd took in a collective gasp. To refuse to answer to God's representative was an act of heresy in and of itself. To speak to him without the use of a respectful title was equally unthinkable.

"I say again, *Milord,* and I advise you to consider the disposition of your immortal soul before refusing, you will respond."

Gilles de Rais was visibly holding himself back from explosion—he was seething, almost shaking.

I swear, Etienne, I thought he would burst—when he could not have what he asked for he held his breath until he began to turn blue. Then, when he let it out, he was all rage, like a young bull who had been poked in the eye! The boy accepts no refusal of his desires without rejoinder. . . . Sometimes I am inclined to take the lash to him myself, were it not forbidden.

Contain yourself, Guillemette. It is not your place to correct the child.

If not mine, then whose? It must be done.

Here before us now was the result of that failing, whosesoever it might have been.

"I will not respond," he vowed again. He looked first at Jean de Malestroit and then at Friar Blouyn. His expression was rife with pride and disdain. "You are not now nor have you ever been my judges."

"In the name of God, who is and always will be your judge, I demand that you respond to the charges that have been presented to you today."

Now Gilles de Rais began to shout at Jean de Malestroit and his judicial compatriots. On the assault of his words, all three shrank back in self-defense. "You are all thieving rogues who have accepted bribes to condemn me," he shrieked, "and I would rather be hanged by a rope at the neck than respond to such judges as you are."

He turned and began to walk toward the door but was stopped by two guards. He struggled against them and for a moment it seemed that he would break free. The courtroom dissolved into pure chaos. Jean de

Malestroit was up on his feet, shouting above the fray as Gilles de Rais was dragged back and placed before him.

"Perhaps you do not understand these charges against you completely, Milord." He turned to one of the scribes. "Repeat the indictments in French," he cried, "so Baron de Rais might understand them, as he seems not to comprehend the gravity of his situation when it is described to him in Latin."

He flailed in impotent protest. *"Je comprends le Latin!"*

"Too well," I whispered under my breath.

I could barely pry *The Twelve Caesars* away from him when he was a child. It was a book whose contents made me shudder. The things these wretches did in the name of sovereignty! Such tales as these might damage a small boy by numbing his soul to carnage. But Jean de Craon insisted that it be part of his education, and Guy de Laval would not override him.

The poor little scribe rose up instantly, parchment in hand, and commenced a shaky impromptu translation. Milord began to tremble, and we all heard him shout, "I am not an imbecile! I understand Latin as well as the next fool."

The frightened scribe stopped speaking and looked to my bishop, whose glower ordered a continuation.

Gilles de Rais stopped struggling finally and glared at his Eminence as the French words were hastily spoken. It was the same look I had seen on his face when he reached his majority and threw off the tyranny of Jean de Craon: pure, cold defiance. His voice rose once again over the timid words of the scribe. "I will do nothing that you ask of me as Bishop of Nantes," he hissed. As he struggled against the grip of his guards, he looked from one to the other, as if to intimidate them with anger. Neither would hold his gaze. Another guard was called forward to assist, and Milord was finally overpowered.

A dreadful, silent gravity fell upon us all as Gilles de Rais made a pathetic attempt to restore himself to nobility. He straightened his garments and smoothed his hair, then looked around the room. He found no support in the observers.

There came over him a calm of the sort that always seems to show itself before a tempest.

I could almost hear Jean de Malestroit's thought prayer: *Father, if this cup can be taken from me . . .* But he pressed on nevertheless, demanding once again of the prisoner if he would respond or object to any of the charges in the lengthy indictment.

And so it continued. By the last of Jean de Malestroit's demands for submission, Gilles de Rais's fatigued refusals had become so hushed and small that we could barely hear them.

Then his Eminence stunned us all.

"By all the saints, Gilles de Rais, you shall force us to excommunicate you from the holy Catholic faith with these heretical refusals."

The Gilles of old returned with a vengeful wrath. He rose up and roared out oaths against his Eminence that I cannot repeat for fear of losing my salvation. Then he cried, "I am as familiar with the Catholic faith as any of you. *And I am no heretic!*" He further declared, "If I had committed the crimes with which I am charged in these articles, then I should be deviant from my faith. From which condition I do not suffer."

"Perhaps not, Milord," Jean de Malestroit said, "but you seem to suffer from the conditions of impudence and lunacy. You feign ignorance, but your denials are not to be believed."

"I would never engage in pretense in a matter so grave as this!" His words were more pleas than declarations. "And I am shocked," he went on, "that *Monsieur* l'Hôpital would give what meager information he has on the events you speak of to the ecclesiastical court and moreover that he would allow me to be so charged on Duke Jean's behalf in the first place."

It was all goose feathers. De Pencoëtdic rose up from his ornate chair and turned to the judges. "On behalf of Duke Jean," he said, "I demand that this man be held in deliberate contempt of this court for his refusal, despite our canonical exhortation, to answer to the charges before him."

Upon which request the judges looked at each other with silent understanding. Jean de Malestroit took up his pen and a fresh piece of parchment, and he began to write on it, forming his letters quickly but with visible care, for the words that the prosecutor read from that page when it was handed to him were as serious as words could be.

"Gilles de Rais, by the authority vested in us by his holiness Pope Eugène, you are hereby excommunicated from the holy Catholic Church."

"I appeal! A pen, a parchment, I shall write my appeal!"

They had anticipated everything. Jean de Malestroit nodded to a scribe who rose up and read from a parchment that must have been written long before. "This appeal is forthwith denied because of the nature of this case and the cases of this order, and also on account of the monstrous and enormous crimes with which you have been charged."

A gasp rose out of the silence, then wails of despair, cries for mercy, pleas to God for salvation, and prayers of thanks, all simultaneously. There followed a state of disorder as great as any we had seen in the proceedings to date. De Pencoëtdic stood and shouted over the crowd in his loudest voice, *"We shall proceed."*

"We shall not!" Milord countered.

"Oh, indeed, sir, we shall."

Yet another proof of authority was read, as Gilles went wild with anger and rage.

"Whereas according to the Apostle, the evil of heresy spreads like a canker and treacherously destroys pure souls if not extirpated in time by the diligent work of the Inquisition, it is meet and fitting to proceed advantageously with all the authority and dignity of the office of the Inquisition against heretics and their defenders, and also against those accused or suspected of heresy and against hinderers and disturbers of the faith—"

Gilles thrashed about like a captured serpent. With unanticipated strength, he broke free of his guards and lunged toward the judges' table. My heart leaped upward into my throat; this was a warrior, bent on attacking a bishop, who had not the skills or the means to defend himself. With his hands alone, Gilles de Rais could tear out Jean de Malestroit's throat. The two guards bolted forward but did not catch him on their first attempt. From somewhere within the folds of his garment came a dagger, which he brought high into the air as if to strike. It was already in downward motion when the guards caught hold of his arm.

My gorge rose and my hand went to my mouth. But as the guards fought with his attacker only an arm's length away, Jean de Malestroit sat, motionless and sure. His eyes burned into Gilles's, delivering the silent message: *Struggle if you wish, but you will be brought down. Such is my power over you.*

I watched in shame and disgust as the guards took Milord away. They dragged him out on his knees, a position he assumed only when absolution was at hand. In that moment, he was as far from absolution as he had been in his life, and more in need of it than ever.

chapter 30

SIX DAYS, NO WILBUR. We had surveillance teams in place at the house and the studio, his two main haunts, but no one had seen him. Employees came, went, and were watched, to the degree that we could get away with it. The land-line phones in both places were monitored, but there were twelve cell phones in use by Angel Productions, and there was no telling which one Durand might have.

We actually talked about getting court orders for every one of them, that's how desperate we were. Fred brought us back to reality.

"He probably walked up to one of those mall carts disguised as a hooker and prepaid for a phone."

It was maddening, the way he could change shapes. There was no guarantee that he was doing that—he was the ultimate nonentity in default mode. But the possibility that he did morph himself into something else colored everything we tried to do to find him.

Description of the suspect: 5'9" to 5'10" tall, medium

to slim build. Mid-thirties to early forties. White. Male or female.

Only twenty or thirty million people in the United States fit that description.

I made sure there was no green food on the table that night.

"Mom," Frannie told me, "we want you to have big cases more often. We like the food when you do."

Everyone agreed, most heartily Evan, whose adolescent predestiny was to despise everything his mother claimed to be beneficial—things like sleep, homework, the OFF button on the clicker, and broccoli.

After the kitchen was cleaned up, we all settled down in front of the TV and watched *Wheel of Fortune*. Frannie kicked our combined butts, once even solving a puzzle with only the spaces, no letters yet.

"The Wind in the Willows," she said. "I just read the book. Piece of cake."

The conversation that followed was not a piece of cake.

"Evan," I said, "shut the TV off."

"But *Jeopardy!* is coming on next," he said. "You always let us watch *Jeopardy!*"

It was true. "Not tonight. I need to talk to all of you, and since we're together for a change, I want to do it now."

A unison groan of dismay rose up. Julia whined, "Oh, no, are we having money troubles again?"

The previous year had been tough; the engine blew on my car, my mother exceeded the limit on her prescription coverage and needed help, and Evan got braces. We went through a cautious period of belt-tightening, which had the unexpected benefit of teaching my kids about some of the economic realities of adult life. "We'll get through it okay," I'd told them, and we had. A lesson learned. They had less fear of money now, and that was good, but that didn't mean they liked it.

I wished it was that simple this time. "No," I said. "Just the opposite. I'm picking up lots of overtime. We'll have a really good vacation this year."

This time the unison noise was a cheer. It was a good omen—perhaps this discussion would go better than I had thought it would.

"But there's a reason why I'm getting all that overtime. You know that big case with the man who directed *They Eat Small Children There?*"

Of course they did. They were all over me with what they'd heard.

"It's my case."

No way that's awesome Mom cut it out you know Wilbur Durand tell us all about him. It all blended into one sentence, the speakers indistinguishable.

"It's true. I've been in on it since the very beginning. I was the one who noticed the pattern."

More shouts of excitement. *Wait till I tell Mrs. Adamy and Mr. Forsyth they'll think it's so cool where's the phone I want to call Samantha and tell her.*

They needed to know, but they couldn't run out and brag—it just wasn't a good idea at this point. I hated to tamp down that glee. "Listen, guys, I know this is a lot to ask, but I'd rather you didn't talk about it any more than necessary. I know that will be hard, and I'm sorry. But it needs to stay that way for the time being."

"Mom, come on, we have to tell *someone*."

I would have to make them understand the danger, to make it personal for them. "Are you prepared for the possibility that it might have an effect on us if you do?"

Silence.

"I would have to deal with the press, people who are his fans, all sorts of nutcakes who don't know how to behave. People might follow us around. I can be much more effective in my job without that kind of interference. So until we catch this guy, I need you to work with me. I'm asking for you all to be like deputies this time. It won't happen if the whole world knows who we are."

The magic word, *we*. There were solemn nods of accord from all three of my blessings.

Two of my blessings retired to their beds, Julia first, then Frannie. Their little heads were undoubtedly full of imagined glory, of the unbelievable things that their omnipotent mother would do. Good. They should have a successful woman as their role model.

In moments like this, I always feel like such an imposter.

Once again, Evan and I were left alone for some precious minutes of companionship. *Dear God,* I prayed, *let these sweet moments never end, let me always be this important to my son.*

It would pass all too soon. With every breath he took, Evan's cells were dividing, his bones were lengthening, his hormones were surging, and he was moving away from me. This is what happens when you feed and water them. But in moments like this, I could imagine his once-tiny arms around my neck, smell his sweet baby breath, know his absolute trust and worship, all vestiges from the time when I was all-powerful, the goddess, the source of his sustenance and knowledge.

It was such a diminishment to simply be his mother.

"Mom," Evan said, his eyes nevertheless alight with admiration, "I know you don't want us to talk about it, but this is just way too cool. *You* figured this out—that's so incredible. Your job is so great. I've been thinking maybe I'd want to be a cop too."

I want to grow up to be just like my mother—an odd thing for a boy to say, but delicious to hear. There was just one problem—becoming a cop isn't the same as it was when I came on. The disrespect for authority that is so rampant now was just starting to take hold in those days. There wasn't the acute danger then; the legal requirements weren't so restrictive.

"You'd still have to go to college. You need to know a lot. They want people with some education these days."

"That's okay. I want to do that anyway."

"I'm flattered, Evan. It makes me feel really good to hear you say these things. But you have lots of time to decide what you want to do with your life."

"Meaning you don't want me to be a cop."

"I didn't say that."

"But you're thinking it. I know you are."

I tousled his hair affectionately. He bristled. "I'm not a little kid, Mom."

How well I knew that. "I know, Evan. I'm sorry. Listen, while the girls are in bed, I want to talk to you about something."

He was quiet for a second, then said, "I know about sex, Mom. Dad told me a bunch of stuff last year."

I covered my surprise with a smile. "That's not what I wanted to talk to you about."

He seemed inordinately relieved. "Good. But what, then?"

"I just want you to be careful. I don't want you to be afraid of the world, because it's a wonderful place, and I hope you won't lose sight of that. But there are people out there, people we can't really understand because there is just something wired wrong in them. They don't act the way normal people do. I just want you to start being aware of what's going on around you. If someone makes you feel uncomfortable, move away from them. That goes for everyone. If someone you know and trust doesn't seem to be acting right, you can just walk away. And please tell me. *Please.*"

He sank back into the cushions of the couch and went quiet.

"Evan?"

His eyes met mine, but he said nothing.

"This is important, honey."

Somberly he said, "Okay."

I caught myself before mussing his hair. "Thanks," I said.

"Quiet morning," Escobar said. "The sharks don't seem to be circling so close for some reason."

It had been ten days since the story broke. The frenzied initial fascination had begun to wear off as other important stories happened. There was a school shooting and a hostage situation at an airport to distract the fourth estate, not to mention the perpetual paranoia over potential acts of bioterrorism. Eleven days passed, then twelve; my kids were back with their father but called frequently, ostensibly to make sure I was okay. But there was a suppressed agenda: When could they start blabbing to their cronies?

Not yet. Soon, but not yet.

On the morning of the thirteenth day, I was sitting at my desk, immersed in organizing the massive paperwork for the Durand case. The phone rang. The caller ID gave a 617 area code. Boston calling.

"All's quiet on the western front, I take it," Pete Moskal said.

"Too quiet," I said. "I wish this guy would show himself already. But he's such a chameleon, if he does show, it won't be as himself."

"Too bad. You could maybe get away with shooting him if he came out made up as some green scaly thing. But listen, I heard something interesting. Rumor has it that his sister is quietly passing most of her cases off to underlings."

"You've got someone in her firm talking to you?"

"Yeah."

"Well, I appreciate knowing who we'll be up against." For some reason I couldn't pin down, I didn't want to talk to him. "Thanks so much—"

"There's more."

It wasn't gossip, I could tell by the tone of his voice.

"I wanted to tell you that I'm going for an arrest warrant."

It had to happen sooner or later. "I guess I can't blame you. You've been pretty patient, Moskal. I appreciate it. Good luck. I hope you have a decent judge to go to."

"A gem."

"Look, just do me one favor if you can. Keep me out of it as much as possible."

"I'm going to have to put your name in the report. The chain of information comes right through you."

"Couldn't you say *an unnamed Los Angeles police officer* gave you the information?"

"You mean like an anonymous informant? I suppose I could, but the case is relatively weak already. Having the name of a referring detective strengthens it. Considerably."

If he got Durand first, it would be because I had opened it up for him. The irony of it just scalded me.

"Is there any way I can convince you to hold off for a few days?"

"Probably not."

"You couldn't give us another day or two to find him out here."

"I'm losing time if I do that. I can get my forces looking for him here."

"He's not in your neighborhood."

"How do you know that?"

There was no logical explanation, only my instincts. "Because the air around here is still foul."

I finally managed to convince him to wait "a few more days," to give me a decent shot at Durand. The reward grew as more of the families of missing boys came forward to join in the public hunt. Predictably, the calls increased again. Following up on bad leads became a blood sport in the division; who could invalidate the most crank calls in one day? Typically it was Escobar or Spence, both of whom were exquisite interrogators who found the bottom line very quickly. We got serious again at the airports and hotels because none of us knew what else to do and because the heightened security in the wake of terrorist attacks made it easier. But there was little hope that we would find Durand that way; he could easily rent a house under an assumed identity, easily charter a jet and bypass the routine airport checkpoints. He hadn't shown up at his home or studio, though his underlings continued to come and go at will. We had no legitimate reason to hold any of them, which did not keep me from teetering on the edge of hauling them all in for a brief cattle-prod demonstration anyway. They were all close associates, perhaps even accomplices—it seemed reasonable for one or more of them to be involved on some level in his doings, but we had no direct evidence of complicity.

We would just have to wait for him to surface.

The phone call came just as I was getting ready to go home. I had my desk straightened and my briefcase loaded. The keys to the car were already in my hand when Pandora's box sprang to life again on my desk.

The ring had that *don't pick up the phone* quality, a jarring, shrill, artificially elongated *brrrrooooooop* tone that sent a bolt of lightning down my spine. A service aide was on the line. She said, quite skeptically, "This is a 911, but whoever it is asked specifically for you."

I touched the flashing red extension button.

"Detective Dunbar."

"Lany?"

It was Kevin. He never called me at work. His voice was full of panic. I stared at the phone. I knew instantly why he was calling.

Or at least I thought I knew.

"God, Lany, he should have been home an hour before and I kept waiting and waiting for him to show up, keeping supper hot for him.... I finally called over to Jeff's house, and his father said he thought it was my turn to pick them up, and I said, no, this was your turn. And then I'd just barely hung up the phone when Evan called and he told me that Jeff's father had come for them but told Evan to wait because I'd said I was going to get him so we could go somewhere, and he just took Jeff and left Evan standing there. Lany, he took Jeff. God. I thought they were too big for that kind of thing, to be kidnapped.... Jeff's so tall, I mean, he's taller than I am, for God's sake...."

"Stay off the phone," I told him. "I'll call you right back." I replaced the handset in its cradle, after which movement of any kind ceased to be an option. My paralysis must have been visible, because Escobar rushed over.

"You're white as a sheet, Dunbar," he said. "You all right?"

"No."

"Speak," he ordered.

"I think Durand grabbed Evan's best friend."

Saying it aloud snapped me out of the stupor. I've been in all sorts of crisis situations over the years, had tons of training, done commendably well under stress. But right then all I could think was *Oh, God, no …*

The troops were summoned for an emergency meeting in Vuska's office.

He told me right out that he had the authority to remove me as the primary and that I had no business continuing in a leadership role on a case where my own safety or the safety of another officer might be compromised by a hasty or emotion-driven decision.

"But it's your call," he said, surprising me. He could have ordered me out of it, and by rights he probably should have.

"Why, Fred? You don't have to let me stay."

He drew me aside, away from other ears. His expression was drawn and pained. "I feel bad for not listening to you in the first place," he confessed. "This might not have happened if I had."

It was an apology of sorts. I acknowledged it with a pursed-lipped nod.

"You know more about this guy than the rest of us combined," he went on. "So we need you. I'm gonna trust you to tell me if you start to falter, and if that happens, I expect you to pull back out of the front line right away and work with the support team. Let Spence and Escobar finish it then."

Before we went out, I knew that Fred would take both of my compatriots aside and tell them to keep their eyes on me, to yank me back if necessary.

There's no logical explanation for the fact that when we all left Fred's office, I was calm again. I guess in my heart of hearts I knew that if Wilbur Durand intended to kill my son's friend, there was nothing I could do at that point to stop him.

The line was busy when I called Kevin back. I was on the verge of sending a squad car over when I finally got through.

He was completely out of control, swearing, apologizing, begging to have the day over again.

"Kevin, calm *down*. Breathe deeply," I said. "Try to concentrate on staying clearheaded. Right now I have to ask you a lot of questions—"

"Jesus, Lany, couldn't someone else ask me the questions?"

Now was not the time for old resentments to surface. "I am the primary on this case and it's my job to do this. We need *not* to get nuts with each other right now. Think of me only as a detective."

I used to talk to him about my cases all the time, or talk *at* him—I don't think he heard much of what I said—but since we've been living apart, the opportunity isn't there. Listening was one of our biggest problems; neither of us was very good at hearing the other. And toward the end it was hard to have a civilized conversation with him about anything at all, never mind the complexities of my work. But I'd always thought that he would have known about the potential risk if I'd told him about this case. Evan had been a good son and had done what his mother asked—he hadn't talked to anyone, including Jeff, about the things I'd told him.

And one thing I should have done right away when I knew the significance of it was to talk to him about the dinosaur exhibit, which they'd taken Jeff to see. But I never did.

Two hours had passed since Jeff had been grabbed, half an hour since we'd learned of it. No doubt the silver Honda Accord Durand had surely rented to feign Jeff's father's car had long ago been dumped.

It didn't matter—he wasn't ever going to need to rent a car again. There's no driving in hell. Or maybe there is—you're stuck in dead-stop traffic on the 405 at 6:00 P.M. on

Friday in one hundred degree heat with no AC, and then there's an earthquake. We'd already sent cars out to tell the watchers at both the studio and the house to be particularly vigilant for anything that looked even slightly unusual. A description of the car did go out on the police radio, preceded by a code to switch to a new channel. Details of what to look for—backpacks, restraint items, disguise components—were revealed to the patrol officers in the private airspace. Every relatively new silver Honda Accord in the city was stopped, especially if it had rental plates. It was a tremendously popular vehicle, and there were occasions where four or five were stopped on the same street at one time that evening. Some of the patrol cops took to putting a soap mark on the upper left windshield after inspecting a car to minimize the problem of repeat stops. Parked Accords of that color were given a once-over and booted if there was the slightest reason to be suspicious, such as a book or sports bag left inside or an extra set of clothes. Returning owners were questioned aggressively before having their cars released. But it all led nowhere.

Jeff's father had e-mailed a photo, which I sent out on the wires immediately. It went to the Teletype and on the computer system so the officers in the patrol cars could see him. We put out a picture of the undisguised Durand, which felt like an exercise in futility. For the next two hours, I sat and stared at the phone, hoping for a new lead, something, anything we could pursue. It stared back, mute, while the food someone shoved in front of me grew cold.

Jeff's father showed up, without his other kids.

It brought the situation home to me in a way I could not have anticipated, to be in the presence of someone with whom I had regular interaction, whose child was now the object of a massive and urgent search because he was in the possession of a monster. His son was guilty of the crime of being with my son, nothing more, nothing less. I didn't know yet whether Jeff himself had been targeted, or if he'd been mistaken as my son. A trip through Durand's security videos might clarify that murk. Had Kevin clowned with Jeff as well as his own son? The two looked like brothers, and Evan favored his father. Durand might have made the mistake of thinking that Jeff was Kevin's child—and mine.

I couldn't say that to him, not yet. It would just complicate things. "You should go back home, be with your other children," I told him.

"I just need to be here," he countered. "He's my son."

"Okay," I said, "but you'll have to go out into the waiting area. I promise I'll come talk to you the second anything happens."

As the door was closing behind him, the phone rang. Spence intercepted the call before I could get to it.

"Durand's houseboy left the house in his own car," he told me. "Opened the garage door, drove out, then closed it again."

"Well, then, stop him and search the car." I was almost shouting.

Escobar's hand was on my arm, gentling me. "And if we find something in the car, will there be probable cause to have searched it?" he said.

We could lose everything on a bad search; it's happened many times before. "Follow him, then," I whispered. "But for God's sake, don't lose him."

I turned back to Escobar. "He almost never leaves the house. Only once in a great while. There have been days on end when we haven't seen him go in or out."

"Lany, calm down. He's the houseboy. He probably just went out for milk."

"But he had stuff delivered this morning. The grocer's van came, remember?"

"So maybe he forgot something."

"We should call the guys at the studio and tell them to keep an eye out for him."

Escobar did just that. He gave them a description of the car and the houseboy himself.

I heard him say, *Five eight to five ten, white or light Hispanic, slender build* . . .

"Shit," I heard myself whisper. "Wait a minute."

Then Escobar's voice broke through the developing mist of realization. "They said that someone who fits that description left there this afternoon just as the shift was changing. Delivered groceries, then left."

thirty—one

ON FRIDAY, OCTOBER 14, there was no court. Outside our dank abbey, which we shared with a host of rare
and unwelcome green substances that came and went
with the damp, there was a hopelessly blue October sky
dotted with high, fat clouds of the sort that simply pass
over without surrendering one drop of rain but wet the
eyes nevertheless with their beauty. I paused in my rush
across the courtyard square to lift my face up to the sky;
the warmth was like God's fingertips caressing my skin.
With one hand I took off my wimple and veil and let the
sun touch my hair as well.

No one in the crowd paid me the slightest attention
as I continued, bareheaded. Once again, a good throng
was gathered around a crier. Yet another vivid, embell-
ished account was being told of the excommunication of
Gilles de Rais. I slipped into the periphery of a group
whose ears were all inclined toward the center of their
gathering; there I stood and eavesdropped as one of them

told what he had heard moments before in the midst of another such group.

Bones, the man said. And skulls. They found more skulls. Forty-nine skulls had been mentioned in the articles of indictment as read the previous day, but those had supposedly been destroyed. I had thought it too many to conceive of at the time.

But now they were saying there were more. And that they had not been destroyed.

⚜

His door was open when I entered the room; I did not try to keep my skirts from sounding, and so their drag on the carpet alerted him to my entry.

"Ah, Guillemette—"

My accounting of the convent's expenses was overdue, so I had hastily assembled it that morning. I slammed it down on the table in front of him. He shrank back in surprise.

"Is it true?" I demanded. "Were more bones and skulls found at Champtocé?"

He did not answer immediately; instead, he looked at me with intense curiosity. "Your hair. It is uncovered."

"The wind has arranged that," I said. "Now, what of this rumor about bones and heads? People in the square are speaking of little else. Is there truth to it?"

At first he said nothing, but eventually he nodded. "Some were found in his private chambers at Champtocé and Machecoul. Well-hidden, probably forgotten by his accomplices in their haste. But only a few—not nearly enough to account for all who are missing. One wonders how many had previously been removed."

"I want to see them."

There was not the slightest hesitation in his voice. "No."

"Eminence—"

"No," he said again. "I forbid it."

"Jean, please—"

"I cannot allow it. My position as judge in this trial would be compromised by such a mishandling of evidence."

"Is that position more important to you than this undying ache in my heart?"

"In asking that question you take unfair advantage of your position with me. I am surprised, Sister; I had thought you above that sort of thing."

I stepped back, hurt and confused. There was nothing more to be said after that last pronouncement of his. I was guilty of some sin no matter what I did. Therefore, I could see no further reason to refrain from committing one.

♔

I returned to my small room and pulled the trunk containing the remnants of my former life out from under the bed. The frocks were sadly out of style and suffering from mildew. I could not have stood to wear any of them. I would have to find something elsewhere, but there was nothing to be had in the abbey without arousing a great deal of suspicion.

The encampments had grown even larger as word of the trial spread through the surrounding countryside. The periphery of Nantes was no longer just farms and trees with the occasional small abode, but a forest of tents and makeshift hovels in which the people of the countryside had gathered. I found Madame le Barbier in one of the cleaner sections of the camps; she was taking a bit of refreshment—cheese and a cup of pale hippocras—when I came upon her. It was a moment before she recognized me sans veil. But then her face lit up, which gladdened my heart.

She bowed slightly. "Mother Guillemette, how fine to see you again."

"*Et vous,* Madame."

"Come, join me. Please"—she extended her cheese to me—"take a bit of food."

I was not terribly hungry, but it seemed an insult to refuse her offer. I broke off a small chunk and gave the rest back to her.

Gone were the gaunt look and sagging attire; she looked much more fresh and substantial. Though I envied her recovery, I said, "You appear to be in good health and spirits, Madame. This warms my heart."

"I am well content that this trial is finally taking place—it was so long in coming, so long! It will not bring my son back to me—of that I am sure. But justice will be done. And in that, I will find some peace."

Peace. Until she said that, I had not realized how deeply I craved it.

She chewed her repast thoughtfully as she regarded me. "You have lost your veil, I see."

"Yes." She would not require any excuses about wind. "For the moment. And that is why I have come to see you."

⚜

She went through what trunks she had brought, tossing skirts and shifts and frocks over her shoulder like so many rags, not the precious jewels they were to one so long deprived as I had been. I had not renounced such things with true willingness, and now they seemed to arouse some aching, ill-defined thirst in me. I stood in amazement as she held first one frock and then another up to me for a quick appraisal—did it enhance or detract from my natural features? Was the style well-suited to my figure? I had quite forgotten that I had a figure which might be flattered by the shape of what was draped upon it.

I left her tent still wearing my cloak, but what lay beneath it was no longer my shapeless habit. Instead, I wore an ordinary frock of an unpatterned fabric in the color blue. I longed for a glass within which I might regard myself, for to me this plain dress was a magnificent gown.

But I made my way through the crowd virtually unnoticed. The rebellion in which I was engaged, my sin of disobedience, was all contained within the cloak.

I retrieved my veil from where I'd stowed it and replaced it on my head. The weight seemed unbearable, but I bore it in silence. I made my way silently through the palace with such purpose in my stride that no one would have dared question me. It would be assumed that I was going somewhere of importance and that I must not be interrupted.

So lovely, so different from the abbey, with its dark stone walls and hallowed air. Though a bishop lived in the palace, he was sometimes a chancellor, who ought to have been surrounded with beautiful things, items that might daily remind him of the importance of his work. Still, the accommodations were just passable in comparison to those to which Milord Gilles had become accustomed.

When I presented myself to the guard outside his private quarters, saying I carried a message from Jean de Malestroit, I was not questioned. For weeks, these guards had seen me following two quiet paces behind my bishop, and there was no reason to doubt me. My manner was prayerful and meek; I told them that Jean de Malestroit had charged me with the important task of providing Lord de Rais some comfort and solace in his hour of darkness. I grasped my rosary fervently between the flat palms of my hands and invited the guard to pray with me for Milord's fallen soul. He let me pass, I think to be rid of the discomfort my feigned religious zeal must surely have caused him.

He spoke a sharp order to another guard, whose expression grew grave on hearing that he was to lead me through the passageway to the lavish central apartments where Milord was quartered.

The guard who went before me walked quickly. I could not fault him for his obvious dread—with every step closer to the inner chambers, my own heart beat a little faster.

Questions of what might occur began to sneak into my mind, and I wondered for a few paces why I had not considered the encounter more carefully before coming. As I was led into a large salon, I felt the strong urge to turn and run away.

But I could not. I breathed deeply to reign in the wild beasts that were scratching and clawing through my innards. The surroundings helped—this was a commodious room, handsomely draped with tapestries and weavings and lushly carpeted with several of the beautiful patterned rugs that came all the way across the Mediterranean Sea on trade boats. I longed instantly to take off my leather shoes and press my bare toes into the thick fibers before the opportunity escaped me.

As I gazed in wonder, the guard tapped three times with the base of his spear and then stood at attention. From another room, I heard Milord bark, *"What?"* Suddenly, all desire for soft carpet deserted me; my feet wanted to take me out of there.

I had seen a rendering of the heart of a man in one of young Gilles's books of anatomy at Champtocé. *Le Coeur,* the inscription beneath the drawing read. It was marvelous, and so simple, but it struck me as odd that there would be two sides to a human being's heart. Of what purpose could it be to have two distinct passageways through which our emotions must course?

In that moment I understood. One side of my heart was entirely filled with anger and the desire for vengeance, the other with immeasurable sorrow.

The guard announced nervously, *"Vous avez une visiteur, mon Liege,"* after which he turned and disappeared hastily back into the passageway.

As soon as he was gone, I pulled off my veil and undid my cloak. I let both fall on a nearby chair, an exquisite piece of furniture on which I would never have dared sit. There I stood, an ordinary woman, when Milord came into the salon. He approached me slowly at first, until the light of recognition crept onto his face. He rushed forward and embraced me. All of my womanly skills went into suppressing the confused revulsion I felt to have his arms around me.

"Madame," he said, "Oh, Madame ... forgive me for not remembering you at first. You must understand, this has been a trying ordeal—and I am no longer accustomed to seeing you in a woman's clothes."

Then he shrank back a bit, his eyes full of suspicion. "Has Jean de Malestroit sent you to speak to me on his behalf? That he should send a woman to do his work—"

I cut him off. "He did not send me. He will be sorely ired when he finds out I have come to you."

"Oh," Gilles said with slight intrigue. "He shall not hear it from me."

The old hatred still existed, then.

His beard was no longer curled and blue, but dark and neatly trimmed. Nevertheless, he played with it as he had the more lush one. There was a madness in his eyes that even the most sublime disguise could not hide. "But if you did not come as Jean de Malestroit's emissary, then why?"

"I am here as Guillemette la Drappiere, though that woman seems long dead to me. There are things I would know. Questions only you can answer."

In that instant I could almost feel him shrink inward.

He knew, then, why I had come.

He forced himself to appear calm. "Surely, Madame, you know as much about me and my life as anyone."

"I do not know whether or not you killed my son Michel."

It was out, at long last. Just in releasing it from my breast, I felt some relief. That alone might have satisfied something within me, but now the answer itself was within my grasp. I wanted it.

I stared directly into the cold blue eyes of my *fils de lait*. Rarely in my life have I felt such discomfort as in that moment. But then, to my wonder, his eyes began to moisten. He shocked me by falling to his knees before me. He pressed his tearful face against my knees and grasped me around the legs. I almost lost my footing, so fervent was his clinging. He wept aloud with the abandon of a child.

Then he began to speak. "Madame, I have committed many unspeakable crimes: I have done nearly all the things of which I am accused. But I did not kill your son, and I am horrified that you could think this of me; am I such a fiend as that to you?"

He went on and on as confusion flooded into my heart. "I do not know what happened to my true brother Michel," Gilles said, perhaps meaning to soften my heart, "though I will always believe it was that accursed boar who dragged him off, the very one who gored my father."

There was such contrition in his voice, such sincerity in his denials. I whispered, "You truly did not kill him?"

"No."

God save me, I believed him. My relief was immense, even though the greater mystery of how Michel had died still plagued me. Had a hunter killed him for some unfathomable reason? I wanted desperately to believe it.

"Milord," I whispered, "God does not abhor you. God loves you, I am sure of it. He will forgive you as He forgives all of His sinners, if only you will confess your sins freely and without hesitation."

I placed a hand upon his head and stroked his hair, as I had often done when he was a child. He clung to me desperately, as he had often done when he was a child.

"Yes, yes," he moaned as he clutched me, "He will. I am a Christian, accepted into His arms by the sacrament of Baptism, and now I am refused His grace. I beg you to help me, *Mère*—I cannot be denied the sacraments." He squeezed me tighter around the legs, until I pried him loose.

"Hear me," I said. "You know what you must do. You must go into court tomorrow and speak freely of the things you have just told me, and all will be well."

He looked up at me as he loosened his grasp and wiped the tears away with one hand. "Is that true?" he said, his voice childlike.

"Yes," I said, the mother once again. "Rise up now. God will make it well."

⚜

Jean, my treasured son,

Please forgive me; I know my laxity in writing has worried you. His Eminence told me of your inquiry via the Cardinal's letter to him. Please put your fears to rest. I am now at least somewhat cured of the cruel affliction that overtook me and kept me from setting quill to parchment.

Today I went to see Milord Gilles in the suite of rooms in which he is imprisoned here at the castle. I confronted him with the question that you know has been haunting me—that of the circumstances of Michel's death. To my eternal relief he denied any complicity and spoke of Duke Jean's hunters, which he has never done before. I believe that he is telling me the truth, for in the same breath he confessed to me that he had committed all the other murders with which he has been charged.

I ought to have been more shocked by this admission on his part, but somehow that upset must have been overwhelmed by the blessed relief of knowing that he had not killed my son and your brother. But his own soul knows no respite; it is desolate and afflicted with confusion and pain the likes of which I have never seen before and hope never to see again. I urged him to confess the rest of his crimes in court tomorrow, when he will appear again before his judges. It is my most fervent prayer that he will do so, for it is only through absolution that he will find comfort.

No doubt you understand that our journey will now be delayed; I am hoping that we can begin it before the weather turns too cold for decent traveling. But perhaps if we leave when the weather threatens, we shall be forced to stay in the warm south! I cannot imagine a more pleasant way to pass the cold Brittany winter than to spend it in Avignon.

Dearest son, remember me in your prayers, as I do you in mine. I am beginning to believe once again that God actually hears me. I did not realize until today how much I missed my faith.

As I miss you, beloved son. I am so glad that we will see each other so very soon.

⚜

My last vision before falling asleep was the blue dress that hung on the back of my door. It was not unlike those that I wore as a wife and mother in Champtocé. I dreamed that night of lying next to my husband, of having his gentle hands upon me. When they brought him back from Orléans, his injuries had already begun to fester and he was in too much pain to chance my brushing against his leg, so I made a separate bed next to his instead. How I had ached to slip under the coverlet with him just one more time before he died. His delirium toward the end was such that he would not have known I was there at his side. But I would have.

I slept beyond dawn. When I came to court that morning, Jean de Malestroit and Friar Blouyn were already seated at the judges' table, poring over parchments. His Eminence regarded me quizzically as I padded quietly to my seat next to *Frère* Demien.

He cast me a glance that I dared not interpret. "I came to fetch you this morning," he said, "but I was told that you were still asleep. Are you ill?"

"No. I was merely fatigued." I glanced toward the front of the court. "I see that Chapeillon is already here."

"He was here when I arrived, which was before his Eminence and Friar Blouyn came in. He has been at his papers all this time."

A buzz of excitement arose, for Milord, once again a peacock, had arrived to take his place among the sparrows. My guilt rose up unbidden and caused me to blush when I saw him, remembering our exchange and the things I now knew unequivocally to be true. I could not speak to anyone of these matters. I followed him with my eyes, hoping he would look toward me, but he did not.

When the whispers died down, Chapeillon rose. "Honored judges," he began, "I ask you in the name of Duke Jean to inquire of the accused if he intends to speak. Further, I ask that you advise him forthwith that even though he has chosen not to speak before now, he may do so at this time, which may take the form either of accession to or objection to the articles of the indictment previously read."

Jean de Malestroit nodded and turned to face Gilles de Rais. "Milord, by request of the prosecutor, I ask if it is your intent to speak."

After a long sigh of resignation, he said, "I shall not speak. But neither shall I object."

This change of demeanor was completely unexpected, by everyone but me.

It took a moment for Chapeillon to regather his composure. "May it please the court," he said, "I would ask our esteemed judges to inquire of Milord Gilles, the said accused, if he will recognize the authority of this court over him."

Again, his Eminence faced Milord. "You have heard the question, Milord. What say you on the matter?"

Gilles de Rais looked as if he had been offered a cup of hemlock. He faced his two judges and said, "I concede that these judges are competent to judge me, and I confirm their jurisdiction over me."

I could not see his face, but I could hear the tears in his voice. His chin dropped as he said, "I will accept any judge you choose to place before me."

He was sobbing freely by then. "I confess before God and this court that I did commit the crimes with which I have been charged, and that I did these deeds within the jurisdiction of these judges."

I could barely hear him for the cries of the observers. I stood and cupped a hand around one ear, and thus I heard his apology. "I do humbly and devoutly ask these judges and any other ecclesiastics against whom I have said offensive things to forgive me."

Jean de Malestroit and Friar Blouyn were stupefied. They looked at each other briefly and came to a wordless understanding. His Eminence raised a hand to quiet the court, then said, "For the love of God, Gilles de Rais, you are forgiven."

Chapeillon found his voice. "If it please the court, I ask for permission to establish proof of the crimes contained in the articles, to which Milord has acceded."

"The articles as submitted are admissible as evidence

and constitute sufficient proof," Friar Blouyn declared firmly.

"Then I would ask Milord to respond to the articles, to confirm that proof."

All eyes went to Milord, who straightened under their stares. He opened his mouth as if to speak, but Jean de Malestroit raised a hand, and he stopped.

"You must first swear an oath of veracity, that what you are about to avow is the truth before God, and nothing but the truth."

Gilles looked down at his feet for a few moments. Then we heard him say, "I so swear, before God."

"Now you may speak."

We sat in rapt silence as Milord Gilles declared his affirmation and accession to articles one through four of the indictment, as well as articles eight through eleven, all of which established the authority of the court and its officers. "And article fourteen, I also affirm. Regarding article thirteen, I acknowledge the existence of a cathedral in Nantes and that Jean de Malestroit is the Bishop of that church. Moreover, Milords, I affirm that the castles of Machecoul and Saint-Etienne-de-Mer-Morte lay within the bounds of that diocese."

There was a momentary lapse, during which we all caught our collective breath.

Jean de Malestroit's voice broke the silence like the tolling of a bell. "Go on," he said.

Gilles cleared his throat, then proceeded anew. But the words he spoke were not what I had expected to hear. "I have accepted Christian Baptism. And as a Christian I swear that I have never invoked or caused others to invoke or summon evil spirits. Nor have I offered anything to be sacrificed to those spirits."

Chapeillon and Blouyn exchanged another glance—clearly, they did not believe him. The air was thick with tension, which Jean de Malestroit only enhanced by saying, "Remember, Milord, that you have sworn a sacred oath."

"I have not forgotten my oath, *Milord*." He then launched into something of an explanation. "I will admit to receiving a book of alchemy from an Angevin knight who is now imprisoned for heresy and will affirm that I caused this book to be read publicly to several people at a room in Angers. I did speak with the aforesaid knight about the practice of alchemy, but I returned the book to him after not having had it for very long. I did engage in the practice of alchemy with François Prelati and the goldsmith Jean Petit, both of whom are known to you. I engaged the services of these alchemists to turn quicksilver into gold. We knew no success in our endeavors."

Jean de Malestroit glared at him and said, "One is told that there were furnaces at Tiffauges built expressly for the purpose of alchemy."

Gilles appeared surprised by this statement, as if the existence of those furnaces was some kind of secret. He countered it immediately. "Yes, I did cause such furnaces to be constructed. But I thought better of it before using them."

"Is it not true, then, as we have been told, that they were dismantled primarily because the Viennese Dauphin had decided to pay you a visit and you did not wish him to see them and therefore suspect you?"

How stiff and defensive his posture became at that accusation. "It is not true, Milord Bishop, I swear it."

Jean de Malestroit leaned back in his chair and considered what had been said. After a few moments he leaned forward again. "Milord, I shall ask you again to respond to the charge of invoking demons, and I remind you of your oath."

Gilles de Rais would not be swayed. "I deny it. Unequivocally. And if there are witnesses who will prove by their testimony that I did invoke spirits, I shall undergo a test of fire to prove them wrong. When such witnesses come forward, I shall use their testimony to illuminate my own position on this matter." He was full of his own certainty. "A broader definition of these matters shall emerge, I assure you."

This avowal of innocence sent Chapeillon scurrying straight to the judges' table, where he and the two judges entered into private conference. All wore looks of combined disgust and frustration, for things had gone well this morning until Gilles decided once again to defy them.

I had so hoped for better after our previous night's encounter. I had prayed sincerely that Milord would enter the court this morning, admit his heresy, and accept his punishment. I was no longer driven toward hatred and vilification of this man by some shapeless rage; he had told me that he had not been the cause of Michel's demise, and I believed him. I longed for him to be relieved of all this, though I knew it meant he would have to give up his life—such was prescribed punishment for crimes of this nature. But perhaps he might be allowed to give it up more easily, with less pain. I could not bear to see him die as Jean d'Arc had.

Chapeillon moved away from the judges' table and made a summoning motion with his hand to a cleric who had been sitting near the front of the court, one Robin Guillaumet, who was also of this diocese. Chapeillon whispered something to Guillaumet, who nodded and walked immediately to the back of the hall. There he spoke briefly to one of the guards, who conveyed Guillaumet's order to others waiting outside the courtroom:

Bring in the witnesses.

The air in the courtroom seemed to have disappeared. But none of us were breathing at present, anyway; we were too busy watching the witnesses summoned by the cleric Robin Guillaumet. One by one, they filed silently into the court, each one looking quickly into the eyes of their liege lord, Gilles de Rais, for one guilty moment. When all were assembled before the judges' table, Guillaumet instructed each one to step forward and be identified as his name was called.

Henriet Griart. Etienne Corrilaut, also called Poitou. François Prelati, cleric. Eustache Blanchet, also cleric. Perrine Martin.

They all stood mute and listened as an oath was read:

"... on the Holy Gospel to tell, depose, and attest to the truth, the whole truth, and nothing but the truth, insofar as it is known to me, on the matter of the articles put forth and expressed by the prosecutor in the case and cases of this order, and also to tell the truth on the thing in general and in specific not expressed in the aforesaid articles ..."

"Do you object to this oath on the part of the witnesses, Milord Gilles?" Jean de Malestroit asked.

Gilles shook his head in stunned silence.

"Let the record reflect the accused's consent."

"I speak now to both the witnesses and the accused," his Eminence continued. "Will you swear to put aside all entreaties, love, fear, favor, rancor, hatred, mercy, friendship, and enmity, ceasing all such behaviors and attitudes during these proceedings, so they might be untainted by such emotions as occur between you?"

All agreed.

"Milord Gilles, will you accept the depositions of these sworn witnesses and any others the prosecutor may produce and similarly swear?"

"I will," he said. His voice sounded lifeless, defeated.

"And do you intend to provoke this court by challenging the character of any of these witnesses?"

"I do not."

"Do you intend, Milord, to interrogate them yourself, as is your right?"

"I shall rely on their consciences to guide them in their testimony."

"Then it shall be as ordained," Jean de Malestroit said. "We shall convene again on Monday next, October seventeenth, to hear their statements."

He reached for the gavel and was about to pound it to bring a close to the proceedings. But Gilles de Rais stepped forward while it was still raised, and when he began to speak, his Eminence set down the wood mallet before sounding it.

"Milord judges," Gilles said, falling to his knees, "I beg you in all contrition to restore me to the sacraments. Rescind my sentence of excommunication, I implore you. I cannot bear to be denied the blessing of God's comfort." His face was wet with tears, and his shoulders racked with the hard motion of sobbing. "Take pity on me, a child of God, and restore me to grace, in writing."

A moment of silence passed before Jean de Malestroit looked at Friar Blouyn. "Will you agree to this?" he said.

Friar Blouyn studied his own hands quite intensely for a few moments, perhaps contemplating the displeasure of Duke Jean at his consent to such a request. But in the end, he, too, had mercy. He nodded his accord.

"Then it shall be done," his Eminence said. He spoke quietly to a scribe, who wrote diligently as he dictated. When the dictation was complete, his Eminence read what had been written and then signed his name.

He handed it back to the scribe. "Let many copies be made, and then post them publicly," he said. "And let the criers know that it is so."

I swear before Christ that Gilles would have kissed his feet had there not been a table between them. The gavel fell.

François Prelati first spoke calmly of the events that had transpired to bring him into the service of Gilles de Rais, of his enticement by Blanchet, and his engagement in the dark arts with his patron. Blanchet himself then came forward and confirmed the accounts of black magic and witchcraft, of heretical conjurings of the devil. Henriet Griart gave testimony that he had taken part in the procurement and killing of many children, and that he had willingly done so.

But it was Poitou whose account was most shocking. He described once again the hurried abandonment of the castle at Champtocé, of the removal and disposal of the forty-six bodies. But he added a new chapter to that tale as well:

That was my initiation into Milord's sins. God save me, I myself later led many children to Milord for use in his debaucheries, perhaps as many as forty. All the while, I knew what he had in store for them. He took such pleasure in this iniquity; he would moan in delight and tremble with lust while the children wailed.

Sometimes, if the wailing became so loud that it annoyed him, or if he feared discovery, Milord would hang a child by the neck until he was almost dead and then take him down again with warnings to be silent. Or he would cajole them into thinking that he was not going to harm them, that he only wanted to have some fun with them in these pleasures. But he always killed them afterward, or had the killing done by me or another of his servants. Mostly we took them from among the poor seeking alms around Milord's various castles, but sometimes they were of better station. He often boasted of finding more enjoyment in the killing than in the lustful activities, that he found his greatest satisfaction in seeing them languish, then cutting off their heads and members. Often he would hold up

*the heads of children he had killed and ask us which of them
we thought most beautiful.*

*And when he was unable to find children suitable for his
debaucheries and killing, he practiced his sodomitic lust on the
children of his chapel, in particular on the two sons of Master
Briand of Nantes. But those boys he would not kill—he esteemed them for their singing abilities, and they all promised to
keep his acts secret.*

*None of us did anything to stop it, and when Master
Prelati came, things got even worse. When word of the Bishop's
letters reached us—perhaps around the fifteenth of August—
I would have run away, but there was nowhere for me to go. I
had no money, for I had not been shrewd as had de Briqueville
and de Sille, who had seen to their own safety by stealing—bit
by bit—a small fortune from Milord. Henriet and I, on the
other hand, had remained devoted to Milord by virtue of our
affection for him, and now his fate would be ours as well.*

*Milord himself grew daily more despondent and con-
stantly repeated his vow to atone with a pilgrimage to the
Holy Land for the grievous sins he had committed. He promised to turn away from his evil life and come to God for mercy
and forgiveness. It came to me in those dark days that God
would never forgive him for what he had done, nor would He
forgive me for my part in it.*

*Yet despite his avowals and promises to God, Milord re-
verted in time to his habits of debauchery. He caused me to obtain this boy—his name was Villeblanche, as I recall—from
his parents with a promise of making him a page and further
bade me to purchase a doublet for the lad. I did these things for
him and then brought the boy to the castle at Machecoul,
where he met the same fate as all the others who had inno-
cently ventured inside with futile hopes of improvement. He
was abused carnally by Milord and then murdered by me and
Henriet. And when the life was gone from him, we burned his
small limp body, which disappeared into the flames, just as all
the others before him had. He was the last that I know of—*

certainly the last for me. I would do no more evil for Milord. I wept that night, for a long bitter time. And I weep now, every night.

May God have mercy on our souls.

⚜

Later that evening, after our meal—for which none of us had any appetite—the court reconvened, and new witnesses were sworn in, as my bishop was eager to get this travesty completed while there was still a bit of goodness in the world. The Marquis de Ceva, Bertrand Poulein, and Jean Rousseau, all of whom had been with Milord at Saint-Etienne-de-Mer-Morte, were deposed. They would testify to the violation of ecclesiastical immunity perpetrated by Milord against Jean le Ferron, rector of that church, who maintained possession of the property in his brother Geoffrey's name. On Wednesday, when court reconvened in another closed session, the same witnesses would reveal to the scribes, judges, and limited observers what Jean de Malestroit already knew firsthand through our horseback observation. They would confirm that Gilles de Rais, who waived cross-examination of these witnesses—it being an act of futility—had assaulted God's servant on earth Jean le Ferron in a desperate attempt at reacquisition that was doomed to failure from the very start. It was, in truth, an attack on God.

God was about to strike back.

chapter 32

IN ONE OF MY PHONE CONVERSATIONS with Doc, he'd uttered these prophetic words:

He goes to enormous lengths to perpetrate his crimes, prepares elaborate disguises and detailed setups—it all seems ridiculous and insane. But this is all about control, and that's how Durand achieves it. Control is supremely important to him. It often is to a person who grows up in circumstances over which he has little or no influence; from what the family friend told you, that's how things worked out for him in the Carmichael household. Throughout his adult life, Wilbur has tried—as have so many others of his pathetic ilk in their own sick, horrible ways—to create a completely controllable life, where everything is ordered and structured exactly to his liking.

Otherwise he can't feel safe. Not even for a minute.

They echoed in my head as I prepared to capture the man who exercised ultimate control over the boys he took, those unblemished canvases on which he practiced his depraved art, the physical representation of his younger self in the hands of Uncle Sean. He destroyed his own sense of helplessness by re-creating it in the boys, then destroying them. He was a power freak on a mission to seize back his lost childhood, and right then he had power over someone who was important to my son.

And, therefore, he had power over me. But not for much longer.

Frantic activity went on all around me. We were almost ready to head out when the front desk called. Spence picked it up.

"For who?" I heard him ask.

He listened for a few moments, then handed me the phone.

A shopping bag containing a pair of blue Nikes was downstairs.

"There are initials inside them—*J.S.,*" the service aide said. "But wait, there's a note too...."

I heard paper crinkling through the phone.

"What the heck. All it says is, *But take your shoes off before you come in the house.*"

I slammed down the phone and swore like a sailor.

"What?" Spence demanded.

"He's got him at the house. I had it in my mind that he would go to the studio—"

"Okay, all right, that's where we head, then," Escobar said. He could not have heard the electricity in his own voice, but I did. You could almost smell the adrenaline; we were all practically bleeding the stuff. Our training and practice, our procedural and equipment drills—it all had a purpose. The rituals of combat, on which we had all been tested, would now be put to the test themselves. In the end, our success would rise and fall on will—if the will to triumph was there, the skills and tools would work as intended. Everything came down to state of mind. Once again I became the huntress in lion skins, but this time I was surrounded by like-thinking hunters. We had sharpened our spears. We were setting out at a trot with our spears in hand. We were hungry.

We would eat.

Jeff's sneakers were an engraved invitation. *Come and get me,* they said.

As we wound through the lower streets of Brentwood, my heartbeat picked up. Trees and fences whizzed by, leaving neon-type trails in my mind's eye; dogs barked in slow motion. The splat of a bug on the windshield sounded like a pile driver. While Spence drove, I tried to concentrate on the layout of the house.

Thinking, thinking. Trying hard to anticipate what he would do. In the end, I could come to only one conclusion.

"He has to have him in his home studio. That's where we have to go first."

"Why do you think that?"

"Because this guy is a control freak, and he wouldn't make that kind of mess anywhere else in his house."

That room had been searched when we went to the house the first time, but being at the end of the hallway, it was one of the last to be surveyed. When the tapes were located in the main studio, everything at the house became an also-ran, so it had gotten only a quick going-over.

"I wish we'd looked at that room better."

"We'll deal with what we find," Spence said. "Everything will work out."

"You think so?"

"Yeah. I do."

He was a better interviewer than he was a liar.

Houses whizzed by in a blur as we ascended into the hills. I prayed that Spence was right.

When we got there, the street was jammed with what appeared to be every car in the Los Angeles police force.

The gate through which the houseboy had to have left earlier in his car was locked again. The observing unmarked police car was still in front of the house next door, though it was now buried behind two layers of flashing blue lights. Beyond the high fence was the modern-day fortress in which the madman holding a boy he assumed to be my son lay in wait. For me. Everyone else here was extraneous to him.

Escobar was out of the unit and deep into the trunk before I knew it; he emerged from the jumble of equipment with a bolt cutter. He headed resolutely for the gate and had the lock broken before I was even completely out of the car.

We charged through the opening and up the driveway. A brick walkway ran from the pavement to the front door, and over it there was an arched canopy. Standing underneath the dark green canvas was an unfamiliar, youngish man whose attire gave me the sense that he was some kind of manservant. Like the houseboy, he wore white pants and a short-sleeved shirt. But he was also wearing a bow tie.

I stopped and took out my gun. Spence moved to within whispering distance of me.

"You seen this guy before?" he said from behind.

I shook my head *no* and began to move forward again. My gun was raised and trained on the unfamiliar new player.

The poor man was shaking. The others stayed a few steps behind while I went all the way up the walk—my hanging-back days were over. With each step I took, the houseboy's eyes widened in deeper terror. I stopped just shy of the canvas overhang and stood there with my gun pointed at his face.

"Raise your arms and step out onto the landing," I ordered. He trembled visibly as he lowered one foot and then the next.

"Come closer," I said.

"Careful, Lany," I heard Escobar say from behind and to my right.

"Always," I said quietly.

And then I did something that confused everyone, especially the houseboy. I spat on the fingers of my left hand and rubbed my own saliva on his face while the gun was about two inches from his nose.

"Lany, Jesus . . ." I heard Spence say.

"I want to be sure it's real skin."

The trembling houseboy was pale as a ghost, and silent.

"Where is Wilbur Durand?" I demanded.

He shook his head almost violently. "I don't know," he said.

"Did you bring a pair of sneakers to the Crimes Against Children division about an hour ago?"

"No, I did not," he said. There was a slight accent, perhaps Hispanic.

The gun was still in his face. "Did you deliver groceries to your boss's studio this morning?"

His eyes widened even further and he shook his head again. "But I heard the garage door open and close earlier."

"What time?"

"I don't remember."

"Approximately."

"Early afternoon, maybe it was—"

I interrupted him. "Going in or coming out?"

"I didn't see. I was in the kitchen. There are many ways to come and go from this house. I mind my own business." He waited a few seconds and said, "They told me he doesn't like to be bothered. So I don't bother him."

He was scared; we would get nothing more of value out of him, and precious minutes were ticking off. "Proceed down the front walk and place yourself into the custody of one of the officers waiting down there," I ordered.

He nodded eagerly and began to move forward. His eyes never came off the barrel of the gun as he slid by me with his hands still raised. He practically ran into the arms of a uniformed patrol officer.

I turned back to the door and looked into the dark open mouth of the unknowable beast who had swallowed Jeff Samuels. *Hang in there, Jeff, just hold on for a few more moments, I'm coming to get you. . . .*

I two-handed my gun, which suddenly seemed to weigh about a hundred pounds. Spence and Escobar were right behind me as I passed through the open door; Escobar started to move forward to get ahead of me, but I put my elbow out to hold him back. I heard the scrambling of footsteps outside—other cops were surrounding the house. Blue light flashed in through the blinds; the whole street was lit up. The sound of radio-squawk was deafening. If Durand was inside, he could not help but know what our intentions were.

Good. It was time for him to get scared.

It was all so unreal to me; I was operating totally on instinct—one minute a mother, the next a cop, sometimes both at the same time. Straight ahead was the living room; the orange glow of the evening sky poured in through the big picture window that looked out onto the backyard garden. As I worked my way down the hallway I leaned into each room and listened with the ears of a fox.

And then I heard muffled human voices from behind a closed door. Spence and Escobar, still both right behind me, also seemed to hear them, for suddenly we all had our guns pointed directly at the door's center. We all stayed quiet and listened intently.

From the diagram, I knew that there were two bedrooms on either side of the home studio. What I didn't know was whether or not there were doors connecting any of those rooms. I whispered "doors" and nodded in both directions. They both understood instantly. Spence went to the left and Escobar to the right to take a look.

But as soon as they left me there, a thin line of very bright light showed from under the door of the workroom, and then I heard a man's voice say, *Action . . .*

I was Arnold Schwarzenegger, Clint Eastwood, and Charles Bronson all blended into one. I kicked in the door with one foot, did a classic drop-and-roll, then came to a crouching position with my Lethal Weapon out in front of me.

Jeff, where are you, we're here. . . .

And there he was, off to the right; he was tied up and gagged, but there was blood on his abdomen. My very first instinct was to rush over to him, but out of the corner of my eye I saw something move. I looked to the left—the light was very poor—and there was Wilbur Durand, but as himself this time, not as the houseboy.

There was a camera trained on Jeff, and behind it was that monster, who appeared to be filming the whole horrible scene. There was a dark object that looked to be a weapon of some sort in one of his hands. He was raising his arm up slowly and very steadily.

Too steadily.

What was I really seeing? I didn't know. And there wasn't time to step forward and check it out more thoroughly. But the movements were too precise, too mechanical, so unhuman. Behind me Spence and Escobar were shouting, both to each other and to me, as we all tried to understand just what it was that we were confronting.

By the books, by the books, play it by the books— it was the prime directive in all of our operations. So I screamed, *"Police, drop your weapon,"* hoping against all logic that it would work as intended. But the arm kept rising.

I hated what the book told me to do next, but I had

no choice. I trained my weapon directly on Durand and pulled the trigger. Twice.

There was smoke and debris flying everywhere in the enclosed space. But it was all wrong, just wrong—no blood, no gray matter, just a shower of sparkling shards. The arm stopped going up, but instead of dropping down as it should have when his head went *kaplowee,* it stayed where it was, right in mid-raise, at about a forty-five-degree angle. Stuck.

When the echoes of gunfire finally stopped, I heard only two sounds: the rush of my own heartbeat, and a soft electronic whir, as if a machine were stuck in a small motion and could not move on to its next task.

I could no longer sustain the weight of the heavy gun; my hand dropped to my side, and I came out of my crouch. As I moved slowly toward the remains of my shooting victim, my feet crunched on bits of shattered plastic. I could smell singed vinyl along with the gunpowder.

"Jesus," I said, when my hand came to rest on the being's shoulder.

I had just killed an Animatronic Wilbur Durand. So I ran over to Jeff—at least what I thought was Jeff, but it was just a mannequin that looked like him. A mannequin with its guts pulled out.

I wasn't prepared for what it would do to me to see that. Everything, and I mean everything, got crisp and clear. It was so real-looking, so perfect. There was pain on his face and he was grimacing horribly. Spence rushed past me. I don't think I ever heard him swear like that before.

"Great shot," he said. "Now let's go get the real guy."

thirty-three

DO YOU INTEND TO GIVE, *propose, allege, say, or produce any justification for these crimes, some motivation through which we might better understand these offenses?*

I know not what to say, your Grace, other than what I have already said.

Once again, the court was adjourned because forward progress could not be made without some agreement from Gilles. With a loud bang of the gavel, Jean de Malestroit set the following day, that being Thursday, October 20, for court to reconvene, and then summarily dismissed the lot of us.

And then he disappeared into his private lair, without another word.

It was well into the evening before he called for his barely touched supper tray to be removed. I found him in a state of obvious distraction. I let a moment pass before speaking. "I understand that your contemplations today must have been torturous. But mind your health. If you do not eat, your stamina will surely wane. And I daresay you could use a bit more rest. Perhaps an early retirement tonight ..."

"Not for some time, I fear. There is more yet to be done. I must still get with Friar Blouyn before we meet with the others."

Were yet more players to be introduced to this crowded joust? "I do not understand. What others?"

He hemmed and hedged for a moment. "Experts," he finally said.

"What sort of experts?"

"In the art of interrogation."

Now I understood the ad nauseam declarations of Inquisitional mandate of previous sessions. They would take care to make this torture legal.

And exquisite.

The finger is to be placed in the device, your Eminence, and then the crank must be twisted. Small motions at first, to give him a taste of the pain, and then more-exaggerated turns should be made. When the bone pops out of the joint, he will speak, unless he is the devil himself. And if he fails to speak, you may take it as a sure sign of his congress with the Dark One.

For this advice, the expert would be paid handsomely. That there should be profit in maiming seemed a terrible thing to me.

"But ... torture ..."

"Has he not engaged in torture of the most vicious kind? On children?"

I could not speak.

"It will be done only if he refuses to admit to what has been proven by the statements of the witnesses. He has sworn to tell nothing but the truth, sworn before God, and yet he insists that he did not do these things. I have no choice, Sister; I must bring it out of him in this way. God must be satisfied in this."

God must always be satisfied.

Long before the cock crowed, my eyes came open. The first thing I saw was Madame le Barbier's dress, which hung on the door like the remnants of some crucifixion, begging to be worn.

I had made up my mind to tell Milord Gilles of his impending torture. Perhaps once he had been a hero, a warrior who could withstand all manner of pain and difficulty for the sake of his cause, but his only cause now was self-perpetuation, hardly noble in view of the vile acts to which he had admitted. He had grown soft and vulnerable, and I hoped that the threat of exquisite pain would bring him to his senses and that he would confess as Jean de Malestroit required of him. It was time for this terrible business to come to an end, for all of our sakes. I whispered only one prayer that morning, beseeching God to sway Milord's heart and spare us the travesty of participating in his downfall.

The dress slipped over my shoulders like a caress. I pulled on my cloak and veil and hurried out into the courtyard. I encountered no one on my silent walk through the passageways to the upper rooms where Gilles de Rais awaited his fate in sumptuous luxury. The first among the sentries, who had acted the gatekeeper on my previous visit, was caught off guard by my arrival, for he began to bare his blade until he realized that the footsteps he had heard were mine.

He shrugged apologetically. "*Je regret*, Madame. But one is ordered to be extra cautious. There are plots afoot to kill Milord, and everyone is suspect."

Then he escorted me through the retinue of other guards, none of whom paid us any notice at all. At the entry to Milord's rooms, he left me alone, without announcement.

"Captain, should you not awaken him?"

"Not necessary, Madame. He barely sleeps."

And, indeed, it was only a few seconds after the guard's departure and my own hasty removal of the veil and cloak that Gilles de Rais appeared in the salon. He did not notice my presence at the periphery. It had been my intention to call out to him, to speak to him of what lay ahead, to try to convince him that it would be best for all if he would simply utter the truth as Jean de Malestroit wished him to speak it.

But in my heart I encountered a coldness that I had never known before. Perhaps it was because Gilles had finally assumed the appearance of something foul; he was disheveled and unkempt, with wild hair and an animal savagery to his movements. Gone was the great lord, the hero, who had been replaced by some dark and vulgar beast.

Gone was the child I remembered.

And gone, too, at long last, was the sympathetic nurse. Without a word, I turned and slipped quietly away.

My return through the courtyard was hasty and I arrived breathless, to be greeted immediately by one of the younger nuns, who seemed quite agitated.

"Sister, calm yourself," I said. "Is there a problem about which I should be advised?"

"Not precisely a problem, *Mère,* but you are required by his Eminence immediately."

So my absence had been noted. "How long ago was his message received?"

"There was no message, *Mère,*" she said timidly.

"Then how do you know that I am required?"

"Because he came himself," she answered. "He left here not ten minutes ago, distressed that you could not be found."

✢

I knocked timorously on the wood panel of his door, which was thrown open almost immediately.

"Well," he sputtered, "here you are, at last!"

"Eminence, forgive me. I did not think that you would require me so early this morning, what with all of your considerations today...."

"Early? Matins awaits us. Where were you when you ought to have been in your room?"

There was nothing I could do but lie and hope that none of his spies had been watching the encampments. "I went out among the gathered; there is much activity so early and I was quite safe."

"And did what, precisely?"

"I walked," I said. "It soothes me sometimes."

"It soothes *me* to know that you are available. And safe. Please, Guillemette, take care not to put yourself in harm's way. This crowd can be quite volatile, as we have seen."

I looked down at the floor. "I shall endeavor to be more cautious."

"Good." I could feel the undercurrent of agitation in his voice, but I did not think he suspected me of lying. Something else entirely was causing his agitation.

"Matins," he said again. "Let us be off."

I followed him meekly to the private chapel; the main church would be filled to capacity with people from the encampments, all wishing to avail themselves of the holiness they believed could be found in the impressive sanctuary. In quiet seclusion, we relieved ourselves of dream-sins through the *kyrie* and were sufficiently cleansed that new sins could be added during that day without fear of crippling the soul. I whispered a special prayer to be shriven of the deception I had committed in the dark hours before dawn, then gathered my skirts and slipped out of the pew.

I stopped in the middle of the aisle as usual and crossed myself before the statue of the Virgin. *Dear Mary, Mother of God,* I prayed silently, *grant that Gilles will be spared the cruelty of torture, and grant that this burdensome trial will soon be over, so that I may see my son.*

I turned and started toward the rear of the chapel. An unfamiliar brother stood between myself and the door. The earliest rays of the sun outlined his tall body. There was something about the silhouette that stirred recognition. I squinted in the pale light, but could not see.

"Mother," I heard the tall stranger say.

Many people call me mother. But the voice, that voice . . .

Mother, I heard again. My heart leaped into my throat.

"Jean?" I whispered.

"Oui, Maman, c'est moi."

♔

I clung to him with all my might, squeezing him to me with such vigor and desperation that I was afraid I might hurt him.

"His Eminence did not tell you?"

I turned around and saw Jean de Malestroit, who had observed the reunion from a distance.

"Wait here," I said. I hurried to the front of the chapel. Jean de Malestroit turned back to the altar and tried to make himself appear busy.

"You might have said something of this," I accused.

He wore a satisfied smile. "I had planned to do so earlier this morning. But you deprived me of the pleasure," he said.

"Hence your upset at not finding me?"

"In part. The rest was genuine concern. Now, as to your son, when his Holiness wrote and requested that the proposed discussions be moved here so as to take place in a timely manner, I specifically requested that Jean be sent among the emissaries. And I did not tell you of the change in plans because I did not want you to be disappointed should it not come about." He paused for a moment to take in my reaction. "I hoped it would please you."

How could I deceive a man who had done something so wonderful for me? Guilt flooded through me, and for the briefest moment I considered telling him of what I had thought to do this morning.

But nothing would come of it, except to foster distrust. "Thank you, Brother," I said with a bow. "I am deeply grateful that you have done this for me."

He smiled almost mischievously.

☙

My bishop relieved me of any attendance upon him, in order that I might devote myself entirely to absorbing the presence of my own dear child before court was called, in less than two hours.

There was so much to speak of—his position, the journey, his health and spirit—but when at last we had exhausted our embraces, all that *Frère* Jean la Drappiere wanted to discuss was the trial and the events that had precipitated it; I spent the better part of an hour explaining the things he wanted to know, based on the letters I had sent him.

As my story progressed, he became steadily more contemplative. "Mother," he said quietly when I finished, "you should have told me of these suspicions as soon as they surfaced in your heart."

"Why?" I said. "What could you have done?"

"If nothing else, I could have been a comfort to you in your distress."

"From Avignon?"

"I take great solace in your letters, as I hope you do in mine."

I had offended him. "Of course I do, my dearest; I anticipate them eagerly and devour them when they come. You need only ask his Eminence." I reached into my pocket and pulled out the last one he had sent. "Here," I said. "See how tattered it is. From so many readings. I memorize them, to absorb all your secrets and intimacies."

He smiled and put an arm around my shoulder. But shortly the smile faded and was replaced by a look of distress. "*Mère,* I have a confession of my own to make."

Rarely had I seen such a look of anguish on his face.

"I never spoke of this when Michel died," he said, "but I must tell you now that I had unholy thoughts at the time."

"Unholy? I do not understand."

"I suspected someone of the crime, someone I should not have considered in that manner."

"Jean—who?"

"Milord Gilles."

My own voice was barely audible, even to myself. "Is there something you know of those events that you have not revealed?"

"Nothing of a specific nature. But there was a jarring quality in the way he comported himself afterward—I saw too much glee in him."

"Glee? He was *glad* of Michel's death?"

"I believed he was, yes."

It was precisely what I had heard from Marcel. "And now it is my turn to ask you why you never spoke of *your* suspicions."

"*Maman,* I was but a boy at the time."

"Thirteen," I countered. "Almost a man. Already committed to studying for your vocation."

There was a look that resembled shame on his face, but not pure shame—some part of it was frustration. "I had not the courage to speak against him. And there was no great love between us—even less after the incident with Michel. We did not speak unless it was absolutely necessary."

"But there were many times when you were friendly with each other, even around the time of Michel's disappearance."

"It was mostly for your benefit, Mère. A ruse, by silent agreement between us. There was no substance to our comradeship other than that which was forced upon us. There came a kind of hatred by the time our paths diverged. I have often wondered if Milord made such sweet arrangements for me in Avignon in order to purchase my silence on the matter. Or because he felt guilt."

I sat back, stunned. "He does not know guilt," I said. "Or at least, he did not, until recently."

He squinted suspiciously. "How do you come by knowledge of what he does or does not feel these days?"

"I spoke with him. I sent word of that to you in a letter, some days ago."

"Its journey must have crossed mine, then. I did not receive it."

The bench was too confining; I rose up and paced around. "I went to see him several nights ago in the suite where he is quartered. Right here in the palace. But you must not tell anyone, Jean," I said in near desperation. "Especially you must not say anything to his Eminence."

By his expression, I could see that it did not please him to agree. But he did, with a nod. "He must have been furious over the role you played in his downfall."

"He does not know, nor shall he. I have given the

responsibility over to the Bishop, and he has made it appear that he brought it about."

"It seems unlikely to me that Jean de Malestroit would allow himself to be caught up in this."

"It is not to my benefit that he does so, but at the bidding of Duke Jean, who would keep his hands clean of the matter." I paced anew. "It would not shock me to know that the two have made a pact with God Himself concerning the outcome of this matter. But regarding the matter of Michel—I am confused by what you are telling me. On my first visit to Milord I confronted him about many things, especially the child killings, and after he admitted to me that he had indeed done them, I revealed my suspicions regarding his part in Michel's death. He had no guard up, but denied any part in it, with great sincerity. He claims that he would never have harmed a hair on Michel's head, that he loved him as a brother."

"There are always unspoken things between mothers and sons, *Mère*. Lies, even. And for that reason, I would suspect some untruth in what Milord Gilles might have told you."

"He is doing a very good job of lying. I watched his every move as a child, and I assure you that I know when he is being genuine and when he is not."

As he rose from the bench to come to my side, his brown robes rustled. The tasseled belt that held the cloth close to his body brushed the ground, leaving a clean trail in the dust. He shook the end of it briefly before speaking. "I must confess that I would like to see Milord myself. I am curious to see what has become of him since we were young men."

"You are a young man *now*."

"*Mère,* I am thirty and seven."

"As I said, you are young."

I walked beside my tall, handsome son, whose unanticipated presence was like an elixir to my blood. Madame Catherine Karle could not have given me a more potent potion to renew the spirit and refresh the soul. But I could not help but notice: His youth was indeed slipping away from him. There were more than a few white hairs at his temples, though the tonsured style did well to disguise it. There was the slightest paunch where once his belly had been taut and flat. He would, one day soon, be elevated to the position of Monsignor, and an even stiffer dignity would be forced upon him. Though he claimed his life with God was joyful, it was a subdued joy. It broke my heart to know that he would never experience some of the happiness that he ought to have had, if he had gone out into the world as most first sons do. I could not help but wonder if he had ever known a woman in bed. His assertion that boys do not reveal such matters to their mothers had set me thinking—what did I *not* know about this man, who sprang from my own belly and was nourished at my breast and in my heart? What manly secrets did he bear in his soul? Had he ever drunk himself into a complete stupor, thereafter to belch and fart around some campfire, roaring with laughter at every inane bit of humor offered by one of his fellows, then to pass out draped over a log and wake up aching and bearded? His father had done so, even after we were married and I was ripe with Jean himself. I would berate him when he came home in such condition, but Etienne always spoke with great affection of those times, for he loved the carefree mood and the camaraderie. Jean had companions, I believe, more like *Frère* Demien—a thoughtful gardener with a wry wit, but no notion of adventure. Jean's one true brother was long gone, and his milk brother had turned into something that none of us could fathom.

We climbed the few steps to the lower hall of la Tour Neuve together and passed among those waiting to be admitted to court. Now and then I would lean toward an acquaintance, be it sister or brother, to whisper, *My son,* whereafter I received many an *ahhh* of approval from these good souls. Jean did not seem to mind being displayed for appreciation.

But he stopped abruptly and stood still at the end of the corridor, and I with him, for around the corner from another direction came Milord Gilles, who by accident of his birth had tasted every pleasure that life offered, including the share that ought to have gone to Jean. He was flanked all around by guards in tight formation, who managed to look as if they were there as an honor, not as the movable prison they truly were. As the accused passed by, he cast glances at those who lined his route; we were plenty in number and diverse in station, but all of us remained equally silent and still. From face to face his eyes traveled, never lingering for more than a second or two. He looked directly into my eyes, and then into my son's, but betrayed no emotion or recognition.

The noisome aggrieved were there, and the fascinated nobility. Diplomats and dignitaries sat shoulder to shoulder with those who had cobbled their shoes and churned their butter, for here all were equally enthralled by the sordid revelations each day brought, may God have mercy on our weak souls. Before us stood the accused Gilles de Rais, who must have conferred with the devil in the time since I had left his presence, for he had been transformed from dishevelment to a state of renewed glory and power and now appeared ready to take on his accusers with uncanny vigor.

Jean de Malestroit and Vice-Inquisitor Blouyn whispered intently back and forth in the midst of all this confusion. It seemed only a few moments until his Eminence commanded the attention of the gathered with his gavel. He stood and looked over Gilles into the crowd as he spoke. "Tomorrow we shall commence at the hour of

Terce, in order to hear whatever objections, defenses, mitigations, or any other words that the accused might wish to speak on his own behalf. The court notes that Baron Gilles de Rais, said accused, continues to indicate his unwillingness to do so."

The scribes began scribbling. Confused murmurs filled the air—was this to be the total of the day's events? It seemed impossible.

And then Jean de Malestroit turned his attention directly to Milord Gilles. "We have decided, Milord, after profound consideration, both legal and spiritual, that even though we have fixed tomorrow as a day on which you might speak your piece to this court, we shall proceed immediately with a course of torture."

A collective gasp rose up from the crowd. The gavel came down again and again on the board. When the clamor was finally suppressed, Milord was left standing alone in the midst of the observers. His lips worked silently, as if he were attempting to absorb the meaning of what had just been said. He might have been saying to himself, *Torture, I am to be tortured.*

He ought not to have been surprised.

My fingers gripped Jean's arm. "He is no longer lucid," I said gravely. "He makes no objection."

The crowd had noticed the uncharacteristic response as well and began to buzz again. His Eminence was once again forced to raise his voice to be heard. "The court shall be cleared in preparation thereof."

The cries of objection were swift and sharp, though one could not say whether to the torture itself or the proposed decent privacy while it was enacted. As soon as the order was given, Milord's guards surrounded him in tight formation. Another group of guards moved from the sides of the room and began to herd out the court observers, myself and my son included.

I stood my ground, depending on the robes of my

station to work their magic for me, and with my grown son in tow, maneuvered into a position where I would be among the last to leave the room. At the judges' table, Jean de Malestroit was already busy again with parchments and scribes and Friar Blouyn. Milord Gilles had been escorted out by his guards but was now being brought in again, looking pale and shaken.

Not a heartbeat later, two very large, stone-faced men entered through a side door, each bearing a satchel. As they set their burdens down, the unseen contents clanked with loud and definite menace; one imagined metal instruments, sharp and exact, with which exquisite pain might be inflicted, all in the name of God the Father Almighty, who required His believers to speak the entire truth to His representatives on earth, which heretofore had not been done by the accused.

Gilles de Rais heard the clank of their falling. His eyes went directly to the two behemoths who had carried them in. He stared in plain horror but received back only cool, narrow-eyed gazes of indifference. He would not need a conjurer to explain that his days as a withholder of truth were numbered. In that moment, I saw the physical breakdown of his resolve—the anger went out of his expression, and the defiance left his stance.

None of this was lost on Jean de Malestroit, who would wield the sword of justice with swift and exacting strokes. Accused and judge were locked in a stare, each measuring the other. It was Milord Gilles who first fell short of the required will, while Jean de Malestroit still possessed it in abundance.

We were the last two in the court, other than the players themselves; Jean and I hid ourselves as best we could behind a tall column and tried to become invisible. We saw Milord Gilles go down on his knees, his hands clasped together in near desperation. "Milord Bishop," he begged, "postpone this torture until tomorrow, which is the appointed time as already arranged. Please, I implore you to allow me this night to think on the matter of the crimes and accusations brought against me. I will satisfy you on the morrow to the extent that it will not be necessary to apply the intended torture to me."

As if Milord had not spoken at all, his Eminence said quietly, "We shall proceed."

"Please, honorable judges, I humbly beseech you to give this matter more thought before proceeding. And further, I implore you to allow the Bishop of Saint-Brieuc and the honorable *Monsieur le President* to take the place of my current judges in hearing my confession, for the sake of fairness."

"I assure you, Milord, your current judges are fair in excess," the Bishop replied.

"Then for the love of God, if you will, please allow the change to take place."

Jean de Malestroit sat statuelike at the table, his face locked in a stern but undecipherable expression. I wondered if he was disappointed that Gilles seemed willing to confess his crimes but not to him; he would be robbed of the pleasure, albeit a shameful one, of hearing Gilles de Rais admit to offenses against God and man that would demand his death.

That death, no matter how cruel, would not be sufficient reparation for the monstrous things he had done. But no one would deny that it was nevertheless right and fitting.

In every one of us, there is an uncanny will to take one more breath, to feel one more heartbeat, taste one more morsel, watch one more bird fly across the blue sky. So, too, did Gilles de Rais, murderer, sodomite, thief of souls, parlayer with dark spirits, want to see one more sunrise. He would do that, most certainly, but beyond one day there was no surety. He knew it as well as any of us.

"Milords, please, grant this, the wish of a man who will soon give up his soul."

Said in those plaintive words, the request could hardly be refused. On Jean de Malestroit's face there was a look of disappointment, of having been robbed of a forbidden pleasure. "Very well," I heard him say. "It shall be so."

He turned to the scribes and said, "Make note. I appoint the Bishop of Saint-Brieuc and *Monsieur le Président* Pierre l'Hôpital to act as judge and Vicar of the Inquisitor in the stead of myself and Friar Blouyn."

The gentlemen in question were present, as they had been called to witness the torture. Now they would be parties instead to the confession. They stood together to signal their readiness.

"The court gives these honorable men its thanks for this effort," Jean de Malestroit said, nodding in their direction. Then he turned to the scribes and said, "One and several public instruments shall be made of these proceedings, and duly posted."

Gilles slumped back in his seat, trembling visibly. *"Merci, merci bien,"* he said, his voice shaky and weak. "I am deeply grateful."

As if he had not heard him, Jean de Malestroit faced the accused and said, "Gilles de Rais, knight, Baron of Brittany, you shall be escorted to your rooms in the upper part of this castle in order that your confessions might be heard on the aforesaid matters and articles, to which you have not yet fully responded. Such confessions shall commence before the hour of two; if said confessions have not commenced by then, the torture as decided shall be applied." He cast a quick glance of disappointment at the two rough-looking experts, whose faces betrayed no emotion whatsoever.

"And now, without further delay, we shall proceed."

chapter 34

IT TOOK US SIX SCREAMING MINUTES to reach the studio. Ellen Leeds's comments about delay echoed in my ears because each second that passed represented another spurt of blood from one of Jeff's veins or arteries. The wave of units that had followed us from the house converged on the parking lot just as we were getting out of our vehicle. Car doors were flung open, in the shelter of which a platoon of cops positioned themselves.

There was already a line of yellow tape around the perimeter to keep the press out of our way, and out of harm's way. A news chopper overhead made it nearly impossible to hear anything; what might the noise be doing to the already crazed and unbalanced Wilbur Durand?

The frustration was agonizing. "If he doesn't get out of here, I'm going to bring him down," I blurted.

Escobar was at my side in a flash. "Look who it would land on," he shouted.

A slew of cops.

Debris and dust were flying everywhere. I looked all

around, in slow motion. A uniformed officer was down about thirty feet inside the line.

"Oh, sweet Jesus, look at that. . . ."

He lay on his stomach in a spreading pool of his own blood. One arm was outstretched and twitching. His gun lay about three feet from the clutching fingers, which grasped futilely in that direction. A crouching EMT worked his way under the line and tried to advance toward the prone cop, but before he'd gone ten feet, a shot ricocheted off the pavement only a few inches away from him. Every time a different EMT or cop tried to get there, the same would happen. But they were never hit, just warned off.

"He has to be trying to miss," Spence said from behind the open door of our unit.

Once again, an EMT crouched downward and set out toward the prone cop. This time the shot was fired directly at the equipment mounted on top of one of the news vans. Metal shards splattered all over the place, hitting people within close proximity. Everyone ran for deeper cover.

"Well, I guess we know he's not a bad shot," I said.

It was a dream, a nightmare, a mindscape—there was no sense of reality. But logic broke through the madness, and a stunning realization came to me.

I rose up slowly and holstered my gun in plain sight, then approached the yellow tape.

Spence reached out and tried to grab me, but I was already beyond his grasp. I heard Escobar calling my name, telling me to get down. Calmly, I turned and said, "He's not going to shoot me. He's trying to draw me out."

In unison, they shouted their protests. I made out the words *nuts* and *crazy* and the phrase *sure about that*. Still calm, I answered their concerns. "He wants me to come inside. He's not going to shoot me before I do that."

Step by step I approached my fallen comrade. When I reached him I rolled him over onto his side; he gave me what help he could by shoving himself upward with one hand.

"What about your back and neck?" I screamed over the chopper blades.

"Okay," he said.

"Then I'm going to drag you out of here. Help if you can, but I can do it without your help if you can't."

He smiled weakly and nodded. I rolled him fully onto his back and grabbed hold of him under the arms. I grunted and pulled, he groaned and shoved with his feet. A trail of blood marked the path of our excruciating crawl to the yellow line. When we were within a few feet, I let go and rushed around to place myself between him and the studio building. Two other cops and two EMTs came out; together they lifted the bleeding young man into the dark safety of the shadows. In a matter of only a few seconds the ambulance flashed off in a haze of red.

Spence and Escobar were all over me. "What the hell are you thinking don't you ever pull a stunt like that again they'll yank your shield for this...."

But they were wrong, and I knew it. I was a free woman, at long last. My biggest professional danger now was that I might be late for the parade they would hold in my honor. I had bought my professional liberty with an act of valor that was probably being broadcast live throughout the world.

A profound sense of lightness accompanied the understanding that this one moment would define the rest of my life, if there happened to be a rest of my life. I thought about my children; how they would do without me, if it should come to that. They had aunts, grandmothers, cousins who would step in and care for them, and an adoring father.

Jeff's father, I realized, had not yet been told of this. I hoped he was still at the division, insulated from this.

I looked at Spence. Confusion, worry, and agonized

concern were all over his face. He had never seen me behave like this before. It must have surprised him to hear
me say, "Have someone call Jeff's father and get him
nearby. Not here; he'll be too much of a distraction. But
he should be available when we bring Jeff out."

"Why don't you go back and get him, Lany? We'll
take care of this from here."

I gave my comrade a sad but grateful smile. "Nice
try," I said. "This is my show, and you know it."

"Lany, don't. Please don't."

I stepped forward into the open, floodlit parking area
that surrounded the studio of Angel Films. I paralleled the
blood smear as I approached the building. As I stepped inside the door, I looked back briefly; Spence and Escobar
were heading in my direction by the same route. Two shots
rang out; neither hit. Soon they were by my side inside the
reception area.

"Did you send someone like I asked?" It was all I
could think to say.

"Yeah," Spence said. His voice was barely audible.

"Thanks." I patted him on the shoulder. I smiled at
Escobar. "You guys are the best."

For three seconds we sniffed and wiped.

"Okay, let's go do God's work."

The door into the main studio area was open just
enough for us to see that it wasn't secured—I guess Durand
thought it would be easier for us just to simply walk in
there instead of having to shoot the lock out. That's really
a movie thing, anyway—if you shoot out a lock in real life,
you end up in a bloody mess of metal shards and splinters,
and more often than not the lock holds anyway.

The reception area was deserted, but there was
one small lamp glowing on one of the desks; it gave off
just enough light for us to make our way across the room

without tripping on anything. There were boxes all over the floor, as if it were moving day. We worked our way to the main door and stood on either side of it to listen for a moment. The sirens, radios, and chopper blades could barely be heard in here because of the sound-stage insulation. I put my ear against the wall, which my comrades repeated in kind. We all listened intently.

I heard thin whimpering—maybe Jeff. And then that girlish voice of Durand's: *Quiet, Evan, your mother will be here any second now to save you, so there's nothing to be afraid of. Everything will all be over soon.*

He'd said Evan. Not Jeff. But how would he know, unless he'd specifically seen me with him? When they went to the exhibit, both Kevin and Jeff's father were there, and everyone had clowned with everyone else. How could he have known?

"Very sloppy, Wilbur," I whispered.

I lost my religion a long time ago, but I prayed more sincerely than I ever have in my life. Not for this to be over, not for this never to have happened, both of which would have been considered reasonable pleas by even the cruelest and most jealous god. Not for absolution from my sins or for another chance to be the perfect cop; there wasn't enough time for either of those wishes to be fulfilled.

I prayed instead for aim, for the missiles that barreled out of the nose of my gun to hit Wilbur Durand in the heart and the forehead and the kidney and the liver until his light went out forever. I filled my lungs with air, then signaled to Spence and Escobar that I was going in.

Again I kicked the open door aside: I wanted both hands on the gun. There was a large wood crate just inside the door; I stepped into its lee and took a quick look around. The lights were incredibly bright and it took my eyes a minute to focus after the low light in the outer area—no doubt part of Durand's plan.

When my vision finally adjusted, I thought I was seeing triple: Three Jeffs were tied up, each to individual posts on the other side of the room in a sort of semicircle. All three had blood on their bellies with protruding entrails—dear God, entrails. I couldn't tell if it was real or fake.

And I couldn't tell which one of the boys was really Jeff. With Evan, I would have known. But this was not Evan, despite what Wilbur believed.

Wilbur Durand stood opposite the three, behind a camera. He was almost laughing. He saw my confusion and said, "I did pretty well, didn't I, Detective Dunbar."

I ignored him and tried to listen to the boys' moans, thinking that maybe the voice would give the real one away. But without the familiar cadence of his words, it was impossible. As I listened, I began to hear the sounds of more people arriving inside the building.

"Stay out," I yelled back. "Don't interfere."

"Good call," Durand said. That nasty little voice of his made me cringe. It sounded as though he had electronically altered it for the occasion.

"Did you like the little exhibit I left for you at my home, Detective?"

"I didn't stay long enough to take a real good look at it."

"Pity. It was a nice piece of work, if I do say so myself. One of my better efforts."

"I guess. You had me fooled for a minute. Had a lot of us fooled. Nice touch with the houseboy, by the way."

"Thank you."

"But, like I said, I didn't stay long."

He gave me the most evil smile. "I didn't think you would. Not with the main event happening here."

I had to keep him distracted. If I did, Spence or Escobar might be able to figure something out. He wasn't going to tangle with either of them; I was his quarry. I looked in the direction of the three boys again. Their

Animatronic movements didn't seem mechanical at all; they all looked alive.

And then I realized that they *were* all alive! The bastard—he'd hired actors!

But I could use that; real people can be *really* frightened. "If he told you this was a film scene," I shouted, "he was lying. These are real guns, we are real cops, and he is going to pull the guts out of all of you before he finishes."

Two of them raised up their heads; with frightened eyes, they regarded each other's bellies and the glistening protrusions that draped forward. I held up my badge—stupidly, because they were probably told to expect that. Then I fired my weapon up into the ceiling; the light fixtures shattered, sending down a shower of glass.

At that point, the two on the right began to struggle against their restraints.

"He's the one on the far left," I called back.

He alone was completely still.

I looked back at Durand and saw on his face the realization that he'd been finessed, that it was time to whip out the trump card. I saw his arm coming up again and the gun was pointed right at Jeff. The motion was smooth and real and utterly believable. In his hand was some sort of automatic weapon—if he just sprayed it he would get all three of his targets. If he swept it around the room, he'd get me, Spence, and Escobar as well.

Spence stood suddenly with his gun drawn and shouted, "Over here!" Durand reacted without thinking; his arm swung around and came to an abrupt halt with the gun trained directly on Spence. By then I was on my feet as well, shouting, *Freeze, police, drop your weapon now,* but only because it's legally required for the shoot to be labeled clean. It was a moot exercise; I fully intended to shoot him whether he froze or not.

I factored in all these considerations in a split second—but Wil Durand didn't have that kind of training. He might have worked with a weapon, but he hadn't learned to live with one as we all do. He had never awakened in the middle of the night and reached for the gun under the pillow when some alley cat knocked over a trash can. He bore no bruises on his hip from where the holster sat. He didn't tilt to the left because the weight of the gun on the right made him so unbalanced. Not to mention the radio, the pager, the badge, and the stick. He would never be one with the gun.

He started screaming to get back, and when Spence and I kept advancing, he raised himself up a little on the camera seat. The camera itself had sheltered him, and it was still big and bulky enough to keep any of us from getting a decent shot.

This would be our best chance to get him. Instinctively I went into a modified Weaver stance, with both hands on the gun and feet shoulder distance apart. I set one foot slightly in front of the other, so my profile shifted and I made a narrower target, which our training sergeants keep telling us is harder to hit.

I was a sitting duck, Weaver or no Weaver. I saw a series of flashes from the muzzle of his automatic before I heard the sound of the shots; this all happened just after I squeezed the trigger of my weapon and hit nothing.

"His shots went wide, wide to the left," Escobar screamed from somewhere behind me. I got off another round that ricocheted against something on the corner of the enormous camera, but I saw Durand wince and grab his shoulder, so I knew he must have been wounded, probably by shrapnel from the camera.

It didn't stop him—he brought the gun up again and pointed it in the direction of the boys. There was that horrible *rat-a-tat-tat,* and then shots from behind and to the right.

Durand's gun went flying across the room. Blood began to spray from his arm. I pulled the trigger on my own weapon and hit Durand again in the same arm. And that was it—the shooting stopped.

Spence rushed toward Durand, and Escobar dashed forward toward the boys as I sank to my knees. I had barely eaten in days, but what little I had eaten came back in the form of a green and bitter-tasting bile. Somehow I managed to find and speak into my radio. Then I staggered to my feet and ran to Jeff.

He was looking up at me with such terror in his eyes, but he was alive, oh, Lord, he was alive still, and there was hope that we could get out of there.

I heard myself asking him if he was okay and then saw him shake his head weakly to indicate that he was not. I was still struggling to get the gag off him when we were surrounded by a swarm of EMTs with their equipment and carts and unfathomable competence. They moved right in and pushed me away. I wasn't a cop just then, I was an intimate of the victim—typically a mild to moderate pain in the ass, but in this case a true menace who could do nothing but get in the way of their lifesaving work.

Spence and Escobar literally lifted me up by the armpits and carried me out of the way.

I stood back, helpless, as they worked on the boy who'd eaten Spaghetti-O's at my dining-room table. It was quickly established that Jeff was the only one of the three boys who had truly been injured. But both of the other two were in shock. One started to rise up; from somewhere behind I heard Fred's voice.

"Don't move!" he was yelling. "We need to clear our officers of any wrongdoing in their shots. You *do* want to cooperate with that effort."

The kid obeyed without question.

Lights flashed in rapid repetition. The clicking of shutters began to rival the sound of chopper blades in my head. I watched out of the corner of one eye as Jeff was gently rolled onto a stretcher, with tubes attached seemingly all over his body. He looked small, young, and terribly vulnerable. The scene swirled around me; I felt a hand on my shoulder. I turned around and saw Errol Erkinnen standing there.

"How did you—"

"It's all over the news," he said. "Your lieutenant let me through when I showed up."

I could feel my shoulders slumping as the exhaustion set in. Somehow his presence made it okay for me to break down. "Oh, God, what a mess ... what a mess I made of this...."

"You don't have to say anything," he said. "You don't have to justify anything right now. I'll stay with you until you feel safe enough to be alone."

This detached, professional assurance had roughly the same effect on me as being cradled in my mother's embrace. I gave myself into his supporting arms for one brief moment and just trembled. And then I pulled away; there was a scene to attend to, my crime scene, and I did not want to let it get away from me.

The whirlwind of activity brought me the strength I needed to plunge back in. As I was demonstrating the views I wanted to the photographer, one of the EMTs came and told me that they were almost ready to take Jeff to the hospital.

The question I didn't really want answered came out of its own free will.

"Too soon to tell." The standard, safe answer. Then he was gone.

I glanced around briefly at the chaotic crime scene, wondering how this one had gotten so out of my control. In the end, it wouldn't matter; there was no "solving" required. We knew what had happened and who had made it happen.

From out of the corner of one eye I saw them securing Jeff's intestines to his abdomen. They wrapped the protrusions in plastic and then strapped everything down.

Incredibly, I found myself thinking, *It's not that much, just a couple of feet, he has lots of feet of intestines, he can spare a couple of feet* . . .

Hope is such a strong force.

I couldn't watch anymore. I went over to where they were working on Durand and observed from a little distance. Dozens of eyes were on me, waiting to pounce if I did something stupid. But I kept my distance, the whole time pleading with the cosmos to let Durand die. I wanted someone to come up with the idea that they should quietly stop treating him so he would just bleed out on the spot. His right arm was literally blown off, and he was still struggling. He was screaming like that bastard Scorpio in *Dirty Harry* that he was hurt, that he needed to be taken care of, and that someone had better do it, because the horrible, violent police had *hurt* him. When he saw I was looking at him he actually grinned up at me and made this disgusting flickering motion with his tongue.

I leaped. Ten hands grabbed me. Durand was laughing and howling and screaming all at the same time. I struggled against my captors, but they held me fast.

"Let go of me," I screamed. "I'm going to kill him, I'm going to blow him away, I'm going—"

Durand howled even louder. "She's threatening me, she's going to hurt me even more—"

Someone finally found the switch for the overheads and threw them all at once. The glare stunned me into submission. Suddenly I felt myself being tossed into the backseat of a cruiser. Erkinnen got in beside me. I heard the click of a belt, the thrum of a starting engine, and then I went under, into some fuzzy place where nothing evil existed, where nothing bad could happen to a child. They would have to mop up this scene without me.

The monstrous Wilbur Durand was secured to a gurney with multiple restraints and transported to the hospital under double guard. Detectives Frazee and Escobar rode along. I would have to read it all later in the report, but I could imagine it in my mind's eye. Spence would be in Durand's face, just a few inches away, and he would be hissing, *You have a right to remain silent, asshole, but you can talk now if you want to, I don't care, because I'm going to nail your one-armed ass to the wall no matter what you do.* Escobar would pretend to try to pull him off, and they would engage in a limited good-cop bad-cop routine, the theory being that if anyone could get something out of Durand, it would be the Father Confessor.

And then at the hospital, they'd take him away from us, because the doctors would want to restrict contact for medical reasons, and then of course Sheila Carmichael would show up with a never-ending list of reasons why we couldn't ask him any more questions. Though he had bled profusely, his vital signs had been brought under control and he was receiving fluids, so Durand was judged not to be in immediate danger of dying from his wound, though his backhand would probably never be the same again, not that it mattered. There are no tennis courts in prison—probably not in hell either.

He was, according to all those in the ambulance, quite lucid during the ride and responded to Frazee's threats with crisp, vulgar invective. There was no longer any need for him to hide the beast that dwelled within him. All disguises were off; he was the naked, nasty Wilbur Durand, who enjoyed his last moments of freedom with abandon, expounding in great detail on the pleasures of pedophilic sodomy and the thrill of evisceration.

Frazee couldn't wait to tell me about it. "Durand was screaming and shouting about how his sister was going to get him out and then he was going to find every one of our kids and pull the guts out of them, and then—God. I can't even repeat the things he was saying he would do to them. Just being in his presence made me feel sick."

And then he told me about the "incident," one that would become part of the internal lore of our division. "The second we got out of the ambulance, one of the patrols let loose on Durand with his fists."

I was so happy to hear that.

"But there were two of them. We can't remember which one smacked him." Neither man included any information on the alleged beating in the reports they themselves wrote later about the ambulance ride, though Durand complained repeatedly that he'd been the victim of police brutality.

As soon as he was stabilized after the completion of his amputation, Wilbur Durand was taken to an isolated room equipped for the treatment of violent criminals and secured to the metal bed with leg cuffs and one arm cuff. Lacking his right arm, there was little chance that even a man of his magical talents could manage an escape. Additional detectives from our division, who had followed the ambulance on the way to the hospital, joined Spence Frazee as he questioned Durand on the matter of the whereabouts of the other children who had been taken over the course of his spree.

Wilbur refused to speak.

I wondered how Moskal could say that Sheila Carmichael maintained a low profile in Boston—she was positively *large* when she swooped down on Los Angeles like the new Johnnie Cochran. But, then, this case was not going to be about the man's guilt or innocence, since that was predetermined—it would be one giant exercise in public relations. The only remaining question, that of the punishment, would be answered as much in the court of public opinion as in the hearts and souls of twelve average citizens.

I started to read up on her. It was not as frustrating to dig into Sheila Carmichael as it had been with her brother Wil Durand—there were plenty of bios, lots of quotes, and a whole slew of articles she'd written for legal journals. The woman had *I want to be a judge* written all over her. Maybe her brother's penchant for mutilating little boys would put a hex on that. Please God.

She was famed within legal circles for taking on defendants for whom no one would reasonably have sympathy. This was just such a case—her brother had been caught in the act of attempting to murder a child after he had already assaulted that child sexually. He committed a portion of that crime while someone who cared about this child, myself, who just happened to be a veteran police officer, watched. He had taped the act in its entirety, which had been legally confiscated as evidence. The most bleeding-heart jury would find him guilty. Not to mention that a body of evidence pointing to his involvement in a number of other disappearances had been accumulated through prior investigation and would probably be deemed admissible.

It was one of the most solid legal cases against a perpetrator I had seen in my career as a cop, and it was a reasonable speculation that if Wilbur had not had a sister who was an attorney, he would have been hard-pressed to find one who would be willing to take him on. Money was not the issue—the real problem was the negative karma of being associated with a criminal the likes of Wilbur Durand. It would be so hard to overcome that few reputable attorneys wanted to be associated with it. Because I, a cop, had more than a passing connection with one of the victims, there might be professional repercussions for an attorney; cooperation from the police department would no longer be assured. Of course, no one would come out and say this—we are supposed to rise above the desire for retribution. But paperwork would become harder to get, calls would be delayed, evidence would disappear for the clients of any in-town lawyer who took on Wil Durand.

Sales and rentals of Durand's films tripled overnight when the truth about how some of them were made finally came out. Critics elaborated on their unsettling and brilliant realism. It all made me want to puke. My nausea was compounded by the stunning public-relations campaign that Sheila Carmichael arranged for her brother. The gory details of his childhood were revealed in a depth that Kelly McGrath could never have contemplated. Stories about Uncle Sean, the abuse by his grandfather, his mother's alcoholism and mental illness. I could hear the shirts rending in Southie all the way in California. But all the players were dead, so who would protest?

The morning after we took him, Wilbur Durand was arraigned in his hospital bed and charged with one count of attempted murder of a juvenile in concert with the act of sexual molestation—physical examination revealed that Jeff had been sodomized prior to receiving his other physical injuries—and two counts of attempted murder of a police officer. He was also charged with the felony kidnapping of Nathan Leeds and a number of other young boys, even though their bodies had not been found, and when the evidence was analyzed, probably the murder of Earl Jackson. It was deemed by all involved with the indictments that there was sufficient physical evidence to move forward without them.

I moved through all of this as best I could. My days could not be classified as "good" or "bad"; the new standard for my existence was "horrible" or "livable." One of my better post-nightmare days was when the prosecutor was named; James Johannsen, who had brought my requests for warrants to the judge and argued so persuasively that they ought to be granted, was assigned the task of seeing that Wilbur Durand was punished to the limit of the law for his heinous acts. He was a tough, resilient former public defender whose sense of right and wrong made it impossible for him to continue defending scumbags for unforgivable crimes. He came over to the good side maybe eight years ago. Jim was every bit a match for Sheila Carmichael, who would still have had a rough road ahead of her even if the prosecutor was a wimp.

Predictably, Sheila dove right into it. When Johannsen filed a motion for a chain-of-evidence blood sample to be drawn so a DNA comparison could be made, she immediately filed a brief with a counterargument based almost entirely on civil-rights issues. Johannsen's request was eventually granted, but his triumph was overshadowed in the press by Sheila's request for a bail hearing. The judge listened quietly to her argument that her brother had "strong ties to the Hollywood community" with a look of sheer disgust on his face. Johannsen, who knew that there was no possibility of bail, pointed out that Durand would have no trouble meeting a million-dollar amount. The cops who were present told me that when the judge denied bail, Sheila went into an immediate snit, at which point the judge walked out of court, leaving her to piss and moan to an empty bench.

The DNA test was rushed through in a couple of days. It came back a positive match to the sample taken from Jeff. I brought Evan to visit him as often as possible, but it was so hard to look at him. The physical problems he faced were terrible. But the emotional problems might be worse. Evan was a loyal friend, a constant source of support. But the strain of it showed on him.

"That was supposed to be me, wasn't it?"

I couldn't entirely deny it, but there was no way to be sure. "We just don't know," I told him. "Durand won't say." Evan's guilt over the matter would probably not surface for some time, but Doc Erkinnen had told me to be vigilant for signs—withdrawal, sullenness, a desire to be alone. Preoccupation with things macabre. No more horror movies for my son; his own reality had usurped them all.

Jeff would never eat another piece of fruit; his shortened digestive tract would deny him that pleasure. For a while, he would have to carry around a portable IV, because he needed a steady stream of antibiotics, the variety rotated regularly, to ward off the infection that was sure to arise from having his intestines exposed to the air. They'd had to cut out three feet, which had literally dried up, but his parents had agreed to let his doctors try to restore a section that had fared better.

Someone's bullet had gone right through his right kidney, and it had been removed in tatters. He had nearly bled out; cops had come in by the hundreds to donate blood for him. He had still almost died, despite several transfusions. So even if he recovered enough to move normally once again, he would never play football or soccer or any other sport where there was the remotest possibility that his remaining kidney might be damaged.

Somehow, mostly thanks to Spence and Escobar, the police work involved in closing out the case moved forward. Warrants were easy to obtain at that point. They got another one for the house, but this time they had a better idea of what they were looking for. In one of Wilbur Durand's sock drawers, they found a single button.

From Earl Jackson's shirt. Durand was immediately charged with first-degree murder in the act of sexual molestation and kidnapping of a child. Off with his head.

thirty-five

WHAT FOLLOWS IS THE CONFESSION of Gilles de Rais, knight, Baron of Brittany, the accused, made voluntarily, under no constraint, and with all freedom of mind on the afternoon of Friday, October 21, 1440.

On the subject of the abduction and death of many children, the libidinous, sodomitic, and unnatural vice, the cruel and horrible manner of killing, and at the same time the conjuring and invocation of devils, oblations, immolations, or sacrifices; the promises made or the obligations contracted with them by him or other things mentioned in the aforementioned articles; Milord Gilles de Rais, accused, voluntarily, freely, and grievously admitted that he had committed and detestably perpetrated on numerous children the crimes, offenses, and sins of homicide and sodomy. He confessed also that he had committed the invocations of demons, oblations, and immolations, and made promises and obligations to demons and did other things that he confessed recently in the presence of the said Lord President and other people.

Interrogated by the said Reverend Father and President

as to the place where and time when he began perpetrating the crimes of sodomy, he responded, in the Champtocé castle; he professed not to know when or in what year, but to have begun doing it near to the time his grandfather, Lord de la Suze, died.

Item, interrogated by the Lord President as to who had persuaded him to the crimes, he replied that he perpetrated these acts according to his own imagination and idea, without anyone's advice or instruction, and following his own feelings solely for his pleasure and carnal delight, and not with any other intention or to any other purpose.

And the Lord President, being surprised that the accused would have accomplished the said offenses of his own accord and without anyone's urging, asked the accused again to tell from what motives and with what intent he had the said children killed and had their cadavers burned, and why he gave his soul up to these heinous crimes, admonishing him to be willing to declare these things completely in order to relieve his conscience and unburden his tormented soul and to secure more thoroughly the favor of the most merciful and clement Redeemer. Whereupon the accused, indignant at being solicited and interrogated in this manner, spoke in the French tongue and said to Monsieur le President, "Hélas, Monseigneur, vous vous tormenter et moy aveques!" *Alas, Monsignor, you torment yourself and me as well.*

To which the Lord President responded, also in French, "I do not torment myself in the least, but I am very surprised at what you have told me and simply cannot be satisfied with it. I want to know the absolute truth from you for the reasons I have already told you, many times."

To which the accused replied, "Truly there was no other cause nor intention nor end beyond what I've told you, which is enough to kill ten thousand men."

Thereafter, the Lord President ceased his interrogation of the accused and commanded that François Prelati be brought into the room. And Prelati was brought forth in person before Gilles, the accused, whereupon he and the said accused were interrogated together by the said Lord Bishop of Saint-Brieuc on the invocation of demons and the oblation of the blood and members of the said small children, and the places where they performed the invocations and the oblations, to which the accused and François had just confessed.

Thereupon Gilles, the accused, and François, responded that the said François had performed several invocations of demons and of one named Barron specifically, by order of the accused, as much in his absence as in his presence, and moreover that the said accused admitted that he was present at two or three invocations, especially at the places of Tiffauges and Bourgneuf-en-Rais, but that he was never able to see or hear any demon, even though the accused had conveyed a note written and signed in his own hand to the same Barron by way of the said Prelati, by which Gilles promised to obey the demon's orders, while retaining his soul, however, and his life. And that the accused promised the said demon Barron the hand, eyes, and heart of a child, which François was supposed to offer to him, but the aforementioned François did not do so.

The Lord President then ordered the said François Prelati to be returned to the room where he was guarded. Whereupon the accused Gilles turned to François with tears and gasps and said to him in French, "Good-bye, François, my friend! Never again shall we meet in this world; I pray that God will grant you patience and understanding, and know well, provided you have patience and trust in God, that we will meet again in the great joy of Paradise. Pray to God for me, and I shall pray for you!"

After saying which, he embraced this François, who was taken away immediately.

༺༒༻

Together my son and I shared one of the first copies of the transcript of Milord's confession. It had been given to me by Jean de Malestroit, who, not having been present himself, likewise had one. Other copies were now furiously being made by a small army of conscripted scribes, who bent over their parchments and worked the letters on the page as fast as their fingers could fly.

I sighed deeply as I read the dry, toneless words. I asked my son, "What can be meant by *grievously* in the description of his speech? Did he weep, as he did when I first spoke to him of these matters in the same room where this confession had been recorded? If so, it has not been described in these words."

He indicated with a shake of his head that he knew no better than I. "*Mère,* you must remember that these pages are not intended to convey the subtleties of his ordeal. They are intended to protect those who ordered his execution from the wrath of Milord's family, and nothing more."

The indignation of his family was likely to be just as dry and toneless. René de la Suze would hardly weep for his brother, but he would tear his shirt and smear himself with ashes to regain the properties that Milord had frittered away in his debaucheries. Little Marie de Rais hardly knew her father, beyond what she had been told by her mother, who had many reasons to hate him. There in his sumptuous quarters, had Gilles de Rais finally broken down and let his deepest secrets out? I could almost hear his voice.

"The child Gilles speaking again in these words. These things he did as a man were no different from the things he did in his early youth, only more grave in nature."

Jean rose up from his chair and stepped away from me. He walked toward the window and looked out into the courtyard for a few moments. His gaze seemed fixed, yet I knew from many years of looking out that small window that there was little to hold one's attention. Something within his own mind was engaging him.

"I would know your thoughts, my son," I said quietly.

I heard him release all the air from his lungs and then take in a new, fresh breath, all very deliberately. He turned toward me with a troubled look on his face. *"Mère,"* he said, "Milord did many things of a very grave nature in his youth. You simply do not know all of them."

I tried to smile. "You have instructed me recently that boys keep many things from the women who care for them."

I heard shame in his voice when he said, "In this case, 'twas not only Milord who did so."

A knot began to form in my stomach. "Have you something to tell me, Jean?"

"Yes, but not for myself, for my long-dead brother."

"Michel? What did he do that he kept from me?"

Jean remained quiet for a moment, as if he could not find proper words for what he wished to tell me.

"It was so many years ago," I said. "There is nothing I could not forgive him, or you."

"It was not what he did, but what was done to him. Or attempted."

It was a few heartbeats before I began to understand. "Go on," I whispered.

"You know that there was something of a falling out between myself and Milord Gilles at one time, that I no longer wished to be in his company."

"Yes. Your paths became divergent, and your interests were very different from his. But I accepted this as just the natural way of—"

He cut short my stream of logic. "It was not a natural rift, *Mère.*"

"Then tell me why." My heart was beating faster, too fast. "And then tell me why you have not found a way to speak of it before, so I might have been better advised."

"It would not have served you to know of these things. Before now."

"But now they will serve me?"

"There is a need now for you to know these things. I know you have loved Milord well, though he has ruined that affection of his own accord. Still it grieves me to say these things. He was not the innocent child you recall him to be. I know you think he was at best an average pupil despite the excellence of his tutors, who benefited Michel and me far more than they did Milord Gilles. That was a matter of self-application; he chose to apply himself otherwise. There was a keenness in him to learn that perhaps you never saw, because he devoted himself to things that he would not allow anyone but a very few close acquaintants to see, myself and Michel among them, his cousins de Sille and de Briqueville as well. I never cared for either of those scoundrels, but I had little choice about associating with them; they were his kin, and he included them among those he allowed to see his secret side. He knew that none of us would speak of what we knew. Michel and I would remain silent because we were not his equals in birth, and he had great influence with you, our beloved mother; there is no greater power than that. De Sille and de Briqueville remained silent because they were jealous of him and afraid of what he could do to their standing in the family, particularly with Jean de Craon, who was so fixed on seeing his grandson Gilles advanced that he barely gave notice to his other grandchildren. And in truth, over time I think they began to enjoy the activities that took place."

I started to raise a hand to make him stop. But I withdrew it. Already it was too late; I had heard just enough that my own imagination might try to fill in the rest, and there was no denying that the truth would serve me better.

So I sat quietly as Jean spoke. His expression was

pained, and I wondered how a cogent man could suffer so in revealing an event from his time of innocence.

Too soon, I understood.

"He was ... *quick* about many things that I and Michel were slower to comprehend. In particular regarding physical matters. There were many times, *Mère,* when he would pull his ... his ... male member out from behind his codpiece and show it to us. He would make it stand first and then ask us to admire it."

I tried very hard not to show too much emotion. "At what age did he do this?"

"Ten, perhaps eleven; it began not long before Milord Guy was gored by the boar. Then he began to engage in acts of self-satisfaction before us. He would apply grease to his hand—I remember once he made me steal a pot of some *crème* from your bedchamber—"

This revelation stunned me. It was a favorite possession of mine, not that the *crème* meant much to me; such luxuries had not the import to me that they had to fine ladies, whose complexions were always under scrutiny. But the pot itself was ivory with a rim of gold, wonderfully carved, and I doted on it because it had been a gift from my husband. *Who has taken my pot de crème?* I can hear myself saying it now, though not with the anger that I perhaps ought to have had. I assumed that one of my sons or my husband had been intent on playing a small joke on me. *Come forward now, and it will go easier on you.* Somehow, the pot magically reappeared, and our little drama came to an end. I never imagined at the time that it had been stolen for that terrible purpose. It rested now in the wood cupboard beside my bed, almost within reach.

"—and used it all up in doing these things to himself. De Sille and de Briqueville did likewise. Michel and I tried to excuse ourselves, but he would not let us leave. He would never let us leave."

"This happened more than once?"

"A thousand times. But I could not speak of it; I was afraid of what Milord might do to me, afraid that you would be disappointed in me."

"Your father could have—"

His words were swift and bitter. "I threatened Milord with such an exposure. Milord simply told me that he would make sure that *Père* lost his position in Milord Guy's retinue if I did so."

That a child of twelve should have to bear such a burden in silence was horrifying to me. That this child was my own son was beyond understanding. I regarded him with the sympathetic eyes of a mother, yet still, his expression was all guilt and regret, his words forced out painfully.

"I could not risk having my family put out in such hard times. So I remained silent. Michel did as well."

He paused. Droplets of sweat had formed on his forehead. "Then Milord began to ask me to touch his member with my hands."

I gasped and crossed myself.

"De Sille and de Briqueville were already doing so, but there came a time when Milord no longer found their attentions adequate—he seemed to tire of them rather quickly. At first I resisted, but eventually I was forced to do as he asked. In time, he asked more of me."

I clutched my sides and moaned, "Oh, most unholy wickedness, what grief—"

"I only did what I had to do, but I swear, I did not do it willingly. Such things as he asked of me and I did for him are against nature, against all that is decent and good. . . ."

He was trembling and his face was distorted in the agony of his remembrances. I could see in his eyes that there was more to say, but the weight of what he had already poured out was such that he had lost his will to complete it. He simply said, "And thereafter I found reasons to avoid his presence whenever I could."

The image of my son Jean as a boy of twelve appeared in my mind. A change had come over him then. There was a time when he seemed to darken before our very eyes, but when I expressed my concern over it, Etienne assured me that it was only the normal course of events for a boy of his age, that he should become moody and want to avoid us. *I did so myself, as I recall. My own mother was none too pleased.*

But he avoids his playmates, I said to my husband. *Do not be concerned,* he told me, *and* mon Dieu, *Guillemette, do not try to keep him attached to your apron strings. He must grow into a man sometime.*

Had a switch been handy, I would have used it upon myself in that moment, so shamed was I by my ancient failing. I was supposed to be my son's protector, and I had failed to protect him from the theft of his innocence.

And then I would have turned that switch on Gilles de Rais, Jean de Craon be damned.

Weariness, shock, and horror ruled me, all deepened by loathing for myself, who had allowed all this to happen. But as the meaning of what my son told me began to take hold in my mind as it had in my heart, a different emotion surfaced; my loathing began to shift to a more fitting target. I was enraged beyond anything I had ever felt in my life, and most of that anger was directed precisely where it ought to have been, toward Gilles de Rais.

◈

I did not bother to don the blue dress that Madame le Barbier had loaned me; there was no longer any need to show myself as someone more approachable than the abbess I had become and doubtless would forever be. I climbed the stairs to the room in which Gilles de Rais now waited for the death that was surely his fate, no longer caring if he was frightened and alone in his last days, wishing only that he would feel those things very keenly in what time remained to him.

It was not enough that he had told his judges of the evils he had done as a man. I would have from him the details of the things he had done as a child. Not since I set out to "market" that morning when I visited Madame le Barbier for the first time had I felt such calm in my heart, such fortitude in my steps, such certainty about what ought to happen. Now was a time for confessions, a time for unburdening the soul. Gilles de Rais had done so more under the threat of torture than of his own free will, as had been recorded in the transcript; the world would never know the true depth of his cowardice. Jean had given his deepest secrets to me in an act of great filial love, similar to the love that had compelled him to protect his father's position at his own expense while still a child of tender years. He understood that it would not serve me to meet my Creator, when the time came, with such a cloud of deception hovering over me.

I was dimly aware of the guards' acknowledgment; I was not a threat to their captive, as far as they knew. The gatekeeper had no reason to suspect that I bore hidden weapons, as he might have of a different visitor. He simply pounded his spear on the tile floor three times and then left.

Gilles de Rais came out of the inner room of his suite immediately on hearing this summons.

I forced myself, through sheer power of will, to maintain a normal visage. "Milord," I said.

"Ah, *Mère*," he said. "Your voice is like God's very own grace. I cherish each sound now as if it would be the last one to touch my ears."

"This is wise."

"Yours was the first I heard; I would not complain if it were to be my last."

He would have that wish. It was all I could do to keep from pulling the pearl-handled dagger from my sleeve and killing him right then. But the knowledge I sought would die with him, and my chance of finding some small measure of peace would be lost forever.

"My lord," I began, "I have read your confession. It gladdens my heart that you have given up these burdens."

"It was not an easy task to do so," he said. "To look these men in the face and speak of what I have done, why, it nearly tore my heart out."

My heart was hard; I felt no sympathy at all. "You spoke of commencing your deeds around the time of your grandfather's death. It surprised me, Milord, to read this."

"I am sorry that you should have to know these things, *Mère* Guillemette."

"Indeed, it is difficult for me. I cannot help but think that my influence upon you might have been stronger to the good than it seems to have been."

"I was but a young man, and willful. You must not blame yourself—"

"Throughout this trial I have looked to my own failings as the cause for your misguided behavior. But I have ceased all such self-incriminations." I reached into my sleeve and pulled out the pot.

He looked down at the accusing item in my hand, and his face transformed from that of the lying child to the thief whose hand was yanked out of the drawer. His discomfort was sublime to me. But it was not enough.

"I will now give you the opportunity to unburden yourself further," I said, quite serenely.

His eyes went to the pot, then rose back up to meet my own. His expression hardened. "There is nothing further to tell," he said.

"Liar," I hissed. There was the devil himself in my

voice, and Gilles de Rais heard it. "Tell me all now, or I shall make it go very badly for you."

He stiffened in defiance, in spite of my threatening manner. There would be no shaking this warrior off his high horse. "By what authority?" he sneered. "Only my judges can shape my fate now."

"You would not have judges at all were it not for me."

He stared blankly.

"It may surprise you, my son, to learn that it was I who began this whole query. Of course, I did not know where it would lead. But your judges owe me a great debt, for without my curiosity, they would not have had the opportunity to put you through this hell. I was the one who went to see Madame le Barbier when she complained of her loss, and I went to Bourgneuf ..."

He remained speechless while I ranted on. I could not suppress a smile of triumph when I finished. I was under no obligation to tell him that only Jean de Malestroit knew of my involvement and that he would not change one hair of a decision for my sake. Let him imagine that I held some power over his fate.

His eyes darted about as if he thought he might somehow flee my presence. But there was no place to hide; guards were only a few feet away, and he would be contained no matter what he did.

I held the pot out closer to him, and when he looked away I brought it up to his face until it was directly under his nose.

"Speak," I commanded him. "Tell me exactly what happened with Michel. Leave nothing out."

The stiffness went out of him.

※

"You know, *Mère,* how I loved Michel. I adored the ground he walked on; he was everything I wanted to be myself. His fair coloring, his beautiful smile, and those sparkling eyes of his—he was a living angel! How could I help but want him?

"But he was good and pure, and he resisted my advances with great vigor. With Jean, it was easier; he gave me what I wanted in part, though I would have had him more completely if he had not resisted. But Michel, sweet Michel, he was the one I wanted to be and to possess, and he would not give himself to me no matter how I threatened him. I told him the same thing as I told Jean, that I would see his father ruined if he did not acquiesce. He would not give in; he told me that his father would accept ruination before allowing his son to be sodomized, and that I should do as I wished, for he would not be a party to my desires under any circumstances.

"I hated him and loved him at the same time; I detested his stubbornness and admired his strength of character, and I envied him a father who would love him thus, as mine did not seem to do. I became more determined to have him with each new bit of resistance.

"I took Michel out of this world, Madame, because he would not be mine in it. It is my sincerest hope that I will meet him in the next world, if God will only permit it. I know that he will have wings and a crown of light, as is his due. By then I had stopped pressing him for favors; he was not afraid of me and there was little hope of achieving my desires with his cooperation. There was a delicate balance between us, one that made it possible for us to remain companions, at least on the surface of things. If I were to have him as I wanted him, it would have to be by force or not at all. I decided that it would be by force, for I could not contain myself. One day I told him that I wanted to hunt with him. At first Michel did not want to go; he had lessons to do before our tutor came, he said. But that excuse was specious, for our tutor had gone to his own home in the wake of my father's death. He made me promise that I would leave him alone, that I would not press him to let me touch him, and I gave my word. He seemed satisfied. We went out that morning with knives and slingshots to bring home a turkey. We were never allowed out without escorts because of the danger of the boar. My usual keepers were occupied in other matters at the moment, and so I was able to escape without them, and Michel with me. The sense of freedom was so very thrilling to me, for rarely could I go anywhere or do anything without someone standing nearby, either to correct me or take care of my needs. Not so much at the behest of my mother and father, or you, sweet nurse, but because my grandfather wished it to be so."

He reached out and stroked my cheek, with the cold fingertips of a demon. I did not move.

"We traveled out as far as the grove of oaks; the stream was high and running fast, for there had been a good deal of rain. The ground was wet still, but our travel was not hindered by it. We were alone, as we rarely were, and though I had given my word that I would not approach him, I could not seem to help myself. In truth, Madame, I did not want to help myself. God save me, I wanted to do to your son the same things that had been done to me, for I had begun to savor them as pleasure."

"But . . . who?"

"Why, Madame, did you not know? *Grandpère, naturellement*. In any case, Michel walked before me, thrashing the brush for birds, and I watched him from behind. By the time we reached the oaks, I was so enraptured by his movements, the suppleness of his limbs, the graceful swing of his arms, that I came up behind him and grabbed hold of him. Oh, he was strong for one so slim and compact; he struggled mightily against my grip and tried to run away from me. I feared that if he got free of me and returned to Champtocé, he would speak of this occurrence and there would be grave consequences. I could not afford to have *Grandpère* know what I had been up to. I could not imagine how he would react.

"So I stilled Michel; I had no choice. I closed my hands around his throat, not long enough to kill him, but certainly long enough to subdue him. I had not planned well; there was nothing with which I could secure him while I had my fill of him. But I remembered the loops of intestines that I had seen protruding from my father's belly when they brought him in, and I knew that Michel would not go far were he secured by his own innards, and so I took out my knife and, while he was still struggling to regain his breath, I slit him up the belly, right through the shirt, so the blood would not spurt all over me. I carefully pulled out a handful of his guts. I needed only a meter or so to secure him to a nearby stump, but more than that came; I could not waste time trying to push them back in again. I turned him over onto his stomach—he tried to raise himself up a bit, I assume to keep his innards off the ground, but it served only to stir me more.

"It did not take long; I was young and excited. I expected that he would scream, but he did not give me the satisfaction. I am not sure just how conscious he was while I was thrusting myself into him, but when I was done and I turned him back over again, his eyes were open, and so full of hate that it broke my heart. He despised me, Madame, and I could not bear it—I loved him so well, and I only wanted him to love me in return.

"But he would not smile; I pushed the corners of his mouth up, but as soon as I took my fingers away, he would grimace at me again. He did not die right then, as I thought he might, though I should have known better in view of what had happened with my father. I tried again to push his intestines back inside him; the blood was warm and wet, and I wanted to smear it all over myself, to wear the essence of him. But I would be found out; it would be trouble enough to remove the blood from my hands alone.

"An hour passed, and still he did not die. I talked quietly to him, but he said little in reply, only that I should tell his mother and father and brother that he loved them well and would wait for them in heaven. And many times he whispered to me that he would see me in hell.

"I slit his throat, finally, and thereafter he died. But in order to keep the blood from spurting all over me, I held his tunic against his neck. I could not see what I was doing, and I cut too deeply. His head was close to coming off—I had not killed before and I did not know my own strength at the time, or I had unnatural strength for some reason, perhaps the excitement of it all. It hung pathetically, and as I began to drag his corpus away for hiding, it bumped along behind the rest of him. I could not bear to think that it might fall off, so I removed it purposefully. I buried him and his head in a cairn by the side of the stream, for there were many loose rocks available, and the spot I chose was behind a large bush, not easily seen except from very close at hand. I tied my own sash around his neck, so it would seem attached still, for I could not bear to look at what I had done to him. I tried to wash the blood off myself in the stream, but it was not possible to remove it all from my clothing. I took the dagger and made a small cut in my arm as a means of justifying it. When all was as complete as I could make it, I ran back to the castle, waving at the lookout as I came into view. I began to scream and blubber that Michel had been dragged off by a boar—you know this, *Mère,* you were there in the courtyard as the riders went out.

"The light was fading, and soon darkness ruled. The riders were forced to come back, perhaps an hour after the sun set, and did not go out again until the following morning. I know in my heart that they must have been only a few feet away from where Michel lay, not that they would have found him—he was too well-concealed, at least then he was. I will never understand why your Etienne did not stumble upon him in his forays out into the woods; he once told me how extensively he had searched. I think perhaps he ranged too far—thinking he was looking for a corpse that a boar or some other animal had dragged off. It was not until a good while later that I went back out again to see if the site was undisturbed. Some of the rocks appeared to have been moved, perhaps by an animal. The head was partly exposed, so I uncovered it. There was Michel's sweet face, at long last smiling at me. I could not bear to leave it there, so I took it with me."

⚜

Madame Catherine Karle and her son had come upon Michel before Milord had taken his head away. Jean de Craon's sudden appearance kept them from coming forward with what they knew, as they feared he would reveal some dark secret of Madame's past. I dare not imagine what secret was precious enough to keep her from speaking of something so despicable. Her son would not tell me, and the lady herself was dead, so I would never know.

But here in front of me was the man who had taken the life of my beloved child, simply because he wanted it. Simply because it came into his imagination to have it, because it was there to be done, and he was there to do it.

I was reeling; I had to get hold of myself. I sat down in the same ornate and beautiful chair that had held my cloak on my previous visit here. I tucked the ivory pot that had brought this confession out of Gilles de Rais back into my sleeve again and felt the near-forgotten dagger that I had brought along with me.

My fingers gripped the hilt and found strength

beyond all my imagining. The pot fell noiselessly to the very bottom of the sleeve pocket as I imagined drawing the knife upward toward the light.

Was this how Milord felt with the *braquemard* in his grip and the neck of a child, or the white belly, exposed to him? He must have felt strong and mighty over these weak little ones, who could not defend themselves against him or his equally depraved cronies. He must have felt like God Himself—almighty, all-powerful, the ruler of all things who could not be denied any pleasure that he dreamed of or saw. With hard and sure strokes, Milord had taken the life out of uncountable small boys and perhaps a dozen young girls who had the inconvenient audacity to be present when he wanted their brothers.

Now I would make one hard and sure stroke and send this evil to the depths of hell for all time.

Milord stood there with his eyes closed, as if savoring his memories. I moved slowly, guarding the rustle of my robe so as not to draw his notice. Just before I pulled out the knife, I prayed with all the sincerity my heart held.

Dear God, forgive me for what I am about to do. And when my judgment comes, remember that I am Your instrument in this moment, that this is Your hand that raises up the dagger, that this is Your will driving it. Let me be the hand of justice, that finds its mark in the throat of this evil one, who offends You and all Your creatures. . . .

Suddenly Gilles's eyes were open and upon me. His mouth tightened into a circle of terror, and he began to shrink back. He brought his hands up as if to guard his face.

But I had not yet raised the dagger.

"Barron," he whispered, his voice barely audible. "Oh, Lord Barron, why have you come now, when all hope is lost?"

What was this sudden madness? "Milord Gilles, I am not Barron—"

"You lie, Demon. You lie, as they have always said you do! Oh, how could I have been such a fool as to think that you would show yourself truly to me, for here you are, in the guise of one I have always trusted, but you are he who I sought with François. . . ."

The knife felt cold and foreign in my grasp; it was no longer the comfort it had been only moments ago when I had planned to use it in the name of God. It seemed an unholy thing all of a sudden. Still, I could not bring myself to let it go.

He saw me as the demon he had sought for so long without success. It had been the mother in me who had wanted to spare him, and now it was the mother in me who would slay him for his sins. If he saw me as the devil, could I not see the same in him?

I looked and saw Satan. But was he lunatic, and therefore inculpable? Was he merely playing at insanity, to invoke my sympathy?

I no longer cared. I pulled the knife out of my sleeve and raised my arm up high in the air. It felt like the staff of Moses in my hand, the sword of God, with power beyond imagining. Milord Gilles did not move but simply stood where he was, welcoming the cut. In his vacant eyes there was no emotion; he did not seem to care if I killed him. He cared about nothing, least of all me.

All my strength rushed to my forearms, and I plunged downward. But before the knife found its home in the heart of Gilles de Rais, I was grasped at the waist and whirled around. I had not heard anyone approach; Milord had not called for the guards, and I had done nothing to attract their notice. It was as if I were dancing in the air. While I was restrained, Milord turned and escaped into his rooms.

And then I was down on the floor in a tangle of black

cloth. The dagger fell free and landed on the carpet, straight up with its point in the deep pile, where it stood, shuddering. I broke free of my abductor's grasp and whirled around to face him, and found myself staring into the eyes of Jean de Malestroit.

He took up the quivering knife and pulled me into the outer passageway. There he placed me against one wall for balance. There were no guards nearby; he must have sent them farther back into the passageway, for surely he would not have dismissed them.

"Guillemette!" he cried. "What has overtaken you?"

"I—I do not know. . . ."

"How could you think to do such a thing as this—have you lost your mind?"

I stared at him for a moment. Then I looked back into the empty salon. "No, Eminence. I am just beginning to think perhaps I have found it."

chapter 36

THE WHEREABOUTS OF THIRTEEN CHILDREN were still unknown. The parents of those boys had most of their hopes for a safe return dashed by the hard reality of what had happened to Earl Jackson and the near-miss that had happened to Jeff. Most of them turned their efforts toward forcing authorities into an all-out push to determine what had happened to the bodies.

Wilbur was about as uncooperative as a murderer could be, almost to the point of taunting. But we knew what he did to them—it was all recorded. He used each of the children he had taken as a forced "actor" in a horror amalgam comprising their filmed tortures and deaths. In the Angel Films studio, a member of the forensic team found a hidden safe built into one of the walls, very cleverly disguised, in which were several reels of film stored separately from the others. I will always wonder why Wilbur never told Sheila of their existence and location. Maybe he had some insane notion that he would get out again and be able to use them.

Wilbur somehow got rid of his victims' bodies, but for some unfathomable reason he kept their sneakers. And can you imagine, a number of film distributors quietly came forward to reveal that Wilbur did in fact discreetly shop this footage around, showing clips and potential scripts in an effort to get someone to pick it up. "It was basically violent child porn," one of them told us, "hardly even disguised. Not my market at all. But the special effects were absolutely unbelievable, that everything looked completely real. I never saw anything like it," he claimed.

It's no wonder the effects were so real-looking. Thank God no one picked it up for promotion and distribution. "It was simply too much, too over the top, for ordinary channels," one distributor said. "But, just watch, copies will sneak out. There'll be a big black market for this stuff."

He was right. The unnamed film eventually became a huge underground hit on Internet porn sites that specialized in slasher-type films and intense pedophilia. It was all part of Wilbur's grand plan.

None of us could ever figure out why the sneakers meant so much to him. Maybe it was the one thing they all had in common, that he could hide in plain sight while he was in the midst of his quiet rampage. It must have satisfied him greatly that people went through that trove regularly without recognizing what they were fondling. Erkinnen had been right in maintaining all along that killers are likely to keep mementos from their victims; Jeffrey Dahmer had a refrigerator full of their heads and a freezer full of their body parts, for when he "wanted a snack." Ed Gein, the real-life basis for *The Silence of the Lamb*'s Buffalo Bill, went so far as to remove and tan sections of skin from his victims. He was in the process of creating a bodysuit for himself from these treasures when he was caught. In the book Erkinnen lent me—it's still at my bedside, if you can believe that—I read about the knight from the fifteenth century, the nobleman Gilles de Rais, who kept the heads of purportedly three hundred victims so he could *contemplate which among them was the most beautiful.*

Dear God.

The sneakers were there in an open box in his studio, in easy view the whole time. It was dangerous and ultimately foolhardy, but Wilbur counted on getting away with it. He did, for a good long time. In the end it was this desire to stay close to remnants of his crimes that did him in.

I can't shake the sense that Wilbur understood the risk of being caught. *He probably wanted to be caught,* Doc told me in one of our post-nightmare conversations. *It probably was not entirely unwelcome to him.* Perhaps there was a part of Wilbur Durand that abhorred what he was doing, some small trace of sane decency that ruled just enough of his psyche to make him put himself in the path of discovery.

Maybe so, but that trace was nowhere to be found on the day detectives began to seriously press him for information on the whereabouts of his previous victims.

What previous victims? he asked them at the time. And Sheila chimed in, *We do not acknowledge any previous victims.*

It was posturing, and it infuriated Spence and Escobar, who were by then officially assigned to the case. The subject of a lesser charge in return for revealing the location of the bodies was raised tentatively with Sheila Carmichael, who listened carefully, then told the police once again that her client had nothing to do with those disappearances. But she offered a caveat, saying that as his attorney, she felt duty-bound to go to him with any offers the police and prosecutors might make, and for that reason she would raise the subject with him—not that it would do any good, since he had absolutely no knowledge of these other disappearances.

"And you know that he's insane," she added, "so he

might say just about anything. I can't predict or control that."

Jim Johannsen met with the families of the victims to explain the discussions that had taken place between the parties. He was seeking the "permission" of the families to press this issue even more vigorously. He was asking delicately if he could have their permission to withdraw the threat of the death penalty as a means of bargaining for the whereabouts of the bodies.

I felt so terrible for all these people. The risk they faced, one they might have to cope with for many years to come, was that they would never know what had happened to their sons if they insisted that Wilbur Durand be prosecuted under the threat of the death penalty.

I don't know if revenge could ever be so sweet that I would be willing to live with such an unknown forever. The secret of what had happened to these little boys would die with Wilbur, were he to die. There would be no closure for thirteen families, who went to bed each night imagining the worst, or hoping for the tolerable best, that the child might by some miracle still be alive, crawling through the cold darkness in a pained attempt to reach home, like a lost dog. It was pitiful, terrible, the worst thing that could happen to any family. Some of the families seemed to be ashamed to face me, ashamed that they would be willing to trade leniency for certainty. I understood what they wanted: closure and finality. My knowledge of what had happened to Jeff was one of life's more bizarre gifts to me. My imagination couldn't take it any further. Theirs could and probably would.

I made good on my promise to my reporter friend and never spoke to any other member of the press after that. It was tough, because they hounded me. But none of the families was bound by the same obligation—they could speak freely. Some of them did. I was really disgusted by one family who sold their story to a supermarket tabloid for an obscene amount of money. Selling this horror for cash was just repulsive to me. Inexcusable.

So many times during the discussions with Johannsen I wanted to speak out. *You don't understand,* I wanted to say to the other families, *this is what we know about this monster, and you want to barter with him? This guy wants all the attention he can get; he's already getting love letters and proposals of marriage from every twisted bimbo out there. He's got every rag sheet in the world beating a path to his jail cell, begging for a story. You're feeding that fire.*

But I couldn't. Professional standards precluded me from revealing the details; it might have jeopardized the case if some part of it had gotten out. And in view of the fact that some of these people were selling their personal stories, I couldn't risk having them sell secrets of the investigation.

Johannsen's decision to go for the death penalty was announced in an elaborate press conference; Sheila Carmichael had few comments, but she did manage to use the prosecutor's own words to her client's advantage: "We are prepared to defend Wilbur Durand against any and all charges to the fullest extent that the law allows," she said in a post-announcement interview. She did her best to pad the jury with the most quirky people available in the pool of potentials. She used all of her objections to remove grandmothers, teachers, parents, anyone with an obvious association with children. But the ideal jury for Wilbur Durand, a cookie-cutter group of childless males with questionable gender identity, an inborn sense of entitlement, and flexible social mores, could not be created even by the most fastidious jury consultant.

The twelve regulars and six alternates selected did not have "that acquittal look," as Sheila was rumored to have commented. She did manage to place two people with personal objections to the death penalty in the group. "I knew it was going to have to be enough," she said in a post-trial interview. "It's funny how things turn out, though. Your strategies don't always pan out the way you envision they will."

In his opening comments to the jury, the presiding judge made a specific point of telling the jury that they should convict or acquit (he never said anything about innocence) based solely on the facts of the case and that the potential for extreme punishment should not in any way enter into their decision-making process. He was careful to point out that additional evidence would be sought and considered in the sentencing phase of the trial, should they return a verdict of guilty, and that it was not a foregone conclusion that any defendant against whom the death penalty is sought, if convicted, would be sentenced to die. Additionally, he instructed them not to allow their religious or political opinions on the death penalty to enter into their decision-making process on the verdict, a warning that is always given and rarely if ever heeded.

I cried like a baby when they found him guilty and sentenced him to death.

thirty—seven

JEAN DE MALESTROIT GAVE ME into the care of a
guard, with the explanation that I was feeling ill and
must not be allowed to move from there until he returned. And then he disappeared into Gilles's suite of
rooms, as if no evil lurked therein. When he emerged
again a few minutes later, his face was grave and dark.

"He told me what transpired," my bishop said. "That
he had confessed Michel's killing to you."

I grasped on to him and clung desperately. "He
taunted me with it, with every horrible detail. And I listened to him; it was as if I couldn't keep myself from
listening. Such blasphemies and horrors as I have never
heard before ..."

Jean de Malestroit crossed himself and placed a
hand on my forehead. "Dear Father in heaven," he prayed
aloud, "take this woman into your special care and bring
her comfort, in this her hour of deepest darkness."

He led me through the passageway to the stairs. "I

went to your *chambre* to find you. But Jean told me that you had gone and that he suspected you were going to see Gilles. I was surprised, but he told me that you had gone there before. Guillemette—is this true?"

I affirmed it with a small nod.

"But ... why?"

"Because there were questions only he could answer. But I wish Jean had not told you. It would not have harmed you to be innocent of these visits."

His face took on the familiar expression of disapproval, in which I found strange comfort. "We shall not speak of that now, Sister; there will be plenty of time later to discuss such things. For the moment, I am glad that he did. God alone knows what you might have done in a few more seconds. For a woman of your station to act in such a—"

"My station be damned! Why must I always live by the laws of my station?"

"Because those are the laws we live by, and it is proper that we do so, to ward off the dark chaos that comes from lawlessness." He paused briefly, then said, "I daresay we have seen what happens when someone tries to live outside the law—in the case of Milord, beyond it. But I think that any merciful judge would acquit you of killing him in view of the circumstances."

"As they did the woman who killed her husband, though he beat her nearly to death himself?"

"That was quite a different matter. What you have been through is far more injurious."

"You do not know the half of what I have been through."

"*Au contraire,*" he said. There was great tenderness in his voice. "I know the whole of it."

"You cannot. Unless Jean told you."

"I do not need Jean or anyone else to know what your suspicions were. I know that you have suspected

Milord of killing your son for some months. And now you know without doubt that he did kill him."

"Why did you not speak of this before?"

"Because, just as yourself, in my heart I was not sure that he had done it until now and because he had committed so many other murders that Michel's was not needed to convict him. For some time I have believed that it could not have been any other way. I wanted to spare you this, if it was within my power to do so."

I had wanted the same for myself, desperately, to the point where my own mind arranged it for me to be spared by simply refusing to believe it all. Somewhere along the path of discovery, the staggering truth had come upon me like rain in winter, cold to the bone. For as long as I could, I wrapped myself in a cloak of oilcloth so the horrible drops would roll off. And they did—I managed to set it all aside for a time after Gilles swore that he could never do such a thing. Why had I believed him? For the same reasons why he had killed—he had wanted to kill, and it was there to be done. I had wanted to believe, and belief was there for me.

We were quiet as we descended the stairs. When we reached the courtyard, I said, "Thank you for trying to protect me, but in knowing the truth I am somehow relieved of its weight. I have carried the uncertainty of what happened to Michel for so many years that I think perhaps I shall miss it when it no longer burdens me. There will be a void in me, where once there was hope."

"You will find things to fill that void," he said. With great tenderness, he tucked stray hairs under the white headpiece that held my veil in place. "We shall keep you very busy here, you can be sure of it."

❧

Jean must have recovered sufficiently to rejoin his group, for when we reached my chamber, he was no longer there.

"I have no idea what the hour is," I said as I slumped onto my bed. "I have never known such complete exhaustion as I do right now. Perhaps I shall sleep for a very long time. But before I do, I beg you, please tell me, what did you say to Milord while you were in there?"

"Now is not the time for such things to be discussed."

"Please, Eminence, there can be no better time than now."

With one hand, he reached out and closed the door, then lowered himself carefully into my small chair. He eyed the blue dress momentarily, but said nothing of it. "I made an agreement with him. Milord will give a deeper confession tomorrow. He will confess to having commenced his crimes in the beginning of his youth, and not in the year when his *grandpère* died."

It was Gilles de Rais's right to say whatever he wanted on the morrow; it had already been granted to him and could not be rescinded. This would be his last chance to speak to the representatives of God in justification of his deeds.

"He will not speak of killing Michel, then."

"No. I can require it of him if you wish."

"No," I said quietly. "It would be agony to hear it all again. But you were there for some time; there must have been more that you spoke of."

"Other arrangements were made, but they are of no consequence just yet and you need not concern yourself." He stood rather abruptly. "I will leave you to your dreams, then. Good night."

"Good night, my bishop."

I was alone with the bitter truth.

I removed everything I wore before slipping into bed—my robe, my shift, the gold chain that hung around my neck. I wanted to be as unadorned and pure as on the day of my birth. In doing so, I hoped I might imagine myself untouched by the burdens of a lifetime. But it was not to be. My mind would not allow it.

My dreams were indescribably dark. I woke up several times, all in a sweat, prompted by gruesome images of my headless son. Sometimes he would call to me and give chase, and I would try to escape, and then in the next dream it would be me pursuing him. Sometimes his entrails were visible, glistening with blood, but then he would trip on them and lose his footing and tumble down the embankment of the stream at the base of the oak grove, there to lie, writhing in agony. In one episode, I held his head in my arms, but the rest of him was not there. We were standing over a gravestone, perhaps Etienne's, and his lifeless eyes were weeping. Mine as well. I awoke with my face wet and my eyes crusted.

♔

Again Milord confessed all, but in this telling he remedied the flaws of the confession he made in his private apartments. He did not mention my son Michel by name, though other children were recalled specifically and in detail—in particular, the boy in Vannes whose headless body somehow had the wherewithal to resist disposal and was finally pushed into the latrine by Poitou.

As promised, he was more specific about the time when he had begun his terrible reign. But he could not seem to resist blaming someone for the wayward path he had chosen.

"...since the beginning of my youth, and that I have sinned against God and His commandments and offended our Savior on account of the bad management I had received in my childhood, when, unbridled, I applied myself to whatever pleased me and pleased myself with every illicit act.

"... that I have sinned against nature in ways not fully detailed in the articles, and let it be published in the vernacular for all men, the better part of whom do not know Latin, to read and to take to heart. Let this record be set forth for my own shame, for it is through this exposure of my sins that I shall more easily attain God's forgiveness and absolution. It was due to my delicate nature as a child—"

Frère Jean la Drappiere sat on one side of me, *Frère* Demien DeLisle on the other. Together they managed to restrain me when I tried to rise up in anger.

My voice was quiet but my words were deliberate. "He was *never* delicate."

"—that I engaged in pleasures and did according to my will whatever evil I could. Please, all you fathers and mothers and neighbors of all young boys, I exhort you to raise them with good manners, by good examples and doctrines, to instruct them in these things and correct them lest they fall into the same trap wherein I have fallen. Because of these passions, and to satisfy my sensual desires with delights, I took and had others take many children, so many that I can not determine the number exactly. I had them all killed, but not until I had vice of sodomy by ejaculating sperm on their bellies, as much after their deaths as before it. De Sille and de Briqueville were there with me, as well as Poitou and Henriet, Rossignol and *petit* Robin. We inflicted various forms of torment on them, including slitting them up the belly and taking their heads with dirks, daggers, and knives. Sometimes we struck them on the head with a cudgel or some other instrument. There were times when we tied them up and hung them from a peg or a hook, and while they languished I had my pleasures on them. And sometimes while they were dying, I sat on their bellies and watched them die, and Henriet and Poitou and I would laugh at them.

"I embraced these dead children and admired their heads and members, so I might contemplate which among them were the most beautiful. I kept these heads, until the time came when I was forced to give up the most part of them...."

He exhorted parents to guard their children against the downfall he had known by raising them to avoid it.

"Those of you present who have children, I urge you to instruct them in good doctrines and instill in them the habit of virtue during their early years.... Watch over your children, who ought not to be too finely dressed or live in laziness. Keep them from developing a desire for delicacies and hippocras, for those desires led me to a constant state of excitement, during which I perpetrated most of my crimes."

And finally, he asked for the forgiveness of those he had wronged.

"I implore the parents and friends of those children I have so cruelly massacred, for the blessing of forgiveness and their assistance in praying for the repose of my soul."

And when he was through, there was absolute silence, until Chapeillon rose up from his seat. "Let a day be fixed for definitive sentences," he said.

"Yes," Jean de Malestroit said. His voice reflected the same deep desire that I felt for all of this to be concluded. "We shall reconvene on the morrow to that end." He sounded the gavel and then rose up himself. Court was adjourned.

♕

That was the last of Milord Gilles's confessions.

"I had not thought I could be more disturbed by these admissions of his," I said to Jean. "But each telling drives it deeper into my heart."

"Our hearts are easily wounded just now, in view of what has been revealed. That he killed my brother is the worst kind of wound he could inflict upon me."

"I think perhaps the first wound he inflicted upon you was equally great," I said. "To be pursued so, and threatened, and forced to touch ... to ... submit—"

I was weeping inside, though I had no more tears left to fall. I could barely say the word; it came out in the thinnest whisper. "To do *sodomy*. Dear God, Jean, I would give anything to have that time back, to have it to do over again. We might have left that evil place and gone somewhere else."

"To do what, *Mère*? To farm? Father was no farmer or herdsman. He was a soldier, and soldiers unattached become highwaymen to feed their families. I could not have that happen to us. All of our hopes and dreams, my education, Michel's hope for soldiery himself, it would all have been forfeit."

He was right, of course. He had protected everyone he loved and everything he cherished. But he should not have had to do so. That he lived as a man with as much grace as he had was miraculous after what had been done to him.

"Come," I said. I forsook the hard stone bench on which we had been sitting, inside the courtyard. The late October wind had freshened and everything about me was cold—my fingers, my toes, my nose. "Let us abandon our sorrows in pursuit of joy."

To that end, we went in search of *Frère* Demien. The arborist–priest had left us immediately after court's session to see to the sorting of apples. The most perfect would be sent to the cold cellar for winter consumption. Those with the misfortune to have been bruised would be sent to the press for the removal of their juice, which would harden in oak barrels for a time, until fermented. Would that I had a glass or two of that delight to soften my memory of the day's events.

The harvest house smelled wonderful when we entered, the air much warmer than that outside, which bore the chill of high autumn and the promise of a cold winter. Barrels and bushels of apples were everywhere. *Frère* Demien had selected out a number of perfect red ones and set them aside. I picked one up and admired it.

"For his Eminence's morning tray?" I said.

"And Duke Jean's cellar," he said.

He looked around the harvest house, surveying the progress. "It goes quite well," he said, "though there have been distractions this year." He idly removed an apple from one barrel and placed it in another. "I have not paid as much attention to it as I ought. Of course, the brothers and sisters proceed without me and do a commendable job of it, but my eye would make the task even more successful."

In other words, if he had been here to supervise, he would not have to move apples from one barrel to another.

"This has been an unusual harvest," I said. "An unusual year."

"And may we have no more such years," *Frère* Demien said. He crossed himself, to enhance the likelihood. "But I daresay that it will become even more memorable, and soon."

"How so?" I asked.

"I have word that Milord Gilles will speak again with his Eminence and l'Hôpital. He wishes to bargain."

"What bargain could possibly be made now?"

"His death."

"But of course he shall be put to death. His Eminence would not entertain the notion of mere imprisonment."

"Of course," *Frère* Demien said. "That is unquestionable. But what I am told he wishes to amend is the manner of his death."

Anger filled my soul; I hoped it did not show. I am

certain that it did, for both young priests, my son and *Frère* Demien, fixed their eyes upon me immediately.

I pulled my hood up over my veil again and, without a word, turned toward the door. I was out and running toward the castle before Jean could even speak.

⚜

My son, on his younger legs, did catch me, of course. But I would not allow him to accompany me on my visit to Jean de Malestroit. In reaction, he behaved in a most unsuitable manner for a priest, with abrupt and unholy curses, the actions of an angry son trying to influence his mother. But I would not yield to his persistent attempts at persuasion.

I found his Eminence with a supper tray before him. Parchments were everywhere on the table; the food seemed untouched. The troubled look melted from his face when I entered, and his welcome was quite sincere.

"I had thought you would dine with your son, else I would have invited you to join me."

"I have no appetite today." I pointed to his untouched tray. "Nor, it appears, do you."

"My stomach is turning and does not want food."

"That is understandable, in view of what I have just been told. Is it true that he will bargain for leniency?"

"Yes."

"And will you render it to him?"

"Only if I am sufficiently compelled by circumstances, which I cannot imagine. Unless something terribly rare develops between now and tomorrow, I shall sentence him to be burned at the stake until he is nothing more than ashes. And then I shall make sure his ashes are scattered into the wind."

It was a terrible, unthinkable fate for one who believed in an afterlife to know that his corporeal remains would forever be blown about like so much unworthy dust. But nothing less would do.

"I am not the only one whose rest would eternally be disturbed if he were to be shown mercy. He had no mercy for my son, or for legions of other lost sons."

"And you are not the only person with such sentiments in this," he said quietly. "But I am bound to hear this request, both as a judge and a man of God."

"When shall you see him?"

"The verdict and sentences will be delivered tomorrow. So it must be tonight."

"I would give you the same advice that I think you would give me were I to ascend to his den of evil."

"Which would be . . ."

"Take care not to allow him to beguile you. The devil is a liar and takes many forms, one of which is upstairs."

I returned to my son, and we pretended to dine. We pushed the food around on our plates; our fingertips grew greasy but our knives went virtually unused. Finally, the young sister who had brought us our food came and took it away again, mostly uneaten.

We went to the evening service together, and when the time came for each of us to pray according to our own intent and desire, I prayed for swift and sure punishment of Gilles de Rais. "Tomorrow the verdict will be given," I said as I came up off my knees. "We shall be there, in memory of your brother and my son, and of all those children who have been taken from us."

"Amen," Jean said.

Outside the chapel, we went our separate ways, he to rejoin his entourage, and I to the convent. As I came through the courtyard a young sister approached me with the message that his Eminence wished to speak with me.

I headed directly for his chambers, without a moment's hesitation.

He bade me sit, which I did, but as soon as I had settled in I began questioning him. "What of your encounter?"

By the pained and drawn look on his face, it was plain that he had acquiesced.

"He will be buried in hallowed ground," he said quietly. "We will hang him first, then burn him, but his corpse shall be removed from the flames before it is destroyed." He looked into my eyes, waiting for a response.

I deliberately gave myself time to think before speaking. "A symbolic immolation." I was bitterly unhappy but could not find a way to express it adequately. "What of the others?"

"He has requested that they be allowed to die after him, so they might witness his execution and know with certainty that he has not escaped punishment; he feels they deserve this treatment in view of his having been the cause of their waywardness, as they were in his service. He believes that without his influence, neither Poitou nor Henriet would have led such a despicable life as they did while his retainers. I agreed that it should happen thus."

It seemed a fitting dispensation for the pages. "And he will die thereafter, as you have described?"

"He will."

I made no attempt to hide my bitter disappointment. "You have made a devil's bargain, Eminence." Disgusted and angry, I stood and faced him directly. "What has he offered? The key to a strongbox full of gold to be delivered to Duke Jean? A formula for transmogrification of metals that is truly successful? The Eucharist cup of Christ?"

"Guillemette, I cannot say—"

"I had thought to expect more of you." Without so

much as another word, I turned and left, my eyes full of tears at yet another betrayal.

☙

I writhed and moaned the whole night through. I tossed relentlessly from side to side and soaked my sheets with sweat. On the next morn, court was convened for the sole purpose of declaring the guilt of Etienne Corrilaut, also called Poitou, and Henriet Griart, both servants to Baron Gilles de Rais, who were sentenced to death by burning. Both stared into the distance without focus; neither said one word in his own defense. They were remanded to the dark, filthy, cold dungeons in which they would remain for the brief duration of their misspent lives, while their shrewd and clever master slept in furs before a fire. Such is God's justice, which is no justice at all.

chapter 38

THE PROSECUTOR JOHANNSEN was kind enough to call me before the news broke.

"Sheila Carmichael filed a motion to reopen Jeff's case based on the fact that you, as a supposed victim, were also involved with the investigation," he told me.

"What?" I was dumbfounded. "I wasn't a victim. Jeff is my son's friend, not my son."

"She contends that because you are an 'intimate' of his—she's defining 'friend of the family' as an intimate—your vigor in going after Wilbur was more than it would otherwise have been. *Enhanced,* I think, was the word she used in the brief."

"Good lord."

"Apparently she found some obscure old case where the verdict was actually overturned because one of the cops who worked on a particular case could also be construed as one of the victims. The opinion cited biased excessive motivation on the part of the investigator."

"It didn't make a bit of difference. Even before Jeff

became involved, I was into this case with everything I had."

"I know that. But they're absurdly careful in capital cases."

"Is there a chance the verdict could be overturned?"

"Not all the verdicts."

"So what's the point, then?"

"It's a negotiating trick."

"What can she get for him?"

"His life."

I couldn't think of anything to say to that.

"My guess is that the judge will think it's as crazy as we both do," Johannsen said. "But you never can tell."

"When will this be made public?"

"She won't be filing for a few days yet—she said it was as a courtesy that she was letting me know."

"Seems like a nonsensical move—you'd think it would be better to surprise you, catch you off guard."

"Sheila likes conflict, I think. And she likes to feel like she's in the middle of it all."

I'd given Pete Moskal a promise that I would keep him informed of every development in regard to Wilbur. The Commonwealth of Massachusetts had not, in view of Durand's death sentence, called for an extradition. I lay awake all that night thinking about what Johannsen had told me—what a travesty it would be if Wilbur walked. I would view it as a personal tragedy if he didn't ride the lightning.

By the time the first thin light was sneaking through the blinds, I had decided to wait to call Moskal, to see how it developed.

I went into the division that day, something I hadn't done in a while. The department had put me on light duty until further notice, but Fred had told me that it didn't matter whether I came in or not—I would get my paycheck anyway. It was almost more difficult to stay away than to be there; I missed the place and the constant swirl of activity. Apparently the place missed me too, because when I came through the door, there was a rush of warm greetings.

After all the niceties were over, everyone went back to his or her own unshattered world. Everyone but Spence and Escobar.

"How you doing, Lany?" Escobar asked, with genuine concern. "You look a little tired."

I had seen myself in the mirror that morning. *A little tired* was a kindness. "Not so good, Ben. I got a call from Johannsen last night." I told them what he'd said.

"Shit," Spence commented.

"Damn," said Escobar.

"Yeah. It would really suck."

We all sat in morbid silence for a little while, until I said to Spence, "Listen, I think I'd like to pay a little visit to Jesse Garamond. What do you think?"

He stared at me for a minute or two, not understanding.

"I think it's time to get him out of there."

"Lany, he's a bad, bad guy. Leave it alone."

"I want to go talk to him at least."

He seemed uncertain but agreed to go. "All right, but I don't like this."

We took the same route to the prison. As we approached the billboard where I'd seen the dripping ad for *They Eat Small Children There,* I closed my eyes. I didn't open them until I was sure we had passed it. It would be a different ad now, but my eyes would disregard the reality and see what they'd seen there before. It was too much for me to contemplate.

Spence had his gun, but mine was tucked in one of Fred's desk drawers, where he'd put it when he took it away from me. "You won't need it on light duty," he'd said. At first I missed it, but in time I came to appreciate the restoration of my balance. I walked taller and felt lighter. One hip did not dip below the other. My back was no longer sore from compensating for its weight. The weapon would stay there until I went back to regular duty. We got through the entry checkpoint that much faster, which pleased me greatly. They didn't pay any attention to the latex gloves I had tucked in my purse, because you can't kill someone with them, unless you stuff them down his throat.

Just as we approached the cell, I turned to Spence. "I want to talk to him alone."

He stopped dead and stared at me. "I don't think that's a good idea, Lany. This is not a particularly sweet guy."

"I'll be all right. I just want a couple of minutes with him."

"Why, for God's sake?"

"Spence. *Please.* I need you to humor me right now. And I don't want you hearing this conversation in case you ever get asked about it."

He stood stiff and unyielding.

"Please," I repeated.

Reluctantly, he said, "Okay."

I sent Pete Moskal two articles from the *Los Angeles Times,* both clipped while I was wearing gloves. They had appeared about a month apart. I sealed the plain envelope in which I mailed them with a sponge and used a self-adhesive stamp. I did not put a return address on the envelope.

The first one read:

> *Convicted serial child-killer Wilbur Durand was found dead late last night in his cell at Los Angeles*

County Correctional Institution, the victim of an apparent homicide. Durand, formerly a noted Hollywood producer and special-effects expert, was incarcerated there last year after being found guilty of first-degree murder, kidnapping, and sexual assault on a minor child in the killing of Earl Jackson, age 12, the kidnap/rape of Jeffrey Samuels, age 13, and on numerous other counts. Attorney Sheila Carmichael, also his sister, was in the process of preparing a motion for the Samuels case to be reopened based on an obscure legal precedent regarding the involvement of a victim in the investigation of a crime. Samuels is a close personal friend of the son of Los Angeles police Detective Lorraine Dunbar, whose dogged investigation of a series of seemingly unconnected child disappearances led eventually to Durand's arrest and conviction.

According to an unnamed prison source, Durand was stabbed multiple times in the abdomen and was then eviscerated. Prison officials have no suspects in the crime and say that the prison population has been unusually tight-lipped with information about the incident. "When something like this happens, there's usually at least one guy who's willing to come forward with information," said the assistant warden. "But so far nobody's saying anything in this case. We have no leads, no physical evidence, and, at this time, no suspects."

Moskal knew all this. But the second article might not have been picked up by the national press, and I wanted him to see the two together. The second one read:

Jesse Garamond was released from Los Angeles County Correctional Institution in Lancaster today on orders from the Court of Appeals. He was con-

victed three years ago in the death of his nephew, who has subsequently been determined to be one of the victims of Wilbur Durand, who recently died in the same prison. Garamond's conviction was unusual in that the nephew's body was never found. Prosecutor James Johannsen says that sneakers confiscated from Durand's work studio have been positively identified by the child's mother as having belonged to her son. They were included among several other pairs of footwear that Durand kept as souvenirs of his victims. Based on this evidence, Johannsen requested that Garamond be released pending a new trial, at which time the charges are expected to be dropped. At the time of his conviction in the death of his nephew, Garamond was on parole after serving four years of a seven-year sentence on a previous conviction for child molestation unrelated to the Durand case.

Pete Moskal got Wilbur Durand back after all. He greeted his casket at Logan Airport.

The last time we'd stood in this spot on the Santa Monica Pier, Errol Erkinnen and I had watched three very lucky young boys cavort in the sand and listened to their exuberant cries. I had told him how much my son Evan liked to come here. This time there was only the gentle sound of the surf and a few errant seagulls, but if I closed my eyes and cleared my head, I could imagine Evan frolicking on the beach with his two sisters.

I smiled and let the sun caress my face. Doc, ever observant, saw it.

"It's good to see you smile," he said. "That's real progress. Didn't I tell you this day would come?"

"You did."

"And that even better days will come after this."

"I guess you were right."

"Hey, that's why they used to pay me the big bucks."

He'd taken a leave of absence from the PD to write a book. The advance had been enough for him to take a full year. My suspicion was that it would be permanent; he would never go back.

I took hold of his hand and squeezed it. "Hey, I want to thank you for everything you've done to help me get through this."

He gave me a little wink. "Just doing my job," he said. "Or what used to be my job, anyway. What a world—who would have thought it would turn out like this."

The sound of the surf was soothing. "You know, I didn't really think Jesse Garamond would do it. He's a scumbag, but he wasn't a killer. At least he wasn't before all this. I hate to admit it, but I'm really glad he did it."

"Maybe Garamond wasn't a killer, but my guess is that he's probably always been a survivor. I don't think it's so terrible, for you to have wanted Durand to suffer."

He *had* suffered. There was more than what was reported in the newspapers. Durand had suffered that certain "thing" the other prisoners did to child killers. Garamond had come up with it on his own; my only request was that whatever he did, he would try to get information about the location of the bodies before he did it. He would have gotten out in time, anyway; we were able to speed it up considerably. And Jesse wanted his revenge, because it was Wilbur Durand's crime that got him thrown back in prison during his parole. He surely got it.

Doc didn't know all the details; there was a silent agreement between us that I would tell him only enough to unburden myself. I don't think he really wanted to know what happened in full detail.

"They found another body," I said. "That makes nine so far."

We would eventually find them all and return them to their families, based on what Jesse Garamond had dragged out of him while the knife was at his crotch.

A condor suddenly appeared along the northern edge of the horizon. He swooped down toward the end of the pier and landed on a piling. The bird flapped its wings and rose up, then soared off free into the sunlit sky. I imagined a phoenix, the mythological representation of our urge toward perfection, which is the ultimate illusion. Beyond even Wilbur Durand.

thirty-nine

MY FINE SON STAYED by my side all through Monday, October 24. His comfort and company were the sweetest blessings I could have known, and much needed, for the morrow would bring the finish of the trial of Gilles de Rais, knight, Baron, Marshal of France, once the intimate of kings and dukes and bishops, now known more truthfully as a sodomite, murderer, eviscerator, and decapitator of children.

Though his death was welcomed, even craved, by many—myself among them—I felt the passing of each minute that remained to him as if it were my own life that was about to end. With each breath came the thought that there was one less in the finite allotment of breaths to be drawn. An indescribably cold fear gripped my innards and paralyzed me against any significant action. I should have been glad to know that Milord was about to die for the crimes he had committed against God, against nature, and above all, against innocent children, who always wanted to trust in the goodness of their betters.

I have come to understand, in these last hours of his life, that my own woe arises largely from blaming myself for his shortcomings. That distress has been present in my heart since the beginning of this ordeal—indeed, throughout Milord's entire downslide—but I have not allowed it to possess me completely until now. There does not seem adequate penance for my failings, but I will try, for as long as I live, to do good works, to live cleanly, to offer succor and aid to small children, to distribute what alms I can so God will once again smile on me.

While he made his confession of these crimes in open court, Milord Gilles was quick to point to culpability of his childhood guardians. But a more perfect admission might have included his own shameless refusal to curb those desires he knew to be vile crimes against nature when they are only imagined and not actually enacted, as he had done. He said nothing in court of how he learned the art of sodomy from Jean de Craon by being the object of the old man's lusts himself. Nor did he say anything about how he had cried hot bitter tears after each encounter with the old monster, almost always in my arms, though I did not understand the reason for those tears at the time. But I suppose that he, too, wanted to believe in the goodness of his betters, or in the case of Jean de Craon, those more powerful. He was no more likely to speak against his grandfather than Henriet was against Gilles himself.

Gilles professed throughout his life to have strong memories of his mother and father, though he was rarely in their presence before they died. He was so young when they departed this earth, both in the same month. They indulged him shamefully, by which excess I think they meant to ameliorate their frequent absences. The gifts, the allowances, the permissiveness—it was all very enticing to a young boy. Those are his memories, not the tears of abandonment. But these riches did him no good, of that I am certain.

☙

On October 25 at the hour of Terce, the prosecutor Chapeillon stood in the upper hall of la Tour Neuve and requested that the proceedings be brought to a conclusion. The judges agreed that it should happen so.

"Gilles de Rais," Jean de Malestroit said.

Trembling and ashen, Milord rose up.

"We find you guilty as charged with perfidious apostasy as well as of the dreadful invocation of demons. Do you understand these charges and our findings?"

With quiet shame, he said, "Yes, your Eminence."

"We also find you guilty of committing and maliciously perpetrating the crime and unnatural vice of sodomy on children of both sexes. Do you understand these charges and our findings?"

"I do, my Lord Bishop. May God save me."

"Gilles de Rais, you are hereby excommunicated from the holy Catholic Church and are forbidden to partake of her sacraments."

I do not know why I was so surprised; it would all be part of the script. Perhaps Jean de Malestroit had insisted on the little drama that was unfolding, for the sake of appearances. In any case, Milord played his role well. He fell immediately to his knees and, with devout tears and moaning, begged to be allowed to confess his sins to a priest so he might be absolved of them before dying.

Jean de Malestroit played his part well too; he was the stern denier of mercy, the rigid and upright defender of the true faith, at least for long enough to create the proper effect. With a great show of sentiment, he called forward Jean Jouvenal of the Carmelite order and bade him hear Milord's confession, which was so passionately and sincerely offered that his Eminence had no choice but to reinstate Gilles de Rais to good standing in the church.

I wondered once again what treasure he had offered to bring this about.

But strangely, when word of this reached the encampments, there was little disapproval; as my son and I walked aimlessly among the crowds later that day, we heard very little grumbling and plenty of accord. These weary people, too, wanted desperately to believe in the goodness of their betters.

⚜

Later that afternoon, Milord was taken by guard to the nearby castle of Bouffay, where he confessed to his part in the debacle at Saint-Etienne-de-Mer-Morte. Pierre l'Hôpital made the final arrangements for him to pay his fine of fifty thousand *ecus* to the Duke of Brittany with a transfer of one of his few remaining properties. That having been settled, there was nothing left to do but to pronounce his sentence of death by hanging and burning, which would be carried out promptly at the eleventh hour on the morrow, October 26.

And then he asked publicly for the consideration to which Jean de Malestroit had already agreed:

"Please, *Monsieur le President,* I beg you to allow my servants Henriet and Poitou to view my death before theirs, else they may not know that I have been punished, and they must not die wondering if I might have somehow been spared that fate."

It was agreed. Thereafter, the sentence of the secular court was given.

"In view of the accused's freely given confessions to the crimes with which he has been charged, and in keeping with his confession of sins and restoration to the divine grace of the sacraments, it is hereby decreed that he shall be hanged to death and then burned, but that his body shall be removed from the flames before it is destroyed, and thereafter it will be buried in holy ground."

And with that, it would seem that there was nothing more to do. But Milord voiced one more request. He spoke directly to Pierre l'Hôpital, who had great influence with Jean de Malestroit. "May it please the judges and prosecutors, it is my great wish and hope that a general procession might be arranged, that I and my servants will be maintained in the hope of salvation as we approach our deaths."

He was arrayed not in his finery, which would soon be divided among petitioners along with the rest of his earthly goods, but in a simple gray tunic of linen, tied at the waist with a rope. He walked slowly through a crowd of thousands who had gathered to see him meet his death. Jean de Malestroit walked a good distance behind the prisoners, and I behind him, accompanied by my son Jean, who prayed constantly as we worked our way to the square, wherein the gallows and pyres had already been constructed. The people who had gathered to watch evinced a tremendous variety of emotions and sentiments toward the man who had killed their children; some called for him to be eviscerated and separated from his head as had their sons; others cried out for mercy on his behalf, saying that it was surely wrong to avenge a lost life with the taking of another. There was no accounting for the behavior of the onlookers, who seemed to have taken on a sort of crazed demeanor, each according to the unwavering belief in his or her heart.

He climbed the steps to the gallows of his own accord as his servants Poitou and Henriet watched. His legs were bowed and shaky, and once he faltered, his hands having been tied behind him, which disrupted his natural grace and balance. He shook his head to ward off those who would have helped him. I watched, with inexplicable tears pouring down my cheeks as this man who had, as a babe, sweetly suckled at my breast and then, as a boy, cruelly killed my son, stepped up on the box and stood below the rope. He looked up momentarily and regarded the instrument of his death but did not flinch as the noose was placed around his neck and tightened. He kept his eyes open as the floor of the gallows fell out from under him. For a few moments, he swayed and jerked, almost as if he were being blown by the wind. Perhaps the demon Barron, who had eluded him for so long, was finally tugging at his feet.

The crowd of onlookers was silent, until his body stopped twitching and he went fully limp. And then the shouts and cries of triumph rose up, to reach heaven itself. The pyre was lit below him, and tongues of flame licked at his swaying corpse. When his clothing began to burn in earnest, pails of water were splashed on the flames, and they fizzled out.

His body was laid into a casket and carried through the streets of Nantes on a simple cart. The wails and cheers of those who walked in this macabre procession could hardly be told apart, for there seemed equal numbers of mourners and celebrants.

I sat numbly through the service in memory of Gilles de Rais, which was held in the church of Notre Dame du Carmel on the other side of the city. Therein he was placed in a tomb alongside other important persons, some his ancestors. Surely all of them were better people on this earth than he; perhaps they even deserved the blessing of being so honorably interred.

But Gilles de Rais did not. I stood outside the tomb in which he had been laid to rest long after the others had departed to such revels or mournings as they would make, and I tried to imagine ways in which I might desecrate it. It was there that Jean de Malestroit finally found me.

"I have something I must give to you," he said.

❧

There is no way for me to describe what I felt when I opened the package he laid before me in his private chamber. It was the last thing I expected, though I cannot say I really had any notion of what this gift might be. Certainly I never imagined what I saw when I undid the silk wrappings.

"He had kept it all these years," my bishop told me. "He told me it was his most precious possession, even more so than the *grimoires* and tomes of alchemy and invocation that he guarded so carefully. Jean de Craon made him bring up the remains from beside the stream and stood over him as he buried them. But he went back to the final burial site to retrieve this."

The broken tooth, that sweet small imperfection—it was Michel. It could be no other.

"He said the rest of his bones would easily be found, even drew me a map. I have already sent a party of men to retrieve them."

So this was the chit on which the bargain had been made—a better death in trade for my peace. I cradled the denuded skull in my arms for a few minutes before I could speak. When I could find no more words of thanks, I said, "Will you go with me to Champtocé? I would bury him with his father."

"Of course. I would insist on going even if you had not requested it of me. This is not a journey one should make alone."

"I should like to leave at first light," I said.

"Yes," he said.

❧

Late the next afternoon, Jean de Malestroit and I laid the headless body of my son in a tomb next to Etienne. With some reluctance, I set his skull, with its familiar chipped tooth, in its proper position. Two strong soldiers from Champtocé had been given to me by the old castellan Guy Marcel, who came out with us to see to the removal of the stones and their subsequent replacement. The Bishop of Nantes said the service in celebration of my son, a child whose birth would not have accorded him such a blessing had he died under less notable circumstances.

But he was Gilles de Rais's first victim—in that, there was a certain importance.

In forgiving him, I was his last.

And in that, there was a certain peace.

ABOUT THE AUTHOR

ANN BENSON, the mother of two grown daughters, lives in Connecticut with her husband. She is also the author of the acclaimed novels *The Plague Tales* and *The Burning Road*. Visit her website at www.annbenson.com.

ELIZABETH GEORGE

"...reigns as queen of the mystery genre."—*Entertainment Weekly*

A GREAT DELIVERANCE _____ 27802-9 $7.99/$11.99 in Canada

Winner of the Anthony and Agatha Awards for Best First Novel

PAYMENT IN BLOOD _____ 28436-3 $7.99/$11.99

WELL-SCHOOLED IN MURDER _____ 28734-6 $7.99/$11.99

A SUITABLE VENGEANCE _____ 29560-8 $7.99/$11.99

FOR THE SAKE OF ELENA _____ 56127-8 $7.99/$11.99

MISSING JOSEPH _____ 56604-0 $7.99/$11.99

PLAYING FOR THE ASHES _____57251-2 $7.99/$11.99

IN THE PRESENCE OF THE ENEMY _____ 57608-9 $7.99/$11.99

DECEPTION ON HIS MIND _____ 57509-0 $7.99/$11.99

IN PURSUIT OF THE PROPER SINNER

_____ 57510-4 $7.99/$11.99

A TRAITOR TO MEMORY _____ 58236-4 $7.99/$11.99

....

Please enclose check or money order only, no cash or CODs. Shipping & handling costs:
$5.50 U.S. mail, $7.50 UPS. New York and Tennessee residents must remit applicable
sales tax. Canadian residents must remit applicable GST and provincial taxes. Please
allow 4 - 6 weeks for delivery. All orders are subject to availability. This offer subject to
change without notice. Please call 1–800–726–0600 for further information.

Bantam Dell Publishing Group, Inc.	TOTAL AMT $_____
Attn: Customer Service	SHIPPING & HANDLING $_____
400 Hahn Road	SALES TAX (NY, TN) $_____
Westminster, MD 21157	
	TOTAL ENCLOSED $_____

Name _____

Address _____

City/State/Zip _____

Daytime Phone (_____) _____